AMARYLLIS FLEMING

To dearest Hen,

Amaryllis Fleming

FERGUS FLEMING

who knows me better than
most! With much love
Amo. x

SINCLAIR-STEVENSON

First published in Great Britain in 1993
by Sinclair-Stevenson
an imprint of Reed Consumer Books Ltd
Michelin House, 81 Fulham Road, London SW3 6RB
and Auckland, Melbourne, Singapore and Toronto

A CIP catalogue record for this book is available at the British Library

ISBN 1 85619 1257

Typeset by Deltatype Limited, Ellesmere Port
Printed and bound in Great Britain
by Clays Ltd, St Ives plc

CONTENTS

ACKNOWLEDGEMENTS

I must first apologise to anyone who has bought this book expecting to learn about the mysteries of music or cello playing. I am no expert in these areas and it would be foolish of me to pretend otherwise. What I have tried to do is to tell the story of a woman who has lived an extraordinary life in the company of extraordinary people. My aim has been to entertain; if I have also managed to enlighten it is due mostly to wisdom received from others.

The bulk of information has been supplied by Amaryllis herself but there are a number of sources which I have used to embellish, corroborate and, occasionally, correct her account. These are listed in the bibliography. A comprehensive introduction to the cello is provided by Margaret Campbell's *The Great Cellists*. For those who want to learn more about Am's two families I would recommend Michael Holroyd's superlative two-volume biography of Augustus John; the biographies by John Pearson and Duff Hart-Davis are definitive on the subject of Flemings.

One omission is the text of E. M. W. Paul's letters. Paul was probably the most important man in Amaryllis's life. But he was also a married man, and his family have justifiably refused permision to quote his words. This is a shame because he had an excellent turn of phrase and spoke beautifully about his research into early Venetian lauters and Baroque composers. When his work is published it will make a fascinating read.

Writing a book is relatively simple compared with the task of finishing it, because only when you come to the footnotes and acknowledgements do you realise – particularly if you are of a chaotic disposition – how much you have forgotten or mislaid over the preceding months. I beg the forgiveness of any who should be mentioned below but are not.

The first person I must thank is my aunt Amaryllis, who sat patiently through interminable interviews, supplied me with sheaves of radio transcripts, concert programmes and reviews, bore with my ignorance and aided me in every way. She all but wrote the description of Fryern Court. I owe her a great deal and hope that the ordeal of preparing this book had nothing to do with the stroke she suffered at its conclusion.

I have received help from many quarters, but I would like to acknowledge particularly the interviews granted by Hugo Cole, Lamar Crowson, Yvonne Hale, Margaret Moncreiff, Geoffrey Parsons, Poppet Pol, Penelope Ram, Joan and Frank Regent, Pilar Torres de Quinhones-Levy, Mary Verney, and Raphael Wallfisch. Their contribution has been invaluable.

I would also like to thank: Amedeo Baldovino; Charles Beare for expert advice on the history of the cello; the literary executors of the late Sir Cecil Beaton for permission to use copyright material from his diaries, both published and unpublished; Christopher Bunting; Michael Burrell for his transglobal wanderings in search of Amaryllis's birthplace; John Engleheart for the use of interview material from a forthcoming memorial to Arnold Goldsbrough; Kate Fleming; Mary Fleming; Linda Freeman; Jean Gibson; Robin Goldsbrough for permission to quote his father; Liz Hodgson for hearth and home; Emanuel Hurwitz; The Kensington and Chelsea Library; The London Library; Joan Mallett; Hamish Milne; Diana Parikian; Geoff Richards; Matilda Simpson; at

Acknowledgements

Sinclair-Stevenson, Penny Hoare and Emily Kerr for their attention to the manuscript; Hugo Vickers; The National Library of Wales; Lady Susannah Walton for permission to quote from Sir William Walton's letters; Vivien White for the use of her memoirs and for permission to quote from the letters of Augustus and Dodo; Camilla Williams; Lord Wyfold.

Without the help of my daughter Romar this book would have been finished much earlier but much less enjoyably. I dedicate it to her. Also to my son Pat who was conceived, at a rough guess, in Chapter Eleven.

ONE

Wild Roses

There is much to say about 1925, none of it very favourable. That was the year in which Hitler published *Mein Kampf* and founded the SS, in which Mussolini seized outright power, in which Stalin ousted Trotsky as leader of the Communist Party, and in which the Ku Klux Klan marched 40,000-strong down Washington's Pennsylvania Avenue. Britain was girding its loins for the General Strike, China was readying itself for Civil War and Japan's military was infusing itself with the drug of ultranationalism. It was a year in which everyone seemed to be stepping off on the wrong foot.

Amaryllis Fleming was born into this world of ill starts and bad decisions on 10 December 1925. But even that is open to question. Nothing is known for certain about her birth, save that it was clouded by the misguided thinking of the age. There were a few who could have revealed the secret of her parentage: that Augustus John was her father. But the only one who knew the full story was her mother. And Eve Fleming was saying nothing.

The beautiful, wealthy, and socially ambitious widow of Major Valentine Fleming – war hero, Member of Parliament, father of her four sons – Eve had everything to lose through scandal. For some years she had conducted a surreptitious affair with Augustus John. But while it was one thing to have an affair with Britain's most notorious artist, it was quite another to have his child. Her solution, therefore, was to give birth in conditions of such secrecy that no one – gossips, friends, family, not even her daughter – would ever be able to uncover hard, factual evidence as to Amaryllis's origins. On 18 June 1926 Amaryllis was baptised at a private ceremony in Eve's home, 118 Cheyne Walk. The certificate reads 'Unknown' in the space allotted for parents' names. A fortnight later, after a second, public baptism, another certificate was issued. It reads more forthrightly, 'Adopted daughter of Mrs Valentine Fleming.'

Until her dying day Eve refused to admit that her daughter was anything other than an unwanted orphan. And until she finally discovered her father's identity at the age of twenty-four, Amaryllis believed what she was told. Domineering, beautiful and musically talented, she never considered that these characteristics might be inherited from a woman who insisted so vehemently she was not her mother.

Evelyn Beatrice Ste Croix Rose was born on 10 January 1885, the third child of George and Beatrice Rose, of The Red House, Sonning, Berkshire. There was nothing exceptional about her background or her childhood surroundings, both of which were rooted firmly in England's new-born middle classes. The town of Sonning, now a traffic-bound satellite in Reading's commuter belt, was then quaint and quietly prosperous, a typical Home Counties settlement on a loop in the River Thames. It was all very English, with its narrow streets, its flinty walls, its picturesque pubs, its roses and willows, its air of mellow tranquillity. And The Red House, an elegant, brick-built Georgian villa, with a large walled garden sloping gently down to the river, fitted perfectly into this atmosphere. It was solid, comfortable, and exuded an air of affluent ease and social standing – words which applied equally well to its occupants. Both George and Beatrice Rose had aristocratic connections – he was the sixth son of Sir Philip Rose, legal adviser to Disraeli and the Conservative Party; she was the second daughter of Sir Richard Quain, Queen Victoria's private physician and one of London's most eminent doctors. They were wealthy, thanks to George's position in Baxter, Rose and Norton, the family firm of solicitors. And as the older generation died, they got even richer; Sir Richard alone, who died in 1898, left a total of over £100,000 to his four children.

With their wealth and rank the Roses were archetypal darlings of Victorian small-town society, a situation George found agreeable. Remembered by one relation as 'a nice old boy',[1] he enjoyed a quiet, respectable existence. He had a passion for the Thames, umpiring at prestigious up-river regattas, and for the last twenty years of his life was president of Sonning regatta. On retirement he moved into a comfortable little cottage called 'Appletree' and eked out his days as the local JP. It was a sleepy world of teacakes and awnings. And perhaps that was a relief to George and Beatrice, for both had grown up in the shadow of giants.

The caricaturist 'Spy' painted a picture of Sir Philip Rose, which he entitled 'Lord Beaconfield's Friend'. It shows a bluff, heavy-set Victorian, his bearded jaw and lowered brow set in a pugnacious expression. This, the picture says, is a well-to-do man with determination and energy, possibly an old sea-dog fallen on better times. In fact, Lord Beaconsfield's Friend was a highly successful solicitor whose services to Benjamin Disraeli (Lord Beaconsfield) earned him a baronetcy in 1874. Four years later he became High Sheriff of Buckinghamshire, and by the time he died in 1883 he was director of a host of public-spirited companies, including the Submarine Continental Railway, a hopeful precursor of the Channel tunnel.

But it is for his philanthropy that Sir Philip is best remembered. In 1841, so the story goes, one of his clerks came down with consumption. Outraged that no hospital would admit consumptive patients, Philip – then just twenty-five years old – set about creating one that would. The result, which he achieved almost single-handedly within only a year, was the Brompton Hospital. Prince Albert laid the foundation stone, Charles Dickens praised the project, and it became a runaway success, doubtless contributing to statistics which proved, in 1871, there was less likelihood of dying in Brompton than in a healthy spa town such as Cheltenham.

'Spy' produced a matching caricature to 'Lord Beaconsfield's Friend'. 'Lord Beaconsfield's Physician' is a slight, sardonic figure, hands in pockets, rocking back on his heels. He smiles wryly at the world from beneath a mop of wavy black hair and a pince-nez rests at a jaunty angle on an enormous nose. This likeable rogue is Sir Richard Quain. Born near Cork, he rose from an unlikely start as tanner's apprentice to become one of London's leading doctors. His talents – for which he was made a baronet in 1891 – were wide-ranging: now he could be found attending the queen, now telling farmers how to deal with cattle disease, now investigating cases of poisoning (in an early sensation he proved that one suspected victim to have been given arsenic *after* his death), now editing the 2,000 double-columned pages of the *Dictionary of Medicine*. He was renowned for his intuitive skill in diagnosis, and if this intuition led occasionally to a 'persistence in error which more detailed examination might have avoided',[2] his patients usually forgave him. Who, for example, could resist a doctor who prescribed 'roastmeat, Carlsbad salt and no thwarting',[3] for suspected malarial fever? Nor did Sir Richard's appeal stop at the surgery door. He was a man of immense charm and geniality, a born raconteur who was a sought-after dinner guest and popular host. He celebrated his birthday twice a year on the pretext that no one could remember whether midnight had struck before or after he was born. Such was his popularity that at his funeral fifty carriages were required to carry the principal mourners alone. As his obituary intoned, 'He may be said to have known everyone worth knowing and seen everything worth seeing.'

There was no competing against such larger-than-life figures. Little wonder, then, that George and Beatrice opted for Sonning, where they groomed their offspring to become decent British gentlefolk. Photographs show cheerful, easy-going parents caught with their two sons and two daughters in spontaneous drollery: George pulling faces over his wife's shoulder while the family pose for a shooting-party snap; beaky-nosed Beatrice cackling away with Eve as she feeds the chickens. They taught them the ways of the river – to swim, to fish, to handle boats and to build them too.

The children's upbringing followed the pattern of their class. Eve's elder brothers, Ivor and Harcourt, were sent to Eton, from where Harcourt advanced to Oxford University and thence to his father's law firm. Ivor, meanwhile, joined the army to fight in Somaliland and South Africa. Eve and her younger sister Kathleen were educated by a private governess and attended a French finishing school which taught ladylike subjects such as music, painting and languages. Eve was good at all three, acquiring fluent French, a proficiency with watercolours and showing considerable promise on the violin.

On paper, George and Beatrice had created four respectable citizens. But only on paper. For it was Quain whimsy rather than Rose conformity which infused their children. Harcourt and Ivor, commonly known as the 'Wild Roses', became rakes of distinction. Before they died – Harcourt in 1955, Ivor in

1961 – both had been declared bankrupt and both had gone through three wives. Early adulthood was marked for both by court appearances relating to charges that ranged from motor offences to manipulation of government contracts. Ivor was a particular offender. When finally dragged into the dock he would produce endearing excuses. A typical Ivorism, in response to one summons, was that he had only wanted to see what a speed-trap was like. Besides, he continued, he couldn't have been speeding because his wife had been sitting on his knee.

The two sisters followed a similar but more subdued pattern. They were independent and single-minded. While Harcourt and Ivor enjoyed the camaraderie of shared misdemeanours, Eve and Kathleen quarrelled vigorously with their parents, their brothers and each other. They were silly on occasions and snobbish always; George and Beatrice had tried deliberately to live down their parents' success, but the Rose and Quain baronetcies seemed to act as social goads to the grand-daughters. They were also vain, Eve exceptionally so. And, to their parents' despair, they had good reason for vanity. Slender, graceful and strikingly beautiful, the Rose sisters epitomised Edwardian society's ideal of womanhood. With their large eyes, high-cheekbones and swan-like necks, clad in vivid colours that repelled and attracted in equal measure (Kathleen preferred vermilion, and Eve a mixture of gold, purple and green) they bloomed like exotic flowers on the genteel lawns of Victorian Society.

The 'Berkshire belles', as they were called, presented the acceptable face of Wild Rosedom – but not for long. Kathleen married briefly a 'cad from Tattersalls', whom she later described in histrionic terms to Amaryllis as a 'sex maniac who gave me gonorrhoea then invited his friends to come and stick hot pokers in me'. Thereafter, she devoted her life to becoming first an actress and then a playwright, but neither career was a success. Eve might well have followed a similar dismal path were it not for Valentine Fleming. The two met at a ball. Exactly when, where and how remains unknown, but the initial introduction was probably made by Harcourt, whom Val Fleming knew from both school and university. Eve fell in love, 'at *first sight*', she later emphasised to Amaryllis. Val felt the same. They were married in February 1906.

Val was the eldest son of Robert Fleming, a shrewd and capable Scot whose financial acumen had brought him from the slums of Dundee to the City of London. Born in 1845, the son of a jute works overseer, Robert had risen in the world at regular intervals of seven years. At fourteen he became a clerk with a major Dundee textile firm, at twenty-one its secretary, and at twenty-eight, having entered the world of finance, he engineered the industrial world's first investment trust. In 1909, when he was sixty-three, he found a partnership which became a fully-fledged bank when he was seventy-seven. Along the way he made huge sums of money, and at the time of Val's and Eve's wedding he was a millionaire several times over. A portion of his wealth had been spent two years before in constructing Joyce Grove, a monstrous red-brick pile which still blights the outskirts of Nettlebed in Oxfordshire. But he still had enough to settle £250,000 on his eldest son as a wedding present: a gift which should be multiplied by about fifteen to gauge its present-day value and which, to put it further in context, should be measured against the payroll of less than £6,500 for Robert's 150 estate workers in the same year.

Money aside, Val was in every respect an excellent choice of husband. Born in 1882, in Newport, Fife, he has been described as 'one of those rare, slightly baffling Edwardian figures of whom nothing but good is ever spoken'.[4] Handsome, charming and brave, he was also honourable, intelligent and impeccably worthy. He had excellent prospects as an Oxford graduate studying for the Bar; he was a freemason and his father wielded enormous influence in the City. A fine athlete, he was credited by Inverness stalkers as being the best walker in that county. Above all, according to Joan Campbell, the couple's housekeeper, he was the only person capable of controlling Eve.

He had good need of this last virtue, for the Fleming family found they had little in common with the lurid bombshell who landed in their midst. Where they were thrifty, she was extravagant. Where they were robust, outdoor types, she was a drawing-room snob besotted with rank and lineage. They maintained gamebooks; she kept a dainty ledger of borrowed *bon mots* and second-hand saws. She quarrelled with all of them save Robert, of whom she became very fond. She flaunted her noble ancestry – besides Sir Richard and Sir Philip she boasted a spurious connection with John of Gaunt – and she sneered at the Flemings' Lowland origins, claiming that her Rose ancestors were true Highlanders.

To give Eve her due, the Flemings could be trying company. They were prodigiously fit – Val's brother Phil was an Olympic gold-medallist oarsman – and expected others to match their standards. Every year they rented a Scottish estate for sporting holidays marked by a degree of bloodthirstiness and physical exhaustion rarely seen out of wartime. After one spectacularly destructive season their landlord, the Duke of Sutherland, felt compelled to bulletin fellow landowners about these fearsome tenants. Occasionally they were joined by their friends the Hermon-Hodges, an equally energetic, slightly eccentric, eleven-strong family of Irish descent into which Val's sister Dorothy had married, whose eagle noses and fierce blue eyes added an unnerving touch to proceedings.

For the unwary, a stay with the Flemings could be a nightmare. Some guests barricaded themselves in their rooms rather than face their hosts' idea of fun. Others fled into the rhododendrons, returning only under cover of darkness. When one Englishman dined with them in Scotland, he likened the experience to eating alongside muscle-bound bolts of tweed. Eve, however, bore these Celtic doings with stoic fortitude and even showed an unsuspected toughness. On her first visit to Scotland, when Dorothy and her sister Kathleen dragooned her into joining them for a 'short stroll', she completed the twenty-mile trek without complaint, in indoor shoes.

Married life had some advantages, however. Eve could now keep at a safe remove from her siblings' misadventures and disastrous alliances – Harcourt and Kathleen married in 1907, Ivor the following year. Moreover, as her husband's career prospered, she could maintain an increasing distance from the Flemings as well. In 1907 Val was called to the Bar as a member of Inner Temple, and a year or so later he joined his father in the City. In 1910 he was elected Member of Parliament for South Oxfordshire (Henley Division), an event that caused Lady Ottoline Morrell, wife of the defeated Liberal candidate, to shake Eve angrily by the lapels.

Eve revelled in her new position. She enjoyed seeing her face on the Christmas cards Val sent to his constituents. And she particularly enjoyed living in Pitt House, the Hampstead residence Val bought in order to be near Parliament. Here she played gracious hostess to statesmen such as Winston Churchill, Val's fellow MP and brother officer in the Oxfordshire Yeomanry. Here too, away from her in-laws, who were cheerfully tone-deaf, she honed her musical skills. She practised the violin daily, and took lessons from two accomplished sisters, great-nieces of the Hungarian violinist Joseph Joachim: Jelly d'Aranyi – to whom pieces had been dedicated by Bartók and

Ravel, and whom Aldous Huxley regarded as 'a bit of a genius' – and Adila Fachiri.[5]

There is little doubt that Eve was gifted. Indeed, given the correct conditions she could have probably become a professional musician. At the time, however, she had other priorities, not least the rearing of her family. She had given birth in quick succession to four sons – Peter in 1907, Ian the following year, then Richard in 1910 and Michael in 1912. It was a happy nursery to which Eve would willingly have added were it not for the sudden outbreak of World War I.

The war for which Val departed in August 1914 was seen by many in Britain as a bit of a lark and a rare chance to prove one's valour; it would almost certainly be over before the end of the hunting season. Eve was one among hundreds of wives who sailed to France to dine with their menfolk and catch a safe whiff of the excitement before it was gone. But as autumn lengthened into a muddy winter, Eve and other civilians stayed at home, relying on daily letters for reports of a war that would be longer than they had imagined and, in scale, quite beyond their comprehension.

'Imagine a broad belt, ten miles or so in width, stretching from the Channel to the German frontier near Basle,' Val wrote in that first November, 'which is positively littered with the bodies of men and scarified with their rude graves; in which farms, villages and cottages are shapeless heaps of blackened masonry; in which fields, roads and trees are pitted and torn and twisted by shells and disfigured by dead horses, cattle, sheep and goats, scattered in every attitude of repulsive distortion and dismemberment. Day and night in this area are made hideous by the incessant crash and whistle and roar of every sort of projectile, by sinister columns of smoke and flame, by the cries of wounded men . . . Along this terrain of death stretch more or less parallel to each other lines of trenches, some 200, some 1,000 yards apart, hardly visible except to the aeroplanes which constantly hover above them menacing and uncanny harbingers of fresh showers of destruction. In these trenches crouch lines of men, in brown or grey or blue, coated with mud, unshaven, hollow-eyed with the continual strain, unable to reply to the everlasting run of shells hurled at them from 3, 4, 5 or more miles away . . .'

Yet somehow the true horror failed to sink in. The letter was passed to Churchill, who replied in rhetorical tones: 'You must . . . look beyond the blasted lines of contact and collision and the suffering troops to the long and glorious years of peace and power which await our country as the result of the victorious issue of the war . . . Tell the squadron what I say about it all coming right for certain and putting England at the head of the river for 100 years.'[6] If Churchill and the rest of Britain's propaganda machine was to be believed in those early years, the British Empire was an unstoppable force which would triumph come what may. As Val later wrote to Eve, 'The papers make me sick with their silliness.'

Of course, the press had no monopoly on silliness. There were also the generals. As the front line wavered back and forth across Flanders to minimal purpose and at unparalleled human cost, faint whispers of their futility reached London. When Haig experimented with high-explosive sapping techniques, the sound of a French hill being vaporised reached Pitt House; when the wind was right, the thunder of Falkenhayn's and Nivelle's artillery could also be heard. One morning Eve's children found a piece of shrapnel on their doorstep.

In war, as in peace, Val was seemingly too good to be true. Passing through a trench in Wulverghegm, he borrowed a rifle and picked off two German soldiers on Messines ridge at the impossible distance of 900 yards. While at Kemmel he walked fifteen miles every night to inspect his working parties. He ran every morning before breakfast in the snow at Senlecques. Bored at Morbecques, he started a competition to cut down a nearby forest until his superiors put him in charge of a trench-warfare school. He was mentioned in despatches and he turned down a DSO. At Vermelles he remained imperturbable when a shell snapped the pipe in his mouth.

At Guillemont Farm, on 20 May 1917, Major Valentine Fleming's luck ran out. Having reconnoitred this newly vacated outpost of the Hindenburg Line he wrote a pessimistic report: it was under direct observation from German positions, there was an adverse salient, and much of the trenchwork was in ruins. Nevertheless, he ordered 1,000 sandbags, 500 yards of barbed wire, 50 sheets of corrugated iron, 100 feet of timber and set to work. It was a thankless task, the men working in forty-eight-hour shifts amid a hail of gas and high-explosive shells fired by both enemy and ally. Occasionally, in the early hours, it was possible to catch some sleep, a period Val spent writing reports for the runners who left for Battalion Headquarters at 6.00 a.m. One report informed his colonel that it would be impossible to hold the farm for more than four days. At 1.00 a.m. on the third day he wrote, 'My squadron holds its locality,' and at 2.30 that morning he began his situation report, detailing mounting enemy fire of all descriptions. Neither message was sent. An hour later he was caught in the barrage and killed instantly.

TWO

The Chelsea Widow

Eve's world, which had once seemed so secure and promising, crumbled around her. Val had meant everything to her. Now, it seemed, she would have to carve a new future. Her options, however, were severely circumscribed by Val's will. He left her almost all his wealth, on condition that she remained single. Should she remarry the money would pass to the four boys, leaving her with a drastically reduced allowance.

Eve was outraged and maintained to the end of her life that it was a formulaic document, signed blind at the outset of war, which bore no resemblance to Val's true wishes. In one respect she was right: the will, signed on 7 August, just three days after Britain had declared war on Germany, *had* been drawn up in a hurry. But supplementary codicils show that her husband had chosen to leave things as they were. Val had taken the then unexceptional step of ensuring that family money stayed firmly within the family.

The document had a startling long-term effect on Eve who, for the rest of her years, teetered between bouts of wild expenditure and elaborate meanness. She knew she was rich, yet at the back of her mind lurked the fear that one day she might not be. She might spend it all; she might remarry and lose it all. Was it hers anyway? Or did it belong to her sons? Should she follow her headstrong instincts or toe a careful

Scottish line? Her compromise was to limit the damage by spending only on herself, leaving her children to fend for themselves. To the four boys she excused her tightness as safeguarding their future inheritance. To Amaryllis she would explain that she was, simply, very poor.

In 1917, however, Eve was too preoccupied to worry about financial affairs. She plunged into deepest, most extravagant mourning. For months her brilliant costumes were replaced by exotic funereal garb, and before selling Val's Scottish estate at Arnisdale she had every room in the lodge painted black, a colour which lingers to this day in the lavatories.

Few were surprised by this theatricality; Eve had never been one for half measures. But even the Flemings, whose reaction to grief was to laugh until it went away, were impressed by the woman who finally emerged from mourning. The silliness which had marked her life was replaced by brisk and forthright capability. Spurning all offers of help – in particular one from Ivor – she shouldered the full burden of raising her four sons, drumming into them the four essentials of life as she saw it: to be tough; to be Scottish; to be successful; and to remember that she was in control. The first two qualities were unspoken Fleming dogma – Val's will had stipulated extra monies for those of his children prepared to spend at least two months of the year at Arnisdale – while the third and fourth were Eve's contribution, reinforced by a clause in the will giving her power to discriminate between the boys as she saw fit.

Despite what must have been an overwhelming inclination to the contrary, she kept her children in regular contact with their Fleming relations. Weekends were spent at Joyce Grove and the summer holidays in Scotland, where, from 1924, Robert and and his wife Katie were based, at Blackmount, a large chunk of Argyll previously owned by the Marquess of Breadalbane and now in thrall to the Flemings and the

Hermon-Hodges. As usual, Eve found these northern visits a trial. Having landed the heaviest salmon ever caught on the estate, she closeted herself in a corrugated-iron shack, a little way from the main lodge, and practised her violin in a peace broken only by the ferrets which Dorothy's children sent beneath the floorboards. At Joyce Grove, however, she enjoyed the seclusion of her own separate wing, and she got on well with old Robert, now afflicted with Parkinson's disease and slipping into early senility. In the evenings she read to him the books his shaking hands could no longer hold. But as the boys grew up and went to boarding school her life focused increasingly on London. In 1923 she sold Pitt House and moved to No. 118 Cheyne Walk, Chelsea.

Even today, Cheyne Walk's western extreme is the dead-end of Chelsea respectability. A traffic-bound squib of a thoroughfare with views which encompass Chelsea Wharf, Lots Road Power Station and a jumble of houseboats, it is noisy, dirty and inconvenient. Or, as estate agents assure their wealthy clients, it is 'bohemian'.

In Eve's day it was truly bohemian. Chelsea Wharf was then in working maritime order and the area was peppered with brothels, ships' chandlers and public houses. The river was filled not with houseboats but their ancestors: true, working barges which hooted through the fog, bearing cargoes of every commodity from coal to sugar, which had been trodden level by barefoot boys in the East End docks. Cheyne Walk was swamped by water whenever the Thames flooded, a disaster attributed by Harcourt Rose in a letter to *The Times* to inefficient dredging. Yet the houses were solid, and Eve took three of them. The compôte, which became her address until the outbreak of World War II, was known to postmen as No. 118 and to visitors as Turner's House.

No. 118 did include J. M. W. Turner's house, to which the irascible, tight-fisted artist – called by his own whim Mr Booth or The Admiral – had retired in old age to paint the Thames, and where he had died. But it also included an adjoining building and the next-door 'Aquatic Stores'. The three were knocked together and transformed into a cedar- and pine-panelled retreat, complete with twelve bedrooms, three reception rooms and three studios, which was ideal for both family living and entertaining. It only remained to cover the walls of the main, fifty-foot-long studio with gold canvas, equip it with a Bechstein grand and a multitude of brightly cushioned sofas, polish its oak floor to mirror brilliance, and Mrs Valentine Fleming was in business.

Business, of course, meant social business, of which Eve was a competent managing director. Hers was not the despairing Gatsbyesque flappery which became a cliché for life in the Twenties. It was instead a carefully conducted campaign to bring all with rank and status within her ambit. Lords and ladies abounded on Eve's guest list, as well as luminaries such as Jacob Epstein, Thomas Beecham, Winston Churchill, Edwin Lutyens and George Bernard Shaw. She wanted the cream. And she wanted it not only for herself but for her sons, whom she bombarded with 'suitable' young girls. But there was one other motive for this vigorous socialising. On a scrap of paper – the back of a letter sent to her by Val's batman in the trenches – she wrote the lines: 'While all melts under our feet we may well grasp at any exquisite passion, or any contribution to knowledge that seems by a lifted horizon to set the spirit free for a moment.' The wider and more exalted her circle of acquaintances, the greater, it must have seemed, her chance of finding this exquisite passion. Opportunity presented itself in the shape of Augustus John.

It was inevitable that Augustus John would sooner or later

be drawn into Eve's circle. Hailed as Britain's greatest contemporary artist, he had long since established himself as a pillar of Chelsea's bohemian society. At his studio in Mallord Street, just a few minutes' walk from Turner's House, a steady procession of sitters, girlfriends, and mistresses testified to his desire to 'sin openly and scandalise the world'.[7] Those words had been uttered many years before, and by the Twenties he was beginning to shrink from his earlier reputation as a womaniser – but only the reputation; he clung to the reality as firmly as ever. In the early years of the decade Eve Fleming became part of that reality.

Born in 1878 in the small Welsh town of Tenby, Augustus was all that Eve was not. He rebelled against social strictures and loathed snobbery. He preferred the rootless existence of gypsies, whose Romany language he spoke, to the orderly life of industrial Britain, and he defied convention in all its forms. With his flowing red beard, his undoubted talent, and his seemingly endless capacity for women and alcohol, he epitomised the public image of what an artist should be. Scandal had always accompanied him, particularly with regard to his hectic sex life. One account estimated his illegitimate children at more than one hundred, and rumour had it that when he walked through Chelsea he patted every child he met in case it was one of his.

The tale was exaggerated. His son Romilly wrote, 'He had a positive dread of . . . meeting acquaintances of his in the street. As a very small "acquaintance", I passed him on various occasions in the King's Road, without receiving a flicker of recognition. Looking neither to the left nor to the right, he would stride onwards to the Six Bells, the lord of creation, in his wide-brimmed hat.'[8] Nevertheless, he was undeniably fond of children: before her death in 1907, his first wife Ida Nettleship had presented him with five sons; Dorelia McNeill, or Dodo, as she was known, his second wife (they were, though, never officially married), gave him another two boys and a pair of daughters; and still he took delight in each new and unauthorised arrival.

While shunning polite society, Augustus knew how dependent he was on its favours. It was the rich and famous who paid for his double lifestyle — that of artist and philanderer in London, and of Victorian paterfamilias with Dodo and his children in the country. So, despite himself, he found it necessary to cultivate the *beau monde* and in the Twenties, as he turned his talents to portraiture, the search for wealthy patrons grew more intense. As Michael Holroyd wrote in his biography of Augustus, 'Mrs Fleming admired him, he admired her and many people came to Cheyne Walk and admired them both.'[9] The symbiosis between patron and client was perfect and they soon became lovers.

Augustus affected to sneer at Eve, ridiculing her pretensions and social aspirations. He later told Amaryllis that the affair started only because he found her so unutterably boring there was nothing to do but take her to bed. And he wrote nostalgically of 'the nice little beer house next door called the Aquatic Stores, which I found so sympathetic', and which Eve had incorporated into Turner's House. If Turner returned, Augustus continued, 'he would have some difficulty in recognising his now transformed little lodging house on the river-side, and it is most unlikely that he would feel at home at Mrs Fleming's luncheon parties, even if he were ever invited to one of these distinguished gatherings. No; for him the simpler and perhaps grosser amenities of Wapping were to be preferred . . .'[10]

Augustus too, preferred the simple life, but beneath his dismissive exterior lay a deep fondness for his extravagant mistress. They corresponded for the rest of their lives, she signing her letters 'Mie', the nickname by which only her children knew her. And in his second volume of memoirs, *Finishing Touches*, published posthumously in 1964, Augustus included an 'Elizabethan Interlude' in which he appears as a young Shoreditch artisan employed by a fashionable Chelsea widow. The widow, he wrote, was 'subject like all young people (and indeed to some extent the old) to the general urge, having been left in affluence as the result of the industry and forethought of her late husband (a highly respected and substantial wool merchant), had already begun to entertain somewhat largely, when having been presented by a common friend, I made her acquaintance'. Despite having 'become a trifle arrogant in her good looks and enviable circumstances', she is described as possessing beauty, amiability and 'superior liquor'. The widow, if not Eve, is someone much like her, and the tone is of affection rather than distaste.

Their relationship produced four portraits, all showing what Eve considered her best side, and differentiated mainly by the sitter's costume. 'Of course the moment you had popped out I looked at the picture,' she wrote after one sitting, 'and it is the best ever done. Simply marvellous. It seems as if the only thing to do is to die, as you say no picture is finished until the model expires.' Augustus replied that she couldn't tell a painting from a cowpat.

In his memoirs he wrote of love: 'Lovers must be free, for the servitude of one enslaves the other. Where no decisions are irrevocable, no engagements binding, an exquisite reciprocity can be the only rule.'[11] This was certainly the attitude he took in his relationship with Eve. While seeing her, he was sleeping with other mistresses and whatever models took his fancy. Dodo naturally resented these attachments, in particular the one with Mrs Fleming. 'Eve would sometimes drive down to Alderney Manor where we lived at the time and take Augustus out for drives in her Rolls,' recalls Dodo's daughter Poppet. 'Dodo hated her and suffered quite a lot. Of all the mistresses she was the one she took exception to. Eve was *determined* to marry Augustus. The pressure grew so intense that he was driven to suggesting to Dodo that he'd *have* to marry her. Dodo's response was to tell Augustus that he'd never see her again. She'd leave for good. But Eve persisted, and in some desperation Augustus suggested to Dodo that he'd marry her in order to divorce her, and return.'

It was an old ruse, and one which Augustus had tried on a previous occasion when chased by a determined and pregnant admirer. Eve, however, was playing a slightly different game. Certainly she admired and loved Augustus, and certainly, for a while at least, she considered marriage. But the ties which bound her to her wealth were stronger than those which bound her to her lover. What she wanted from the relationship was a child, a living memento of her brush with genius and, perhaps, of a time when she had been ruled by passion instead of social ambition. Such a child – preferably a girl, to counterpoint her four boys – would be hers in a way that the father never was.

She liked to be in control; she liked to dominate. And this was probably another reason why she chose to have a child, for even in those days the choice was hers. Admittedly, birth control was not what it is now, and abortions, besides being illegal, were crude. But precautions and solutions were available, particularly to those who had money. Eve made no use of them. In her late thirties, with her sons growing up and her fertility waning, she had a chance not only to have a daughter but to prolong a dominance which, as her sons matured, was slipping from her grasp.

That the child should be genetically hers was of no consequence. She wanted a child, any child so long as it was fathered by Augustus. And what she wanted she usually got. Chiquita gave her the chance she needed. One of the many models who had succumbed to Augustus's charms, Chiquita gave birth to his daughter, Zoë, in March 1922. Eve moved fast and with Augustus's approval, he having decamped to Spain shortly after Zoë's birth. She offered to adopt the infant. She offered to buy her. She plied her mother with clothes, all bearing Fleming name-tapes. And finally she kidnapped her from the family she stayed with in Islington, and took her off to North Wales. It was not until Augustus returned from Spain that the whole sorry business ended with Zoë's return to her true mother's arms.

Eve had lost a battle but not the war. When she had recovered her composure, she resumed the campaign. The final victory came in the spring of 1925 when she accompanied Augustus on a trip to Berlin. As Europe's acknowledged sin city it seemed a typically John-ish destination. From the British Embassy, where he and Eve were billeted with Lord D'Abernon, Augustus sallied forth by night to indulge in 'solitary exploration of the monstrous city'.[12] But somehow the German capital failed to appeal, and as for embassy life, he found it 'too strenuous for me . . . there are hours of *intense* boredom'.[13] When an encampment of gypsies arrived on the outskirts of town he seized the opportunity for escape. Eve, he insisted, should stay behind; she would be bored in the company of Romany-speakers. Eve insisted otherwise. To Augustus's chagrin, she had a splendid time surrounded by gypsies who spoke 'perfect South Kensington English'. There were other diversions too. Years later Augustus recalled Eve's knickers. Hand-made to order by a French seamstress in gold thread and lined with pink crepe de Chine, they were magnificent. But Augustus found them irritatingly scratchy. He removed them.

About three months later, Eve called together the staff at Cheyne Walk and announced that she was going for a cruise. The house would be closed and they were all to find new positions. No compensation for loss of employment was offered, but Eve promised that their old jobs would be available when she came back. The house was put in mothballs and in due course Eve set sail.

At the end of the year she returned with an 'adopted' daughter wrapped in a shawl. The following summer, after a brief period of mourning for old George Rose – who had died in February 1926, having outlived his wife by fifteen years – the baby was christened Amaryllis Marie-Louise Fleming. The name Amaryllis had no history in either the Rose or Fleming families, and was probably chosen for precisely that reason; Marie-Louise was added in honour of Eve's friend Princess Marie-Louise, who had been cajoled into acting as godmother to give the ceremony a gloss of respectability.

Eve did, in fact, go for a cruise in those last months of 1925. One acquaintance reported seeing her, hugely pregnant, on a boat somewhere in the Mediterranean. Otherwise nothing is known of her movements. In those days Britons frequently travelled without passports, feeling that ownership of one-fifth of the globe gave them the right to do so, and, since no documentation was required for infants, Eve and her baby could have come and gone across frontiers as they wished. She sent Augustus a postcard announcing the safe birth of a daughter, as her father told Amaryllis later. But by then he was unable to remember anything save that the postcard showed snow-capped mountains. Was it sent from Switzerland, perhaps from Lausanne, which Eve knew well having taken her son Peter there several times before the war to be treated for a childhood ailment?

If anyone knew the full secret it was Lord Dawson of Penn, the royal physician through whom Eve claimed to have arranged the adoption. In later years Dawson became famous for the words, 'The king's life is moving peacefully towards its close,' a message repeated at fifteen-minute intervals by the BBC on the night of 20 January 1936, as George V lay dying. But at the time he was attracting attention for his espousal of birth control and his insistence that sex was more than just a means to procreation. His message was delivered to the Lambeth Council of Ecclesiasts in 1921 and was still causing a stir four years later when Eve called for his assistance. But apart from his daughter's recollections of unexplained lightning visits to Switzerland there is nothing to confirm Amaryllis's place of birth.

Nobody could disprove Eve's story, but not everybody was convinced by it. Peter's friend Rupert Hart-Davis described in a letter to George Lyttleton in 1962 'the appearance of this baby when Peter and I were at Eton, and even then in my innocence I thought Mrs F's account of how she adopted the child unnecessarily protracted'.[14] Adila Fachiri commented that no adoption on earth could make a woman's breasts swell so dramatically. And when the news reached the Hermon-Hodges, Dorothy Fleming's father-in-law lay back and 'laughed for a week'.

THREE

A Rare Bird

At the age of four, Amaryllis was asked by Eve to spend the night in her bedroom – an area normally off limits. Even at that age she felt suspicious and, as mother and daughter lay together in bed, her suspicions were realised. In a normal, conversational voice, Eve told her that her mother had died, her father had disappeared, and that she was an adopted child. It was a devastating shock, but Amaryllis's uppermost thought was that she must not cry, must not show she minded. 'Oh really?' she replied. The two then went to sleep.

In her clumsy way, Eve probably thought she was acting in everyone's best interests. The stigma of illegitimacy would have been as damaging for her daughter as for her sons and herself. To be known as adopted, however, especially after the introduction of the first Adoption Act in 1926, was far more acceptable for a young girl trying to make her way in 'society', as Eve fully expected her daughter to do. But the only result of Eve's decision was to make Amaryllis deeply unhappy. She felt she was living on charity; that she was a nobody; that she had no family at all, certainly not the one she was living with. And for the next seven years she had, night after night, a recurrent dream. She dreamed she was walking through a beech wood, a forest of tall, bare trunks, whose foliage was hidden far above, out of sight. She walked and walked, until she came to an invisible boundary. In her mind she knew that if she crossed this boundary she would return to wherever she had come from. She would no longer have a name, especially not the name Fleming. She would merge with eternity and no longer have to endure this existence. And once she had acknowledged these facts she turned away from the boundary and woke.

The dream, which some might interpret as suicidal, never worried Amaryllis. To her it represented an alternative, a possibility of escape that made life bearable. She never crossed the boundary, yet its presence was a comfort. It was only when she was eleven and lost the dream that she began to worry, her fear being that she was going to become one of 'them', part of the family to which she knew she did not belong. But if the dream faded, the knowledge of her adoption remained. From the age of four Amaryllis was determined to do something in her own right, to prove that she was somebody, to shrug off the sense of being a burdensome dependant. The feeling grew that it was somehow undignified to be a child, demeaning to accept orders from others – even as an infant she had regarded her pram as being infra dig. But, however much she wished not to be, the fact remained that she was still a child, and her reaction took a typically childish form. She developed a fearsomely rebellious streak. Life became a progression from one temper tantrum to the next, punctuated by the slamming of doors. Her rages were terrible and uncontrollable. She hated the clothes Eve gave her and occasionally tore them to shreds. At every step, mother and child were at loggerheads. Stubborn, proud and strong-willed, each had an instinctive knack of rubbing the other up the wrong way. In Amaryllis's words, 'It was as if we were two bulls with a red rag in the middle.'

*

The world of Turner's House was an ideal setting for rebellion. Eve lived by a strict regime. Mornings were spent in bed catching up on her correspondence, at noon she ventured into the outside world and, unless she had guests, she was in bed by 8.00 p.m. But, as a chronic insomniac, she was often up again for a punishing cure of a cold bath, then wrapping a towel around herself and getting straight back into bed. She had definite ideas about food and adopted a spartan diet. The cook – a mannish woman named Louis, who warmed her feet in the oven – baked her a special brown loaf every day and prepared her minute dinner of a lettuce leaf and a bowl of yoghurt, which she took in bed. Guests, however, were expected to eat what was put in front of them. As her housemaid Joan Regent recalls, 'You had to brave it out whatever it was.' No one was immune from Eve's cuisine. She dismissed her architect for refusing a bowl of strawberries and cream. That they gave him a rash was no defence. Even Bernard Shaw, a vehement vegetarian, was served a ham omelette. 'I've been betrayed!' he moaned as the offending meat lolled from the tines of his fork.

The opinions of others mattered little to Eve. Not for nothing did her maid, Hilda Gee, dub her 'The Great I Am'. But, if she wanted, she could make most people like her (she was, after all, Sir Richard Quain's granddaughter) and she was especially good with young children. Many of Amaryllis's friends and relations recall her as a witty and generous person. But power, rather than affection, was the keynote in her actions. As her sons matured she tried to control them with childish tactics, such as telling them their father's spirit had visited her with specific warnings against whatever venture they had in mind. And the staff at Cheyne Walk were expected to spy on her children's movements, delivering their reports to Eve's bedroom every evening.

She brought the same degree of control to her household staff, using carrot and stick in rigorous and effective combination. Joan Regent summed it up: 'With Mrs Fleming you were either in or you were out.' Now one might be the apple of her eye, now the worm beneath her heel. Those who thwarted her went; those who succumbed stayed. To thwarters she was hell on earth, to succumbers the most wonderful person in creation. The result was an infantilising autocracy where obedience was all and dissension an unforgivable heresy. Those who wore the uniform and obeyed the orders prospered. Those who showed independence were outlawed.

Eve's chauffeurs suffered the most. She set strict standards and tight speed limits, making it almost impossible for them to get anything right. Too fast, too slow, or too ignorant and their fate was sealed. One terrified man spent his nights walking the streets to gain a footsore 'knowledge' of districts Eve might wish to visit. It was a futile task, and every night, until he was sacked, he could be heard crying himself to sleep. There was one, however, who made a stand, having driven his employer and her daughter from Cheyne Walk to Joyce Grove. During the whole journey Eve fulminated in French – the era of *pas devant* still flourished – against his failings. On arrival he turned in his seat and said simply, '*Madame, vous savez, je comprends français.*' Then he quit.

Life at Cheyne Walk continued in its matriarchal fashion. Every year Eve sorted out bundles of cast-off clothes for the staff, each bundle carefully selected for its recipient in terms of size and suitability. Some contained truly magnficent gifts in almost pristine condition. As Joan Regent says, 'Mrs Fleming would put on a pair of shoes, walk to her car, and never use them again.' But other donations were less welcome. After her retirement to Switzerland, Amaryllis's French governess was surprised to receive a brown paper parcel from London. It contained Eve's ancient dressing-gown, patched to oblivion, and with mole-pelt inserts peppering its withered mink trim.

While seeking to reduce her employees to dependence, Eve also sought the complaisant, unthreatening company of older men. Even in her seventies she was pursuing the Marquess of Winchester, a man twenty years her senior. Some may have been her lovers. She kept, for example, a photograph of Lord D'Abernon by her bedside until she died. And occasionally the gold knickers (which she washed in private by hand) could be glimpsed drying triumphantly on her bathroom towel rail. But her affairs, if any, were kept a close secret.

Amaryllis's childhood was spent in a state of perpetual organisation. There were French lessons, dancing lessons, music lessons and a host of different tutors coming to and from the nursery, but it was in music that she excelled. Eve had her on a piano stool at the age of three and shortly afterwards she was sent to school to learn the Yorke-Trotter method – through which one gained a sense of rhythm by repeating over and over 'Ta Ta Taffy Taffy Ta! Ta Ta Taffy Taffy Ta!' In fact, Turner's House was filled with music. Eve practised daily, and Amaryllis soon learned to recognise the piece by Kreutzer with its multitude of bowings which her mother used as a warm-up before serious playing began. By this time Jelly d'Aranyi had settled into a performing career and her place had been taken by a Hungarian violinist, Louis Pecskai. Not that Adila was forgotten; Eve called on her for tuition and for support at her rare charity concerts, because she was too nervous to play alone. But Pecskai was now the senior tutor, and Turner's House resounded as he and Eve indulged his favourite pastime of racing through a piece.

Amaryllis listened and learned, and did her best at the piano under the eagle eye of a Miss Robinson. 'When I was four I thought I was a very good pianist,' Amaryllis told the *Sunday Times* some forty years later. 'Then I found out it wasn't true.' By that age, however, she had attained a modest competence and would commandeer Hilda Gee as a reluctant audience, offering a choice of 'something fast or something slow'. Hilda, keen to get away, invariably chose the former. 'You know, Hilda, you have very bad taste,' Amaryllis admonished; 'slow pieces are much more moving.' Miss Robinson had high hopes for her pupil but it was not until her career as a cellist had taken off that Amaryllis discovered how high those hopes had been. In a sad little post-concert encounter the ageing piano teacher asked if she could possibly have Eve's address. Her tuition had obviously been useless, she explained, and she wanted to repay the fees.

Amaryllis never took to painting. Eve showed her how to use watercolours and paid for professional tuition, but the tutor insisted she paint only still life – which she hated – so his wisdom did not take root. Later, school offered another opportunity for Amaryllis to learn art but, through some arcane piece of curricular dogma, only at the expense of music. Music won, and whatever artistic talent she might have possessed, given her father's ability, remained stillborn.

Most of Amaryllis's friends came from among the staff, and her happiest days were when Eve was out and she could call them up to the nursery, where, seated under a tablecloth on a row of chairs, she made them play trains. Her constant companion was Nanny Towler. A sad woman, herself illegitimate, who shuffled round the house wearing two dresses for warmth, she was constantly in tears because of the treatment she received from Eve. She was also bedevilled by migraines during which she went pale green and collapsed on the nursery floor, whereupon Eve would berate her for eating too much mutton fat. Poor Nanny Towler got even shorter shrift from her charge. When Eve was away Amaryllis feigned sickness to get off school, then flew at her sympathetic nanny. 'You fool!' she would cry, 'don't you know I'm lying through my teeth?' When Nanny Towler protested that surely her sweet thing would never do that, the grim reply was, 'Oh yes I would!' Every other week Nanny Towler announced her imminent departure, but never mustered the courage to give notice.

One who did have the necessary gumption was Mademoiselle Chabloz, a Swiss governess who gave Amaryllis French lessons. This capable and kind-hearted woman started Amaryllis on *The Three Musketeers*, reading a chapter to her each night in the bath. As Amaryllis gained in fluency her excitement mounted. When Mademoiselle Chabloz left for her rooms in the King's Road she stole the book for secret reading by torchlight under the blankets. She was never caught, which was fortunate because Mademoiselle Chabloz had an iron will to match Eve's, and whenever she had had enough of her employer's whims she would leave. Then, after a brief pause for honour to be satisfied on both sides, she would return on Eve's humble insistence.

Appearances were all at Turner's House and even Amaryllis's pets had to be pedigree. There was Misty, an amber-eyed grey Persian cat, who ate liver delivered from Harrods. Ahmed, a ludicrous Afghan, devoured Eve's paisley shawl then fell into the garden pond, caught pneumonia, and had to be spooned brandy until he recovered. Mercury, an equally stupid Dalmatian whom Eve had had neutered, was successfully sold to a dog breeder. Less select but no less adored were the clumps of slugs and snails which Amaryllis kept in her bedroom.

In the general scheme of things Amaryllis identified more with the slugs than the pedigrees, yet for much of her childhood she was forced to assume the role of the latter: an unruly household pet, pretty but flawed, who was brought out for show but otherwise hidden from view. When guests arrived she was dressed in a curiously old-fashioned costume made by Eve herself, and called to dance in front of them. At lunch or dinner she was required to circle the table, curtsying to each diner in turn while receiving their kisses with turned-away cheek. And Eve always introduced her with the words, 'This is Amaryllis, my adopted daughter.'

She was already showing signs of becoming a striking beauty: red-haired, slender, with high cheekbones and un-settling eyes whose huge brown irises were surrounded by a thin blue corona. But it was at Eve's annual set-pieces of two lunch parties and two cocktail parties that Amaryllis was expected to look her finest and behave her best. A society column caught the contrived nature of one such event: 'There – in the big golden walled studio – a balalaika orchestra played, and guests divided their time between having their palms read and eating early strawberries and clotted cream . . . The hostess, a striking and graceful figure in lime green with a turquoise and silver lamé coatee, had three if not all four of her sons, as well as her litle adopted daughter, with her.'

Although Augustus's attentions had strayed since Berlin, he was often to be seen at Cheyne Walk, his excuse being that he wanted to paint another portrait of Eve. The resulting 'Lady in the Red Dress' was completed – or, rather, left unfinished – in 1933. On these visits no acknowledgement was made of any connection between him and Amaryllis. He merely went into the studio with Eve, and Amaryllis was given strict orders not to disturb them. Even when Amaryllis answered his phone calls, Augustus never divulged his paternity. Later he admitted that when she asked who it was, he longed to say 'It's your dad!' but fear of Eve's wrath stopped him every time. On the occasion of the pudding-pink dress, however, he made a stand. Eve was trying to make Amaryllis wear a new dress for a party, a hideous blancmange-hued creation which clashed violently with her red hair. Amaryllis recognised the mismatch and threw a tantrum. Augustus, who happened to be in the house for a sitting, was called in to add weight to Eve's authority. To her dismay he was as horrified as his daughter. 'No!' he cried, 'it doesn't suit her at all. Take it off at once!' Eve retired abashed and the dress was never seen again.

If Amaryllis saw her father often but did not know who he was, the opposite held true for her uncles Ivor and Harcourt, of whom she heard plenty but saw little, thanks to Eve's determination that her children be protected from their baleful influence. She need not have bothered, for almost all her offspring developed their own strain of wildness. As she wrote to Lord Esher on 25 May 1938, after Richard's wedding to his cousin Charm Hermon-Hodge, 'I've just married off another of the four madmen to whom I gave birth. Mad because he and his bride have gone off to Persia at the worst moment . . . with a little tent and a hold-all.' Ian, in particular, had much in common with the 'Wild Roses'. When he joined White's Club, in St James's, an older member approached and, introducing himself as 'your Uncle Ivor', presented him with a selection of pornographic postcards. Ian was delighted.

A dim echo of this incident can be found in Barbara Skelton's description of Christmas lunch at Ian's home in 1952. 'Ian distributed a collection of sexy mottoes and a dummy Lucky Strike carton he'd brought from the States; when holding it up to the light and turning a small lever one could see a succession of nude girls . . . After tea, presents were given – always an embarrassment. From Ann a box of Floris soap, talcum powder and eau-de-cologne. From Ian, a used pencil, a used lighter and a dirty motto.'[15]

Eve's attitude caused considerable resentment among her brothers. The two were not inherently bad, merely a touch irresponsible and a little unreal in their expectations of life – as Harcourt's lawyer told the Bankruptcy Court, his 'client started life with the misfortune of being the son of a rich father'. They saw no real reason why they should be excluded in such a fashion. Harcourt had, after all, been one of Val's close friends and a named executor of his will. And Ivor was notably aggrieved, his genuine offer to help with the children after Val's death having been rejected out of hand.

The resentment was deepened by their dependence on Eve. Until the 1930s, the two brothers had survived well enough on inherited wealth. Ivor lived in The Red House at Sonning, spending his time and money on unprofitable business ventures, yachting holidays in the South of France, and a succession of fast cars, whose radiator grilles he made his teenage daughter, Camilla, paint vermilion 'to enable people to see how fast he was coming'.[16] On occasion he would drop in to visit 'Harky', who resided at nearby Whitchurch with his Swedish second wife and from whose bedroom window, conveniently overhanging the river, the 'Wild Roses' could enjoy a peaceful afternoon's fishing.

By the middle of the decade, however, their money had run out. In 1936, the Official Receiver reported that Harky's 'ranking liabilities amounted to £20,044 and the only asset was a ring which had realised £1.15s'.[17] Ivor was little better off, debts having forced him out of The Red House and into the coachman's cottage. Reluctantly, they petitioned Eve for funds.

These visits to Cheyne Walk were Amaryllis's only childhood contact with her uncles. And even then she saw nothing, only hearing muffled voices pleading with her mother behind polished cedarwood doors. Later in life, however, like Ian, she had a curious introduction. One winter's evening a stranger arrived on her doorstep, announced that he was her Uncle Harcourt and said he had come to see what she looked like. He peered closely, nodded, then presented her with a large chicken. 'This is all they seem to have in Norfolk,' he said before disappearing back into the night.

Of her aunt Kathleen, Amaryllis saw a little more. After nursing her father through his last illness and having finally gained a divorce from her husband – 'I was fed up with all that bouncing about in bed,' she announced defensively – she had gravitated slowly but surely towards Eve. And there she stayed, orbiting gently round the lodestone of her sister's wealth. The two enjoyed each other's company – Kathleen liked having a sister to moan at, Eve liked having a sister to put down – but only to a degree. They quarrelled, parted, made up, then quarrelled and parted again. But Kathleen's was not a presence which could easily be banished. During the periods of separation she wrote a number of plays which she sent to an embarrassed Peter for his comments.

Cut off as she was from the rest of her relations, it was lucky for Amaryllis that she got on with the Flemings. From the very start her half-brothers had welcomed her into the family – 'It seems quite a humorous brat,'[18] Peter had reported in his offhand way to Rupert Hart-Davis – but due to the age difference and the fact that they had all fled their domineering mother at the earliest opportunity, their contact with Amaryllis was relatively limited. Ian spent the most time at Cheyne Walk, periods memorable for his unique ability to charm the staff into bringing him breakfast in bed, and for the clinging aroma of Turkish tobacco which emanated from his bedroom. Occasionally Richard, the most Scottish of all Val's children, might swirl through the house in a kilt. Peter, too, made intermittent appearances fresh from the outer bounds of nowhere. On these domestic sabbaticals he irritated the staff by complaining loudly if his bath had not been run to near boiling point. Joan Regent, the lady at the tap, never understood how a man who had spent cheerful months without so much as a glimpse of a bath could set such exacting standards; nor could the rest of the family as they shivered before the windows and doors Peter was forever throwing open.

Peter was Amaryllis's early favourite and although 1932 marked the beginning of his transglobal wanderings, at which date he was twenty-five and Amaryllis only seven, the two exchanged a cheerful stream of insults. In a letter of 15 February 1935, headed Peiping, China, he wrote:

> My Dear Toad:
>   Thank you very much for your witty letter. You are clearly not worth writing to, so I am dictating this letter. I don't suppose you have ever had a letter dictated to you before but you needn't feel grown up about it, because everyone knows you are no better than a baby, and a pretty ugly one at that.
>   Tomorrow I am starting home, first of all in the sort of train that little girls who can't draw straight lines make pictures of, and eventually on either a camel or a yak or a mule, all of which have something about them that reminds me of you.
>   Anyhow I shall see you very soon. They tell me that you have got fatter and more repulsive than ever. Give my love to Mrs F.
>   Your arch enemy
>   Peter

At midnight on the day of writing, Peter embarked on a perilous trek that he would later describe in his best-selling *News from Tartary*.

Eve was inordinately proud of Peter, for whom she

envisaged a glittering future in politics, and she was equally fulsome in her praise of the other three – a weary Augustus nicknamed all four 'the shiny boys'. She was proud, too, of Amaryllis, but she drew a careful line between her legitimate and illegitimate offspring. In conversation with Amaryllis she pointedly referred to 'my sons', never 'your brothers', a distinction which would have been disclaimed by all the boys had they known of it. Nevertheless, Eve brought Amaryllis up to fit the same Fleming mould as her half-brothers. She was taught to be tough, to laugh off misfortune, to be successful and to recognise her mother's authority, especially in matters of money. She was also taught, with less success, how to speak Gaelic and how to use a shotgun. And every weekend she accompanied her mother to the heart of Fleming clandom, Joyce Grove.

Joyce Grove was the perfect place for a child. Amaryllis could go riding with Flynn the groom, play tennis on 'Master Ian's' hard court which had been splashed ostentatiously across an otherwise fine piece of lawn, or explore the orchard where myriad strains of apple tree sprouted beyond a gate made of whale ribs. Alternatively, she could clamber through the wooded heights of the Himalayas, a vast, artificial bank of earth constructed to hide the village of Nettlebed, or clean out Michael's pigsties, a chore for which she was paid sixpence. And if the immediate policies palled, there were always another 2,500 acres of Fleming-owned farmland and beech woods to investigate.

It was, as Peter summarised in a report on estate wages in 1968, 'a small empire whose benevolent rulers saw nothing unusual either in its dimensions or in the fact that they themselves spent only a comparatively small fraction of the year within its boundaries . . .'[19] Robert having died in 1933,

Joyce Grove was now the undisputed domain of Granny Katie, under whose rule events followed a routine of generous parsimony. 'Eat the *cut* food! Eat the *cut* food!' she exhorted the family at teatime. And as the raging hall fire, surmounted by an elaborately enamelled Parisian clock, cast its light over the acres of hardwood panelling, the grotesque ormolu piano, the hothouse palms, the Persian rugs and the expensive paintings – including a portrait of her by William Orpen and one of Robert by Augustus John – she nervously eyed the less perishable food that might be saved for tomorrow.

Later in the evening she disconcerted guests with the news that their sheets had been kept carefully unwashed since last they came, often months before. In a house whose vast, marble bathrooms were equipped with three different taps – hot, cold and rain water – this stinting came to many as a surprise. To the staff, however, it was nothing new. Peter's report detailed a curious system whereby ('doubtless for some good reason') wages not only stood still but, as national earnings rose, actually fell. 'For instance in 1920 the son of the head-keeper Wykes . . . was taken on at £2.0.0 but almost immediately reduced to £1.16.0. Similarly D. Hall started as a clerk in the Estate Office at £4 a week in October 1921 but dropped back to £3.10.0 in the following month . . .'[20] Most alarming of all was the fate of Brown, the chauffeur, who in 1938 had his wages reduced from £4.0.0 to £2.10.0, the same amount he had earned in 1915 which was a pound less than he had been getting in 1910.

Economy and extravagance competed in Katie's muddled list of priorities, but both dwindled into insignificance against the great god of exercise. She did physical jerks every morning and, given a suitably frigid expanse of water, swam before breakfast. She played golf whenever possible – Ian enjoyed telling the story of how she once tipped her caddy with a toothbrush – and if the green was too damp she went for twenty-to-thirty-mile walks across the surrounding countryside. An unfortunate peer who joined her on one of these marathons was so exhausted that he retired to bed after tea and was carried out feet first the following morning, having died of a heart attack during the night.

The Fleming boys adored their grandmother for her vigorous eccentricity. In *Goodbye to the Bombay Bowler*, a collection of articles written under the pseudonym 'Strix', Peter fondly remembered her letters, a honeycomb of illegible script covering every spare inch of every sheet; if they enclosed money, they were posted in an unstamped envelope. They 'gave you', he wrote, 'the impression that, possibly owing to her house being under some form of siege, she found herself obliged to husband her writing materials with the utmost care.'[21] Katie seemed quite divorced from reality and when, shortly before the first war, Joyce Grove caught fire – giving her an excuse to add a new wing – it was accepted as fact that she only realised what was happening when she leaned out of her bedroom window to shoo spectators off the front lawn. She was, in the words of one acquaintance, 'kind, very simple, and a happy, childish snob', and nowhere was her uncomplicated nature better revealed than in her friendship with Queen Mary.

In her old age Queen Mary had discovered the useful art of 'admiring' people's possessions, a practice which, thanks to unspoken laws of etiquette, usually resulted in her accepting the admired object. Such was her reputation that one desperate man, hearing that she planned a visit, hid all his best furniture in the attic, where it was duly discovered and admired all the more for being unwanted. The Flemings, however, were oblivious of such English niceties. When

Queen Mary admired a fine French table recently installed at Joyce Grove, Katie swelled with pride and gave her an intriguing chunk of rock she had found on the hill at Blackmount.

Katie was, in essence, very like Eve but more powerfully distilled and much, much wealthier. For some reason – forgetfulness or a belief that Val's family had funds of their own – Robert had left his entire fortune to Katie and then in trust to his three remaining children. Eve hated her for it. And, from the separate wing that she occupied with her children and staff imported from Cheyne Walk, she taught Amaryllis to hate her too. On rainy days Amaryllis amused herself by cutting Katie's head out of old photographs.

Although Amaryllis did not realise it at the time, it was Granny Katie who made Joyce Grove such a perfect antidote to Turner's House. Under her aegis it became, in a way, a select holiday camp where enjoyment of life was a law no one, not even Eve, was allowed to break. This was in stark contrast to Amaryllis's 'real' holidays. During her first seven years she rarely went away with her mother. There was a fortnight in Portofino, a week in Ireland, a few visits to Blackmount, but in the main she boarded with nannies in Bexhill or Bognor while Eve took the boys on trips to Scotland, Scandinavia and the Continent.

At home or abroad, Eve remained her magisterial self. Rupert Hart-Davis recalled a typical vacation with the Flemings when he was dragooned into carrying Eve's luggage, of which there was a great deal, 'the most tiresome piece of it an elaborate and heavy tea-basket for one, containing a spirit-lamp, a kettle, a teapot, one cup, one saucer and one plate'. Having hauled this impractical article halfway across Europe he longed to see the last of it. But back in London, 'when I had safely deposited Mrs F in a taxi with all her luggage she graciously presented me with the tea-basket, as a reward for "being so good with Ian" '.[22]

By the early Thirties Eve could no longer count on the company of her sons, so she took Amaryllis instead. Their first foreign destination, in about 1933, was Venice. With them went Mademoiselle Chabloz, who had long since established herself as the only one who could control Eve's unruly daughter. For all its glories, Venice in the Thirties had major drawbacks. In the preceding eight years Italy had undergone a dramatic modernisation but the heavy hand of fascism had yet to reach the Rialto, which was becoming more raddled and less romantic with every year. 'The bathing, on a calm day,' wrote Robert Byron of Venice in 1937, 'must be the worst in Europe: water like hot saliva, cigar ends floating into one's mouth, and shoals of jelly-fish.'[23] Augustus, in 1933, complained that '. . . the place is full of bores, buggers and bums of all kinds'.[24]

Amaryllis's first impressions were not of bathing, bores, buggers or bums, but of the stinking canals and the ubiquitous mosquitoes. She was horrified to see the Venetian urchins scampering about half-naked, their scrawny bottoms peppered with bites. And even in the marbled splendour of the Daniele Hotel, where Eve had booked rooms for the three of them, beds were swathed in nets – except the bed belonging to Mademoiselle Chabloz. In her old age, the Swiss governess recounted how she had left Amaryllis in Eve's care on her day off. Amaryllis had behaved with her usual rowdiness, exasperating Eve and driving her to a peak of jealousy that she should fail where Mademoiselle Chabloz had succeeded. In an act of petty revenge Eve ordered the Daniele staff to remove the governess's mosquito net. At breakfast the next morning Mademoiselle Chabloz's face was a mass of bites but she did not utter a word of complaint, bearing this insult with a fortitude that enraged her employer even further.

As Amaryllis grew older she went on more foreign holidays and, despite the claustrophobic atmosphere engendered by her mother, they provided a welcome change of scenery. At the end of the day, however, such holidays, and even the weekends at Joyce Grove, were fleeting escapes from a prison where, as Augustus remarked, she was kept as a 'rare bird'. Through the bars of her Cheyne Walk cage a brief glimpse of reality was afforded by the neighbouring council estate whose children occasionally lobbed footballs into the small, over-shadowed garden behind Turner's House. When Eve spotted them climbing over to retrieve their property she topped the wall with broken glass. After that Amaryllis spent much of her time loitering in the garden, hoping for a chance to throw back stray balls and to talk with real people.

The council block also gave Amaryllis her first taste of true embarrassment. Every Monday, Turner's House was adorned with flowers from Granny Katie's Joyce Grove hothouses and borders. But by Friday, when it was time to depart once more for the country, they were withered and rotting. Amaryllis was deputed to carry them over to the estate. 'It was the most awful thing in the world,' she recalls. 'I'd ring the bell, then hand over the flowers. "These are for you," I'd say. "Do what you want with them." Then I'd run.'

FOUR

Cellist in a Djibbah

By 1934 Eve was tired of spending weekends in a house that was not hers and with a mother-in-law she detested. In that year, when friction between the two Mrs Flemings was becoming unbearable, she began to look for an alternative. Donning a withered mackintosh and instructing Amaryllis to look poor, she set off with her daughter in search of a bargain Shangri-la. They did not have far to travel. Standing only three miles from Joyce Grove, Greys Court was a beautiful gabled mansion steeped in history. The main block was of Tudor origin, but there were ruined fortifications dating back to the thirteenth century. Along one side of its outer walls stood a derelict stable block where Cromwell had housed his cavalry. With its flinty, ivy-clad walls, its sweeping views towards the Chilterns, and its romantic disrepair (all the more romantic because of its effect on the price), Greys was precisely what Eve had in mind.

Its purchase was conducted in a circuitous fashion, the bargaining taking place from Venice where Eve was once again holidaying with Amaryllis. The author Cecil Roberts, whom Eve had recently met, was deputed to act as her intermediary. 'The Henley agents imagine all the Flemings are millionaires,' she told the startled man. 'Will you act for me and bid for it in your name?'[25] Roberts agreed, and with an offer of £10,000 against an asking price of £17,000 – he predicted a sale at £11–12,000 – haggling commenced.

As cables flew between Henley and Venice, Amaryllis found plenty to occupy her attention. Three years earlier Eve had written her a postcard from Venice describing how she 'met two little Princesses Zozo and Ariel & they asked after you & want to come to tea when they come to London'. To her delight, the princesses turned out not to be imaginary characters invented to please a lonely child, but Isabel (Zozo) and Ariel, aged nine and eight respectively, daughters of Parisian *haut-mondaines* Prince and Princess Faucigny-Lucinge. The tenor Lauritz Melchior was also in Venice and his daughter joined them in a foursome which overcame its linguistic differences with a pidgin of dog Latin. They built sandcastles on the Lido, toured the canals by gondola and ate ices at Florian's.

Other entertainments were more interesting to the adults. One was the sight of Mussolini, dressed only in a bathing costume, striding through the lounge of the Excelsior Lido Hotel where Eve and Amaryllis had rooms. Roberts described his bullet-headed progress through cheering ranks of Italians. 'Unresponding, grim, he strutted on down to the beach. He went straight into the sea and vigorously swam out beyond the pier, followed by a boat-load of camera and Press men.'[26] On a more edifying note there was also a chance to hear Beniamino Gigli in a performance of Verdi's *Requiem*.

Il Duce postured, Gigli sang and the Henley estate agents dropped their price, first to £15,000 and then to £13,000. Roberts stuck to his original offer, encouraged by the prospect of divine intervention. He recorded, 'Excitement had been added to our bargaining by little Amaryllis who, during an excursion to Padua, had put her small hand on the shrine of St Anthony and made a wish. She kept it secret but we guessed what it was. "We shall get Greys Court," said Mrs Fleming. "St Anthony never fails!" '[27] But the bargaining ended on a tragic note. In late September, while congratulating himself on the certainty that the agents would drop to £11,000, Roberts received a letter from his friend the Marchesa Nadja Malacrida, who, with her husband, was renting Roberts's cottage near Henley. It described, in glowing terms, a house for which they had just made an offer: Greys Court. Roberts barely had time to digest the news when he read in *The Times* that the Marchesa had been killed in an automobile accident. It was little comfort when a few weeks later the agents came through at the price he had predicted. The whole business had gone sour. Roberts later met Katie Fleming and, while admitting to an acquaintance with Eve, forbore to mention his part in the Greys Court purchase. As he noted sagely, 'Mothers-in-law often do not appreciate the enterprises of their daughters-in-law.'[28]

Eve's original intention had been to use Greys as a weekend residence, near enough to Joyce Grove for the boys to visit their grandmother, yet secluded enough to give her a sense of independence. But as the place worked its charm, so weekends stretched into weeks, which stretched, in turn, into months. For almost a year Turner's House lay fallow as Eve turned her full attention to Greys, painting several rooms gold, initiating a thorough excavation of the ruined fortifications, and converting Cromwell's stables into a self-contained writer's studio for Peter. One visitor was astonished to find Greys' new chatelaine distressing the mullions with chains.

Amaryllis too fell under Greys' spell. She had always enjoyed the freedom offered by Joyce Grove, and it now seemed as if her whole life was going to be transformed into one long, happy weekend. The confining spaces of Cheyne

Walk receded further and further into the past. She explored the grounds barefoot, relishing the feel of springy turf beneath her feet. She rode over the surrounding fields – conveniently part of the Joyce Grove estate – on a New Forest pony named Firefly, and smoked hay cigarettes rolled by Richard's groom. In her room she kept boxes full of worthless but exciting treasures from the excavations.

The true discovery of this period, however, was of a musical nature. Stringed instruments had always attracted Amaryllis, and at first she wanted to learn the violin. But Eve, declaring that no house was big enough to hold two fiddlers, would only countenance the cello. She searched for a tutor willing to travel and came up wth John Snowden, then teaching at Reading University. Amaryllis took to the instrument immediately and before long she was playing trios in the Cromwell stables with Eve and Lady Esher, a pianist friend of average ability.

'Playing with my mother was a disaster,' Amaryllis recalls, 'because neither of us would admit that we'd made a mistake, and then we'd start arguing over who it was that had come in wrong. There was really no future in it.' While the others argued, Lady Esher hammered on wearily at her piano. But there *was* a future in the cello, and Amaryllis soon realised what she was going to do with her life: she was going to become a professional musician. For the first time she had a sense of her identity and her destiny.

These were golden days, and by the beginning of 1935, when Turner's House was put on the market, they looked set to continue indefinitely. Even Eve seemed to have been softened by country life. When, later that year, the conductor Eugene Goossens fled from his rented studio at Turner's House, Eve made no fuss at all. She waived the arrears and even paid off his creditors who queued at her door for restitution. The happiness, however, was not to last. For some time Peter had been torn between his love for Celia Johnson and his feelings of loyalty towards Eve, in whose eyes this beautiful, talented, but woefully untitled actress was simply not good enough. On 10 December 1935 Peter made his choice, marrying Celia at a ceremony so sudden that Eve was powerless to prevent it. It was Amaryllis's tenth birthday and, although disappointed not to be a bridesmaid, she was happy to have been invited. 'I thought Am had the other celebrated beauties licked into a cocked hat at the wedding,' Peter wrote to Eve. 'Give her our love . . .'[29]

But Eve was too angry to pass on any such message. Her eldest son had successfully disobeyed her, therefore he must be punished. She uttered wild threats of disinheritance and promptly put Greys Court up for sale. Neither act had much impact on Peter, who was never much worried about money and had been appalled at the thought of working in his mother's gilded caravanserai. But the sale of Greys was a terrible blow for Amaryllis, who found herself, in 1936, back at Cheyne Walk, being educated in the Francis Holland Church of England School For Girls.

Her temper became ever more uncontrollable. Nor was it helped by Eve, who reminded her after one dreadful outburst that she was lucky not to have been brought up in a Dr Barnardo's home. By 1937 her mother could stand it no longer. In the early months of that year, halfway through the Lent term, Amaryllis was sent to Downe House, a select boarding school for girls near Cold Ash in Berkshire.

The headmistress of Downe House was Olive Willis, a formidable, square-jawed lady, very much of her time. Looking at her pictures one cannot help feeling that Ealing producers had her in mind when casting Alistair Sim as headmistress of St Trinian's. A thyroid disorder from which she had just recovered gave her an air of bulbous-eyed omniscience. One pupil wrote, 'We were constantly, if much of the time sub-consciously or at least indirectly or even hazily, aware of Miss Willis. We were convinced that she Knew All. *How* she knew appeared to be somewhat occult . . . By chance, by blunder, we might cross her line of vision. To attract her gaze, actually, was rare and memorable.'[30]

Miss Willis was perhaps aware of the effect she had: 'Headmistresses acquire large faces,' she liked to say, 'so that their expressions can be seen at a distance.'

Her methods were unorthodox. On discovering a group of girls having a midnight feast – her pet abomination – she made the whole school rise at midnight for the following week to eat a meal of dry biscuits. On another occasion she decided to cure a girl's homesickness by auto-suggestion, having her dormitory neighbours whisper while she slept: 'You are quite happy here . . . you like school.' Originality was cultivated to such an extent that any sign of normality in a pupil was regarded as eccentricity by the others.

Miss Willis had a fondness for lame ducks. Many teachers were hired more out of pity than professional scrutiny, a case in point being Miss Nickel, an exiled Pole whose early years had been spent as companion to a Russian aristocrat's daughter. During subsequent peregrinations she had trained herself in medicine, entomology, forestry and the use of electricity in treating rheumatism, as well as finding time to invent and patent a novel form of metal tyre. This curriculum vitae qualified her, in Miss Willis's opinion, to teach geography and chemistry, a remit which soon stretched to include cookery, conducted on the science lab's bunsens, and carpentry. Later still she was put in charge of the school's heating (she pioneered a new form of electrical plant), its drains, the construction of new classroom extensions, designing a chapel and the care of Miss Willis's Samoyed dogs.

By 1937 Miss Nickel had been banished from the classrooms but could still be seen around the school, a stocky, stomping figure in rubber boots, with a packet of cigarettes protruding from the breast pocket of her khaki overalls, who disappeared now and then to check the personal possessions she kept in a variety of shacks about the grounds. It was widely rumoured that she slept like a guard dog on the floor outside Miss Willis's door. This was very near the truth; after a brief flirtation with the bathroom lino Miss Nickel had taken to sleeping on a board atop the tub, which she claimed was an excellent cure for rheumatism.

Miss Willis was noted for dealing with 'difficult' children, bringing stupid and rebellious girls into the mainstream of school life, and she often admitted pupils for greatly reduced fees. Downe House also laid strong emphasis on art and music; one pupil recorded, 'We were surrounded by music at all times.'[31] All these qualities would have appealed to Eve, searching for somewhere to send her troublesome, musical daughter.

Flammy, Flam or, to give her her full nickname, Flamaryllis Eming, neither knew nor cared about Miss Willis's reputation. What mattered was that she had escaped one prison only to land in another. Compared with the freedom of life at Greys, her existence was now governed by bells, Nickel-contrived electric buzzers which marked out the daily routine. She ran panting from one class to another, always to be greeted with the words 'You're late!' She wept with frustration to hear the trains that puffed through the valley below her dormitory window. She yearned to be on them, going anywhere so long as it was not home.

If she had resented the costumes Eve forced on her at Cheyne Walk, it was nothing to the horror she felt at having to dress up in Downe House's uniform, the djibbah, a one-piece, short-sleeved tunic based on those worn by North African tribesmen. Never one to go to unnecessary expense, Eve ensured that her daughter would never have to buy more than one. When she arrived at Downe House, Amaryllis was clad in a long, dark-green djibbah that came down to her ankles. By the time she left, it had mutated through age and washing into a pale yellow mini-skirt held together at the hem by safety pins. This meanness on Eve's part was all the more noticeable because of the trouble she took over her own clothes. Throughout their schooldays her sons had been embarrassed by their mother's outlandish garb: 'Oh look! Fleming's mama's wearing a bath-towel!' was one taunt that greeted Richard when Eve arrived at Eton sporting a huge yellow terrycloth turban. Now Amaryllis too was subject to the jeers for, although Eve was in her fifties, her wardrobe was as wild as ever.

Amaryllis's first term at Downe House was an unmitigated failure. Bad behaviour was awarded 'stripes', and the average bag was six or seven per pupil per term. At the end of her first short term Amaryllis had amassed an awesome seventy-six. Every Saturday afternoon was spent cleaning cutlery for repeated offences such as talking after lights, wearing her uniform in bed (so that valuable sleeping time need not be wasted in dressing), being late for meals, late for classes, late for church – late for almost everything. The cause of this unpunctuality was, of course, the cello, which she practised in every spare moment. But while Miss Willis was well acquainted with musical instruments – in her youth she had squeezed a tortoise through the F-holes of her father's cello – she was not going to let them disrupt school life. By the end of the Lent term she was threatening expulsion, and Amaryllis was clamouring to be taken away.

Eve acceded to her daughter's demands with good grace. She even allowed her to choose her own school, the only stipulation being that she be able to spend weekends at home, in the mistaken belief that Amaryllis was homesick. Together they toured a variety of establishments, mostly convents, all of which appalled Amaryllis with their pious regulations. After visiting one institution, where nudity was forbidden and pupils had to bathe wrapped in a sheet, Amaryllis gave up. Opting for the devil she knew, she returned to Downe House, having elicited from Eve a promise that she could leave when she passed her School Certificate.

Gradually, Miss Willis and her recidivist charge came to terms. Amaryllis's unpunctuality at mealtimes, previously punished by banishment with bread and water, was now greeted with a weary wave of the hand. 'You were practising,' Miss Willis would say. 'Go and sit down with the others.' And when staff members complained about Amaryllis practising in her room, which was situated directly opposite their common-room, Miss Willis stood up for her. There were still moments of rebellion. For a good few weeks Amaryllis managed to dodge Sunday chapel, and hid behind a piano in one of the music rooms listening to concerts on the radio. When it was too icy or rainy to play games, and the school formed into a crocodile for a walk through the woods, Amaryllis lingered at the back until she got a chance to jump over a wall and return to her cello. And there were still the bells.

On one occasion, late as usual, she tripped running up a flight of stone steps and fell on her cello. The instrument, borrowed from John Snowden who had borrowed it from a friend, was protected only by a canvas case and was badly cracked. Although Eve had it mended by Hills, the top firm in Bond Street, it was considerably devalued. Eve, however, refused to offer Snowden any recompense, claiming that the repair made it sound better. When the cello was returned, a shame-stricken Amaryllis bought a heavy, wooden coffin case. Lugging this weighty monster around the school, her time-keeping became even worse. 'It does seem a pity to waste a good brain on music,' sighed Miss Willis, 'when she could be so good at history or some such subject.'

Her wilfulness also became apparent in her cello playing. Almost on arrival she had been put in a Haydn piano trio with two girls who would become firm friends: Anne Davies and Mary Vestey. The trouble as far as Amaryllis was concerned was that the cello played only a light background role, while the violin and piano had all the tunes. The trio soon turned into a musical battlefield, the two stringed instruments competing for precedence while Mary played manfully through the storm. Lady Esher would have sympathised.

It was Mary who helped give form to Amaryllis's un-channelled ambition. Possessed of great talent, bubbling enthusiasm and a vast record collection, she opened Amaryllis's eyes to the possibilities before her. They spent hours listening to works such as *The Magic Flute* and *Don Giovanni*. Their pleasure was increased by Amaryllis's ploy of stuffing the horn and resonance box of her wind-up gramophone with sweets. The turning-point came a few weeks into one term when the sticky baffles had been eaten and Mary put on the Dvořák Cello Concerto with Pablo Casals as soloist. 'God!' cried Amaryllis, 'I wish I could play like that!' 'You could,' was Mary's laconic reply, 'if you tried.' That slight push, the unsolicited, offhand comment from a kindred spirit, was all that Amaryllis needed to tilt her professional urge into artistic determination.

She had a low opinion of the teaching at Downe House, where isolation and an idiosyncratic regime did little to encourage high-calibre staff. Those who stick out in her memory include the Misses Moses, a pair of Jewish refugees who gave one-to-one German lessons. Admirable in most ways, they were let down by short-sightedness and halitosis. There was an ineffectual maths mistress whose wig the pupils liked to knock off as they chalked equations on the blackboard. English classes were rendered incomprehensible by Mamie Poor, who invited her twelve-year-olds to discuss Wordsworth's philosophy of life.

The only subjects Amaryllis truly enjoyed were French and Music. Already fluent in the former, she could sit back and enjoy the antics of Mademoiselle D'Agobert, a bombazine-clad martinet who was 'fierce in inverse proportion to her small size',[32] and much given to hurling objects around the classroom. Having told Amaryllis she was brought up in the gutter, she once threw a full inkwell at her. To her target's joy it hit the girl behind. A favourite D'Agobert trick was to invite pupils to write on her swivel-mounted blackboard, then slam it down on their heads when they made a mistake. Another, for mumblers, was to stuff balls of paper between their jaws to show just how far their mouths could open. This confrontational style appealed to Amaryllis and she was disappointed when Mademoiselle D'Agobert left, to be replaced by a more vapid teacher. The newcomer did have one advantage: she became infatuated with Amaryllis and insisted on giving her individual tuition in French literature, with the result that her pupil won medals two years running in a national competition.

Music, however, was one subject where Amaryllis could not afford to be complacent. She thought the teaching execrable, and when Eve heard her daughter playing, so did she. A phone call to Miss Willis elicited for Amaryllis the privilege of travelling to London once every three weeks to get personal tuition from John Snowden, who was now at the Royal College of Music. Nowadays such a course of action would be considered ludicrous – one or probably two lessons per week being the usual quota for serious musicians – but at the time it was a rare privilege which Amaryllis accepted without hesitation. Dressed in her purple uniform coat, and with strict instructions not to remove her hat lest she catch nits, she boarded the Paddington train with excitement. At the other end she was met by Nanny Towler who chaperoned her to the RCM, where John Snowden personally lugged the coffin-cased cello to his room on the third floor. There, to her delight, he would make his older students, aged around nineteen or twenty, come to hear his flame-headed prodigy.

Then came the war. Up went the blackout curtains, out went the lights, and down clumped Miss Nickel from her bathroom to the front hall, where she slept Cerberus-like on the floor in anticipation of the Hun.

The conflict was barely a year old when it claimed its first casualty among the Fleming family: Michael, who died of wounds as a prisoner-of-war after Dunkirk. Eve, for whom, like so many, the second war was repeating the horrors of the first, was stricken. 'Peter, poor Peter, came and told me. It is the second time in his life that he has been with me in my sorrow,' she wrote to Lord Esher on 8 December 1940. 'If he had been killed outright it would not be so hard to bear, but for anyone with any imagination the thought of those months of suffering alone and dying alone without hands to hold are too pitiful to contemplate. If only I could have *got* to him! I feel that with my strength and healing in my hands I could have saved him. Sometimes there comes a tiny gleam of light like a very small star in a vast sky of blackness and I think he has escaped with the connivance of the doctor and that it isn't *true*, but I fear this is only sent me to help me through the night, like a child with a night light.'

The drama passed over Amaryllis. Of all the brothers, Michael had been the one with whom she had least in common. He had been a distant figure, marrying early and vanishing with extraordinary rapidity into the City. His death was a loss but not so great as to interrupt her cello playing. Or, as Miss Willis told Mary Vestey, Amaryllis was too selfish to care what happened to anyone but herself.

At night the dormitories of Downe House were lit by a single blue bulb, their windows draped in blackout curtains. The skylights of the music rooms, however, were open to the stars. Undisturbed by buzzers, unable to see her watch or even her music, Amaryllis practised blind beneath the sky, learning the invaluable art of memorising a score.

Since air raids prevented her travelling to London she had to rely on the tuition provided by Downe House. Fortunately things had changed for the better. The old tutor, Edith Vance, had left to be replaced by Effie Richardson, a capable and well-known teacher who had studied in Paris with Diran Alexanian. By this time, however, Amaryllis was beginning to outstrip the teachers. When Effie had a prolonged spell of illness shortly before the Associated Board exams, it fell to Amaryllis to coach the pupils through their scales and repertoire. On her recovery Effie was furious to discover that not only had her girls passed the exams without her, but that their playing had improved dramatically.

If Amaryllis was gallingly good, Effie could console herself that it was partly due to her teaching. Certainly the school orchestra, in which Amaryllis had been principal cello since her first term, had done nothing to improve her playing. This ramshackle organisation – run by Miss Gunn, another St Trinian's archetype who wore tweed suits and stamped out the rhythm in heavy brogues, bellowing, '*One*, two, three, four, *one*, two, three, four,' – played nothing but Haydn's simplest symphonies and, due to a shortage of violas, Miss Willis often stood in with her violin, tuned for her by Amaryllis. Periodically, however, its cumbersome progress was halted by visits from professional musicians who did much to hearten the more talented members. One visitor was the famous cellist Emanuel Feuermann, of whom Amaryllis remembers, 'At first I got the giggles because he pulled such excruciating faces while playing, but I was soon overcome by his performance.' Another was the pianist Myra Hess, whose lunch-hour concerts in the National Gallery were Londoners' main access to live chamber music during the war. On two occasions she hoisted the school orchestra from its bland diet of Haydn and into the realms of the Bach D Minor Concerto. Beethoven was introduced by the Menges Quartet whose cellist, Ivor James, also gave an invaluable pre-performance explanation of the music. Amaryllis seized on these opportunities for enlightenment, attending even when ill – ice cubes were a handy way of fooling matron's thermometer.

So preoccupied was Amaryllis by her music that it seemed she would never gain her School Certificate. Many were taken aback when, in the summer of 1941, Amaryllis not only passed but did so a year in advance; not least Eve, who had been expecting another twelve months of peace. But a deal was a deal and Amaryllis packed her bags and left Downe House in a 'blaze of excitement' for the wider world.

FIVE

An Unproductive Paddock

The excitement of leaving school soon wore off. A lot had happened since that first disastrous term at Downe House: Michael was dead; Richard had married his cousin, Charm Hermon-Hodge – the gold pin they gave Amaryllis at their wedding held her djibbah together for a while – and he was now at the front with the Lovat Scouts; Ian was working for Naval Intelligence; Peter was running a street-fighting school in Battersea. The Flemings seemed suddenly very distant. Moreover, in 1937, Granny Katie had died intestate, with the result that Robert's fortune now passed irrevocably to his surviving children, Phil, Dorothy and Kathleen. Eve took it badly, as did Ian. 'Never mind, Mama, we'll make our own,' he comforted her. But Katie's worst offence was the smallest: she had left none of her jewellery to Eve. This was especially irritating, since Eve's jewel-case, containing everything Val had given her, had been stolen on the train during a pilgrimage to his grave in France. Determined to right this, she delved into the law books, emerging with an ancient piece of legislation which covered just such an eventuality, and to the Flemings' annoyance they had to sell the gems and split the proceeds.

It made little difference to Amaryllis whether Eve received her pound of flesh or not. Of far greater importance was the fate of Joyce Grove, to which she and Eve had reverted after the sale of Greys. This ludicrous but likeable enterprise now belonged to Phil, who had neither the inclination nor the extravagance to keep it afloat. Like an oil tanker, however, Joyce Grove could not be stopped just like that. It needed to slow down gradually, and, while it did, the younger Flemings continued to use it as their country base.

Shortly after Katie's death, Queen Mary made a surprise visit to Joyce Grove, learning only on arrival that her old friend was dead. The only Fleming in sight being Amaryllis, she summoned her to the royal presence. Curtsying to Her Majesty and then to her entire entourage (lest they too be majesties), Amaryllis accompanied Queen Mary into the hall, along whose walls hung a lugubrious collection of stuffed rhino heads, mementoes of a brief excursion by Dorothy and Kathleen to Africa. 'To think Mrs Fleming shot all these!' Queen Mary said in awe. Even in death Katie's scatter-brained vanity lived on.

It took a year before Joyce Grove ground to a halt; in 1938 Phil donated the house to St Mary's Hospital, Paddington, giving the rest of the estate to Peter in a generous act to redress Robert's omissions. The following year, when the outbreak of war made London an impractical base, Eve moved to Appletree Cottage in Nettlebed. By 1941, when Amaryllis left school, she had moved once again, this time to the dark, reputedly haunted Abbey at Sutton Courtenay in Berkshire.

Wartime restrictions had wrought a curious but agreeable change in Eve's character. Despite her leisurely lifestyle she had always claimed to be practical, and liked to tell people what a good working-man's wife she would have made – 'We were all sceptical, except for the men who were rather frightened,' Joan Regent recalls. But the Abbey gave Eve a chance to prove herself: she gardened, she cooked, she milked the goat, she stripped the Abbey fireplaces with a blowtorch.

The goat was a pedigree – Eve sat on a stool reading it poetry because it hated to be alone – and the cleric who exorcised the house of its ghost was a bishop, but much of Eve's pretentiousness had disappeared. The woman who had once decked herself in gold lamé and thrown away shoes she had barely worn now wore dungarees and fixed her footwear with Rhinosole ('available from Woolworth's for 6d,' she boasted). Gone were the chauffeur-driven limousines, the housemaids, the cooks, the tweenies, the nannies. Eve now drove a Hillman Minx and employed one maid, Hilda Gee. The Cheyne Walk hostess who had entertained London's finest with balalaikas and fortune-tellers was almost unrecognisable in the semi-recluse of the Abbey. Amaryllis recalls, 'We lived together like hermits, dreading callers. At the sound of a car approaching or footsteps on the gravel, I'd put my cello down and crawl along the floor screened from view, and Mamma would dash out into the shrubbery. Hilda Gee was left to deal with the visitor.'

Among those who made it through the front door were Jelly d'Aranyi and Adila Fachiri, who had moved to nearby Ewelme. Another was the accompanist Yvonne Hale, upon whom Eve had made a lasting impression when they first met in Portmeirion, with her bedroom parties and the bottles of champagne she cooled in the basin. Yvonne saw a different Eve from Amaryllis. 'She had a good sense of the ridiculous and we had some great laughs. She invited me to the Abbey, and one morning announced that the strawberries were ready to pick. She had a tremendous canning apparatus in the kitchen and I helped her can the strawberries. Avalanche, the grey mare, put her head through the kitchen window, which rather took me by storm. She took me in a canoe up the Thames to Abingdon, and I remember her handling the paddle with great skill.'

Occasionally Ian descended from London to charm Amaryllis up and down the river in a canoe. Augustus, too, braved the trains to the local whistlestop, Appleford Halt, cadging return lifts from Joan Mallett, a Chelsea friend who was wartime chauffeur to the Ewelme-based attorney general, Sir Donald Somerville, and whose Priority 21 boards allowed her to sail through police checks with impunity.

Otherwise it was Eve alone with her daughter, arguing, bickering, at every step barking their shins on each other's personality. Whenever Eve spotted Amaryllis reading a book she made her peel potatoes or scrub the floor. The experience left her with a guilt complex which still prevents her reading during the day. Sometimes they went for outings in the Hillman Minx. Thanks to petrol rationing and Eve's inexpert driving, these excursions were often truncated by an empty tank, whereupon Amaryllis would have to push the car home.

The image of Abbey life is full of contradictions: a rebellious adolescent acquiescing meekly to her mother's demands; an ambitious girl submitting to the tedium of everyday chores; a society leopard changing her spots, possibly in the hope of reaching a rapport with her daughter; a woman in her fifties reverting to the riverine backwaters of her childhood. Against the contradictions are the similarities: both women were forceful, selfish and talented; they were beautiful, with the same high cheekbones, slight frame, large smile and large eyes; they shared a liking for green and purple. It is almost as if the Abbey were designated as a testing ground, an opportunity for discovery.

There was testing but there was no discovery. Amaryllis still believed she was adopted, even in the intensely inquisitive period of adolescence. Accepting the differences and ignoring the similarities, she saw Eve only as a figure of authority, never as a mother. Similarly, she made no connection between herself and Augustus John. It did not strike her as odd that this strange bearded man should hover so persistently on the outskirts of her life. He sent postcards to her at Downe House, missives unique in the school postbag for being plastered over with economy labels – 'it was either beyond or below Augustus actually to buy a new card' – and memorable because she enjoyed deciphering the message that lurked beneath his scrawl. He gave her birthday presents, one of them a book of Eskimo folk tales, *The Eagles Gift*, by Knud Rasmussen. He kept up a regular correspondence with her mother and visited the Abbey in the teeth of wartime travel restrictions. None of this meant any more to Amaryllis than that Augustus was a family friend.

Eve had brainwashed her daughter well, but the deception was becoming increasingly irrelevant to Augustus. One Friday, having collected Augustus from the Abbey, Joan Mallett remarked on Amaryllis's beauty. 'He turned to me and said, "Of course she's beautiful. She's my daughter and Mrs Fleming's her mother." I told him he was pulling my leg but he assured me it was true.'[33] Against Augustus's indiscretion, however, stood the considerable strength of Eve's personality, wealth and social standing. 'I once said that Mrs Fleming had a daughter by Augustus John and I was told I would be had up for slander.' Joan Mallett, like others, learned that Eve's secret was public in a very private way.

Had she known of it, Amaryllis would have appreciated Augustus's description of the English country in wartime: 'a paddock which one grazes in, like a cow, but less productive'.[34] Unable to travel to London, she fell back on Oxford, where, after an abortive term at a finishing school with Mary Vestey, she found herself playing once a week as principal cello in the Oxford Amateur Orchestra. It was pale stuff, but the conductor, Thomas Armstrong – later to become Sir Thomas, and principal of the Royal Academy of Music – recognised that his leading cellist was in a class apart. He suggested that she return to Downe House for regular tuition.

Miss Willis disagreed. She flatly refused to countenance the idea unless Amaryllis reformed and participated more fully in school life. Miraculously, her wish was granted. Through a mixture of artifice and genuine application, Amaryllis convinced the headmistress of her good intentions. Indeed, she carried the part so successfully that she was given a reward: the opportunity to attend a London concert of her choice. She immediately opted for the longest on offer, Bach's *St Matthew Passion* at the Albert Hall.

After another year at Downe House Amaryllis had had enough. She decided to audition for the Royal College of Music to study under Ivor James, who had thrilled her in the Menges Quartet. Effie Richardson, who looked to a time when the war was over and she could return to London with Amaryllis as her pupil, was obstructive. She refused to coach her through any of the set pieces, with the result that she had to learn them by herself, a process which gained her the Associated Board's top scholarship.

In an unaccustomed burst of generosity Eve insisted on paying fees, feeling that the scholarship could be better used by a poorer musician. But, reverting to type, she granted Amaryllis an allowance of only ten shillings a week, which was expected to cover everything from food and travel to new strings and music. Amaryllis was unfazed. Equipped with her Ruggieri cello and Dodd bow – a combination acquired at the age of fourteen and which would last through to her late twenties – she commuted three times a week between Appleford Halt and Paddington.

But the relationship between Downe House and its

reluctant pupil was not quite over. The coda came some twenty years later when Amaryllis was invited back to perform at the school. In a *faux pas* unique in her career (she still believes it had psychological overtones) she double-booked. While staff and pupils waited with growing impatience, their star was driving happily north to another engagement. When she telephoned the next day to apologise, the music mistress said three words: 'That's absolutely typical.'

SIX

The Royal College

Designed in the 1890s by Sir Arthur Blomfield, one of Ivor Rose's fathers-in-law, the Royal College of Music juts imposingly amid the Muscovian heights of Prince Consort Road. There is something of the Kremlin about it, with its turrets, its red-brick façade and its central position staring up towards the Albert Hall. Once inside, however, all trace of autocracy disappears. The marble-pillared entrance hall aims at stateliness but achieves only shabby intimacy. The maroon-and-blue carpeted lobby invites visitors to ask the porter for popcorn. And even the RCM's imposing concert hall, lined with portraits of past directors and famous alumni, feels more like a recently vacated schoolroom than a breeding ground for genius. It is quite unlike other Victorian institutions, and in part this is due to the pupils themselves. Young, fresh-faced and self-possessed, they move along the terrazzo-floored corridors with an air of patient superiority. The professors may know best for now, their expressions say, but our day will come.

The Royal College of Music today is much as it was in 1943. The teaching rooms are the same, with their stained-pine doors, their discreet gold numbers and their glazed inserts — 'to stop any hanky-panky', Amaryllis explains. The walls are still painted corporation cream and their pointing-finger signs

(To the Registrar, To the Director, To the Vice-Director) indicate exactly the same directions as they did fifty years ago. The students of the Forties had all the confidence of their modern counterparts; the four female cellists who entered the RCM in the autumn of 1943 – Amaryllis, Joan Dickson, Eileen Croxford and Anna Shuttleworth – are all now professors at their old alma mater. But according to the music critic Hugo Cole, who was also studying the cello, Amaryllis was no ordinary student. She was 'one of the few girls around with a dress sense, full of enthusiasms, apparently without any sort of diffidence, and knowing very well what she wanted of life'.

This confidence was due mainly to Ivor James, or 'Jimmy', as everyone called him. A kindly and talented man, Jimmy had begun his thirty-four-year career with the RCM in 1919 and at his death in 1963 was acclaimed as an elder statesman of English cello teaching. His realm was chamber music, in which he gave Amaryllis her first vital grounding in phrasing and balance. He lacked experience as a soloist and while he was able to explain the music was cheerfully unable to illustrate it; most demonstrations ended with a disclaimer, 'That's how *not* to do it.' His forte, however, was personal contact. According to one obituary, 'He truly felt music to its very depth and centre . . . [and] communicated his musical intention to his pupils in some remarkable way which seems impossible to put into words.'[35] He reached a close rapport with Amaryllis and before long she knew him so well 'that I could tell what he was going to say from the lift of an eyebrow'. Throughout her studies he was an invaluable source of support and encouragement.

It was James who, immediately after her enrolment, suggested Amaryllis join the First Orchestra – where now there are five, there were only two in 1943 – which was an almost unheard of promotion for a first-termer. 'I had to be given special permission,' she remembers, 'and wore a hole in the corridor floor from the amount of times I was sent between the Registrar's office and the Director.' The Director was then Sir George Dyson, a beaky-faced, piercingly blue-eyed ex-organist who had a wry sense of humour and was cherished by his students for never being able to remember their names and for having written a book on hand grenades during World War One.

Her first orchestral task was to perform Vaughan Williams's *The Wasps*, a daunting piece conducted by Adrian Boult. For someone whose experience had been confined mostly to Haydn, stamped out by Miss Gunn on the rostrum, it was nerve-racking. But she survived and very soon became principal cellist, replacing Martin Lovett who went on to play in the Amadeus Quartet. Indeed, she was soon dominating the others. During one rehearsal of Sibelius's Fourth Symphony the conductor, Basil Cameron, brought proceedings to a halt. 'Amaryllis,' he said, 'I know you only deigned to come and join us because there's a good tune, but you don't have to drown the whole orchestra.' Whereupon the wind section, who were on her side, began stamping their feet in protest. 'Rather gusty,' was how Hugo Cole remembered her playing, 'but she was a real communicator.'

The cello occupied only part of Amaryllis's three days each week in London; there were also piano lessons and lectures on harmony, history of music and acoustics. Although she enjoyed these, they were subsidiary to her time with Jimmy James. And while she persevered with the piano for a full year – the teacher, Kathleen Macquitty, had ambitions to turn her into a concert pianist – she escaped the history and acoustics lectures after a few weeks. As the lecturer Sir Percy Buck explained, she was far too advanced for the slow pace he had to adopt for the other students. 'I see those black eyes of yours looking at me piercingly,' he said, 'and I can't bear it. Please, do me a favour and stay away!' That left only harmony lessons to distract her, and she soon escaped those as well.

Her route to freedom lay, paradoxically, in the college's constraints. Designed for a different generation and a different approach to music, Sir Arthur Blomfield's building allowed ample space for teaching but none for practice, the original concept being that students practise at home between lessons. But with a growing catchment area, wartime travel restrictions and the shortage of nearby lodgings, Blomfield's plan began to show its flaws. To compound matters, the teaching rooms were locked between lessons lest the pianos be played into a state of uselessness. Accordingly Amaryllis drafted a petition demanding that the teaching rooms be opened and threatening a mass boycott of a forthcoming concert before the Queen unless her demands were met. None of the students dared sign for fear of incurring Dyson's wrath, but, undaunted, she signed her letter 'The Students' and handed it in. The next day a note was pinned to the board: AMARYLLIS. THE DIRECTOR DOES NOT ACCEPT ANONYMOUS LETTERS.

Nevertheless, the teaching rooms were unlocked, the students were able to practise and Percy Buck was delighted. 'I hear you're a rebel!' he said. 'That's wonderful! Keep it up! And if you do – I know you don't like harmony lessons – I'll pretend you've come and tick your name off.' The extra time gave her a chance to practise and to make friends. She soon fell in with fellow students Alan Loveday, Neville Mariner and Cynthia Freeman, with whom she made up the College Quartet. Alan Loveday was the one with whom she formed the strongest bond. 'His arrival at College caused some excitement,' Amaryllis remembers. 'Word went round that a violinist had arrived who couldn't play out of tune!'

Born in New Zealand, Alan was the product of natural ability and extraordinary parental vim. He had been taught by his father – himself a violinist, who had practised finger exercises on the butt of his Lee Enfield during World War I – and the result was so good that he was playing concerts by the age of four. When the visiting Budapest Quartet heard him, they raised the money to send Alan and his entire family to England. Arriving in 1939, he was given free lessons by Albert Sammons – remembered by Amaryllis for his refusal to go abroad in case the *Evening Standard* was not available – and he practised under the supervision of his father, who had taken a job as a Woolworth's nightwatchman to leave his daylight hours free for this task. Sometimes Alan joined his father at work, bringing with him records of famous violinists, which the two played through the shop's loudspeakers.

Eve viewed most of her daughter's friends askance, invariably because they came from the 'wrong' backgrounds. Students, however, were no real threat to her authority. When young men telephoned, she simply put down the receiver. What really worried her was Amaryllis's attachment to André Mangeot.

Born in 1883, Mangeot had been brought up in a family of musicians and had studied at the Paris Conservatoire before becoming a British citizen after World War I. He subsequently founded the Westminster Music Society and went on to form the International String Quartet with John Barbirolli as cellist. Christopher Isherwood, who worked as his secretary during the Twenties, described him as being uninterested in 'some showy personal interpretation of a piece of music'. His aim was to achieve accuracy and anonymity, a faithful reading that captured as closely as possible the composer's original vision. 'To this aim he had sacrificed all prospects of stardom and big material success – had sacrificed them as a matter of course, without any complaint, or posing, or fuss.'[36] This music fundamentalist sailed into Amaryllis's life when she was eighteen: 'After a students' concert at the College he came into the artists' room and said in a heavy accent, "You are very talented. You must come and play quar-r-rtets with me in Crez-well Place." ' So she did.

When Amaryllis walked into 21 Cresswell Place she found herself in a new and amazing world, a French household transplanted to a South Kensington mews. Isherwood described it in his book *Lions and Shadows*: 'As we drove up, all the doors and windows were standing open, so that you could see right into the downstairs room; and the whole place with its gay check curtains and steep miniature staircase looked like a big doll's house. In the bright sunshine its appearance was so disarmingly cheerful that I felt myself, after the first glance, already quite charmed.' Inside, Isherwood found it even more charming. 'This is how real human people live, I thought, as my eyes wandered over the comfortable untidiness of the large room; the music stacked on the grand piano; the pencil, pipe, orange and block of resin beside the keyboard; the violin on the chair next to the tennis racket; the fishing rods in the corner; the photographs with scrawled inscriptions; the Japanese prints on the white-washed brick walls; the Breton cupboard crammed with music stands, pictures, books, clothes. People living together, busy, friendly, intent upon their work, had created an atmosphere in this house; nothing was planned, forced, formal, consciously quaint.'[37] Isherwood's secretarial duties bore the same hap-hazard stamp. Mangeot lugged a trunkful of letters from beneath a bed. ' "These", he told me, "are extremely urgent." He opened a cupboard: letters poured out in an avalanche. "These are not so urgent: we should answer them by Christmas." '

At the centre of this mess was Mangeot, 'a thin, youthful-looking man of about forty, with plentiful grey hair brushed back from his lined sunburnt face, and a pleasant rather sleepy smile'.[38] André loved company and welcomed people from all walks into his home. Indeed, he had such a gripping fear of solitude that his first wife left him on the grounds that it was impossible to be alone even in the lavatory. In her place came hordes of 'pretty girls, enthralled by André's charisma and the fund of delectable stories he told with the French accent that was part of his charm'. The house was a convivial forum. John and Evelyn Barbirolli, Julian Bream, Eugene Goossens, Vlado Perlemutter, Sandor Vegh and the members of the Kolisch and Loewengruth Quartets all found a ready welcome at Cresswell Place, as did the friends of André's journalist son, Sylvain.

Amaryllis joined the circle with joy. 'Although I'm sure there was little money to spare, there was an overflowing warmth of hospitality. André and Sylvain produced delicious meals, and I learned never to forget that "*Un repas sans vin, c'est une journée sans soleil*." ' But more than the excitement she felt from entering a truly adult world, one so different from that which she shared with her mother, there was the glow she received from the musical environment. At André's memorial concert in November 1983, she recounted, 'He created a vibrant atmosphere of musical *joie de vivre*. Through him one seemed to become part of a great tradition of French music and musicians.' Not, of course, that André rested on tradition; informality was his keynote. Au pairs often found themselves pulled from the kitchen to receive an impromptu violin lesson, and the direst musical amateurs were greeted at Cresswell Place provided they were willing to enjoy themselves and take life casually. But the bonhomie was underpinned by a deep seriousness. 'He was a very good musician,' claims Amaryllis, 'who changed many people's lives.' A fascination with the interpretation of Baroque music, long before it became fashionable, led him to spend whole days in the British Library Reading Room. He edited all the Purcell Fantasias, which were published by Curwens for the first time in the Twenties. And he arranged for Amaryllis a Purcell piece for cello, an achievement which sowed the seeds of her own love of Baroque.

Meanwhile, André or no André, life carried on in all its wartime dreariness. Although the blitz had come and gone, London was now subjected to a spasmodic drizzle of doodle-bugs, one of which narrowly missed the RCM while Amaryllis was playing in a College chamber concert. There was little food, little money, little warmth – in winter Alan Loveday went once round the Circle Line to warm up before College – little music and little transport. The trains between Paddington and Oxford were packed to bursting, and Amaryllis's cello was ill-appreciated by other travellers, especially when she chose to practise in the compartment. Sometimes she kept people out by sprinkling food on the floor and pretending she had just vomited; at other times they swarmed in regardless. But whether she was alone in her compartment or not, the journey was always interrupted by a long struggle with her cello through crowded corridors to the front of the train to tell the driver to stop at Appleford Halt. Her return was greeted with the bulbous-eyed outrage of a Bateman cartoon.

In 1944 that burden at least was removed, when Eve moved back to London, the better to keep an eye on her wayward daughter. A bomb had split Turner's House neatly up the middle, so Eve took a flat in Knightsbridge. The smallness of its rooms did little to endear mother and daughter. Eve, now she had learned to cook, took great trouble contriving elaborate menus, but as Amaryllis was usually rehearsing or out with friends (the former being an excuse for the latter) Eve often ate a solitary meal before going to bed at her usual early hour. But some of her fire remained. When Amaryllis was practising at 11.00 p.m. she emerged from her bedroom to rip the bow from her hands, shouting, 'I can't stand it a second longer!' And when she once returned with Alan Loveday in tow, having narrowly escaped violence at the hands of two Piccadilly drunks, Eve refused to countenance the idea of his having sheets. 'Blankets will do for him!' she commanded in night-gowned splendour. It went unsaid that the sofa would do for her daughter.

Conditions improved towards the end of the war, when Eve left Knightsbridge for the grander environs of Mayfair. Her new abode, 21 Charles Street, was a fine three-storey house, with comfortable, panelled reception rooms and a grand staircase leading past Georgian murals to spacious bedrooms, the whole furnished to Eve's luxurious taste: exotic, many-branched Italian wall-sconces sprouted from either side of marble fireplaces; fine rugs lay over oak floorboards; deep sofas beckoned in the library, extravagant Venetian mirrors in the bedrooms; at the top of the stairs a blackamoor statue stood theatrically before rich swags of pre-war-quality curtain; John paintings hung everywhere.

The building gave mother and daughter greater scope for avoiding each other. It also had, in Amaryllis's eyes, the advantage of proximity to Ian. Her dashing half-brother had left his Ebury Street home for a three-roomed apartment in nearby Hays Mews, where he lived a life of luxury made possible by his immense charm and the procession of doting au pair girls who scurried to answer his every command. They ran his bath; they fetched his lighter off the mantelpiece; and they cooked salmon kedgeree, which he sent them to learn from his mother.

But Mayfair was not bohemian Chelsea and, come V-Day, Eve began to investigate the possibility of salvaging her previous life in Cheyne Walk. Her discoveries made depressing news. Turner's House had been ravaged by a 'burst water main, bomb just by the front door, and incendiaries, blast, and fly-bomb in the Thames', she wrote to the Eshers. 'Theft has been very bad since, in spite of every effort on my part. I don't know whether the balcony which Turner had changed to the roof to make it safer for him to paint there has gone, it *was* there. The beautiful old carved hand-made roof tiles have been stolen except the broken ones, some of the panelling and the whole of the old oak block floor of the studio. Much damage has been done by rain and snow. The lead memorial plaque by Walter Crane is with the builder, saying that he lived and *died* there, and this is supposed to have taken place in the bedroom on the second floor. I wrote two letters to the *Telegraph* and I enclose them . . . The inside of the house makes it seem an impossibility to put the place back as it was, and the outside wall can only be done by someone who understands it . . .'

There was no going back. Eve received substantial compensation from the government for bomb damage and sold the remains of her home as it stood. Amaryllis's childhood cage had now gone.

SEVEN

'La jeune fille que je n'ai jamais rencontrée'

By the end of the war Amaryllis was more than ready to leave College. She had gained plaudits from all quarters and had won every prize available for students. In addition, she had gained valuable experience in the outside world.

Her first public engagement had been on radio: a seven-minute BBC broadcast on *Children's Hour* in October 1942, for which she had received one magnificent guinea. The following year she had appeared at the Wigmore Hall in a recital given by Effie Richardson's pupils and Ivor Newton, one of the country's most distinguished accompanists. In November 1944, she made her solo début performing Elgar's Cello Concerto at Newbury. It earned her a glowing review from the composer Robin Milford and her first piece of fan-mail. 'I do not know the lady and should you publish this little note in your paper, it may not be good for her to read it,' started a letter to the press. 'Now, as one who has heard all leading cellists in the last fifty-five years, I (seconded no doubt by other experienced concert-goers) aver that ... Miss Fleming, young as she is, must even today be classed with the great among the cellists of the age. Technique (and hers is flawless) can be developed to a remarkable degree by many gifted in that direction, they astonish us, but their "turn" is soon forgotten. Miss Fleming, however, is first and foremost a musician, with the cello as her medium of expression. Hence her Casals-like tone, her perfect ear, her natural, honest presentation of music wholly assimilated by mind and soul, with no vestige of extravaganza. I am not given to prodigality of praise, but let readers watch Miss Fleming's career and see whether I have said too much.'

The RCM took a stern view of most outside engagements, considering them detrimental to study and practice, and those who performed without George Dyson's permission did so at their own risk. Martin Lovett, whose place she had filled as leading cellist in the College orchestra, had been expelled for just such a reason. Amaryllis, however, found it easy to get permission, the cause being that 'The Canterbury Pilgrims' required a good cellist, that the composer wanted it to reach as wide an audience as possible, and that the composer was George Dyson. He took it all over the country with amateur choirs 'who were mostly good', and with amateur orchestras 'who were mostly not so good', and for the first time Amaryllis experienced the power of indispensability. 'We were playing somewhere in the Midlands or the North and because of wartime trains I was late. Dyson had already started rehearsing and got tremendously cross when I walked in. "Well, if you don't want me I'll go home again," I said. It was *so* nice to see him jump off his platform and scurry to bring me back.' She also played quintets with the Mangeot Quartet, a nebulous motley whose members came and went like gypsies.

But while experience was important, one factor was still lacking in her education. As she said on a BBC broadcast for the French Service in December 1953, 'I believe there comes a time in every musician's life when he needs a teacher who not only knows how to explain the principles of music but who can illustrate them as well. I also believe it's a waste of time picking a teacher just because you admire his technique. So many times I've heard some young hopeful say he's working on his bow with X and learning fingering from Y, under the impression that he knows exactly what he's aiming for and lacks only the technical ability to achieve it. That's all wrong. I believe an artist's goal and the route to its realisation are inseparable.' For Amaryllis, the person who combined end with means, explanation with illustration, was Pierre Fournier.

Pierre Fournier was born in 1906, and had established himself during the Thirties and Forties as one of Europe's leading cellists. Like Amaryllis, he had started on the piano and had taken to the cello at the age of nine, but disability rather than rebellion had driven him to the instrument. While on a family holiday in Normandy he had been struck by polio, a tragedy which calipered one leg for life and effectively extinguished his nascent career as a pianist. His doctor advised him to choose something that needed less legwork, and the cello was his answer. Unable to run about with other children, he channelled all his spare time and natural determination into music.

By 1944, however, when the Allies landed in Normandy, he had fallen into disgrace. Feelings ran high in liberated France, fuelled in the north by anger and in the Vichy south by guilt. The punishment of so-called collaborators was widespread, vicious and arbitrary, and scores of French men and women suffered. Pragmatism became a crime, and Pierre Fournier had been pragmatic. The first charge against him was that he had stayed in occupied Paris, accepting the position of Professor of Cello at the Conservatoire in 1941; the second that he had accepted the Germans' offer of a chauffeured car; the third, and most damning, that he had accepted an invitation to perform in Berlin under the legendary conductor

Wilhelm Furtwängler; the fourth that his wife Lyda was rumoured to have had an affair with a German officer. He was suspended from teaching or performing abroad for six months and subjected to the indignities of a trial. He emerged an innocent man but his name was cleared only in 1953 when, in a burst of revisionism, the authorities awarded him the Légion d'Honneur.

His first foreign performance following the expiry of his six-month sentence was in 1946 at the Albert Hall, where he played Tchaikovsky's *'Rococo' Variations*. Londoners, hungry for good music and international artists of Fournier's calibre, flocked to hear him, and among the audience was Amaryllis.

'I was bowled over by his playing. The colour and nuance he produced with his bow, and the subtlety of emotional shading, particularly with his vibrato, was a total revelation. It was like the chiaroscuro of an Impressionist's brush.' When she met him afterwards in the artists' room, with her escort Ivor Newton, admiration turned to adulation. She found a soigné, broad-shouldered man, impeccably dressed, immaculately coiffured (she later discovered that he slept in a hair-net), with an easy but slightly thin-lipped smile. 'I was so enthusiastic that he asked if I would like to hear him play the Lalo Concerto the next day. Again I was bowled over. It was the most musical, sensitive playing I'd heard.'

He invited her to play to him, so she made her way to his room at the Hyde Park Hotel clutching her cello and the piano score of Haydn's Concerto in D Major; she already knew the cello part by heart. Fournier was impressed, so impressed that he offered to give her free lessons in Paris. Amaryllis leapt at the opportunity. She had done three years at college and although she had been offered another year the prospect was insipid.

All that held her back was her affection for Jimmy James. At their next lesson James, at the piano, found Amaryllis's score overwritten with cello bowings. He asked who had written them and Amaryllis replied that it had been Fournier. James immediately suggested that she take lessons from Fournier, whereupon the rest of the lesson dissolved into pathos. Amaryllis played the entire concerto, tears streaming down her face, while Jimmy James accompanied her stoically on the piano, refusing to let emotion dent his habitual reserve. The separation came that summer at a Promenade concert which James attended with Amaryllis and his cellist wife Helen Just, an ex-pupil some years his junior. It was Helen who prodded him into action. In the artists' room he nervously approached Fournier, and suggested that he teach Amaryllis. '*Mais naturellement!*' replied the baffled virtuoso. And that was that.

There remained one final disappointment for Jimmy James. He sometimes invited students to his home in Clarendon Road where play-throughs were followed by discussion and buns. Amaryllis was a frequent participant. One night, during the discussion, Fournier rang from his hotel. 'I need you here,' was all he said. Amaryllis went. Jimmy James introduced a new topic and someone else ate her bun.

The love affair which began that night in the Hyde Park Hotel between Amaryllis and Pierre Fournier was superficially one of mutual self-interest. Fournier was flattered by the attentions of a younger woman – '*la jeune fille que je n'ai jamais rencontrée*', as he called her in a sad allusion to his blighted childhood. Amaryllis, for her part, was flattered by the attentions of such a great artist. Neither was remotely faithful to the other: Fournier had a keen eye for the opposite sex, and Amaryllis an even keener one. Nor did they have any illusions as to where the affair might lead. But once the initial passion had subsided there remained a genuine affection and a shared devotion to music, which kept them together for some ten years.

The relationship was invaluable to her musical development. Particularly helpful was Fournier's instruction in the use of the bow. Coming from Paris, which was then the world centre of cello playing, he was horrified at what he found in London. 'The bow is the soul of expression,' was his favourite maxim, and the English school of bowing technique was, in his opinion, non-existent, with musicians concentrating on the accuracy of their left hand while paying no attention to their right. For Fournier the remedy lay in the violin, which had always been a more popular instrument and for which there existed a massive body of music. As he told Amaryllis, he had learned far more from violinists — of whom there were many famous virtuosi at that time — than from any cellist. Accordingly he put her on to the Ševčick violin-bowing exercises, transcribed for the cello by Feuillard, which he himself played every day. '*Très simple*', he assured her, though they were anything but, progressing through the most basic to the most complicated movements. Nor did he neglect the left hand: '*Il faut varier le vibrato!*' was his constant refrain. And he helped her achieve a measure of his immaculate phrasing by teaching her mentally to divide difficult passages into sections, using points of reference to make the music less daunting and more manageable.

It is an old saying that good players make bad teachers. Fournier used to remark, 'There are no good teachers, only good pupils,' — a half-truth, as Amaryllis later wrote, 'which only a fine player could indulge in and to which only a very talented student might wish to subscribe! Perhaps a certain useful shift in responsibility was implied . . .'[39] Certainly there was a shift in responsibility, but such shifts are useful only if the pupil knows exactly what he or she is responsible for. In that respect Fournier was insensitive. His crippled childhood had left him enormously strong in the wrists, arms and shoulders, and thus ignorant of the strain suffered by weaker players. He gave Amaryllis the Ševčick exercises but made the fatal error of never watching her play them. She fell victim to the temptation to aim for immediate results, putting her energy into attaining the audible end while forgetting that the real achievement lay in understanding the physical means. As she practised unsupervised, she built up severe muscular tensions which would ultimately be damaging. 'Don't be afraid of a little pain,' was one of Fournier's favourite lines, according to another pupil, Margaret Moncreiff. But in Amaryllis's case it was misplaced advice.

For the moment, however, such concerns were far from her mind. She had found a teacher who could not only instruct but demonstrate magnificently the ultimate goal of his instruction. Soon Amaryllis was travelling with him all over England as he sped from performance to performance. On the train he gave her lessons, and at each concert she digested their value. He was tireless in his dedication, constantly reworking studies, repeating scales over and over with elaborate fingerings he had invented to exercise his hand to the full, and practising every aspect of a forthcoming piece. As Amaryllis explained in one French broadcast, 'He liked to play Bach's Suites slowly, mezzo-piano, almost without expression, from one end to the the other, in order to gain perfect intonation and rhythmic precision. It was the same with every difficult passage he played, whether in sonatas or concertos. Having Pierre Fournier as an example was a godsend because knowing how to apply yourself to your work is the biggest secret of all.'[40]

Fournier sometimes feared he had set too good an example.

'Do you really want another lesson?' he would plead. 'Couldn't we go to the cinema instead?' Amaryllis always insisted on the lesson, her only compromise being to skip the slow movements. Fournier's face would light up. 'And then we can go to the cinema?'

On 10 December 1946, Amaryllis came officially of age. As she puts it, '*I* realised I was twenty-one but nobody else did.' There was no party – Eve pointed out with justification that Amaryllis hated organised gatherings – but Ian was summoned at the last minute for a celebratory drink before he went out to dinner. And there were few presents: from Eve a cheque for £21 and from Ian a ring of 'Victorian paste masquerading as an emerald'.

The day was disheartening but unimportant. Although still a student, Amaryllis had one foot in the adult world and the other itched to follow. She finally pulled it from the mire of domestic life when André Mangeot invited her to accompany him to France to play quintets early in 1947. It was the first time she had been abroad without Eve, and the experience overwhelmed her. They took the ferry to Dieppe and boarded a train for Paris. In that brief period between boat and train, Amaryllis became a confirmed Francophile. The smells, the markets, the people, the atmosphere, all bewitched her. 'I could almost have fallen out of the train with excitement,' she recalls. Even the unfamiliar experience of a unisex toilet, where men and women perched atop their poles chatting freely to each other, separated only by a thin curtain, fascinated her.

Their repertoire, the Schubert quintet and the Brahms quintet, had a slightly surreal quality. The Brahms had been written originally for piano, cello, viola and two violins. But André's ensemble was playing with an additional cello, the other cellist being Joan Dickson, following a score written by one Sebastian H. Brown who claimed to have received his interpretation from the spirit world. Nowadays, such a statement would perhaps be greeted with scepticism, but then it was a matter of serious debate, and Brown's Brahms played to packed houses and was broadcast by Paris radio. One possible reason for its enthusiastic reception was that the Vieille Salle du Conservatoire, where it was performed, had been advertised as *Salle Chauffée* (though Amaryllis remembers it as anything but) and in that freezing post-war winter any hall which claimed to be heated was guaranteed full attendance. However, the same could hardly have been said of the hall at Valmondois, yet that too was packed.

Standing some forty kilometres north-west of Paris, Château Valmondois was occupied by André's friends the family Geoffroy Dechaume, an ensemble of near-fanatic music lovers consisting of ten children, an overwhelmingly matriarchal mother and a shell-shocked father whose last full night of sleep had been during the World War 1. Their lives were devoted to the concerts they arranged at their home, in a huge music room *chauffée* to the extent of a single open fire. This was not big enough for the Geoffroy Dechaume boys, who enlarged the venue by single-handedly erecting a gallery and stage in a nearby barn. André's group was booked to play the Schubert and Brown's Brahms at its inauguration. The family was virtually penniless but by dint of its connections had persuaded the authorities to lay on special trains to shuttle audiences from Paris. On performance night the carriages were even fuller than usual, and their occupants provided a practical test of the Geoffroy Dechaumes' building skills. Halfway through the piece, Amaryllis noticed that the crammed gallery was beginning to sag. She played on, hypnotised, as the floor dropped lower and lower until it was on the point of collapse. Then, as she was about to scream, people realised the danger and moved to safety. The concert continued without interruption.

Thanks to post-war rationing and her hosts' poverty, conditions at the château were primitive. Food was in short supply and the daughter, Marie-France, foraged daily on her bicycle for such finds as two carrots, a cabbage and a yellow loaf of maize bread 'that went stale as you looked at it'. Besides the music-room fire, the château's only heat source was a stove in the hall, but on her first night, in a fit of Englishness, Amaryllis left her bedroom window open. After that she slept cocooned in her sheets, blankets, every article of clothing she had brought, and the rug from the bedroom floor.

Despite these hardships Amaryllis loved her time in France and returning to London was a dreary comedown. As she mooned disconsolately around 21 Charles Street, the old tensions resurfaced. Before long she and Eve were 'sparring like two old cats'. Hugo Pitman came to the rescue. A close friend of Ian, he was also an admirer of Amaryllis and an avid collector of Augustus John's work, buying a number of his paintings particularly when the artist was hard up, for which Augustus rewarded him by repeating that, like Eve, he 'couldn't tell a drawing from a cowpat'. Pitman's solution was that Amaryllis should study in Portugal under the famous cellist Madame Guilhermina Suggia.

EIGHT

An Iberian Interlude

Suggia had attracted a sizeable following in Britain, where she had lived from 1912 to 1923. Her professional career had started in 1900, when she was twelve, as principal cello in the Oporto Symphony Orchestra, and in 1906 she began studying in Paris with Pablo Casals. Before long the two were living together and appearing at concerts in which she billed herself as Madame P. Casals-Suggia. Eugene Goossens recalled their appearance at a musical evening in the Chelsea home of Paul and Muriel Draper. 'Always there were new faces and unexpected happenings, as when one night Suggia and Casals took their cellos behind screens and made us guess which of the two was playing. Most of us failed in this.'[41]

Casals's biographer, H. L. Kirk, described her as possessing 'an explosively gay laugh and an instinct for centre stage. Exuberant and attractive, although not beautiful, she had an independent mind and spirit as well as bohemian tastes her teacher [Casals] did not approve of.'[42] She was physically striking at performances: seated grandly astride her instrument, she fixed her eyes on some unfortunate man in the front row and stared hypnotically at him until he began to shrink visibly. There was, however, a small sweetener for her victims: Suggia had very short legs and an extremely long back, so when she rose to receive the applause she seemed hardly any taller than when she had been seated.

Although little known outside Britain and Portugal, Suggia was idolised by British audiences for her exoticism. Augustus found her irresistible and the portrait he painted of her is arguably the best he ever did. Certainly it was the one that required most effort. Its creation took three years, from 1920, and involved about eighty sittings. So often did she make the trip to his studio in Mallord Street that people assumed they were living together. Suggia wrote of the experience, 'In a picture painted like this, a portrait not only of a musician but of her instrument – more of the very spirit of the music itself – the sitter must to a great extent share in its creation. John himself is kind enough to call it "our" picture.'[43] Augustus, for his part, swore never to paint a cello again.

The portrait captures Suggia's dramatic stage persona, her pale, haughty features accentuated by her ruby red dress. The accompanist Gerald Moore wrote, 'Her striking appearance, caught and emphasised so superbly by Augustus John's portrait . . . gave an impression of boldness, romance and colour. She persuaded you her playing was passionate and intense, but the reverse was the case: it was calculated, correct and classical . . . She was far from being the fiery prima donna she appeared.'

The truth was that Suggia was a better performer than musician: her main fault was that her bow-hold, as clearly depicted by Augustus, could not deliver enough power. An example of this was graphically demonstrated by Emanuel Feuermann, as Moore relates: 'She had two instruments, a Stradivarius and a Montagnana. She played to him at his request first on one and then on the other but he only allowed her a few notes before seizing the 'cello from her hands and eliciting twice the volume she was able to produce . . . Suggia felt deflated and secretly resentful of Feuermann's tepid appreciation of her, while he afterwards dismissed her to me as a "drawing-room player".[44]

When Amaryllis met Suggia in 1947, however, it was on a tidal wave of adulation. Eve rated her highly because she had played in a piano trio with Jelly d'Aranyi. And Hugo Pitman had once proposed to her, 'but fortunately for him', Amaryllis believes, 'he was turned down'. Instead Suggia had become engaged to the owner of *Country Life*, who had presented her with an island in Scotland and a Stradivarius. When the engagement was broken off, Suggia returned the island but kept the Strad.

It was arranged that Amaryllis should play to her at Queen's House, Hugo Pitman's home in Cheyne Walk. Having heard her, Suggia insisted she study with her in Oporto, not only because of her talent but because with a foreign pupil she could advertise her classes as being truly international. Eve pressed her to accept, and even offered to pay for the trip, hoping it would get her away from Fournier. Fournier offered the same advice, though for a different reason: it would, he suggested, get her away from Eve. Accordingly, that summer, Amaryllis boarded a plane for Lisbon clutching her cello and £75, the maximum that currency restrictions permitted.

She spent her first night in Portugal at an expensive Lisbon hotel, which she would have been unable to afford had not a besotted fellow-passenger offered to pay her entire bill. The next day she made the long train journey northwards to Oporto, a precipitous town on the River Douro, supposedly built, like ancient Rome, on seven hills. Its steep streets echoed to the rattle of trams, the burbling of limousine exhausts and the ceaseless cries of poverty – '*un testao* to save your soul'. But Oporto under Salazar, who had seized power in 1932, was no place for the poor. Instead, it was the grand old port families who ruled the roost. For three hundred years Oporto had been the centre of the port wine trade, and the English merchants who were its mainstay were a prominent social element. They formed a little colony centred on the imposing granite bulk of the Factory House, a clubman's delight built in 1790, which contained billiard rooms, sitting and smoking rooms, a ballroom, and a banqueting room, plus a separate dessert room for the port.

It was as a guest of this colony that Amaryllis found lodgings in Oporto. The Misses Tait, Muriel and Dorothy, were elderly maiden sisters whose father had come to Oporto in 1851. They were friends of Suggia and it was through her blandishments that Amaryllis found herself at their home, *Entre Quintas*, a magnificent house filled with antique furniture, overlooking a camelia-crammed garden that jutted into the Douro. She felt at home with these kindly old ladies who were interested in music and who allotted her a separate room for practising. She also became friends with their servants, having learned a few words of Portuguese from a teach-yourself book.

Lessons began almost immediately at Suggia's home, where she lived with her radiologist husband José Mena and a petulant lap dog, Mona Lisa. Amaryllis saw nothing at all of Mena, who had been badly burned in an early X-ray experiment, had had a leg amputated and was now having an arm taken off. Whenever he entered the house there was a hurried scuffle and the slamming of doors as Suggia spirited him away. Later she confided to Amaryllis that he kept her awake at nights with his moaning and groaning. 'If only he were English he wouldn't make such a fuss,' she complained. The wretched Mona Lisa, however, was constantly in evidence. Suggia doted on the beast, which had only to snuffle for its mistress to cancel a concert. But Amaryllis hated it, because it began yapping whenever she played. When the noise became too insistent, Suggia summoned her chauffeur, and Mona Lisa spent the rest of the lesson being driven round Oporto resting on a silk handkerchief spread over a velvet cushion.

Suggia 'liked Amaryllis very much', according to one pupil, Pilar Levy, 'and used to say she was passionate and that her tone was fat and beautiful'. Once, Pilar recalls, Amaryllis left early and Suggia rushed to the vacant chair to turn the cushion. 'She is too hot!' she told the others admiringly. She knew that Amaryllis was Augustus's daughter and believed that, possessing her father's fire, she would become a great cellist. She arranged for her to play in a broadcast, which came out in June, starring 'Amarylia Flemin', and took her along whenever she played at a concert. These events, held at provincial music societies in northern Portugal, were remarkable for their lack of organisation. Suggia, undecided what she should wear, took at least three dresses; the cello platform was inevitably the wrong height so a local carpenter would be hastily summoned to rearrange matters; then, as like as not, he would be called back to alter the height of Suggia's chair.

Amaryllis enjoyed the concerts, but Suggia's lessons were a different matter. Although she never had to play side-saddle, as did one poor girl whose husband thought the standard position indecent, Amaryllis was forced to change her bow-hold, which was almost as damaging. Her bow-hold had developed from a mixture of influences, the last being that of Fournier; it was flexible and allowed power to be put into the tip of the bow. Suggia's method was stiff and limiting. Worse still, it put additional strain on Amaryllis's arm muscles, which were now forced to act against her body's natural movement.

Becoming increasingly disillusioned with Suggia's teaching, Amaryllis was also tiring of life with the Taits. Much as she liked the sisters, she found life too easy in their semi-colonial milieu. The port families were suffocatingly insular, dividing their lives between their grand town mansions and the rural *quintas* where the wine was produced. Their main form of entertainment was interminable lunch parties which began at noon and continued with course after course and port after port until about five o'clock. They saw in their success proof positive that 'the natives' were a bunch of idle layabouts, and many, though their families had lived there for generations, could not speak a word of Portuguese. Not that the English of Oporto differed in their lofty isolation from wealthy people anywhere in Salazar's dictatorship. In 1955 Mary McCarthy wrote, 'The rich in Portugal are said to be the richest in Europe. As you watch them in the hotels – silent, like sharks, endlessly masticating, with their medicine bottles before them – you form a new feeling of what cold selfishness can be.'[45]

Amaryllis felt keenly the massive gulf that separated have from have-not, and although she had little enough money she was vastly better off than the poor who filled Oporto's streets: the workmen whose lunch-pails contained nothing but thin cabbage soup; the women who carried goods on their heads, unable to afford a donkey; the crowds who clung to the outside of trams because they lacked money to pay the fare; and the families who maimed their children to give them a start as beggars. Augustus inveighed against the system in his attack on Roy Campbell's book *Portugal*, published in 1954. 'According to better historians than himself the stench of the poorer quarters of Lisbon, during what Campbell calls her Third Renaissance under its dictator, rises to heaven, but none may hear the groans of the unfortunates who languish in the filth of medieval dungeons without trial or hope.'[46]

*

Driven by a mixture of guilt, rebellion and inquiry, Amaryllis quit *Entre Quintas* and found accommodation in a less refined neighbourhood. The glimpse she got of Portuguese life was unnerving. The couple with whom she stayed were drab martinets who treated their fourteen-year-old maid like dirt. Having unpacked, Amaryllis was horrified to find the girl ironing the tissue paper that had protected her clothes. Later she discovered that the maid, who never had a day off, rose at five in the morning and remained on duty until she had performed her final task of the day: to switch off her employers' bedroom light. Amaryllis made a point of thanking her for everything and the maid repaid this small courtesy by warning her that the Senhora was reading her letters and eavesdropping on her telephone conversations. The latter Amaryllis knew already, having 'seen the ear coming round the door', but from then on she took care to lock her drawers. Perhaps the Senhora needed some diversion because she and her husband talked solely of their *intestinos*, whose disorderly state they palliated with a carefully restricted diet. Their lodger, being British and therefore iron-bowelled, was served nothing but *bacalhau*, the national dish of dried cod which Amaryllis was dismayed to discover could be prepared in 360 different ways.

'Real' Portugal palled very quickly. When Amaryllis left in the mornings the street fluttered with twitching curtains. In the evenings a furious shouting match erupted between her and the Senhora, centred on the beggar who had taken to serenading Amaryllis outside her window. She soon found different rooms. Her last words with the Senhora concerned the holes her cello spike had made in the bedroom's ancient lino. The woman had counted them on her hands and knees. 'Buy new lino,' Amaryllis advised and left for a *pensao* by the sea.

The beginning of the end came when the cellist Gaspard Cassadó arrived in Oporto to play at the Teatro Rivoli, accompanied by the Italian pianist Carlo Busotti. Suggia, who had a permanent box in the theatre, took Amaryllis to hear them. At the end of each piece Busotti leaped to his feet and bowed vigorously in their direction. Suggia responded with a gracious wave of the hand. The interchange continued for some while until Suggia suddenly began laughing. 'It's not me he's bowing to,' she told Amaryllis, 'it's you!' When they met afterwards in the artists' room, Cassadó said they were performing next in Lisbon, and suggested that Suggia and Amaryllis come too. Suggia was enthusiastic; she had examining to do at the Lisbon Conservatoire, she could give Amaryllis lessons while she was there and then the two could travel back to Oporto together. In the event, Mona Lisa caught a cold, Suggia cancelled and Amaryllis went alone.

Cassadó, she discovered, was a celebrity musician given to collecting rich old women. In Lisbon he soon latched on to Dona Eliza de Sousa Pedroso, a rich old woman who ran the prestigious Circulo de Cultura Musical and who, in admirable symbiosis, collected celebrity musicians. A few days after her arrival Amaryllis partnered Cassadó to one of Dona Eliza's much-vaunted dinners. It was a daunting occasion. Amaryllis could find nothing to wear, arrived late, and made a grand entrance by falling up the stairs into the hands of one of the white-gloved footmen who sentried every tread. The evening was difficult, with none of the diners sharing a common language. Portuguese, Spanish, Italian, English and French washed to and fro, with a single German guest, understood by and understanding nobody, remaining silent throughout. Meanwhile the diamond-encrusted hostess gleamed regally over her catch, her white face framed by a black wig as she puffed energetically on a fat cigar. Afterwards, Amaryllis was flattered to be asked to add her signature to the famous scrawls which covered the inside of Dona Eliza's piano lid.

As soon as Cassadó heard Amaryllis play he attacked her new bow-hold. Everything he said went in the face of what Suggia had taught. Bewildered, and lacking confidence to analyse her actions, Amaryllis began to flounder. Cassadó suggested that she join his international class in Siena's Accademia Chigiana. He would arrange for her to do some broadcasting which would pay for her accommodation, and the classes would be free. But she refused. Her mind was reeling from the conflicting advice she had received, and she needed time to sort the matter out. Cassadó departed for Siena while she remained in Lisbon to explore the city and her own musical identity.

In the late Forties, Portugal's capital was a beautiful city possessing an almost rural charm. Fishing boats dotted the harbour, donkey-loads of fruit and vegetables yawed through narrow streets amid ancient buildings whose tiled roofs glowed orange in the sun. It was hard to connect this sunny city with the period, just a few years before, when it had been a neutral haven for spies of every denomination.

Ian had visited Lisbon in 1941 with Admiral Godfrey, head of naval intelligence. The two had gone to the casino, 'a grey-walled, melancholy-looking building along the Tagus'[47], where Ian had been seized by the fantasy of out-gambling potential Nazi agents. While a disgruntled Godfrey looked on, Ian played a consistently bad game of cards against a few bored Portuguese punters and lost heavily. Not until 1952, when the incident was reversed to form the basis of his first James Bond novel, *Casino Royale*, did he begin to recoup his losses.

In 1947 Ian was Foreign Manager of Kemsley Newspapers,

and had written to their Lisbon representative, Cedric Salter, asking him to keep an eye on Amaryllis. Salter was an entertaining guide; he had covered the Spanish Civil War and possessed an apparently encyclopaedic knowledge of the Iberian peninsula. He invited Amaryllis to his villa in Estoril and took her several times to the casino. On one occasion, like Ian before him, he lost all his money and made Amaryllis hand over her own minuscule funds. Certain that she would never see her money again, Amaryllis was amazed when Salter won back all he had lost.

As she listened to his tales of journalistic derring-do Amaryllis began, for the first and only time in her life, to question her choice of career. She was confused by the tuition she had received, disillusioned with the cello, and depressed by the world she saw around her. Political journalism suddenly seemed a real alternative. She had enough contacts: both Peter and Ian worked for newspapers, as did André Mangeot's son Sylvain, who had introduced her to plenty of his colleagues at Cresswell Place. But the urge soon faded. By now Suggia was telephoning her daily – each time reversing the charges – to persuade her to go back to Oporto. Amaryllis realised that the real solution to her problems was to leave the country.

The excuse she gave Suggia was that she had run out of money, a story that was, alas, all too true. However, Salter came to the rescue. Insisting that she see something of Spain, he gave her a bundle of black-market pesetas to cover her journey home via Madrid and Barcelona. As a further favour he telephoned a hotelier friend in Madrid to ensure she got a room. Stuffing the precious currency into her shoes, Amaryllis survived a frontier search and hobbled triumphantly into Franco's Spain.

It was an exhausting but exciting experience. In Madrid she

made friends with the editor of a leading royalist newspaper, who took her to a number of shady nightclubs which were the haunts of newly released political prisoners. In Barcelona she fell in with an officer of the Secret Police who taught her to dance the *paso doble* and gave her a forged sovereign as a memento of her stay. There was, however, the disadvantage of being a woman alone in a Latin country. During the train journey from Lisbon to Oporto it seemed to her that every man on the train queued outside her door to stare at her, and things were little different in Spain. Whenever she ate out, the waiters asked if she had lost her companion and, on learning that she was eating alone, gawped in astonishment. Walking through the street, she was tailed by lines of Spaniards.

Then there was the problem of money. Salter's hotel in Madrid had proved wildly expensive but a gallant Scandinavian stepped forward, announced that she was the most beautiful creature he had ever seen, and paid the bill. The Kemsley representative in Madrid had advanced her fare to Barcelona. And in Barcelona the hotelier had waived her bill with the assurance that he would collect it the next time he was in London; he also lent her the money for her fare home. Riding high on a wave of credit, Amaryllis cabled Ian to alert his Paris man, Stephen Coulter, to her imminent arrival, and set off for France.

When the train pulled in to the Gare d'Austerlitz at five o'clock in the morning, Coulter was there to meet her, clutching an irate telegram from Ian instructing him to send her home on the next train and under no circumstance to give her any more money. Like Salter, however, Coulter felt it would be a waste for her not to see Paris since she was there. So he put her up in his apartment for a twenty-four-hour furlough before sending her home to face Ian's wrath.

In fact, Ian was not very angry, having passed all

Amaryllis's bills to Eve for payment, and so the Iberian interlude came to a peaceful close. The loose ends were soon neatly tied. The Scandinavian sent a few hopeful letters before falling silent; the hotelier in Barcelona never arrived to collect his money; and the forged sovereign, to its credit, was later stolen.

That left only Suggia, who first learned that her pupil had walked out when a letter arrived from Eve in London. The break rankled and, two years later, after Amaryllis had just given her first lunchtime recital in the Wigmore Hall, a familiar figure appeared in the artists' room. 'But my dear,' Suggia said in her deep voice, 'what has happened to your tone? It has *van*-ished!'

NINE

London, Jamaica and Paris

After the trauma of studying under Suggia, Amaryllis was in need of a musical tonic. She received it courtesy of the BBC, which was holding six commemorative concerts to celebrate the 150th anniversary of Schubert's birth and the 50th of Brahms's death, both of which fell in 1947. Among the participants was Pierre Fournier, who, with Joseph Szigeti, William Primrose and Artur Schnabel, was playing the chamber music of the two composers. Reunited with her lover, Amaryllis found herself carried along with a project which Szigeti later described as including 'peaks of musical experience'.[48]

Amaryllis was fascinated to meet these performers, all of whom ranked among the highest in their fields, and in the case of Schnabel and Szigeti were almost living legends. Viennese-born Schnabel was possibly the world's most distinguished pianist at the time. As a youth he had walked with Brahms in the wooded hills surrounding his birthplace and the great composer had once praised his youthful companion's playing, a story which became so exaggerated in the telling that Schnabel was driven to remark, 'Perhaps one day I shall read that I played billiards with Mozart.'[49] Szigeti could claim no such accolade, but was renowned for his superb violin playing – made all the more amazing because of his near-impossible posture: a bow-arm clamped so tightly to his body that he was known as 'the telephone-booth violinist'.

Given their sponsorship by the BBC, it was ironic that Schnabel and Szigeti shared a mistrust of recorded music. Schnabel objected on grounds of etiquette: an imperial Austrian of the heel-clicking variety, he was aghast at his music being played before an audience who might be behaving improperly – 'not knowing how they would be dressed, what else they would be doing at the same time, how much they would listen'.[50] Szigeti took a more lenient approach but still pleaded artistic *angst*. 'How loth we all are to be faced with material proof of our former musical statements!' he wrote later. 'One hears stories about some of the greatest musicians of our time who are roused to frenzy when they listen to one or another of their recent test-records, roused to the extent of stamping the inert platters of shellac in fury under their heels; while some of their older recordings may excite even greater horror in them.'[51]

Szigeti suffered excruciating attacks of nerves at live performances and was plagued by the 'pearlies', musicians' jargon for the muscular tremors produced by anxiety. The pearlies are particularly distressing for string players, striking as they do on long slow notes or at the start of a concert – those times when control is most needed and audience attention is keenest. Few are immune – Amaryllis recalls an occasion when she had to make fifteen bow changes during a single note – and once the pearlies have been experienced, the fear of recurrence is enough to produce a further attack. So deep-seated was Szigeti's phobia that at the beginning of a concert his bow would often jump to the wrong side of the bridge. On one occasion at the Albert Hall the realisation of what was to come made him refuse to go on to the platform. His manager sympathised and said he needn't play but he *would* have to go on to apologise. Szigeti saw the vast audience gathered before him and chose the pearlies he knew. The concert went without a hitch.

Schnabel, conversely, was imperturbable. During one performance of a Brahms piano quartet, Primrose broke a string. Seconds later, Szigeti broke a string. Fournier, seeing the impossibility of continuing, stopped as well. But Schnabel played on, and not until Szigeti jabbed him in the back with his bow did the elderly pianist admit anything was amiss.

Apart from one concert in Westminster, the performances took place in Scotland at the inaugural Edinburgh Festival. But the offstage action centred on the Hyde Park Hotel, where Schnabel had installed a Steinway grand in his bedroom, and Chez Charles, a cosy, check-cloth bistro across the road in Knightsbridge Green. Amaryllis was intrigued by the personal interplay among these great musicians. The quartet, she learned, was organised on a tyranny of age. Fees were carefully divided according to birthdate, with Schnabel, the eldest, claiming the largest cut and Fournier, the youngest, receiving the least. The same system worked in rehearsals, with Schnabel treating the others like little boys, and telling them precisely how the music should be played. Come the concert, however, each went his own way. She also discovered that Schnabel was an incurable bore. At Chez Charles he embarked on lengthy, tedious stories which his wife tried gamely to halt. But Schnabel, never one to be headed off at the anecdotal pass, forged on triumphantly to a non-existent punchline.

His artistry was supreme; hearing him play the opening chords of Beethoven's G Major Concerto was for Amaryllis 'unforgettable. It was the most precise, the most perfect interpretation. The balance was extraordinary.' But it was Szigeti who really interested her. He was '*the* great violinist, an extremely intelligent musician who made the most wonderful sound'. She admired the genius with which he overcame his self-imposed handicap, and his performances, which she attended whenever possible, became a source of profound inspiration. Szigeti reciprocated the interest. Once, Amaryllis took his bow to be re-haired, in return for a bar of soap, an item only recently lifted from the rationing lists. Fournier was outraged. 'SOAP?!' he cried. 'Well, if he can't think of anything better to give you, then don't go running errands for him.' Amaryllis returned the bow to Szigeti's hotel room where he was practising Schubert's notoriously difficult Fantasie in C. He invited her to sit down and listen. Like a restaurant gypsy, he sidled up until his bow was practically in her ear. She moved. So did he. She moved again. He followed. Together they shuffled around the room, Szigeti playing ever more insistently, until Amaryllis was finally pinned against the wall. Just then the phone rang. Szigeti had a brief conversation, then replaced the handset. 'I think you'd better go down,' he said. 'That was Pierre. He sounds rather cross.'

Szigeti never lost heart. Years later, shortly before his death in 1973, he had dinner with Amaryllis and a mutual friend, Manoug Parikian, with whom he had adjudicated at the Moscow International Competition. 'Ah, it's so sad,' he sighed; 'when I was younger you always put your cello between us. Now, at last, you haven't brought one and I'm past it!'

Before the BBC concerts were finished, Szigeti introduced Amaryllis to 'the great Mrs Tillet' of Ibbs and Tillet, the agents who handled many famous musicians, including Szigeti and Pierre Fournier. In the artists' room after one performance Szigeti said, 'You must hear Amaryllis. She's wonderful!' Amaryllis thought he was joking. But she did have an interview with Emmy Tillet and was taken on to her books, albeit reluctantly. 'If only you were a tenor,' Tillet sighed, 'what we could do for you!'

The excitements of 1947 ended on an exotic note. Eve, at her doctor's suggestion, had decided to take a trip abroad. Her chosen destination was Jamaica, where Ian had just built a house on the north shore at Oracabessa, or 'Goldeneye', as he called it, and her chosen companion was Amaryllis. In December, mother and daughter set sail on the *Queen Elizabeth* to New York, thence to Kingston and the Myrtle Bank Hotel (the Turtle Tank, in local idiom) before moving on to Goldeneye.

Augustus had visited Jamaica in the late Thirties, drawn by images of 'rum, treacle, white devilry and black magic', and had relished his trips into its interior. 'In my idle daydreams,' he wrote, 'I imagined myself heading an uprising of the Island, driving the whites, the good Governor and all, including a number of my new friends, into the sea and inaugurating a reign of Harmony in this potential Paradise.'[52]

After a short spell at the Turtle Tank, Amaryllis began to have similar daydreams. During her stay she accepted an offer to perform at the Institute of Jamaica. 'All I can offer you', wrote the man in charge, 'is an enthusiastic audience of rather humble folk of all colours, shapes and ages. "Society" is not usually interested in the Institute's activities unless we invite one of its high lights in whose exalted radiance they imagine they shine more gloriously.' It was a short recital with a black pianist, Miss Foster Davis, whom Amaryllis later invited back for lunch. But as they took their seats in the Turtle Tank dining room, the other, exclusively white, guests rose and left the room without a word. 'Take no notice,' Eve whispered. They continued their meal accompanied only by the waiters. It was one of the few times Amaryllis felt proud of her mother.

Before long Eve and Amaryllis headed for Goldeneye. The newly built house was, even to Ian's friends, a monstrosity. Ivar Bryce described it as 'a masterpiece of striking ugliness'.[53] And Noel Coward, another north-shore neighbour, directed visitors: 'Straight on for miles, and it is the nearest ear, nose and throat clinic on the right.'[54] Built of concrete around three sides of a square, Goldeneye comprised a huge sitting room, flanked at one end by servants' quarters and at the other by tiny sleeping cubicles which gave uninspiringly on to the courtyard and a mass of tropical bushes. The furniture, constructed to Ian's designs by a local carpenter out of indigenous green mahoe, was bitingly uncomfortable. Bed legs stood in saucers of water to keep ants at bay. There was no refrigerator. The absence of baths became academic because there was no hot water to put in them. And the food – mostly curried goat, served by Ian's maid, Violet – soon palled. The location, however, was superb. The sitting room had panoramic views over the ocean and opened on to a small garden from which narrow paths led down to the golden sands of Goldeneye's private beach, where Amaryllis practised in the boiling heat, wearing only a bikini and a towel to protect her cello from the sweat which poured down her body.

She longed to explore the island but had little opportunity to do so. She had managed to escape the Turtle Tank once or twice to stay with a friend of Ian's in the British Council whose sole purpose in life, as far as she could see, was lecturing Jamaicans on Elgar, birth control and how to make crème caramel. Now at Goldeneye she was marooned. It was an isolated place, and Ian had jacked up his car on bricks, leaving guests reliant on taxis. Those were rarely summoned, due to Eve's paranoia that Amaryllis would be raped if she went outside the property. Accordingly Amaryllis passed her days practising the cello, swimming and reading. The only excitement was when a maybug settled agonisingly in her ear one night. With great presence of mind she seized a bottle of brilliantine from Eve's dressing table and sluiced the insect out.

Sensing that her daughter was getting bored and herself feeling the pinch of Ian's domestic austerity, Eve booked them both into the Hotel Casa Blanca in Montego Bay. Here they met Noel Coward, who doubtless sympathised with their move, having once stayed at Goldeneye, and who recommended it wholeheartedly as a 'perfectly ghastly house'.[55] To Amaryllis the Casa Blanca was as oppressive as the Turtle Tank. The beach was reserved for whites only, which made her uncomfortable, and when Eve caught her exchanging glances with a handsome black waiter she insisted on sharing her bedroom. This gave Amaryllis the chance to note that her mother, who always claimed to be an insomniac, slept very soundly indeed, retiring early and turning the lights out at 9.30, a curfew which forced Amaryllis to rig up a screen of clothes and blankets between their beds so that she could read without disturbing her.

They returned to Britain on a banana boat shortly before Christmas. It was a five-day journey of stultifying boredom, with cocktail parties every evening followed by polite conversation at the captain's table. Come Christmas Day, she played carols on her cello while the forty or so other passengers croaked away in dismal unison. Augustus had journeyed home by the same means, had suffered the same monotonous routine and on leaving the vessel, like Amaryllis after him, had felt nothing but 'an intoxicating sense of relief!'[56]

It took several months for Amaryllis to shake off Suggia's influence entirely. Fournier helped where he could, but as his workload increased so his London appearances became few and far between. He was now at a peak, releasing all the creativity stifled by the fallow war years. Szigeti, who had not heard him since the Thirties, was struck by his 'immense talent', and wrote admiringly of the 'Apollonian beauty and poise'[57] his playing had acquired in the intervening period. If Amaryllis wanted to receive the benefits of this talent, her only option was to follow him to Paris.

As always, money was a problem. Fournier did his best by supplying free lessons – though when Eve grudgingly offered to pay he was happy to take her money – and even offered Amaryllis free access to his account at Ibbs and Tillet. But she refused to take handouts. By dint of saving her allowance, now £1 a week, and the occasional piece of paid work, she was able to fund not only the journey, then about £8 return via Dieppe, but lodgings in Paris.

Among them were hotels, her favourite being the Hôtel Beaujolais, a gimcrack conversion overlooking the Jardin du Palais Royal. The spacious rooms of what had once been a grand town house were crudely subdivided with plywood partitions, and on the ground floor a male concierge lifted his long nose from a volume of Maeterlinck to inquire lugubriously, 'Alors, le Monsieur est parti?' The novelist Colette, a friend of Pierre Fournier, lived a few doors away and now and then Amaryllis glimpsed her walking beneath the flowering chestnut trees which lined the gardens. But not even the Beaujolais, shabbily charming as it was, could compare with the rue du Mont Thabord.

The apartment had been discovered by Hugo Cole, who was then studying composition with Nadia Boulanger. The previous occupant, an old woman, had just died and the new owners were undecided whether to sell the place or keep it for their teenage daughter. While they dithered, it was let at a rent equivalent to about ten shillings a week. It was a magnificent bargain. The street, although dark and narrow, was in the heart of fashionable Paris, leading directly off the rue de Rivoli. The apartment was on the second floor and comprised a large sitting room, three bedrooms and a kitchen, all excellently equipped and furnished. On the minus side, it was exactly as the old woman had left it, with dusty bundles of this and that sitting on every shelf; as there was no bath they had to wash in the kitchen sink, and directly opposite was an architect's office, whose inhabitants spent their days shooting paper darts at Amaryllis as she practised in the sitting room, then shouting to her to give them back.

These were trifling disadvantages. In 1948, S. J. Perelman wrote: 'The character exists, unquestionably, who managed to have a rip-roaring time in Paris in the summer of 1947, but who he is, where he did so, and how he found the inclination, I cannot imagine.'[58] He should have asked Amaryllis. For her, Paris was a dream. Not only could she study, but the cafés were cheap, the people friendly and the atmosphere, even in post-war trauma, had a youthful vibrancy. She collected admirers by the bistro-full and gave the concierge a blacklist of men who were on no account to be allowed upstairs. Then, too, there were also more work opportunities than in London, most notably the soirées, financed by wealthy patrons, from which some musicians made their entire living.

One of the most sought-after social venues was in the rue Barbet-de-Jouy at the house of Comtesse Marie-Blanche de Polignac. An accomplished amateur pianist and singer, the *comtesse* was the latest in a line of distinguished musical patronesses. Her family's salons had been a fixture since the nineteenth century, and Marie-Blanche continued that tradition in an ambience enriched by her superb collection of Impressionist paintings. Describing a pre-war visit to Paris, Salvador Dali gave a thumbnail sketch of one such gathering.

'In the spring it was very pleasant at the Comtesse Marie-Blanche de Polignac's, where from the garden one listened to string quartets played in the interior all aflame with candles and Renoir paintings and with the malefic coprophagia of an unsurpassable pastel by Fantin-Latour – all this accompanied by *petits-fours* and much candy and other sweets.'[59]

Amaryllis got her first taste of this somewhat precious world when she was invited to the rue Barbet-de-Jouy to hear Fournier play in a chamber group. There were hidden undercurrents: Fournier had taken a fancy to a fellow performer's wife while he, in turn, had taken a fancy to Amaryllis. After the rehearsal the man drove her home and saw her up to her apartment. A minute or two later the concierge was interested to see him tear down the stairs and into the street, where he then had to dodge a shower of furniture rained on him from the second floor.

The soirée itself was a claustrophobic affair. Paris's finest were there, decked to the gills in the latest modes. They laughed and chattered in the Polignac salon, surrounded on every side by artworks so numerous that even Cézannes were propped against the walls. When the performance began they slumped to the floor, nestling comfortably against priceless paintings. Amaryllis, dressed incongruously in Eve's hand-me-downs, and ignored by all, was revolted. She felt literally suffocated ('Scent, scent, scent, until you could hardly breathe') and was reminded of one of André's favourite anecdotes concerning the Belgian violinist Ysaye, who had remarked to his pianist at just such a soirée, '*Dis donc, Raoul, si l'on pétait pour changer l'air.*' Fournier's wife, Lyda, sensing her plight, did her best to help matters by introducing her as Peter Fleming's sister. The blank stares which followed made things worse. In desperation she tried one more introduction and, 'For the only time in my life,' Amaryllis recalls, 'I was glad to meet an Englishman abroad.'

The Englishman was Ashley Clarke, First Secretary at the embassy and, in time, one of Amaryllis's best friends in Paris. He took her to lunch, to the ballet, to the theatre, and introduced her to Margot Fonteyn, who she found 'sweet, and very natural', though Amaryllis was too shy to utter more than a few words. His greatest gift, however, was a recital he arranged for her in his grand apartment at 101 Avenue Raymond Poincaré on 7 December 1948.

He had enlisted the support of Gerald Moore from London as accompanying pianist, and Marie-Blanche de Polignac as wardrobe mistress. They both performed well. When Moore arrived, they all went out for lunch at Maxims then repaired to Lanvin's – couturière Jeanne Lanvin had been Marie-Blanche's mother – where Amaryllis was offered her pick of mannequins' dresses. Thin-waisted and slender, she was the perfect mannequin size, but the cello demanded a full skirt. The only one available was a magnificent strapless edifice of tiered black silk. Moore suggested she jump up and down to see if it would slip. 'Jump again!' he suggested half-heartedly after fifteen minutes.

The recital, which consisted of works by Purcell, Fauré, Samuel Barber and Herbert Howells, was not a success. Amaryllis was too inexperienced, unready for that kind of close event which requires nerves of steel. But it was a taste of the grand life, and she felt downcast when she had to return the dress, Cinderella-like, to Lanvin's, and even more abashed when Ashley bought her a bouquet of flowers as a thank-you gift for Marie-Blanche de Polignac.

On this occasion she was spared the embarrassment of Fournier's presence. Not all Amaryllis's time was spent in Paris, thanks to a growing number of engagements in Britain, but she was so enamoured of it that she went there whenever possible, even if her tutor was away. But Fournier still figured large in her life. And his wife knew it.

Lyda Fournier was no fool. A White Russian who had been married to, and deserted by, the great cellist Grigor Piatigorsky, she had openly declared her intention to marry an even better cellist. In the event she found a different cellist, and although she played no instrument herself she promoted Fournier's career assiduously. Not even the best-willed person in the world could have said the marriage was held together by fidelity, but Lyda had a sharp eye for her husband's misdemeanours and an acid tongue for his admirers. Strangely, though, it was the admirers rather than the lovers who called forth her wrath. She was outraged by one horse-faced English cellist who pestered her husband and who once camped overnight in the lobby of the Hyde Park Hotel, forcing a desperate Fournier to escape through the kitchens. But she took Amaryllis in her stride. This did not mean, however, that she gave her an easy time.

One Christmas while Amaryllis was studying in Paris, she was invited to dinner with the Fourniers. It was a grand family affair and it was arranged that she would rendezvous with Lyda and Pierre at their apartment in rue le Sueur. 'Right, Amaryllis,' said Lyda, 'I give you ten minutes on the sofa with my husband while I dress. Ten minutes! No more.' The two sat motionless at opposite ends of the sofa, nervously eyeing the door that led to the adjoining bedroom. Later, at the dinner, Amaryllis found herself sitting between Fournier and his seventeen-year-old son Jean-Pierre. 'Do you know,' Lyda suddenly announced, 'I do believe Jean-Pierre is still a virgin. I think, Amaryllis, you could do something about this. It would be a good turn.' Amaryllis politely declined. But later in the evening she felt Jean-Pierre's foot creeping over to hers. At the same time Fournier's foot was advancing from the other side. As she sat making polite conversation, and playing footsie with the two of them, Lyda hoisted the tablecloth. 'That's a bit much!' she cried indignantly. 'Both my husband and my son playing with your feet!'

TEN

Escape

It was only a matter of time before Eve uncovered her daughter's affair with Fournier. Whether at home or abroad, Amaryllis wrote regularly to her lover, who, because of his increasingly busy schedule, could be reached only via a series of *postes restantes*. One revealing letter missed its destination and was returned to Charles Street. Eve steamed it open.

Nothing was said. But when Fournier was next at the Hyde Park Hotel he received a visit from Peter. Amaryllis, whom Fournier had warned in advance, was told to wait in the park until he gave the all-clear: his bedroom light flicking on and off. She paced up and down the Serpentine in freezing fog, then, when the signal came, dashed back to the hotel.

Fournier was a wreck. As he sat shaking on the bed she tried to piece together what had happened. Peter had been very cold – all the brothers could be icily terrifying – and had refused to shake hands, an insult Fournier found unforgivable. He had asked if Fournier's intentions were honourable, 'which, of course, they weren't,' Amaryllis scoffs; 'anyone could have told him that!' Fournier took it very seriously. 'We can never meet again!' he declared dramatically. 'Wherever we go, one of your brothers may be hiding under the bed with a revolver!' And then he left for Paris, to spend the best part of a week prostrate with shock. The affair continued on his recovery but things were never quite the same.

Although neither Peter nor Eve mentioned the matter, it had its inevitable repercussions on life at Charles Street. On one occasion Eve summoned the family doctor to show her daughter the error of her ways. Unfortunately Amaryllis interrupted them as her mother was coaching the man on his forthcoming lecture. Eve fled the room, Amaryllis burst into tears and the doctor muttered nervously about 'misunder-standings'. There were fleeting periods of freedom when Eve went abroad but they were made illusory by her habit of returning a day or two in advance to take people by surprise. Once she returned early from South Africa, to find that her sister Kathleen, whom she had left to house-sit, had let Amaryllis go to Paris for the weekend. Enraged, she chased Kathleen out of the house and down the street, pelting her with potatoes from a bag she had snatched from the kitchen.

Eve's attitude was ambivalent: she wanted Amaryllis to go out and earn a living but hated the thought of being left alone. Comparisons with her sons, who had flown the nest at an early age, were readily forthcoming, but funds for Amaryllis to do likewise were not. Peter, as usual, was the one pushed forward to have a word. 'He once had a great session with me, saying that I expected to be given money while I was starting this career and why couldn't I get a job in an orchestra, as my mother wanted me to do. I explained that playing in an orchestra was nothing to do with what I could do, or wanted to do. So he asked "How good are you going to be?" To which I replied, "As good as I possibly can be. I haven't got a crystal ball and cannot foresee that, but I intend to try to the best of my ability." He retorted, "Well, no one but a sergeant-major could deal with you!"'

Even Fournier must have felt the same on occasions. For all

his closeness to Amaryllis, he had an old-fashioned view about her career. The showdown came after Fournier had concluded a live broadcast for the BBC's Third Programme at which Amaryllis had been page-turning. He told her that being a soloist was far too demanding for a woman, and that her best option would be to marry a rich man and play part-time for her own pleasure. Marriage, in his eyes, was no obstacle to their continuing to see each other. Amaryllis erupted. 'I'm not the kind of person you wrap up in cotton wool!' she shouted. Only then did they discover that the microphones were still on and their argument had been heard by the producer.

Fournier and Amaryllis were too selfish to be compatible. He was utterly absorbed in his work and spoke of little save himself and his various troubles with agents, gramophone companies and critics. He was a closed man, unable or unwilling to listen to others. Although Amaryllis loved him she never considered moving in with him on a permanent basis. He misread her ambition and was too terrified of her family to help her cope with Eve. It was his talent she was after. As he himself told her, she would never have taken any notice of him had he not been a splendid cellist. And as Amaryllis readily concedes, she has rarely fallen for anybody from whom she cannot learn.

Another who fell into that category was Denis Fry, Professor of Experimental Phonetics at London University, whom Amaryllis met during a musicians' summer school at Downe House, the school having disbanded for the holidays. They were short of a viola player for quartets, and Denis Fry, a talented amateur musician, came to the rescue. He was a remarkable man, an expert in his subject and fascinated by music, eventually dovetailing the two interests in *Some Effects of Music*, a pamphlet which analysed the elements of music and their aesthetic appeal. He shared his knowledge with

Amaryllis and infused her with his enthusiasm for esoteric philosophy. He introduced her to the works of Ouspensky and Idries Shah, and placed her in an Ouspensky group which taught self-awareness. 'It was very formal – no one was ever called by their Christian names – and deeply esoteric. Questions were not allowed unless properly formulated. From time to time we were given tasks – one week it was to write about Energy. We were taught self-remembering – to be aware of oneself. After a while "it" had crystallised and the group suddenly collapsed.'

More important, however, Denis Fry helped Amaryllis articulate her feelings towards her mother. For some time she had been torn between the guilt of leaving Eve on her own and the strain of persuading herself that she 'should' cope with life at Charles Street. Fry's response was that this pattern of aggravation was doing nothing but harm. The relationship could get no worse if she left, and might even improve. 'There comes a time,' he told her, 'when you tell yourself that you can't cope with something. It's no use your saying you should, or you can, when you can't. Therefore you leave.'

Her first attempt was an ignominious failure. She leased a furnished bed-sit in Earls Court Road which was so un-pleasant that she had to slink back to Charles Street, tail between legs. Her second try was more successful. In the summer of 1949 she moved into 49 Cranley Gardens, where she had found space in an attic flat with Penelope Ram, an after-care officer for Borstal girls, whose cellist cousin had alerted her to Amaryllis's plight. It was a crowded and uncomfortable place owned by a professed music lover who lived on the floor below and sang scales loudly and badly. Having claimed to 'simply adore' the cello, and to have no objections to Amaryllis practising, he soon changed his mind and banished her to a gloomy, booming basement bathroom where she was unable to hear the telephone which rang with increasing frequency with offers of work.

It was lucky, therefore, that Penelope met a woman who had just found for her butler what she described as a 'wonderful little house' in the Fulham Road, and doubly lucky that the man had refused point-blank to live in it. Certainly, the maisonette at 455 Fulham Road had its disadvantages. It was next to a pub on the intersection with Gunter Grove, and almost every night there was an accident; when lorries squealed to a halt at the lights, the whole house shook on its foundations. The rooms, reached by a flight of rickety stairs, were small and in bad repair. Below lurked the premises of British Typewriter Supplies, whose landlord-owner braved the treads to inform tenants of grand Masonic functions – 'Mansion House, my dears!' or 'Duke Street St James's! Duke Street St James's!' – which he had attended or was about to attend. Nevertheless, compared with Cranley Gardens it was heaven. Penelope and Amaryllis took it at a rent of three pounds a week.

From the start there was a disreputable air about 455 Fulham Road. Borstal girls were always coming in and out, arriving with a police escort and departing with some stolen memento such as scent or clothing. Sometimes, the girls were delivered into Amaryllis's hands. Some became good friends, such as Cosy, 'a tremendous character from the East End who once asked the conductor Richard Austin which route he worked', and Joan, a fifteen-year-old French prostitute, 'enormous, very tall, very butch and frightening', for whose services American soldiery paid a princely £200 a night in Park Lane hotels. One day Amaryllis passed on an unwanted present of a pair of pink knickers. They 'went down very well'. And they did so in Hyde Park, whereupon Joan was rearrested and caused a furore by naming the magistrate as one of her clients.

Others who made regular trips to the flat were Pierre Fournier, who struggled gamely up the stairs in his caliper, and the landlord, who, like the Cranley Gardens singer, had discovered a new aversion to the cello. While Amaryllis practised Beethoven, he rattled the doorknob, begging her to stop playing scales. There were also many boyfriends and admirers, for, like her father, Amaryllis had developed a healthy sexual appetite. Whenever the bell rang, Amaryllis crept downstairs and raised to the fanlight a home-made periscope, consisting of a broomstick with mirror attached. What she most commonly saw was a man bending over to peer through the letterbox. 'Men fell in heaps around her,' recalls a friend. Penelope Ram concurs, 'The telephone never stopped ringing when Amaryllis returned from abroad. We'd have parties with an extraordinary mix of people. To me her beauty was not so apparent until I saw her on the platform. I remember people gasping when she walked on. I was so proud of her that I used to burst into tears.'

It was a chaotic, student-like atmosphere, made all the more so by lack of funds. Meals often consisted of kippers and cornflakes, furniture was other people's cast-offs and curtains were scrounged from friends. Eve gave Amaryllis a bed which none of the servants would sleep on, and refused her request for lampshades – bare bulbs, she pointed out, used expensive electricity more efficiently. Penelope alleviated their finances by taking in a lodger, Rosemary Whiffin, whose days were spent on a bicycle herding recalcitrant VD patients into St Mary's hospital. The household budget rose; the moral tone slid deliciously down.

Outside Fulham Road, Amaryllis was kept busy. Lessons continued with Fournier, either in Paris or in his room at the

Hyde Park Hotel, and she often page-turned for him at the BBC. He became good friends with the BBC accompanist Ernest Lush and the two played at concerts around the country. Once, while Amaryllis was page-turning for Lush she had to whip out a large picture of a naked girl which Fournier had slipped between the pages. Lush took his revenge. At the next performance, with only a few minutes to get changed and make himself presentable, Fournier discovered his shirtsleeves had been tied into knots of Gordian complexity.

Amaryllis also had her own engagements. In March 1949 she had formed a piano trio with Alan Loveday and Peggy Gray, and though it received high critical acclaim, it was hard pushed to make ends meet. Their schedule, which consisted initially of school concerts, was unremitting, sometimes demanding two or three performances a day. For some children the Loveday Trio was their first experience of live classical music, and their reactions to the carefully planned programmes were mixed. In Great Yarmouth, the headmaster asked a small boy which bit he had liked best. 'Please sir,' came the reply from the front row, 'the bit that played the cello.'

She also gave a growing number of solo performances. In September, she appeared at the Bournemouth Winter Gardens, playing Dvořák's Cello Concerto with the Municipal Orchestra. She had spent the preceding night with Nanny Towler, who had retired to eke out her days by the seaside. It was as if Amaryllis had been bundled back to childhood. Nanny Towler insisted she sleep between blankets, as that would be warmer – 'frightfully uncomfortable' in Amaryllis's recollection – and after the performance accosted Sir Charles Groves, the conductor, in the artists' room. 'Now, you will look after my girlie, won't you?' she admonished; 'you will give her another engagement?'

Eve, meanwhile, looked upon her daughter's activities with vague disappointment. For all that she had urged Amaryllis to go forth and earn there was a part of her that wanted her to fail. Eve hated the thought of her last child leaving home, leaving her control, leaving her to a lonely widowhood. Secretly, she hoped that this was only a temporary defection and that before long Amaryllis would be driven back to Charles Street by lack of funds. As yet, however, there was no sign of that happening; Amaryllis was doing far better than Eve had expected. And in 1949, in grudging recognition of her daughter's talent, she held a musical soirée for her at Charles Street.

It was a far cry from Nanny Towler's blankets. Full evening dress was required, butlers were on hand to keep the champagne flowing and the two eldest 'shiny boys' had been dragooned into attendance (though Ian tarnished his sheen by falling asleep on the sofa). 'Mrs Fleming was beautiful,' Penelope recalls; 'stunning, for a woman of her age. Her elegance, her dignity, her enchanting house, all combined to make a magic atmosphere for someone like me . . . when she was entertaining she was a wonderful hostess and appeared concerned about everyone in a superficial kind of way.' But there was sadness in the magic. Eve remained aloof, not haughtily but in an unhappy, remote fashion. Passing graciously through each pine-panelled room, greeting Britain's post-war youth with a distant handshake, she must have remembered the parties she had hosted in Turner's House under the same Italian candelabras, on the same oriental rugs. She must also have reflected, once the guests had gone, that if her daughter now knew what she was, how long would it be before she discovered who she was?

ELEVEN

Discovery

Rumours of Amaryllis's parentage had long been circulating in London. It was commonly understood that Augustus was her father, because he made no attempt to hide the fact. But who was her mother? For a while the finger of gossip pointed at Suggia. After all, *eighty* sittings for a portrait . . . and Amaryllis *was* a very good cellist. Then, with a slight waver, it slid back to Eve. Lord Dawson, the only reliable third-party source, had died in 1945, so there was no solid proof either way, but circumstantial evidence was too strong to be ignored. All one had to do was look at the two women to know that they were mother and daughter. If Amaryllis was fooled by Eve's argument that people who lived together grew to look like each other, she was the only one.

Even students at the RCM had heard the talk, string players in particular, and it was Penelope Ram's cellist cousin who first brought her the news. But so strong was the spell Eve had woven that none dared break it. As Penelope recalls, 'I did hear people say it quite often, although I didn't pass it on. And, since I'd never asked Amaryllis, as far as I knew it was hearsay, a rumour, and I'd say "I don't know", when asked.'

Not even Augustus had brought up the subject, though he had long kept a watchful eye on Amaryllis, and was beguiled by both her talent and her beauty. In 1946 he had invited her to his studio in Tite Street, and two red conté portraits emerged from this encounter, one of which he gave to Eve as a Christmas present. Two years later, in April 1948, he wrote to Amaryllis announcing a forthcoming show at the Leicester Galleries. 'I would so like to have a drawing of you in it. Can it be done?' he inquired, adding, 'I long to see you.' Maybe he was tiring of the charade. In May, after the exhibition, he wrote trying to arrange another meeting. As he explained, 'Conditions at the Leicester Galleries were not favourable for a tête-à-tête.'

Rupert Hart-Davis wrote of Augustus, 'He knew he was a genius and came to think it was his duty to people the world with others.'[60] But his sense of duty usually stopped at the peopling. The upbringing, education and, often, explanation, was left to the mothers. It was not that Augustus disliked children; on the contrary, he adored them. But if their mothers wished to present his many illegitimate offspring as children of later husbands (in Chiquita's case) or as adopted (in Eve's), Augustus would toe the line. With Eve, however, agreement verged uncomfortably on extortion. He later told Amaryllis, 'Oh, she put the fear of God into me! I can't remember what she said she'd do if I ever told you, but whatever it was I thought I'd better not risk it.' Nevertheless, by the late Forties her parentage was common knowledge. Amaryllis was, in her own words, 'the last person in London to know', but no one had the courage for open disavowal of Eve's myth. Fittingly, the impetus was supplied by Eve herself.

Late in 1949 a letter arrived for Amaryllis at 455 Fulham Road. Written in block letters, it carried a message that said roughly, 'You have no talent, play out of tune and have no tone. Leave the filthy men alone and go back to your mother, who by all accounts is quite a decent old stick.' Behind its feeble disguise, the writing was recognisable as Eve's.

The note, meaner than most of her mother's tyrannies, had a shattering effect on Amaryllis. Possibly she still felt guilty about leaving home, or perhaps it was just the last of many straws, but she blocked its consequence from her mind. When asked about it now, she says that she found it amusing. She claims that when she laughingly confronted Eve, her mother said she could only write since Amaryllis refused to talk to her.

Penelope Ram tells a different story. 'Amaryllis was *terribly* upset by this letter, so I suggested going out for some lunch. We went across the road to a café and had lamb chops and peas which cost 1/6d each. I tried to soothe her by saying that we say awful things to our own flesh and blood because we feel safe in the relationship. At first I thought her mother couldn't have written it, but Amaryllis had no doubts. Again I tried to console her by saying that parents do say terrible things to their children, things we'd never say to anybody else because we're so sure of our relationship. Amaryllis said, "But she's *not* my mother!" My eyes came out on stalks – I can still feel the shock – and I must have gasped. She leaned forward and said, "Didn't you know I was adopted?" I must have gone white. I couldn't believe that she didn't know what I'd been hearing. She picked this up and asked me, "What are you thinking?" There was a silence which I can remember as if it was yesterday. Then I said, "I suppose you ought to know what people say." '

' "What *do* they say?" she asked.

' "That your mother *is* your mother and that when Augustus John painted her they had an affair and you were the result."

'She was amazed, very shocked, and she asked me what she ought to do. I suggested that she talk to Ian or Peter.'

In the end she went to neither half-brother, but to Hugo

Pitman, who, as a friend of both the Johns and the Flemings and an intimate of Augustus, seemed a suitable arbiter. A meeting was arranged at the Queen's Restaurant in Sloane Square, where, over dinner and amid a great deal of embarrassment, Pitman confirmed that the rumour was true.

The next step was to confront her father. A lunch was arranged with Augustus, again at the Queen's. Augustus certainly knew what it was all about, but he made it no easier when the moment came.

'I hear you're my father,' Amaryllis said.

'Nobody knows who you are except Lord Dawson,' thundered Augustus, bringing his fist down on the table, 'and he's DEAD!' After a moment's pause he added, 'You were found in a ditch!'

Just as when Eve had told her she was adopted, Amaryllis refused to cry or show any emotion. But now the reason was not childish pride but the knowledge that Augustus hated scenes: if cornered he might deny it all; if given time he would come round. 'We chewed our way through the meal and Augustus kept leaving the table to go to the gents. Then, when we got up to leave, he gave me a great slap on the back and said, "So you're my little girl, are you? Well, don't tell your mother!"'

It remained for Amaryllis to do just that.

Eve, possibly forewarned by Augustus or Hugo Pitman, took the initiative by inviting Amaryllis to Sunday lunch. The invitation arrived on the Friday, and for the next two nights Amaryllis and Penelope sat up discussing the forthcoming conflict. 'She looked so ill when she left I thought she'd be sick on the bus,' Penelope recalls.

The lunch was as traumatic as anticipated.

'Why didn't you tell me you're my mother?' Amaryllis demanded.

'Because I'm *not!*' came Eve's emphatic reply, and she produced sheaves of papers to prove her point.

There were letters to adoption agencies inquiring about a baby girl; there were letters in reply, confirming that there was or was not one available. But there was nothing to say that Eve had visited any of these places, nothing to show that she had made a formal adoption. As Amaryllis scanned this lack of evidence, she heard Eve mutter in a near inaudible whisper, 'It was only for the best.'

The truth was out. When Amaryllis looked up from the documents, the Great I Am had disappeared. In her place was a frail old lady with grey hair and stick-thin limbs whose pointless pretence had finally been exposed. Not that Eve had any intention of abandoning her life's work. She insisted until her dying day that Amaryllis had been adopted, and refused to hear otherwise.

In the summer of 1950, while staying in a rented villa in Opio near Cannes – to which he had been taken to disentangle him from one of his more attractive sitters – Augustus wrote Eve 'a drastic letter . . . to which she hasn't replied yet. The subject was *veracity*.' A little later he informed Amaryllis that '. . . my exhortation seems to have horrified her. I will be writing back to Mamma at once with all the tact I can summon, though her view of me seems uncomplimentary.' If there was another letter, it had no result.

The news of Amaryllis's true identity struck the Fleming brothers in different ways: Richard was the least surprised, having already caught a whiff of scandal as any good banker should; Peter was astonished but indifferent; whereas Ian, who had once made a vigorous pass at his 'adopted' sister, was decidedly shaken. But they were accustomed to their mother's eccentricities and, loyalty prevailing, they toed the party line. Thus John Pearson, whose *Life of Ian Fleming* was published in 1966, refers to Amaryllis as adopted, as does Duff Hart-Davis, in his 1974 biography of Peter.

It was only when Michael Holroyd embarked on his second volume of Augustus John's life that the truth became inescapable. Richard, by then the last surviving son, fought a rearguard action. On 31 December 1973 he wrote to Sir Caspar John, another of Amaryllis's half-brothers, that although 'Peter, and the rest of us, had aided and abetted Mamma in her rather transparent subterfuge . . . the Fleming brothers owe a great deal to my mother who resolutely refused to acknowledge that Amaryllis was anything but adopted and as the last of the brothers I am damned if I want to let her down if I can help it . . . Needless to say I should welcome your support in my efforts but have no reason to claim it.' The letter was filed by Sir Caspar with a scribbled note: 'Wilco – but do Richard and Amaryllis feel the same way?' As it transpired, they did not. Amaryllis had no objections to the truth being revealed and Richard, having discussed the matter with Holroyd, gave his go-ahead. In 1975 the second volume was published, and so, exactly fifty years after her birth, Amaryllis's parentage became official public knowledge.

In 1949, however, such intrigues were far from Amaryllis's mind. Her immediate concern was to find out more about her father. Shortly after Eve's confession Augustus invited Amaryllis down to Fryern Court, the Johns' New Forest home near Fordingbridge. She went via Bournemouth, where she played the Dvořák Concerto conducted by Rudolf Schwartz, and stayed as usual with Nanny Towler. The following morning she boarded the bus for Fordingbridge, to be met by Augustus in his grey Wolseley. She presented him with the bouquet of amaryllises which she had been given after the concert, and they set out on the final leg of her journey. When they arrived, Dodo was waiting outside the porch in an ankle-length gathered skirt with a long-sleeved bodice buttoned to the waist, her grey-white hair pinned up, 'looking unutterably graceful'. Amaryllis took one glance and knew she had found a kindred spirit. She seized the flowers from her father and presented them to Dodo, then she went into the house. Fryern's unique atmosphere enveloped her and for the first time in her life she felt utterly, completely, at home.

Fryern Court had been home to the Johns for more than twenty years and until Dodo's death in 1969 it became Amaryllis's home too, in a spiritual and often a physical sense. Every weekend, work permitting, she drove out of London following a route which soon became engraved on her mind: down the road to Guildford, over the Hog's Back with its panoramic views, through the twisty Winchester by-pass, along the switchback road from Stockbridge to Salisbury, where the first signpost to Fordingbridge appeared, and then the final turn-off into the drive of Fryern itself. In winter the lights would be on in the dining room and the curtains drawn back, and she could glimpse Dodo moving past the long, scrubbed refectory table on which sprawled Dinah, the doyenne of Fryern cats. She had arrived.

Built in the fourteenth century, Fryern had evolved from friary to farmhouse to manor, and its orderly Georgian façade hid a rambling arrangement of eight bedrooms, two sitting rooms – the smaller of which was Augustus's den – a dining room and an ancient kitchen, the whole linked by a maze of uneven, creaking staircases and corridors. It offered space for wild parties and space for solitude. The meeting-ground between the two was the dining room. With its oak table scrubbed until the grain stood up in sharp ridges, its sofa, its huge dresser, its desk above which hung a portrait of Dodo by Augustus's sister Gwen, and its long windows looking on to a gravel forecourt, this was the one room that was never empty, the heart of Fryern to which everyone gravitated whether food was served or not.

If Fryern's heart lay in the dining room, its soul lay in the garden. In springtime the shadows of two large copper beeches danced on a carpet of snowdrops and aconites, beyond which was a secluded lily pond. Across one side of the house grew two tall magnolias which produced huge-stamened yellowy-green flowers, sometimes picked as models for Augustus. In the middle of the large lawn a small oak was at the centre of a round flowerbed ringed with *fraises des bois* for the delectation of grandchildren. On one side was a mellow brick wall covered with clematis, gnarled wistaria and a profusion of roses which hung over a wide herbaceous border dotted with flowering shrubs. On the other, a path led to the orchard and kitchen garden, shaded by fruit trees whose roots were garlanded with miniature cyclamen, fritillaries and grape hyacinths. In the kitchen garden, once-neat box hedges enclosed beans and potatoes interspersed with hosts of Japanese anemones. Sorrel, rosemary, parsley, chives and thyme grew outside the back door in the stable yard. And in the background, trying to hide behind trees and shrubs, glinted a small mountain of empty bottles.

The bottles were one sign of Augustus's presence. Others were his two studios: the 'new' studio, set in a corner by the lily pond and reached by a flight of steps where for a time Dodo kept a hive of bees to deter unwelcome visitors; and the 'old' studio, his favourite, to which sitters were directed along the mellow brick wall, snatching their skirts from the plants which tumbled haphazardly from the herbaceous border. But the garden was essentially Dodo's, and Amaryllis relished it as such. She thinned the lilies, waist-deep in mud, then sat on the stone bench watching goldfish dart among the nymphaea. She gathered fruit, picked vegetables and experienced 'a feeling of joy and deep peace'. In summer, she had tea with her new parents in the shade of an ilex and an old apple tree, Dodo occasionally wandering off in her conical straw hat to pull a few weeds, bending straight-legged from the waist like a human deck-chair.

It was in these surroundings that Amaryllis met her extraordinary second family. Augustus had eleven surviving children, four by his first wife Ida Nettleship, three by Dodo, and at least another four illegitimate ones, including Amaryllis – although, since work pressure seemed always to prevent a visit to the registrar, all Dodo's children were officially illegitimate.

Of Ida's surviving sons there was David, a talented musician who played first oboe in the Sadlers Wells orchestra but later abandoned this career to become a postman. There was Caspar, later Sir Caspar and First Sea Lord, one of the few Johns to opt for a relatively conventional life. The third was Robin, who, as Augustus told Amaryllis, was 'silent in seven languages' and spent his time creating a scale of colours equivalent to that in music, blissfully unaware that one already existed. Edwin, a boxer turned watercolourist, gazed into the distance with pale blue eyes, dreaming of the girl who was for ever beyond his reach.

Eccentricity also reared its head in Dodo's offspring. Romilly, born in 1904, three years before Ida's death, wrote poetry, played the guitar 'not very well' and, like Robin, spent his time inventing things someone else had already invented. There were two girls, Vivien and Poppet, the former an accomplished artist whom Augustus had allowed to attend the Slade, on condition she be taught nothing, and the latter a bouncy, outgoing *bon viveur* with whom Amaryllis formed a close bond. Augustus once took a photograph of the two swimming naked in the South of France and was so delighted by the result – one white skinny beauty, one brown buxom beauty – that he kept it in his wallet to show his friends until one of them stole it for his own wallet.

Finally there were Augustus's extramarital children: Zoë, who had grown after her kidnapping by Eve into a striking actress with high cheekbones, slanting eyes and a one-armed boyfriend, with whom she slept alongside an adopted piglet in a gypsy caravan at the bottom of the orchard; Gwyneth Brownsword, a painter who caused general delight by renting a house in Spain 'with swimming-pool' to an Olympic swimmer who found the pool to be a brackish pond; and Tristan De Vere Cole, the teenage son of Mavis De Vere Cole, one of Augustus's long-time lovers. But, as Amaryllis recalls, 'Mavis seeeemed incapable of telling the truth', so Tristan was equipped with a roving ancestry. In one of her wilder moments she let slip that he was the son of Edward VIII.

There were two sides to Fryern. The first was its conviviality. Daniel George, Augustus's mentor for *Finishing Touches*, caught the atmosphere neatly when he arrived to cajole his dilatory author into parting with a much reworked manuscript. 'We pulled up at a pub at which, judging by the landlord's greeting, he was no stranger. It was there that I was initiated into the mysteries of shove-ha'penny ... Thus delayed we were late in reaching Fryern Court for lunch. Mrs John, unsurprised and uncomplaining, presided over a table at which – indeed *on* which – three or four cats joined us. "Don't mind red wine with fish, do you?" said Augustus, filling a tumbler for me. Later I was glad to have it confirmed that I had seen a herd of white goats straying about the lawn.'[61]

The second, the darker side, was recorded by Cecil Beaton, a distant neighbour, who sensed the aggressively anchorite aura

Augustus could emanate. 'Fryern', he wrote in his edited diary, *Self Portrait with Friends*, was 'like an island surrounded by a dangerous sea. Only the most intrepid visitors were able to make a landing.'[62] He was right, for, although Fryern was an open house where almost any stranger could wander in and partake of its hospitality, no social quarter was given. There were no introductions, no gestures of welcome, nothing. The dining-room windows may have shone warmly, but they did so only because Augustus hated the new curtains and refused to have them drawn. Newcomers, and occasionally family, were expected to fend as best they could, battling a surf of indifference to prove their worth.

Amaryllis sailed ashore with consummate ease, to the slight resentment of other Johns. 'I did experience a twinge of jealousy when the red carpet was always put out for her and very special attention was paid her,' wrote Vivien. But there were a great many others who foundered. Although generous to a fault, Augustus was a man of strong dislikes, and the closer the acquaintance the more critical his attitude. He seemed to hold most of his sons in varying degrees of contempt and with Edwin, in particular, he was at loggerheads. Strangely, Edwin insisted on making regular visits, occasions which plunged Dodo into despair. Fryern's atmosphere became thunderous as father and son tacked menacingly from room to room. The common suspicion was that Edwin pillaged the house behind Augustus's back looking for pictures to remove. However, Romilly recorded, 'One of my brothers complained that a certain person had stolen a number of his drawings. His reaction, unexpected as so often, was to remark that at least this showed they were appreciated by someone. "A pity none of you ever stole any." '[63]

Augustus was just as scathing about his daughters' boyfriends and husbands. It took Poppet three marriages before she found a partner her father approved of. Vivien's husband, a doctor who enjoyed potholing in Yorkshire, was simply not tolerated in the house. Augustus could not even bring himself to say his name, referring to him as Vivien's 'medical attendant' or 'the potholer'. A reconciliatory lunch was eventually held on neutral ground, at the Queen's Restaurant in Sloane Square, but as Amaryllis stiffened her father's resolve in the nearby Royal Court Bar his nerve broke. 'I can't bear to see that bloody man!' he bellowed. Amaryllis and the barman — who always said he would lay down his life for Augustus — calmed him down, and the lunch scraped along without any scenes, the two protagonists sitting at opposite ends of the table saying nothing to each other. The reconciliation effected, John White was allowed to stay at Fryern for occasional weekends.

Like an ageing lion, Augustus clearly felt threatened by other, younger men, but he retained a keen eye for beautiful women. Dodo, accustomed to Augustus's ways, turned a blind eye to his bedroom antics, which were by now merely half-hearted attempts to recover the lost vigour of youth — 'an inebriated joke', Amaryllis recalls. His advances, Dodo advised, could easily be discouraged by putting a chair behind the bedroom door, but Amaryllis developed her own method of dissuasion. From time to time, when in London, Augustus told her she allowed her life to be ruled by megalithic taboos and flung her with gusto on to a nearby bed. Whereupon Amaryllis quoted a few passages from Plato's *Republic*, one of Augustus's pet abominations and a source of instant distraction and irritation. His original purpose forgotten, he would give her a half-crown for the taxi home and remain to fulminate in solitude.

Vivien once complained that while Amaryllis was allowed to bring her boyfriends to Fryern, she could not even bring her husband. But not all Amaryllis's friends were welcome. A weekend with Julian Bream was a disaster. They found her father in a dark mood and as soon as Bream opened his mouth Augustus denounced his Cockney expressions as a poor simulacrum of trench slang. When he tried to talk about the history of the guitar, Augustus rode him down with a set of cock-and-bull theories invented on the spur of the moment. It took all Amaryllis's charm to get Bream out of bed the following day for a cello and guitar recital which they played to family and friends in the hall. On the return journey, Bream's windscreen wipers broke. They drove on in silence, Amaryllis pulling the wipers back and forth from inside the car with a piece of string. Later, Augustus could be heard quietly boasting that none other than Julian Bream had played in his home.

Dodo was the opposite of Augustus. Where he was boisterous, she was shy. His presence filled a room, hers slipped evanescently through the corridors. He spoke in a gruff bellow, her voice was small and scarcely audible. He exuded an aura of Old Testament solidity, she looked as if the slightest breeze would carry her away. She tended to avoid people she did not want to see, particularly the large numbers who gathered round Augustus's drinks table in the evening. Often the only indication these visitors had of her presence was a loud bell ringing outside the sitting-room door to signal that dinner was ready and their time was up.

Yet for all this it was Dodo who defined Fryern. It was she who gave the house, with its vibrant colours, its flowers and its faded upholstery, the atmosphere of untidy beauty which linked it so perfectly to the garden outside. It was she, too, who fixed the timetable around which life revolved. Meals were served punctually at the same time every day, and Augustus's drinking hours were strictly monitored. If Dodo caught him with a glass of wine before the magic hour of six o'clock she tore it from his hand and tipped it into the nearest flowerpot. Augustus said nothing but sat quietly with a book, occasionally looking at his watch. Even painting took second place to Dodo's routine. 'I used to be sent to fetch him from the old studio at one o'clock precisely,' Amaryllis recalls. ' "Augustus! Lunch!" I'd bellow. And to my amazement he stopped whatever he was doing, dropped everything, and came meek as a lamb. It was extraordinary.' Nothing and nobody was allowed to get in Dodo's way. When Amaryllis once tried to help her with a heavy coal-scuttle, she had the door kicked shut in her face.

Amaryllis adored Dodo and, as her visits increased in frequency, this affection was returned, manifesting itself in a rapid promotion through Fryern's hierarchy of bedrooms. Beginning next to the lavatory in a room which had once been Caspar's, she progressed through a variety of chambers, including one bisected by an open bell-pull which quivered from the kitchen below to the attics above, until she reached nirvana in the shape of a room at the front complete with four-poster bed, 'the cello', Vivien recalls, 'being placed in the room next door'. Other touches measured Dodo's esteem: an electric fire switched on in the bedroom, or clean sheets on the bed. These were important privileges by Dodo's economical standards of housekeeping. 'Oh Am, darling, I had your sheets!' Caspar telephoned after he had slept in her five-week-old shrouds. 'They smelt so deliciously of you!'

Dodo also gave Amaryllis her first driving lesson, outraged that Eve should not have already done so. It was not a success. She showed her how to start the car and how to change gears, but forgot to tell her how to stop. The car ploughed sedately across the forecourt, over the lawn, under the beeches and, as its terrified driver let go of all the controls, glided to a halt at the edge of the lily pond. 'Thank goodness Augustus wasn't looking,' Dodo murmured. She never gave Amaryllis another lesson. But if Amaryllis's association with Fryern did little to improve her driving, it did provide her with her first car. The vehicle, a Hillman Minx which Julian Bream labelled 'a suburban housewife's car', was the gift of Colonel Philips, a wealthy Canadian whose wife's portrait Augustus was painting. He assumed the role of unofficial godfather to Amaryllis, forever pressing £10 notes into her hand and lavishing on her expensive presents, of which a piano and the Minx were just two. When the car arrived, Amaryllis was rehearsing with the clarinettist Gervase de Peyer, who insisted on giving her an immediate driving lesson. After they had disentangled its front bumper from the railings in Chelsea Square, Gervase, like Dodo before him, decided to leave well alone.

Augustus was an enthusiastic driver, but cars seemed out of place at Fryern. It was essentially a rural home which harked back to Augustus's fascination with Romany life and a natural existence unfettered by twentieth-century technology: central heating consisted of one tepid radiator in the hall; the house had no fridge but a tiny cold-box where Dodo kept the milk; there was just one bathroom; the single telephone was hidden in a cupboard with the wine. In the night, New Forest ponies clip-clopped up the drive to eat the rampaging garden. By day the goats did whatever damage had been left undone, while Augustus looked on approvingly and vowed to paint them. The field beyond the orchard was periodically decked with gypsy caravans whose occupants trooped over in the evenings to drink with Augustus and to hear Amaryllis playing. Sometimes it seemed as if the garden, house, caravans and orchard, the staff, the family and their London guests, the wildlife, the gypsies, were one big natural occurrence, a self-contained and self-sustaining unit which defied the outside world and all its manifestations.

When Amaryllis first arrived at Fryern, Dodo was helped by Mr and Mrs Cake, gardener and cook respectively. Mrs Cake was a magnificent cook who complained Amaryllis was too thin and did her best to remedy the problem. She made a delicious semolina using goats' milk, and goats' cheese and goats' butter – not to everyone's taste – were always to be found on the table. Indeed, the making of the butter formed a regular mealtime routine. A jug of cream was passed around the table with every diner shaking it vigorously, save Augustus, who gave the container a single cantakerous jolt before shoving it along to his neighbour. Very often that neighbour was Amaryllis, who was seated next to her father to protect first-time guests from his moods and deafness. To strangers the old man could seem utterly terrifying and one poor girl, who asked him if he wanted more potatoes, received such a thunderous '*What?*' that she fell silent for the rest of the meal.

Meals took a slight downward turn when the Cakes retired, to be replaced by Antonio, a Neapolitan whose dialect Dodo found incomprehensible but whom both she and Augustus adored. He cooked a bit, cleaned a bit and gardened a bit, sometimes helped a bit by his sister, who had, as Augustus enthused in a letter to Amaryllis, 'had a *misfortune* with one of her compatriots which took the form of a *baby*'. Possibly this was the same compatriot for whose manslaughter Antonio, as he confided to Amaryllis, had served a prison sentence.

Amaryllis invariably brought her cello to Fryern. 'It was very exciting to hear her playing for Augustus and Dodo, and practising for hours upstairs,' Vivien recorded. 'I never tired of hearing those profound notes repeated over and over again.' But as Amaryllis became more in demand, the visits became fewer. 'These occasions became important. Her remark-able infectious laugh and individual manner were missed by me and to pay homage after one of her memorable concerts, ploughing bravely through the circle of possessive admirers, was no substitute for the rollicking evenings at Fryern.'

One rollicking evening Amaryllis never missed was Christmas, a big event at Fryern which always drew a large crowd comprised mainly, as far as she could tell, of Mavis De Vere Cole, whom Dodo had invited, and Mavis's friends, whom Dodo had not. The family contributed to the fun according to their skills: Amaryllis played her cello; Tristan, destined for the BBC, did amusing skits and impersonations. Habitually the festivities ended with Mavis sinking under the dining-room table with a local farmer. Sometimes Tristan too would be infected by the general spirit. One Christmas, after his mother had attributed him to yet another famous father, he brought Amaryllis a hot-water bottle and tried to follow it into her bed. 'But it's all right, Am!' he protested. 'I'm *not* your half-brother after all!'

Augustus always dominated these occasions – a huge bearded figure dispensing tumblers of wine with abandon. But while he was the centre of Fryern's life, it was not the centre of his. He was always making plans to get away, to go somewhere, to visit someone, to find new scenery, another sitter, different faces. When Amaryllis got her Hillman Minx he repeatedly suggested she chauffeur him over to paint Bertrand Russell, a scheme which like so many others came to nothing. But she did drive him to see Cecil Beaton, who lived in Reddish House at nearby Broadchalke – and to visit the MacNamaras, again close neighbours, whose eldest daughter Caitlin had married Dylan Thomas and whose second daughter Brigid became a close friend of Amaryllis.

For a brief period Augustus's search for variety led him to take up sculpting, to which he was introduced by the Italian sculptress Fiore de Henriques, who, in 1954, embarked on a life-sized statue of Amaryllis playing the cello. Amaryllis was appalled by the result and dreaded the prospect of being given it. But she was spared the ordeal; the effigy was bought by a Member of Parliament.

Sometimes, frustrated both with life in the country and with Dodo, whom he saw in his more jaundiced moments as a prison warden, Augustus escaped to London. Whenever possible he called to take Amaryllis out to dinner or to introduce her to friends over lunch at the Queen's Restaurant. One such was Dylan Thomas, who, after a long monologue on the shortage of milk for Welsh mothers, looked blearily at Amaryllis and said, 'What a pity you're a young cow instead of an old one.' She was still puzzling this out at the end of the meal when he ordered her to drive him back to the Hyde Park Hotel. Another was Lucian Freud, whom Amaryllis later chased all over London to retrieve an overcoat belonging to Augustus which had mysteriously left the restaurant on the wrong artist.

Mavis was frequently present and she and Augustus would shout at each other like fishwives until Amaryllis threatened to walk out. Augustus and Mavis enjoyed a stormy love-hate relationship. Recording one foray to see her in London, Augustus wrote to Amaryllis: 'The night before a doctor friend of mine gave a little party at his flat and seized the opportunity to inject me with some frightful up-to-date stuff which aroused my murderous instincts and almost caused me to punch Mavis on the nose when she exposed her person to the company. Though quite familiar with the landscape itself I thought her popularisation of it among strangers ill-advised, and the effects of the drug reappeared the next day . . .' Yet the two seemed irresistibly drawn to each other. 'I cannot bear the sight of her,' Augustus reiterated in a letter, revealing that he had invited her down to Fryern yet again.

Augustus never stayed long in London. A night or two was enough before he tired of the company and returned to Fordingbridge, expecting Dodo – whom, as like as not, he had been vilifying a few hours before – to collect him from Salisbury station. As he never remembered to tell her which train he was catching, she performed this chore with remarkable clairvoyance, predicting his arrival by hanging a gold ring on a strand of hair over the timetable.

From Fryern he kept in touch with the capital, using Amaryllis as a convenient errand-runner. Letters arrived asking her to inspect new studios, to deliver pictures to the Royal Academy, to get portraits framed, to put up friends for the night, and when, in the late Fifties, Augustus developed a passion to own a black straw hat of the type once favoured by Whistler, she was deputed to scour London's hatters. She searched in vain and compromised by painting a white one black. Her father was delighted. 'You are a wonder,' he wrote. 'The hat fits perfectly and will be an important event in my life.' He wore it constantly, occasionally dabbing on more paint as the old wore off. 'Painted it myself,' he boasted to a friend at a funeral. 'Best thing you've done for years,' was the reply.

One summer Amaryllis let her house in London and moved to Fryern to spend the season with Dodo and Augustus. It was a mistake; although welcome, she fell foul of Dodo, who was determined to do things her own way. 'You seem to be trying to run the house,' Augustus murmured casually, and possibly to himself; by this time his hearing aid infuriated him so much that he rarely wore it. Nevertheless, her housework yielded one treasure. During a summer shower she caught the unmistakable aroma of cat excrement. She followed her nose to the attic but soon forgot the mess she had intended to clear when she saw row upon row of canvases stacked beneath a dripping window. As she moved the paintings to safety, she found a portrait of Dodo. She put it to one side and continued shifting, then went down to show the sitter her prize. Dodo was impressed. 'It's good!' she said. 'I'd forgotten all about that one. It's Augustus's birthday in three days' time. Show it to him then and maybe he'll give it to you.'

Amaryllis did as she suggested. 'It's good!' Augustus echoed Dodo. 'I'd forgotten all about that one. Fetch me a tube of brown paint.' Amaryllis did as she was told and waited in suspense. By this stage Augustus was on the wane, struggling so hard to produce a picture that every canvas became a tortured mass of overpainting. She envisaged the once-perfect portrait emerging in smears of brown revision. Time passed. Then came a bellow from the sitting room. She entered. The portrait was signed but otherwise untouched. Augustus had been struggling to find room for a dedication but had been unable to do so without destroying the composition. A simple 'John 1959' adorned the upper right-hand corner.

TWELVE

Prades and Casals

The revelation of Amaryllis's origins had almost as profound an effect on Eve as on Amaryllis. Since Val's death she had been marking time, holding herself back until her sons had matured and found their way in the world. In 1933 she had written them a letter admitting that her job was as good as done and hinting at the prospect of remarriage. 'I think the time has come when I should tell you that my task as far as you all are concerned is practically finished. I can do little more for you . . . You are grown men and for all the faults in your upbringing or in me I would ask your forgiveness and ask you to remember that the task was a great one for a woman alone, and without any real help and a good many hindrances.'[64]

Possibly one of those hindrances was Amaryllis, but it was for her sake that Eve extended her deadline, delaying a new life until she too had found her feet. That time had now come, and with her last responsibility discharged Eve could make a fresh start. And where better than in a foreign country? It would be easier to maintain the pretence that Amaryllis was adopted, which was becoming well-nigh impossible in London. Besides, her financial advisers assured her that the only way to avoid Britain's crippling death duties was to live abroad – and, the unspoken message ran, to die there.

She had three criteria for her new home: 'that the climate

was suitable, the inhabitants polite, and the country the sort of place she would enjoy'.[65] Her final choice, on the advice of Ian, who oversaw the transfer with assiduity, was Nassau. In July 1950 she settled into the prestigious environs of Cable Beach. Ian's friend Ivar Bryce recalled, 'Among these houses and, believe it or not, almost next door to a house called Oodles of Poodles, one called Emerald Wave had been bought by Mrs Eve Fleming . . .'[66] Here she practised her violin, searched in vain for a suitable accompanist, made at least one recording and swam every day from the exclusive, mile-long silver beach. The climate and country were suitable but she had doubts about the inhabitants. 'Both my neighbours illegally cut my hedge when I was away,' she complained to the Eshers. 'I now open a window and play scales in front of it, and exercises, one of which has 120 different bowings to one horrid little hideous theme. So good for me too.' In another letter she ominously instructed Ian to procure fresh ammunition for her pistol.

Before leaving Britain, however, Eve had one final stab at separating Amaryllis from Fournier. Her suggestion this time was that she study with Pablo Casals. Amaryllis was at first doubtful, being quite happy where she was, but when Eve offered to pay for the lessons she saw no point in looking a gift horse in the mouth. In the summer of 1950, she set out for Prades.

Casals was then seventy-three and had been living in the French Pyrenean village of Prades since 1939, forced from his home in Barcelona by Franco's victory in the Spanish Civil War. Vowing never to return while Franco remained in power, he lasted out World War II in this tiny village helping the refugees who had been billeted in nearby camps and resisting Nazi blandishments to play in Berlin. Nineteen forty-five brought an end to hostilities but not, unfortunately, an end to Franco. After a concert tour in England, Casals realised just how lightly morality weighed in international affairs. 'I really thought I was nearing the end of my exile,' he later said, 'since the victory of the Allied Nations was logically bound to put an end to the Franco regime. But my deception soon began.'[67] In despair, he cancelled his British engagements for the following year and packed his bags. Before he left he received a request to discuss the matter with Sir Stafford Cripps. 'No,' replied Casals, 'you would speak about politics and I about morals – we would not understand each other.' Myra Hess arranged an interview with King George VI's secretary, to whom Casals explained what he saw as Britain's duty. Then he left for Prades and an indefinite period of self-imposed silence, the greatest protest within his power.

It was not a new stance. Casals had refused resolutely to play in Mussolini's Italy or Hitler's Germany and, unlike Fournier, had turned down an invitation to play with Furtwängler and the Berlin Philharmonic. Now that ban was extended worldwide, and was maintained in the face of astronomical fees offered by the Americans. Music lovers began to fear that they would never again hear the man who was acknowledged as the world's greatest living musician.

Relief came in 1950, the two-hundredth anniversary of Bach's death. To commemorate the event, an international consortium of musicians persuaded Casals to host a festival at Prades, the proceeds going to help Spanish refugees. After some hesitation Casals agreed, and on the evening of 2 June 1950 the first Prades festival opened in the Church of St Pierre. For the next three weeks Casals played and conducted his way through thirteen concerts, accompanied by a troupe of celebrities. Throughout it all the audience remained silent; not until the last note had died away did they respond with an ovation that lasted twenty minutes. The festival was a resounding success, transforming a sleepy Pyrenean outpost into a musical focus of the world.

The village was still in a state of stunned elation when Amaryllis arrived some six weeks later, and even before she stepped off the train from Perpignan she had secured a performance. A fellow passenger, who opened with 'the usual perspicacious question: "Do you play that thing?" ' happened to be the owner of Prades's only nightclub, La Pergola, and had offered to make her *L'Attraction du Samedi Soir*, in return for which she could have a free meal. Amaryllis accepted, and having booked into Le Grand Hôtel — twenty-seven bedrooms, one bathroom, and a manager recently retired from the French Foreign Legion — walked up the dusty track to La Pergola, where she found a Marseilles band whose pianist, it was rumoured, could sightread. After rehearsing a few light pieces, she returned to take a nap in her hotel room only to be roused by loud knocking on the door. It was the butcher, who had heard of her planned performance and brought the news that Casals would disown her because he disapproved of drinking and dancing. No sooner had the butcher gone than the baker arrived with the same message. Then came the postman, followed shortly after by the doctor, and another and another until it felt as if the whole 4,000-strong population of Prades was knocking at her door. They all said the same thing: that if she appeared at La Pergola it would be the end of her studies with Casals. La Pergola's owner had received a similar string of callers, so the project was cancelled just in time to halt an announcement already placed with the local paper. La Pergola lost its *attraction* and *L'Attraction* lost her Saturday dinner.

The next day she met Casals for an audition which included the Schumann concerto and some movements of Bach. 'Le

Maître', as everybody knew him, was short, stocky, and astute-looking, with lively eyes, a pipe clamped constantly in his mouth, and a pullover whose stained front was a history of recent meals. Casals was impressed with Amaryllis's playing. 'You are extremely talented,' he said, 'and I would like to teach you for nothing.' A brief pause while he sucked on his pipe and Amaryllis's spirits rose. 'But unfortunately,' he continued, 'I cannot afford to do so.' He named his fee and told her that she should have two lessons each week. But this time it was Amaryllis who could not afford it; a compromise was struck at one lesson every five days.

Having settled the matter of tuition, her next problem was to find new accommodation. The manager of Le Grand Hôtel had taken exception to her eating out at a cheap restaurant in the village. As she overheard him tell one of her fellow guests, '*Madame est jolie mais les affaires sont les affaires et je ne paie pas deux chefs pour rien!*' Casals's brothers-in-law, Pepito and Ramón, came to her aid and found her a soothingly damp room (the summer heat was intense) adjoining an old outhouse, with a three-inch gap between the floor and the bottom of the door which let in a nightly carpet of cockroaches. The landlady, who refused to let anyone into her kitchen, insisted on serving Amaryllis breakfast in her room. This had its drawbacks since the landlady worked in the fields and, possessing neither watch nor clock, relied solely on church chimes to tell the time. She was also slightly deaf, and could not count. Breakfast, Amaryllis found, might arrive any time between six and eleven in the morning. The family opposite had better hearing, but luckily had no objections to Amaryllis practising. When she apologised in advance they merely shrugged their shoulders and responded philosophically that her profession made a noise; theirs happened not to; what did it matter?

Lessons were in Casals's home, El Cant dels Ocells (The Song of the Birds), a little cottage which had previously housed the gardener of a nearby estate. Conditions were cramped, for the house contained not only Casals but his companion and erstwhile childhood love, Frasquita Capdevila, and sometimes his teenage niece – another cellist, who ran errands for Casals and envied Amaryllis her damp but private lodgings. The tuition took place in Casals's bedroom – a tiny space which harboured a bed, two chairs and an upright piano – and concentrated on Schumann's Cello Concerto, which Casals once described as 'one of the finest works one can hear – from beginning to end the music is sublime'.[68]

Amaryllis had already studied it with Fournier, but Casals offered an entirely new interpretation, changing every bowing and every fingering. It was neither easier nor more difficult, just different. His constant refrain was that a musician had to look for the true feeling of a piece. 'Poor Schumann,' Casals said to her, 'think of the horror of his impending madness, his uncontrollable mental agony, the dreadful noises in his head. Hear the surging emotion, the restlessness reflected underneath the wonderful melodic line.' He never stopped stressing the limitations of printed symbols, and the importance of understanding what lay behind them.

This emphasis on pure emotion underlined his teaching methods. 'His lessons were a very good exercise in concentration,' Amaryllis recalls, 'because he didn't give you time to write anything down at all. He was always on to the next phrase, so you had to remember every single thing he'd said, go home, and *then* write it in. Often he would say, "Yes, I like the way you play that, but this is how I do it," meaning "You do it like me!" ' At the time Amaryllis was too young to observe and question properly, so she did as she was told. In retrospect, however, it was a flawed method, one that led to imitation rather than comprehension.

Not, of course, that there was anything wrong in imitating Le Maître. It was inspiring just to hear him play. 'Everything must sing,' he used to say, 'even the fast passages,' and in his practice he was a paragon of dedication. He started each day with a Bach prelude and fugue on the piano, his own private benediction on the house. One morning Amaryllis listened to him playing the prelude of the E*b* cello suite. 'I was early and for about half an hour I sat under his window in the garden, during which time he only covered eight bars, going alternately to the piano and back to the cello. He repeated intervals for absolute intonation, terribly hard in that particular prelude because it is really keyboard writing. You have to cope with very difficult string crossings which don't lie easily on the cello. It was a lesson in concentration and perfectionism.' Casals was, above all, a perfectionist. He was known to say, at the end of a concert or a recording session, having practised one passage for an entire day, and for days before that, and for previous months and years, 'Today I was lucky. It came off.' He expected the same application from his pupils and seemed to be clairvoyant about their extramural activities. One day Amaryllis went with Pepito, Ramón and a local farmer to climb Le Canigou, the largest mountain in the district. It was a wonderful experience, with the three men cooking eggs and bacon on the summit before manhandling Amaryllis down a precipitous return route. At the next lesson Casals gave her a piercing look and said, 'I hear you took the day off.' On another occasion, she bathed naked in the river, having checked carefully to make sure nobody was in sight. The precaution was useless. 'I hear that you have been swimming . . .'

*

Augustus John
self portrait, 1920
(© *Vivien White*)

Eve Fleming by
Augustus John, early 1920s
(© *Vivien White*)

Amaryllis on holiday
in Ireland

Amaryllis skating with
Eve in Switzerland

Pablo Casals

The Loveday Trio;
l. to r. Amaryllis, Alan Loveday,
Peggy Gray (© *Angus McBean*)

Pierre Fournier by the Serpentine

Augustus and Dodo

Peter Fleming in China
by Ella Maillart, 1935
(© *News Productions*)

The Prom début; Amaryllis
plays Elgar's Cello Concerto
(© *Picture Post.*
Photography by Thurston Hopkins)

After the Prom at 21 Cresswell Place; l.
to r. Sir John Barbirolli, André
Mangeot, Augustus John, Amaryllis (©
*Picture Post. Photography by Thurston
Hopkins*)

Guilhermina Suggia, a preliminary
sketch for Augustus John's portrait of
1923 (© *Vivien White*)

Amaryllis with Enrico Mainardi

Amaryllis plays Màtyàs Seiber's *Tre Pezzi* in the Teatro Fenice
at the 1958 Venice Biennale. Philharmonia Hungarica with Antal Dorati conducting
(© *Giacomelli, Fotografia-Eliografia*)

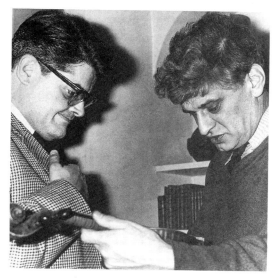

Paul (r.) and Norbert Brainin (l.)

Amaryllis and Paul
in the music room at
Old Church Street

Vlado Perlemutter and
Amaryllis give a recital
(© *Erich Auerbach*)

Ian Fleming
by Cecil Beaton
(© *Sotheby's, London*)

The Paganini Trio in its last incarnation;
l. to r. Amaryllis, John Williams, Alan Loveday

Augustus's studio sale. A front row of Johns;
r. to l. Caspar, David, Vivien, Edwin, Tristan De Vere Cole's chin.
In the second row, far left Amaryllis, and the top of Hugo, Pitman (© *Reuters*)

The Fleming String Trio; l. to r. Emanuel Hurwitz,
Kenneth Essex, Amaryllis (© *Donald Sutherland*)

Amaryllis with Sir Peter Maxwell Davies
at Dartington summer school

The revised Trio; l. to r. Manoug Parikian,
Amaryllis, Hamish Milne (© *Donald Sutherland*)

Despite Le Maître's disapproval Amaryllis often escaped into the surrounding countryside, which, with its magnificent Romanesque architecture, was a soothing balm after the heat of Prades and constant practice. One day she was offered a lift on the back of the garage hand's motorbike to the abbey at Serrabonne. It was an arduous journey: they were overtaken by a thunderstorm and drenched to the skin; Amaryllis was hard put to it to stop the lad carving his initials into the abbey pillars; and the motorbike jumped around like a goat, the mechanic having, he later confessed, inflated the tyres to their fullest as a gesture of respect. By the time they returned Amaryllis was unable to move and the proprietor of her favourite Catalan restaurant had to carry her off the motorbike and into his bar, where she recovered only after a large glass of cognac. After this the restaurateur became so excited and his wife so jealous that Amaryllis was forced to stop eating there. 'It's a wonder you came back whole from that expedition with the sportive Spaniard,' Augustus wrote. 'You should always wear a shock absorber on such occasions.' Casals took a dimmer view: 'I hear you have been to Serrabonne . . .'

By this time she had quit her cockroach-infested lodgings for a larger, healthier, cheaper and more solitary room which Pepito and Ramón had located nearby. The landlady was hardly ever there, and when she was she had no objections to her guest practising. *'Je vis d'une façon bohème,'* she said, which, Amaryllis soon learned, meant that she never cleaned the place. When a rat got caught in a trap in the courtyard, it lay rotting in the sun for days before she finally removed it, while Amaryllis sprinkled herself with eau de cologne and filled her windows with mountain herbs to keep out the stench. *La vie bohème* also meant that the landlady never stocked enough wood to fuel the open fire which was her kitchen's sole cooking appliance. Although the woman put in weekly appearances bearing a gargantuan basket of fruit from her brother's farm, Amaryllis chose to dine out in the cheap but cheerful Catalan restaurant – until she went to Serrabonne. Thereafter she ate with Pepito and Ramón, who were almost as destitute as she. She adored Casals's two relations; although known as his brothers-in-law they were in fact the brothers of his sister-in-law. They took her to dances in neighbouring village squares and taught her how to spout wine into her mouth from a *peron*, but the meals they cooked in their minute two-room apartment were less thrilling. The unchanging menu was paella, into which Pepito and Ramón threw what ingredients they could find – predominantly snails, the small, everyday variety, which they hunted by torchlight in the gardens of Prades. 'It was', Amaryllis remembers, 'very much like eating pieces of hosepipe.'

Besides taking care of Amaryllis, Pepito and Ramón also looked after Le Maître. They fed his pet Alsatian, took it for walks, and performed endless odd jobs about the house. The whole village venerated Casals and, as Amaryllis had learned from the experience of her first day, they seemed to live for his approval. The butcher, for example, would reverently recommend a certain cut of meat because Le Maître had chosen the very same earlier that day – ignoring the fact that the notoriously careful musician had chosen it for its cheapness. Not only the villagers bowed to Casals; there were the students, young and old, who had travelled from afar to worship at Le Maître's altar. Among them was a group of Americans, the only people whose wallets bulged in those tight, post-war years, who could be found most afternoons eating large chunks of steak smothered in strawberry jam.

The elder statesman of Le Maître's seasonal entourage was a Swiss named Von Tobel, who had been studying with him since before he had arrived in Prades. Von Tobel clung like a limpet to Casals, and when Amaryllis was there he was engaged in compiling a biography. In her recollection it was a sorry task, marked by constant requests for Le Maître to repeat the same anecdotes he had recounted the day before. Von Tobel, however, far from being swept away, became a useful adjunct to Casals's life. Amaryllis remembers the embarrassing occasions before performances, when Von Tobel would be called upon to tune Casals's instrument, it being supposedly beyond his arthritic capabilities. As the Swiss leaned over his shoulder to manipulate the pegs, Casals stared stony-faced at the audience, commanding, '*Plus haut! Plus bas! Plus haut!*' Then finally, to everyone's relief, '*Oui!*'

Prades seemed to be in danger of becoming a musical Lourdes, to which everyone swarmed in search of the miracle that might improve their condition. One such was Pauline Maze, the daughter of French Impressionist Paul Maze, who had lived at Swan House on Cheyne Walk and who had taken French lessons with Amaryllis under Mademoiselle Chabloz. Amaryllis was surprised to see her, not only because she was a long-lost face from childhood but because she was now in a wheelchair, having tried to shoot herself but succeeding only in paralysing herself from the waist down. She must have been a tough woman, because when her mother subsequently committed her to an asylum she brought a legal action that secured her release. Like many invalids, she had developed the knack of making people do things for her and it was not long before Amaryllis was wheeling Pauline around Prades and even scaling the walls of her convent lodgings to rouse the key-holding nun when she had been locked out.

Augustus was delighted that his daughter was studying with Casals. 'So glad to hear from you and to know you're getting on so well with the Master,' he wrote to her on 17 August. 'I'm overjoyed for I felt sure that he and he alone was It. You'll have to go back.' Augustus admired Casals as much for his moral stance as for his musical genius, sharing with him a hatred of the Spanish dictator; 'Franco is beneath contempt,' he wrote to his son Caspar in 1955. Amaryllis, however, found Casals's attitude slightly repugnant. 'How wonderful!' he exclaimed, on hearing that anti-Franco terrorists had blown up a trainload of innocent citizens.

None of Augustus's political feelings emerged in his letters to Amaryllis. Paramount was his insistence that she learn as much as she could, regardless of cost. 'I will write to Mama. She has written from Nassau & says it is so difficult – or impossible to send money in these times no matter how much one may have. But I believe for educational purposes it can be done. It *shall* be done anyhow . . . Dodo says it's now a *crime* to send money abroad. I don't mind a spot of crime provided it's successful. *Nous verrons*.' In the same letter he expressed a strong desire to paint Casals. The money never materialised; neither did Augustus.

It was while in Prades that Amaryllis learnt of the death of Suggia, at the age of sixty-two. 'Poor Guilhermina died of cancer,' Augustus wrote. 'She seemed as merry as a cricket when I last saw her.' If the news affected Casals in any way, he chose not to show it. His relationship with Suggia had come to a stormy end when he arrived unexpectedly from abroad to find her in the arms of the Edinburgh musicologist Donald Tovey, whom he had invited to stay at his home near Barcelona. The explosion of shattered windows and smashed furniture was reported by his cleaning lady to his accompanist, from whom it eventually found its way to André Mangeot, who added it gleefully to his repertoire of anecdotes.

Amaryllis had never mentioned her previous tuition under Suggia, and Casals had never broached the subject. Nor had she mentioned Gaspard Cassadó, whom Casals despised for having remained 'apolitical' over the Civil War and for having performed in Hitler's Germany and lived in Mussolini's Italy. Fournier too figured on Casals's blacklist, outwardly for his alleged collaboration with the Germans but more personally because he had replaced Casals in the famous Casals–Cortot–Thibaud piano trio following Le Maître's resignation in 1933. One day, Amaryllis received a letter from Fournier, addressed c/o P. Casals (Fournier had often been called 'the second Casals' and was slightly jealous that Amaryllis had gone to Prades), consisting of a single piece of paper. At the top it said, '*Cher ex-maître et ami,*' while at the bottom were the initials AF. The intervening space had been left blank for her to fill in. Casals, who had opened it by mistake, handed it to her without a word.

Despite the depth of emotion in his playing, Amaryllis found Casals a remote man with a highly developed sense of propriety. He rarely smiled. One of the few times Amaryllis caught a glimmer of amusement in his eyes was when Pauline Maze was carried up to his room by a pair of village stalwarts for a piano lesson. Amaryllis and Casals played the cello part together while Pauline, unable to use the pedals, lumbered chaotically through the Beethoven F Major Sonata. At the end of the recital Casals said, 'Well, Pauline, you played very beautifully. Thank you for coming.'

But what really made him smile were his evening games of ludo, to which Amaryllis was sometimes invited to make a foursome with the local butcher and the doctor. Casals cheated, with great seriousness and apparent lack of self-consciousness, throughout every game. There were few rules that he did not invent on the spur of the moment, and fewer still that did not contribute to his final victory, when, his face wreathed in innocence, he faced his opponents and announced: '*J'ai gagné!*' Then came an ecstatic grin.

Amaryllis's lessons came to an end in September. As a finale, Casals decided they should play through the Schumann Concerto together. She found it a challenging battle of wits: 'I just had to guess what he was going to do next. He was quite old by then and had become very personal in his interpretation. Sometimes he made rather exaggerated rubati and I had to know by intuition what he was going to do.' Casals was pleased and praised her for her intonation in the difficult parts, but criticised her for carelessness and lack of awareness in the simpler ones. 'In the very first lesson he talked to me about intonation – expressive intonation – sharp leading notes, flat minor thirds. "You've understood very quickly," he said. "Now practise it for the rest of your life." How right he was!'

Despite his doubts about her days off, Casals admitted that Amaryllis needed a rest and offered her the run of his villa in San Salvador, some seventy kilometres from Barcelona, a place which held deep emotional ties for him and which he had last seen in 1939 overflowing with refugees. Designed by his mother, and subsequently remodelled by Le Maître himself, the villa was a uneasy combination of the grand and the homely. There was an enormous, marble-pillared music room capable of holding an audience of several hundred. Then there was Casals's Salle de Sentiments, in which were pictures of his family and friends as well as souvenirs, such as the windowsills from the room where Beethoven had been born. A third addition comprised an ornate salon lifted entire from an eighteenth-century Catalan palace. The gardens were landscaped with pools, terraces and specially commissioned marble Catalan statues.

The intended grandeur was lost on Amaryllis. Certainly the villa came as a relief after her train journey in a wooden-seated third-class carriage surrounded by farmers and their chickens. But she was taken aback by the plethora of glass cases displaying letters from kings, queens and heads of state from around Europe, all praising Casals. The statues she thought hideous. And there was an uncomfortable atmosphere of desolation except in the kitchen, presided over by Casals's brother Luis and his wife Teresina, the latter warmly capable, the former charmingly incompetent. One evening Luis left the tap of the wine barrel open, and its contents poured over the cellar floor all night. Amaryllis was relieved to see another opened the following day. Breakfast at ten o'clock consisted of a tepid tortilla – 'I never knew whether it had been left to go cold then put out to warm up in the sun, or the other way round, and that had to last us until four, when lunch arrived.' In between times she bathed, chatted to Luis – whose conversation centred on Pablo's refusal to send enough housekeeping money – bicycled the four kilometres to see Casals's birthplace at Vendrell, and revisited Barcelona to meet his other brother Enrique. In one of his many idle moments Luis asked Amaryllis if she felt she had got to know Le Maître. When she replied in the negative, Luis gave a gloomy nod of the head. 'Even though he is my brother, I, too, never really knew him,' he said, 'and I doubt if anyone ever will.'

After a few weeks, Amaryllis bade farewell to her hosts and journeyed back to Prades to collect her cello for the trip home. In her baggage she carried a bottle of wine so that Casals could taste the produce of his vineyards. His parting words to her were, 'I don't doubt that with your temperament and talent you can play the Dvořák splendidly. The Haydn D will present more of a challenge of discipline. Study it with much care.'

THIRTEEN

Milestones and Mirrors

Amaryllis had heard nothing from her mother during her stay at Prades. The only time she thought of Eve was when Casals admitted that he too used the cold-bath-and-towel treatment for insomnia and advised her to try it. She did so and decided that if she were going to be awake, she would rather be warm and dry.

Eve, too, had more than Amaryllis on her mind during those first months in Nassau. She had made a remarkable discovery: the Marquess of Winchester, a 'harmless but indigent old aristocrat'[69] who had left Britain as a bankrupt in 1929. They became engaged the following year, much to Augustus's amusement. 'How pleased you must be to hear that Mama is about to join the aristocracy,' he wrote to Amaryllis in October 1951. 'Most gratifying, isn't it?' But the engagement was doomed. While the prospect of being England's premier marchioness (the marquessate, created in 1551, was the oldest in the land) held obvious appeal, the prospect of poverty – Val's will still held good – did not, and by June 1952 Eve was writing to Augustus, 'We are still unspliced and I have given up all idea of it although my young man insists it will take place.' That month, 'on her doctor's advice', Eve dropped out of the running and the Winchester baton passed into the hands of Miss Bapsy Pavry, daughter of a Parsee high priest and, after a whirlwind courtship, the new Marchioness.

Eve began to have second thoughts. In September 1952, just two months after the marriage, Augustus wrote, 'I have just heard from Mama who tells me Bapsy is divorcing the Marquis and has been refused a seat at the Coronation. M. is chortling with glee!' Eve, as usual, got her way. Soon she and her ninety-year-old lover were reunited at Emerald Wave, where, according to Bryce, she 'had caused to be built a special swimming-pool, six inches deep, for him to enjoy', and where 'there was almost always an overweight Indian lady clad in a dingy sari, pacing the main road as firmly as Eve paced the cellar, but occasionally pausing to raise and shake her fist towards the house. This lady was none other than the Marchioness of Winchester herself . . .'[70]

The raised fist soon turned into legal action, and for much of the decade Eve was embroiled in unseemly court disputes over the Marquess's attentions. The situation gave Augustus a certain sense of satisfaction. In the past Eve had reprimanded him for his ruinous lifestyle; now it was his turn. 'I get frequent news by air from Mama,' he wrote Amaryllis loftily. 'I am rather tired of her domestic embroilments and have told her to snap out of this before she gets into a worse pickle. She should drop that discredited old ass and choose a better 'ole.'

Amaryllis had little interest in her mother's activities. Work was picking up with the Loveday Trio. She was getting a number of solo broadcasts and recitals. And early in 1951 she joined the newly formed Fidelio Ensemble, whose members included the clarinettist Gervase de Peyer, sopranos April Cantelo and Ilse Wolf, and Peggy Gray, who, when she became pregnant, was replaced by the American pianist Lamar Crowson. They embarked on what was to be the first of five annual tours of Scotland, organised by the Scottish Arts Council, and concentrating on the small repertoire for clarinet trios plus works for clarinet or cello and piano and some vocal arrangements.

These northern excursions, conducted invariably to a tough itinerary and under dreadful weather conditions, were testing times. Scottish pianos were perhaps the worst aspect. Once, after a city-hall venue had been unexpectedly cancelled, the ensemble found itself playing in a hotel festooned with an embarrassing plethora of decorations. Lamar Crowson recalls Gervase seated among the paper chains ('we could only see his clarinet') and the piano suffering from 'halitosis' as the temperature crept from '0° to heat'. 'By the end of the recital the ivories were on the floor and I was playing on wood!' On another occasion the piano had been tuned a semitone too sharp, a manageable problem for string players but one that had Gervase scurrying to the artists' room, where he held his clarinet up to the single, wall-mounted electric bar to raise its pitch. Amaryllis, meanwhile, explained to the audience that although the piano was sharp they would do their best to complete the programme. Her announcement brought an unexpected riposte. The piano tuner was in the audience and he and Amaryllis argued to and fro like pantomime characters – 'No it isn't!', 'Yes it is!' – until the recital started and he had to sit down.

Even the local press bemoaned the poor conditions under which the ensemble had to perform. In 1955, after Crowson had played de Falla's *Ritual Fire Dance* at the Mechanics' Hall in Brechin, a review complained that although his rendition showed 'great alacrity and animation . . . a good piano is essential to a cultured community. It is a pity that the *Ritual Fire Dance* did not burn the piano on Saturday!'

Fire, or the lack of it, marked the Fidelio tours. Hotel

bedrooms were usually without any heat whatsoever, and a hot dinner was an eternally elusive grail. For the most part they survived on high teas of smoked haddock or kippers and tinned peas. When snow came, as it often did, and traffic was reduced to a single crawling line, they drove to each performance amid the fumes of an ineffectual chemical heater, playing solo whist on Gervase's clarinet case and laughing automatically at the jokes delivered in an incomprehensible brogue by their Glaswegian chauffeur. These journeys became a source of deep anxiety for Ilse Wolf, whose whist skills were minimal and who was once overheard wailing in her sleep, 'Oh dear. Shall I play high?' A pause. 'Or low?'

With the weather came illness. One year, in Fort William, April Cantelo caught 'flu, causing Amaryllis, who was page-turning, to display her Fleming fortitude. 'There's nothing wrong with you at all,' she declared. 'The show must go on.' And amazingly it did, even though April passed out halfway through the performance, to be dragged offstage by Amaryllis and dumped unceremoniously on the artists' room floor. The next day Amaryllis gave the same advice to a pregnant Peggy Gray, who collapsed before the show had even started. Their chauffeur, who sat through every concert, remained uncomplaining until the end of the tour, when he died of a heart attack.

Despite such setbacks, the show always did go on; no concert was cancelled through illness or poor weather. Indeed, some people struggled ten miles on foot through the snow to claim their seats. The Fidelio continued to entertain music lovers for twelve years, until Gervase's wife uncovered a brief liaison between her husband and his cellist. The only souvenir that Amaryllis retained – albeit briefly – of those frost-filled years was Gervase's string vest.

In June 1952, when the Fidelio was barely a year old,

Amaryllis's reputation was further enhanced when she won the Queen's Prize, an open competition for British subjects under thirty, described by one of that year's adjudicators, the music critic Richard Capell, as 'the blue riband of the profession so far as the younger generation of executive musicians goes'. More than just the blue riband, it was virtually the *only* riband, there being no other major prize for cellists in the whole country, and the competition was, Capell noted, 'extraordinarily severe'. After the field had been whittled down to three finalists, Amaryllis found herself competing against Christopher Bunting – 'magnificently equipped' – and one other. 'Women cellists are handicapped by nature,' Capell later wrote in the *Daily Telegraph*. 'They have to toil harder to make up for the lack of a man's physical strength. But this dazzling young person glowed with the sacred fire. There was charming imagination in her playing, the music was illuminated; and the prize is hers.'

With the Queen's Prize, a cheque for £100, in her pocket, Amaryllis felt confident enough to take her next big step forward: a performance at the Wigmore Hall. A musician's first Wigmore is a milestone in his or her career and Eve, who had responded to the whiff of success by matching the Queen's Prize with another £100, hired the hall for the evening and followed it with a lavish reception at Fortnum & Mason. Augustus was unable to come. 'I am so hustled over some pictures promised for two or three coming exhibitions that I feel I couldn't leave them, greatly as I shall miss the concert. I am praying hard for its success all the same . . . I hear there's a gathering after the concert with lashings of champagne. I shall miss that too. Perhaps you should come here to rest after your labours,' he concluded wistfully, 'I could do you on your back.'

The recital, scheduled for the evening of 14 May 1953 with Gerald Moore as accompanist, included Bach's Third Suite, Brahms's F Major Sonata and Bartók's First Rhapsody. All were familiar pieces, but Amaryllis was nervous none the less. 'Don't worry,' Moore reassured her, 'there's only one thing worse than your first Wigmore: your second.' In the event, her nerves disappeared and she played beautifully, attracting glowing reviews for her treatment of the Bach and placing herself, according to *The Strad*, 'among the most accomplished lady cellists of her generation'.

Augustus was impressed. 'What a howling success!' he wrote. 'How I wish I'd been there! Dodo was absolutely delighted and full of praise without reservations – unusual for her. I heard from Mama confirming it all. Did you hear the tender Fiore, seeing an old lady seated all alone, sat down with her for company – it was your noble godmother!' Eve had pulled out all the stops. Not only Princess Marie-Louise had been hauled into the Wigmore but the family doctor, complete with top hat and frock coat, and all three Fleming brothers. None of the boys had much of an ear for music. According to one observer, they remained in a huddle around their mother, looking rather lost; but they voiced their criticisms freely.

Peter, who had dabbled in theatre in his youth, was baffled by the difference in presentation. In particular, he could not understand why, since eye-contact was so important in acting, Amaryllis should keep hers closed. During the interval he sent her a note: 'TOAD! Keep your eyes open!' The lighting arrangements left him similarly confused. 'I went to a concert last week,' he wrote in his *Spectator* column on 22 May. 'It was held in one of the better-known London halls, and I was greatly interested by my first view of the conditions under which musicians perform in public. The platform was lit by –

in addition to footlights – one powerful bulb suspended centrally and encased in a large shade in black. Flanking it on either side, and facing the audience, were two doors over which appeared the illuminated legend EXIT, in massive capitals; and at the side of each door shone a small but brilliant light rather like a gas-mantle. The effect of all this was naturally to distract the eye and to make it less easy than it should have been to concentrate on the central figure of the musician: and I came away wondering whether in all concert-halls there is the same lofty disregard for the elementary principles of stage-lighting; and if so why.'

Ian's comments were more practical and centred not on the lights but on Amaryllis's ring, which flashed distractingly as she moved. Ironically, this was the same paste bauble he had given her on her twenty-first birthday and which she had worn ever since. It made no difference to Ian. 'I don't care,' he said, 'you shouldn't wear it.' Nor did she from that day on.

Rings, lighting and closed eyes regardless, the Wigmore was a success, and it was followed by another. One day, at Cresswell Place, André Mangeot introduced Amaryllis to Sir John Barbirolli, the diminutive, Cockney-accented son of an Italian father and a French mother who had worked his way up to become one of the world's great conductors. She played to him, and was overwhelmed when he offered her a Promenade concert with the Hallé Orchestra in the Albert Hall. While a Wigmore is a major step, the hall can be hired by anyone with enough money and the approval of the management. A Prom, on the other hand, requires an invitation. This Amaryllis now had, with an expected audience of 6,000, a fee of ten guineas and a prospective date of 25 August 1953.

Barbirolli was the perfect conductor for Amaryllis. In his youth he had been a cellist, playing both orchestral and chamber music, and he used his experience to excellent effect.

The conductor Daniel Barenboim, Jacqueline du Pré's husband, wrote, 'It was not just the way he studied the scores but the fact that he personally bowed every string part of every piece. His great knowledge enabled him to propose bowings to the string section which automatically made them produce the sound and articulation he wanted. He could produce the "Barbirolli sound" with almost any orchestra he conducted.'[71] He was known — and, in phlegmatic England, rather distrusted — for being an emotional conductor, a trait which appealed to Amaryllis. This intuitive streak came out to best effect in the works of Edward Elgar, for whom he had great affinity. It was almost inevitable, therefore, given Barbirolli's background and musical taste, that Amaryllis's first Prom appearance should be as soloist in Elgar's Cello Concerto.

Brian Dowling and photographer Thurston Hopkins from *Picture Post* recorded the entire day for posterity. From Amaryllis's arrival at 11.30 a.m. for the rehearsal, they followed her to her chaotic room at 455 Fulham Road — described euphemistically as 'very lived-in' — then back to the Albert Hall artists' room. They took in the Hallé's warm-up, 'the noise jumbled into bumps and booms like a next-door-neighbour's radio', and noted the 'dismal brightness' with which Amaryllis detailed the number of times she had been sick and the weeks she had spent without sleep. Finally they witnessed the terrifying suspense as her cue approached. 'During a performance, the dressing room must be the loneliest place in the world. You sit there practising on your own, and listen to the garbled sounds from the hall. Amaryllis went further and further from us. At last, after a clatter of applause, Sir John came in. Amaryllis was waiting at the door. Barbirolli plucked a string: she plucked it: Barbirolli straightened his tie in front of the mirror. "Have a good time," he said. She was on.'

'On' in the Albert Hall means different things to different people. When Celia Johnson recited a Thanksgiving poem at a November 1944 celebration entitled 'To you America', starring, among others, Barbirolli and the London Symphony Orchestra, she wrote: 'The Albert Hall has the effect of making one feel the size of a small worm but an ultra-conspicuous one, and when empty it echoes so that you have to wait between each syllable to let the boom die away but when full does nothing of the sort, thus disconcerting one to start with.'[72]

Amaryllis was well acquainted with the Albert Hall's acoustics, which gave it the reputation of being the only place a first-time composer could count on hearing his music played twice, but the small-worm feeling Celia Johnson had experienced was absent. Backed by an orchestra, distanced by lights from her massed audience, she could give her full attention to the romantic music.

'Miss Amaryllis Fleming proved well suited to Elgar's Concerto,' wrote *The Times* later that week. 'Her tone is cool and singing, if not quite strong enough for the Albert Hall, and her fingers are quick enough to deal with every technical problem presented in the finale, and to catch at the shivering leaves of the allegro molto. It was an unhurried performance, liberal in its use of expressive, but never distorted, rubato. Thus the autumnal melancholy of the work had time to make itself felt . . .' Amaryllis took four calls and when the photographs were published they drew letters commenting on the similarity between her rapt expression and that in Augustus's portrait of Suggia. Augustus was the only one of her relatives present, and although unable to hear much he was excited by the spectacle and counted the number of people in tears during the slow movement.

After the performance he and Amaryllis returned to

Cresswell Place with Sir John Barbirolli and his wife Evelyn to celebrate André Mangeot's sixtieth birthday. On their heels came the indefatigable journalists. 'At 2 a.m. the Ravel Quartet starts. Amaryllis takes the cello, Barbirolli the viola (played cello-wise on his knees), André Mangeot and Arthur Davison the violins. At 2.30 Max Ward arrives and the instruments are reshuffled. Amaryllis sits it out, a little tired, more than a little elated, and, most of all, at peace.'[73]

In later years Amaryllis became even better acquainted with the Elgar Concerto and went on to give its German première in Hamburg. Curiously, although many of Elgar's pieces had their first performances in Germany, the nation's music-lovers associated him only with popular works such as *Pomp and Circumstance*. When audiences heard Amaryllis play his more serious work they were astounded and delighted. She also became well acquainted with Barbirolli, who had played in the orchestra at the Concerto's première in 1919 and who made the piece distinctively his own. She soon found that Sir John did a lot more in an artists' room than twang a string or straighten a tie. 'He was a bit of a show-off and just when one wanted to collect one's thoughts he would come into the artists' room, seize one's cello and rattle off all his old chestnuts. He had been a very good cellist and had played in André's quartet, but when I knew him he was terribly out of practice. The worst thing was that he always left the door open and I was terrified people would think it was me playing.' Many years later she sat with him on the panel of the Suggia Award, a foundation established after her old tutor's death to help cellists under the age of twenty-one. After a few seasons, however, a clause was discovered in Suggia's will stating that 'no woman cellist should be employed in the decision-making of awards from this gift'. Amaryllis was dismissed amid great hilarity.

Two months after the Prom, on 30 October 1953, she was back in the public eye, receiving an award at the Festival of Commonwealth Youth following a concert at the Royal Overseas Club in St James's. The occasion was noteworthy not so much for the prize – 'a medal and a bit of money' – as for the person who gave it: Princess Marie-Louise. Amaryllis had always been slightly apprehensive about her royal godmother, whom she considered just another instance of Eve's snobbery and who, apart from giving her a sentimental religious wall plaque for her christening, had stayed very much in the background. When she announced to the audience how glad she was to be giving the prize to her goddaughter, Amaryllis shrank.

On meeting her after the ceremony, however, she was pleasantly surprised. 'Agonisingly old, but still athletic',[74] according to Cecil Beaton, who had met her at the Coronation a few months earlier, Princess Marie-Louise showed her eighty-two years. Her face was long, thin and deeply lined, her limbs frail, yet her features were full of character and she impressed Amaryllis with her wit and her attachment to what looked like a large glass of gin. Moreover, she was genuinely glad to be giving her goddaughter the prize and had a real interest in music. Between the wars she and her sister, Princess Helena Victoria, had held musical soirées in their Pall Mall salon with guests such as Leon Goossens and Lauritz Melchior, and she was also a close friend of Eve's two teachers, Jelly d'Aranyi and Adila Fachiri. For Amaryllis it was a delightful revelation, but they were never to meet again. Princess Marie-Louise died four years later, and joined, with Granny Katie Fleming, the list of those Amaryllis wished she had known better.

The last in this string of accolades came in September 1955 when she and Lamar Crowson entered the important Munich

International Competition. Lamar had already won the chamber-music prize in 1953, but this time he and Amaryllis were battling for the cello and piano section. The pair were billeted in the Hotel Am Markt, overlooking the bustling market place near Munich's central Marienplatz, and were allotted practice space in a suburban school to which they travelled daily by the *Kleine Fünf* tram. The competition entailed a deal of preparation: the duo had to prepare nine different sonatas, not knowing which the judges would choose on the day itself, and as a result they had little time to admire all that Germany's southern capital had to offer. Lamar, who had strict ideas about what a woman should or should not do, was overwhelmed by Amaryllis's approach, which was both authoritarian and bohemian. She frog-marched him resolutely past the cafés – he had a passion for cream cakes – on the grounds that they were a waste of time and money, and did so, to his horror, in bare feet while smoking a cigar.

'Munich was fun, *but* a battle,' Lamar recalls. 'We were up against a "ferry" academic German team. The test piece was Beethoven Opus 69. I kept saying to Am, forget about *soixante-neuf*!' The competition was held in two rounds, after which the judges would deliver their verdict. Amaryllis expected everything to run with Teutonic efficiency. On the contrary, the competitors were left for four hours in a single room, clutching nervously at their instruments, with nothing to eat but a plate of sandwiches for which they had to pay. Amaryllis grew angrier by the minute and by the time they were called, at ten o'clock in the evening, her nervousness had been replaced by fury. The two played brilliantly – 'Casals reincarnate' was how the jurors later related their impression – but the following morning, when she and Lamar appeared at nine o'clock for the second round, her confidence had gone.

The only woman in a host of male competitors, she was assailed by self-doubt and her playing suffered accordingly. So astonished were the judges that they took the unprecedented step of ordering a third round. This went better, and the British duo carried the day. 'The two "professors" ', Lamar later recorded with sympathy, 'couldn't cope with "Suggia" Fleming.'

'Magnificent!' Augustus wrote. 'Of course you've won and you always will! We are overjoyed. I couldn't think of any other end to it.' Dodo had predicted the result by her pendulum method and sent a congratulatory telegram which arrived before the competition had finished. The Bavarian press, while noting that its talented countrymen had been faced with an unnecessarily harsh jury, was much taken by the pair's 'admirable formal discipline'. And at the post-competition concert, which was broadcast live, the judges insisted they play the Beethoven A Major Sonata 'because you play it better even than the Germans'. But for Amaryllis the finest accolade came from Lamar – a cigar, which he implored her not to smoke in public.

After the success at Munich, Amaryllis was riding high in critical opinion. The next sensible move would have been to capitalise on her achievement. She had the talent, she had the looks, and she now had the reputation to become an immediate star. But commercialism had never been Amaryllis's strong point. If she thought at all of success it was in terms of artistry rather than in the social and financial context her mother had always espoused. Rather than advance her career Amaryllis decided to postpone it.

For many years she had been worried by her posture. In the *Picture Post* Prom photographs she had been presented as the epitome of a cellist – head flung back, eyes closed, right shoulder raised to throw the whole force of her body into the bow. But the popular image of musicianship jarred with reality. While a raised shoulder looked the part, it radiated tension throughout the whole body. Instead of allowing her arm to move freely below a relaxed joint, thereby achieving far finer degrees of control, she had fallen into the common fault of constricting her body around her instrument. Her back hurt, her arm hurt, and her music, like her body, was in danger of shrinking into itself.

Joan Dickson introduced Amaryllis to her own personal guru, the celebrated Italian cellist Enrico Mainardi. Born in 1897, Mainardi had been a child prodigy whose glittering career was interrupted by World War I. When, after five fallow years, he went back to the cello he discovered he had forgotten how to play. The ensuing period of re- learning made him acutely aware of how much technical and physical information he had absorbed unconsciously as a child, an awareness which in later years he was able to pass on to his pupils. Joan Dickson described him as 'of tremendous personality and exuberant vitality, with a wonderful gift for expressing musical ideas in illuminating, if sometimes un-grammatical, language'.[75] He was an imposing figure with a great mane of white hair (Amaryllis later discovered a bottle of blue rinse in his bathroom) and, like André Mangeot, he hated to be alone. Mainardi invited Amaryllis first to supper, then in rapid succession to tea, lunch, breakfast, a master class, and his hotel room whenever he was practising. He also invited her criticism – and even listened to it – while at the same time offering advice. It was he who first noticed that she had double-jointed thumbs, something she shared with her half-sister Vivien and which she had considered perfectly normal. He advised some thumb-twiddling exercises, but they were ineffectual. When Amaryllis reported the discovery,

Fournier shrugged and said that everyone had some disadvantage and she might as well forget about it. It was not until many years later that an expert cured the problem by clicking a bone which had probably been out of place since childhood.

Mainardi was fulsome in his praise of her playing. 'If you cure those double joints there isn't a man in the world who can stand up to you!' he announced, imploring her to accompany him to Rome and enrol at the Accademia Santa Cecilia. She refused, but the two stayed in touch, Mainardi sending her studies and scores inscribed with flowery dedications. Shortly afterwards, the cellist Amedeo Baldovino was at a dinner party with Mainardi in Rome; halfway through the meal Mainardi beckoned him outside and produced from his pocket a photograph of an attractive woman. Only much later when Baldovino met the woman in the picture did he realise he had been drooling over Amaryllis.

Having dispensed with Mainardi, Amaryllis was still in need of someone who could help her with her shoulder. She journeyed to Bologna to enlist the aid of Ricardo Nani, to whom she had been introduced a few years earlier by a mutual oboist friend, Henry Shuman. Nani, who played in an opera orchestra, was not an outstanding cellist but he was a rarity among string players in that he had come to the cello relatively late in life. For most people, unless they start on an instrument in childhood, it is physically impossible to get the necessary flexibility in their fingers; when, for example, Alan Loveday learned the piano at college he found himself unable to make a flat hand. Nani was fortunate in that he had played the double-bass in his youth and the change to cello-playing, which he made in his twenties, was within the bounds of possibility. Even so, the switch was hard – when Amaryllis knew him he was still exercising his fingers with elastic bands to achieve the wider groupings of cello technique – and in the process he had learned, like Mainardi, the importance of self-observation.

Together he and Amaryllis scoured Bologna for a bedroom with full-length mirror. The landladies were astonished by this bizarre request, but eventually one was found and for the next two months life settled into a weary routine. Every day Amaryllis practised naked in her bedroom, studying her movements in the mirror. In the evening Nani would come to analyse what she was doing. Then she ate alone in a nearby restaurant, where she soon became known as La Signorina and as a mark of favour was served *Rosbif a l'Inglese*, a lump of meat seemingly waved at an oven before being placed raw and purple on her plate. Fortunately, there was usually a stray dog to hand. The *padrone* stood in slight awe of his new regular. 'La Signorina eats like a bird and drinks like two men,' he commented admiringly.

There were moments of relief. Nani introduced her to his son, who took her on a side-saddle motorbike tour of the city. Side-saddle was then the rage – fortunately, since Amaryllis was wearing a strip of batik large enough only to make a very tight dress – but when the boy turned a sharp corner she found herself standing in the middle of the rush-hour traffic. Nani also introduced her to the splendours of Italian opera, which she adored but was intrigued to see how it differed from the more staid English performances. The stars were adulated; one exceptionally lissome tenor was nicknamed *Il Cocce d'Oro* (Golden Thigh), and applause was immediate and unrestricted. Every aria was cheered to the roof then and there, and for an encore the singers would do whatever sprang to mind, accompanied by a piano rather than full orchestra. When free tickets were unavailable, Amaryllis witnessed this exuberant mayhem from the pit, perched on the double-bass player's stool.

Nani was an easily shockable man. Having learned to make shoes during the war, he designed for Amaryllis a pair with velvet-soft leather and stiletto heels. When he took her on a trip to Florence to meet his old teacher, she felt compelled to wear them. But on the return journey, when they missed the bus and had to walk to the station, the compulsion faded. She took them off and walked barefoot. Nani crossed to the other side of the street and pretended not to know her. On her return, Amaryllis found a short-cut to the restaurant that took her past a military brothel. Nani was horrified. 'You shouldn't notice things like that!' he remonstrated. He was even more appalled when she noticed that in the Via del Fossato, where he had a workshop making synthetic resin, it was possible to discern the original street name beneath the overpainting. It had been called Via Fregatete, from old Bolognese dialect *fregare*, to rub, and *tete*, tits. 'I don't know how you find this!' Nani cried in anguish. 'Nobody else does.'

Currency restrictions were still in force, and when a British ballet company arrived Amaryllis took the opportunity to cash a sterling cheque for Italian lire. 'To do this I was obliged to attend a performance. The two oboists in the orchestra had had a flaming row that morning and one had hit the other on the nose so that he couldn't play. Throughout the entire performance the conductor never noticed he was one oboe short.'

Part of the cash went towards a new cello, a Testore which was delivered under the vendor's arm, in its canvas case, on a motorbike in a thunderstorm. It was badly cracked but played beautifully. She wrote a glowing report of her progress and her new acquisition to Augustus. 'I find your news most exciting,' he replied on 3 October 1955. 'In an artist's life such encounters are of the first importance. As in religious conversion, you feel as if reborn, and in your case, your instrument, an extension of yourself, has undergone a corresponding renewal! Maybe you'll return to Bologna . . . I don't know if the seeds were sown there, but Bologna can claim the egg and there should be joy in its arcades.'

There was little joy. Life became a chore that often reduced her to tears: the endless repetition of bowing exercises; the *rosbif*; the men who approached, jangling their keys; the others who tried to corner her under bridges with their cars; the regular visits she made to the post office and the police station to register her presence; and, nastiest of all, the policeman who came to her lodgings announcing that he had the right to enter her room at any hour of the day or night. Her departure, after two months, was a glorious release.

The most memorable souvenir Amaryllis retained of Bologna was a gift from Ricardo Nani's workshop: a retractable end-pin set in a bakelite socket which she felt obliged to fix on her new Testore. It lasted until December 1956, when she and Lamar Crowson were playing in Dublin. Two concerts were scheduled, one in the afternoon and one in the evening, at the Royal Society, which also arranged horse shows and whose matinée programmes had, until recently, begged members of the audience to refrain from knitting. At the time Amaryllis had a theory that if any of the end-pin were left in the cello it would affect the air-space and therefore the sound. Accordingly, she pulled it out as far as possible. The pressure was too much and on the last note of the Boccherini C Major Sonata Nani's bakelite fixture exploded. With it went the strings, the bridge and the sound-post.

'The contented peace which was spread over the audience by the recitalist's lyrical and elegant playing of the Boccherini sonata', reported the *Irish Independent*, 'was abruptly shattered when the spike of Miss Fleming's cello broke.' A replacement was summoned from the university which, with its hairy strings and warped bridge, was little better than the broken Testore. On this monstrosity she completed the programme, with 'some astonishing feats of dexterity', to the *Independent*'s satisfaction.

FOURTEEN

New Departures

With a Wigmore, a Prom, the Queen's Prize and Munich under her belt, not to mention the naked-mirror months in Bologna, Amaryllis began to receive invitations to première new works. In the normal course of events musicians commission composers to write a piece for them. Alternatively, composers write pieces for their favourite musicians. But with Amaryllis's lackadaisical approach to publicity, it was left to the enterprising Howard Hartog to arrange matters. Hartog, who worked for the music publishers Schott, had devised a canny system whereby he sent Amaryllis a new work with a note saying that if she didn't want to play it all she had to do was send it back. The trick, which has made millions for mail-order publishers, worked its usual magic for Hartog. In spite of her reservations towards modern music, she found the chore of re-packing and posting a score even more onerous. So she played Hartog's suggested premières.

The first, on 1 February 1956, was Arnold Cooke's Sonata, performed in Paris with Lamar Crowson. It was an inauspicious start. Amaryllis forgot the score and received it in time only through the joint efforts of her cleaning woman and a British Airways pilot who ferried it over in the cockpit. But Hartog was undeterred. In October, she and Gerald Moore broadcast Racine Fricker's Sonata, commissioned by the BBC for the Third Programme's tenth anniversary, an achievement they repeated in 1957 at a Wigmore with pieces by Brahms, Fauré and Hindemith. Then, at the Cheltenham Festival of 1958, she gave the English première of Màtyàs Seiber's *Tre Pezzi*, or Three Pieces for Violoncello and Orchestra, with Sir John Barbirolli and the Hallé. It is a sad work with a sad history. Seiber, a Hungarian, had written the last piece in memory of his friend the German-born pianist and composer Erich Kahn, who died in a New York car accident in 1956. Ironically, Seiber himself was killed in a car crash four years later in South Africa, when his driver fell asleep and drove into a tree. Kahn and Seiber had last met in Germany in 1955 and 'There is a symbolic reference to this last meeting in the Epilogue', according to the 1959 Prom programme, where Amaryllis performed the piece with Seiber conducting: 'the harmonic C on the cellos, a few bars from the end, which appears together with the tolling of a single bell, is the last note of Kahn's Actus Tragicus.'[76]

By this time, Amaryllis had gained a vague sense of financial reality. She soon discovered that concert promoters were keen to put on new works, and, once she had performed those, the management would invite her back to play whatever she wished. There was no point starting with Elgar or Dvořák, which everyone else could do, so she pursued the Seiber and it paid rich dividends. Before long she had played it in virtually every European country and under a wide range of conductors including Colin Davis and Hans Schmidt-Issersted. The most memorable of these was Sir Adrian Boult, who seemed the antithesis of anything modern. With his English reserve, his handlebar moustache, his custom-made batons and his polished turn-out, Boult was one of a dying breed. 'My dear,' he told Amaryllis, 'you have to remember that when I was a young man Brahms was still alive, and you can't really expect me to know what this piece is about.' Nevertheless, he did his best and Amaryllis admired him for it. Unlike most conductors, he insisted on a piano rehearsal with the soloist before the main rehearsal, and during a performance he kept a keen eye on the soloist's bow, ready to bring in the orchestra if it seemed like reaching its limit. Collared, cuffed, and starched to the hilt, he was uninspiring but unwaveringly supportive.

'Gentlemen,' he said during the Seiber rehearsal, 'Miss Fleming tells me this particular passage has never yet gone right. I, of course, told her that this was going to be the first time it did. Now I know it's not going to go right tonight either.' The passage in question was fiendishly difficult, alternating between wind and cello, with the wind, far to the back, unable either to see or to hear the soloist. The conductor's timing therefore had to be perfect. Boult, fortunately, was a perfectionist – even in his sleep: when a barge hooted outside his Thames-side apartment in Dolphin Square he was reputed to have mumbled, 'Ah, my dear! F sharp'.

Boult never failed to impress Amaryllis with his old-school manners. At a performance in the Swiss Cottage Odeon, conductor and soloist shared a tiny artists' room at the top of a narrow flight of concrete stairs, up which he had insisted on carrying her bag; Lady Boult, who always accompanied her husband, carried the cello. All would have gone well had not a drove of Amaryllis's friends appeared unexpectedly in the interval to congratulate her. They poured into the tiny room in which Boult was trying to collect his thoughts for the second half. 'That's quite all right,' the conductor said, as she apologised helplessly. 'Lady Boult and I will go into the lavatory.' Which they did, squeezing immaculately into the adjoining WC.

Other 'carvers', as they are known, Amaryllis found less

appealing. 'Conductors are usually the bane of one's life,' she says. 'There are so many bad ones who just get away with waving their arms in the air.' Those who raised her ire included Sir Malcolm Sargent, whose vanity extended to cutting off all applause not directed at him and under whose guidance the BBC Symphony Orchestra was referred to as 'The Sargent's Mess'. Sargent, however, never suffered the fate of his successor, the Hungarian conductor Antal Dorati, of whom it was joked that when he once fell to the ground in a faint the entire orchestra rushed to stop him getting up again.

Amaryllis first met Dorati in September 1959 when she was invited to play Seiber's *Tre Pezzi* at the Venice Biennale with the Philarmonia Hungarica. Proceedings began amicably enough in London with conductor and soloist singing through the piece sitting on the grass in Hyde Park. But, at the subsequent rehearsal in Vienna, tension arose between the two when Amaryllis insisted, over Dorati's objections, on playing from music instead of from memory. He shrugged condescendingly and continued with the rehearsal.

In Venice, on the day, everything went wrong. The orchestra's instruments failed to arrive, then their clothes got mislaid. By the time both had been retrieved the concert, which was being broadcast live, was already three-quarters of an hour late. Then Amaryllis discovered that the microphone had been moved from its carefully calculated position. 'I quickly shifted it into what I hoped was the right place. And thank the Lord I had decided to play with music. Dorati, who couldn't see very well but was too vain to wear glasses, conducted one bar of four in three and one bar of three in four, which caused an absolute shambles. It's a very tricky piece and if I hadn't had the music I wouldn't have had the presence of mind to carry on and keep the orchestra with me. Poor Màtyàs was in the audience and he must have died a thousand deaths. Afterwards, Dorati never apologised or even mentioned it.'

By the end of the performance Amaryllis was looking forward to leaving Venice. There had been high spots — playing in the splendid Fenice, where Verdi's operas had first been performed; walking through the Piazza San Marco, followed by a porter carrying her cello on his head, and seeing the Florian Café band stop to wave their bows in admiration. But these did little to compensate for her miserable hotel, to which the Italian agency had welcomed her with a surly note detailing its percentage, or the loneliness of being surrounded almost entirely by Hungarians. Salvation, however, came at the post-concert party in the unlikely form of Sandor Vegh.

A huge bear of a man, very much of the old school, who considered himself the spiritual descendant of the great Belgian violinist Ysaÿe, he had been present in the audience to support his fellow Hungarians. Amaryllis had met him once before, with André Mangeot at Cresswell Place, and his presence came as a welcome break in the roomful of Magyar-speakers. He scoffed at her miserable billet and ordered her to join him forthwith in his very cheap, very good *pensione* on the Lido. Amaryllis did as he commanded, thus starting a long and instructive friendship.

Sandor was leader of the Vegh Quartet, a group of emigré musicians who had been allowed out of Hungary in 1946 to play in the Geneva International Competition. All four had been yearning to escape but their fate rested on winning the prize. They were penniless, and only if they won, securing prize, kudos and future engagements, could they survive in the western world. 'Little Sandor', the second fiddle, was down-cast and as the day got closer his spirits sank lower. 'If we win this thing I'll eat my socks!' he cried one night. But they did win, they did get the money and they did get the engagements. They were free. Later 'Big Sandor' went to 'Little Sandor's' room, and saw the violinist hunched over a table on which lay an apple and a strange grey mess. He was eating his socks.

Amaryllis had great respect for Sandor Vegh. After the Prades festival of 1962 she wrote, 'I am more bowled over than ever before. He *is* music. Listening to him has given me a new lease of life, a fresh enthusiasm and an infinitely wider horizon.' When he suggested they play the Brahms Double Concerto together, 'I was so excited by the idea that I came home and wept.' Later, 'he conducted a hair-raising performance of the Grosse Fugue and then proceeded to play Vivaldi's *Seasons* so superbly that it brought tears to my eyes. One no longer thought about pitch, or old bows or style – it simply was Vivaldi and Vivaldi as a more fresh, humorous, sad, profound and joyful composer than I could have imagined. After it, Casals playing the Adagio and Allegro of Schumann was a bit of an anticlimax.'[77]

Vegh was certainly talented, but his personality was too large for the close confines of a quartet. The others, with whom Amaryllis soon became friends, resented his high-handed attitude. Rehearsals got fewer, arguments fiercer, and when Amaryllis did eventually play with Vegh the ensemble was scarcely on speaking terms. The occasion, at Claydon House, home to Amaryllis's old school friend Mary Vestey, marked the quartet's thirtieth anniversary – 'our Thirty Years' War' – and was almost its last performance.

By the time Amaryllis met Vegh in Venice she had already widened her field by forming a guitar trio with Alan Loveday and Julian Bream. Although there was just one piece written specifically for such a combination, the Paganini Trio, they were able to adapt a Vivaldi lute trio and a few other works written originally for harpsichord. These they interspersed with solos and some Spanish piano pieces arranged for guitar. The programmes made unlikely reading, but the music was popular in a time when everyone owned a guitar – and if none of them was a rock star, the trio at least included the right instrument. They played to capacity houses and on one occasion had to abandon their instruments and flee through a lavatory window to avoid autograph hunters.

Their success was due largely to Julian Bream. 'He really brought things to life,' Amaryllis recalls. 'He was excellent on the platform and had this uncanny ability to bring the audience into the music. He was a really imaginative accompanist.' In fact, Bream, already an established soloist, found the trio hard work; cello and violin are much louder than guitar and the strain of the combination affected all three. Amaryllis and Alan were playing 'on one hair and halfway up the fingerboard', while Bream was struggling to play as loudly as possible without breaking his fingernails.

The trio never performed outside Britain, but the Continent provided Amaryllis with some of her most enduring memories of Julian Bream. One foray to Italy – she had a cello for repair, he guitars to buy – took them over the Brenner Pass on its first open day of the year. At the snow-covered top they had a puncture and were forced to call the rescue service. They descended, freezing in their Geneva clothes, Amaryllis trousered in a jersey hand-knitted for Bream by Tom Goff (devoted admirer, harpsichord maker, and illegitimate son of Edward VII), only to find that the cello repairer was no good. Such was the perplexity of Italian customs when Amaryllis returned with her broken cello, for which she had had to complete an export form in quintuplet, that they did not notice Bream smuggling through his three new guitars.

Another Italian venture brought the misfortune of a composition dedicated by one of Bream's friends, Reginald

Smith-Brindle-Borsi, who heard them give an impromptu performance in Florence. The piece was accepted by the BBC and there was no way they could avoid playing it. They both hated it. It was thoroughly modern, involving 'squeaking on the cello, banging on the guitar and all that nonsense', and, although only minutes long, it took hours to rehearse. Playing in Bream's house, with barely an hour before they had to be in the studio, Bream rose in frustration and flung his part on the fire. Amaryllis stared in horror. Then Bream went very, very slowly to a drawer and produced another copy. They struggled unwillingly through the piece, but heard nothing from Smith-Brindle-Borsi until he met Amaryllis at the Venice Biennale. 'What did you think?' she inquired. 'It was timed for three minutes forty seconds,' he scowled. 'You took four minutes.'

Bream's place in the trio was eventually taken by John Williams, recently separated from his wife and lodging, ironically, in Turner's House with Yehudi Menuhin's son-in-law, the Chinese pianist Fou Ts'ong. Once again the combination of guitar, cello and violin did well and an album was released by Columbia with a 'truly dreadful photo of the three of us on the cover'. But despite the thrill of LP royalties the group eventually disintegrated. The repertoire was too limited and Williams was receiving more lucrative offers. Amaryllis was left with a memory of guitarists scraping oil from behind their ears to lubricate their nails, and a re-released Columbia album whose sleeve now showed three pieces of fruit.

FIFTEEN

The Young and the Old

Amaryllis was not the only Fleming to prosper during the Fifties. Even more successful was her half-brother Ian, whose first James Bond book appeared in 1953. Amaryllis and Ian had always been close; of all Eve's children they were the most alike, sharing an animal magnetism and a love of the good life quite alien to the other brothers. Ian, too, despite the suave and debonair image he projected, was the only one whose passion came close to matching Amaryllis's fiery temperament. There had been times, as Ian admitted, when he was sorely tempted by his beautiful half-sister. But in 1953 there was a slight friction between the two, the initial cause being Ian's marriage to Annie Rothermere on 24 March 1952.

Amaryllis had never warmed to Annie, whom she regarded as a brittle society hostess, a 'phoney' who was not good enough for Ian, and her temper rose when she learned that Ian was getting married because Annie was pregnant. 'I thought Flemings were tough!' she stormed. 'It's too late,' Ian replied flatly. 'It's settled and there's nothing you can do about it.' The son, named Caspar after Amaryllis's half-brother whom Ian had met and admired during the war, was born that August.

The second source of discord was the Bond books themselves. The family was enormously proud of Ian's achievement, even if Richard made his wife Charm use brown-paper dustjackets when reading Bond in public. Ian was highly amused: 'You needn't lock this one away!' he wrote in Richard's copy of *Thrilling Cities*, one of his few non-Bond books. Amaryllis, however, had always respected Ian's intellect and thought him capable of more than mere thrillers. Ian took umbrage when she told him so. 'So what do you want me to write?' he snapped. 'Long-winded philosophical treatises that no one will buy?' This brief hiccup in their relationship was soon smoothed over, but from that day Ian never sent her any of his books. Later, however, he offered something far more valuable: the royalties of *From Russia With Love*, first published in 1957. When Amaryllis protested that they should go to Caspar, Ian replied that Caspar had far too much as it was and he wanted her to have them. But then he forgot all about the offer.

It came as small recompense when Amaryllis discovered that Ian, following his habit of using the names of friends and relations, had included her in a short story, 'The Living Daylights', written in 1962 and published posthumously with *Octopussy* four years later. Bond is following a cello-playing Russian sniper, code-named Trigger, whose hair 'shone like molten gold under the arcs at the intersection. She was hurrying along in a charming, excited way . . . Everything was flying – the skirt of her coat, her feet, her hair. She was vivid with movement and life and, it seemed, with gaiety and happiness . . .'[78] Whether or not Amaryllis was the model for the twenty-three-year-old Trigger, Ian's description is a good sketch of her at the same age. Later on he pokes fun at her profession: 'Why in hell did she have to chose the cello?' Bond wonders. 'There was something almost indecent in the idea of that bulbous, ungainly instrument between her splayed thighs. Of course Suggia had managed to look elegant, and so did that girl Amaryllis somebody. But they should invent a way to play the damned thing side-saddle.'[79]

By the late Fifties Ian's name was cropping up in the Press with monotonous regularity, though he ruefully recounted that he had once been asked at a party if he was 'by any chance related to Amaryllis Fleming'. But in 1957 his thunder was stolen when Eve made headlines over her entanglement with the Marquess of Winchester. Bapsy Pavry's case opened before Mr Justice Devlin on 30 October, the Marquess's ninety-fifth birthday. It charged Eve, in essence, with husband-theft. Mrs Fleming, it was reported, had 'conducted a campaign of hate, jealousy and venom'[80] to secure the Marquess, with whom she had been living since 1953 in Nassau 'as man and wife, or to all appearances as such'. The case lasted ten days, 400 letters were produced in evidence and the judgement ran to forty-six pages of transcript.

It was a colourful contest. In the one corner was fifty-four-year-old Bapsy Pavry, described in 'Profile of a great and gracious lady, in honour of her fiftieth birthday' (a document circulated by herself to the Press) as an unofficial 'Ambassador for India' who was 'recognised for her beauty and grace' as well as her 'wealth and fabulous jewels'. In the other was seventy-three-year-old Eve Fleming, a wealthy 'viper' who, if reports were to be believed, had a gun, a bottle of vitriol, and the potential for murder. In between was the penniless figure of 'Monty' Winchester, pulled one way by Eve, who, he assured his wife, 'was trying to help him as a friend and wanted to give him £100,000', and the other by Bapsy Pavry, who wrote assuring him that 'this shameless woman wants to keep you as a filthy gigolo', adding, perhaps as extra encouragement for his return: 'May a viper's fangs be for ever around your throat and may you sizzle in the pit in your own juice.'

The proceedings provided ample fodder for public intrigue. Why did the Marquess and Marchioness of Winchester spend their wedding night in separate hotels? Why did Bapsy buy 300 copies of their marriage certificate? Was it true that when Monty left to join Eve in the Bahamas he gave his wife a farewell gift of two old pairs of his pyjamas – 'one of parachute material and the other of flannel'? How did a birthday cake from Bapsy bearing ninety-one candles survive the postal service from London to Nassau? Did Eve really follow the Winchesters to Cannes, checking in at a nearby hotel under the pseudonym Mrs Lancaster? And did she expect anyone to believe that her only interest in Monty was to see that he got enough food?

Mr Justice Devlin was having a difficult time. 'If there are any more of these silly gusts of laughter, I shall clear the well of the Court,' he admonished. 'The public in the gallery are behaving perfectly well.'

Neither Bapsy nor Eve acquitted themselves well in the witness box. Bapsy proved on occasion so impossibly voluble that one sub-head in the *The Times* report read 'Witness Stops Talking'; at other times she refused to speak at all. Eve was, in the prosecuting lawyer's view, 'evasive, opinionated, worldly, snobbish and untruthful', having 'carefully avoided practically every question she was asked'. Eventually, the judge found against Eve, pointing out that while she claimed to be acting on charitable impulses she was not, in his opinion, 'of a type which naturally sought fulfilment in good works'. Undaunted, Eve took the case to appeal.

The Fleming children reacted to their mother's latest escapade with weary discomfiture. To Amaryllis the whole affair was ludicrous beyond belief, and she made no secret of her opinion. Although Eve took her mockery in good style, Amaryllis refused to take any part in the charade, leaving her half-brothers to sit awkwardly by their mother's side throughout both hearings. Annie Fleming described the lighter side of their ordeal in a letter to Evelyn Waugh: 'The Fleming brothers are having a tough time with their mother, she inclines to dress like Lady Ottoline Morrell or the Casati, so every morning Peter, Ian and Richard go to her hotel and force her into hospital matron clothes. On Friday the poor old thing wished to wear a yellow satin picture hat with grey pearl hatpins the size of tennis balls – they had her out of that in a trice.'[81] Augustus, meanwhile, offered tea, sympathy and (to Amaryllis) the revelation that he had once painted Bapsy's portrait and had been overwhelmed by a desire to verify the rumour that Parsees shaved their pubic hair. His revelation did not include what he had discovered.

On 17 July 1958, three law lords reversed the previous year's decision, leaving Bapsy outraged and Eve serenely cock-a-hoop. Having gained her elderly but undivorced prize, she retired with him to the Hotel Metropole in Monte Carlo, where she spent her days shopping in the market for meals which she cooked in the tiny lobby connecting their rooms and ensuring that Vivaldi, the chauffeur, kept her rarely used Rolls-Royce in tip-top condition. Once, as he was buffing the car to lustrous magnificence for the thousandth time, he jokingly asked his employer if she wanted him to black the tyres with boot polish. '*Naturellement,* Vivaldi,' Eve replied, looking neither right nor left as she strode off to buy aubergines.

Sometimes she and Monty came to London and on one occasion Amaryllis joined them for dinner. Like others before her, she was surprised to find the Marquess an engaging companion with a twinkle in his eye and a host of anecdotes which covered lion-hunting expeditions with Cecil Rhodes, his five-year chairmanship of Hampshire County Council and his experiences as an amateur jockey. She would have liked to see her mother on her own, but Eve said that Monty would only order champagne and caviare from room- service: 'It's cheaper this way, dear.'

By this time Amaryllis had left the flat at 455 Fulham Road, for more salubrious accommodation in Knightsbridge at 41 Ovington Square, a fine white stucco house whose end-lease Eve had purchased for £2,000 and which had ample room for Amaryllis and a number of paying lodgers. But 'The Ovaries', as she and Augustus called it, never appealed; it was too proper, too conventional for her taste, as well as being in a decidedly unmusical neighbourhood. Her neighbours thumped on the walls and tacked peevish notes to the front door. One man from the other side of the square ordered her to keep her windows closed at all times. At this, the others rallied round, instructing Amaryllis to keep her windows wide open because much as they hated her music they hated the man opposite more – besides, they suspected him of beating his wife. The only ones who didn't complain were the call-girls who lived on one side of her above a doctor's apartment. Indeed, they thanked Amaryllis for redirecting the clients who knocked furtively at her door.

The Ovaries did have one compensating factor in the form of Mrs Virgo, who lived in the basement and cleaned for Amaryllis while moonlighting for Poppet John at her flat in Percy Street. A large, talkative woman with a passion for painting, Mrs Virgo strengthened the bond that already existed between the half-sisters, borrowing from the one whatever the other needed. Glasses, cutlery and plates flowed from The Ovaries to Percy Street, and on the return journeys Mrs Virgo brought Poppet's books (one an unexpurgated French edition of *Lady Chatterley's Lover*) and an unending stream of gossip. Guests at either establishment were reported on in savage detail. 'And when I looked in her cupboard, there were all her clothes, each one drabber than the last!' Mrs Virgo informed Amaryllis after one well-known pianist had stayed at Percy Street. Then, having delivered her news, she would retire to the basement and attack a canvas. Sometimes she climbed the stairs, arms smeared with paint, to brief her employer on her progress. 'I'm painting a magnolia just like Mr John!' ran one Virgo bulletin, before she disappeared triumphantly back to her palette.

When Poppet moved to the South of France, Mrs Virgo continued to clean for the people she let Percy Street to. One was John Russell, then the art critic of the *Sunday Times*, to whom Amaryllis formed a brief attachment. Mornings became a slight problem. 'Oh, it was such a foggy night I couldn't come home!' Amaryllis explained from the hastily occupied spare bed in Percy Street. 'Yes, dear,' Mrs Virgo replied, tidying the undrawn curtains. 'I quite understand.' There were many who would have paid for Mrs Virgo's knowledge of events at Ovington Square and Percy Street, among them Russell's Russian girlfriend Vera, who consulted a medium to discover what he was up to. The spirit world revealed with astonishing accuracy that Russell was involved with a redheaded woman connected with the stage. Vera, who had met Amaryllis, immediately circulated a rumour that she was lesbian. The ménage eventually dissolved but it was Vera who had the last laugh. When Amaryllis visited the artist Matthew Smith, an old friend of both herself and Augustus (each painter swore the other was colour blind), he gave her a pair of gouaches he had fished out from under his bed. But instead of letting her take them there and then he offered to get them framed to save her the expense. Unfortunately, Amaryllis later discovered, he was seeing Vera. She never got the pictures.

The Ovaries was the major financial coup of Amaryllis's life. In the late Fifties she had it valued by a surveyor, who pronounced it to be worth £4,000. She had the lease extended for another forty years, at no cost, and put the property on the market at £9,500. There was no difficulty finding a buyer. For some time she had been troubled by her female lodger who had a rich, older lover. Every night it sounded as if they were banging each other's heads against the floor and on pre-concert nights, especially, their skull-cracking reached such a crescendo that Amaryllis was tempted to call the police. It was lucky she didn't because the lover, persuaded by his penniless companion, bought The Ovaries at full asking price. Amaryllis left them to crash about in Knightsbridge and moved with relief into 137 Old Church Street, a tall, thin, eighteenth-century house in the heart of Chelsea.

Amaryllis was no stranger to Old Church Street. The house had been occupied by the artist Anthony Gross since before the war and one summer she and Penelope Ram had moved in to house-sit when he was away. She fell in love with it and after Gross moved out in 1959, when it came on the market at £4,500, she snapped it up. It took all the profit from the sale of Ovington Square to bring the building up to scratch, but the expense was worthwhile. Much of the money went into turning the top-floor studio into an acoustically perfect music room complete with hardwood panelling and a vast Venetian mirror for muscle analysis. Nothing was done to alter the house's character, and with its rickety front porch, its uneven floors and its steep, winding staircases it soon developed a Fryern-like feeling of its own. 'The house had an atmosphere of peace,' a friend remembers. 'It felt lived-in and was filled with beautiful objects. In summer, trees outside the windows cast a subaqueous light across the living room and a fountain splashed in the garden.' Towering over the fountain was a pear tree whose magnificent blossom is the leitmotif of 'Bliss', a short story written by Katherine Mansfield, who had once taken rooms in Old Church Street and who had also, coincidentally, trained as a cellist.

The neighbours were more accommodating than in Ovington Square. On one side were Sir Edward and Lady Maufe, he an architect who had designed Guildford Cathedral, among other achievements, and she a designer for Heal's furniture store. They were both, Amaryllis later discovered, slightly deaf, which probably accounted for the note they sent inviting her to practise day and night as much as she liked. On the other side lived Michael MacOwan, a retired actor who gave private lessons and positively encouraged her to play late hours on the grounds that it would set his pupils a good example. Directly opposite was the publisher Denis Cohen, who occupied a house built by the German Modernist architect Erich Mendelsohn – 'the one that looks like a laundry', he told taxi drivers – which stood next to a pink building designed by Bauhaus-founder Walter Gropius, home to Denis's cousin and his actress wife Constance Cummings. Amaryllis was introduced to this cosy family gathering by Augustus, who had studied at the Slade with Denis's nephew Michel Salaman, and who engineered a dinner with the Cohens on the understanding that she would encourage Denis to publish a book on Gwen John. From that first meeting they became close friends, with Denis inviting her to meals almost every day. When he eloped with a much younger woman named Mary, Michel was astonished. 'I just can't understand why he wants to get married,' he told Amaryllis. 'He has Mary for lunch and you for supper. What more could a man want?'

Old Church Street was Amaryllis's home for the next twenty years, and it was filled with a seasonal variety of guests who came for weekends and invariably ended up staying much longer – one and a half years was the record. There were Poppet and her husband Pol, who stayed on their visits to London. There was Lady Maufe who took a room as a workshop for her design work and to make tapestries and altar cloths for Guildford Cathedral. There was a Chinese girl who came to interpret for Sylvain Mangeot and remained at Amaryllis's house in a prolonged limbo after Sylvain's interviewee, outraged at her anger when he pinched her bottom, refused to speak to her. There was an Italian boy who refused to go anywhere without Amaryllis and when sent alone to the barber had to take her poodle for moral support. And then, of course, there were those who just came for a good night out. One particularly fraught gathering included Sylvain Mangeot, Queen Kukola, who had a porcelain hand and was the reigning monarch of Sikkim, Ashi Tashi Dorji, the King of Bhutan's aunt, and her Manchurian friend Lobsang, who had escaped from prisons in both China and India and who was, as Amaryllis discovered when he made a pass at her in the kitchen, frighteningly strong.

Sometimes, on one of his rare trips to London, Peter Fleming would drop in for a bath – 'a quick rinse', as he put it – and David John could be seen most evenings walking unsteadily to his lodgings in Cheyne Walk. Several times Amaryllis followed him in her nightgown to make sure he arrived safely. When she once hauled him in for a nightcap, he was astonished to see her cello standing in a corner. 'But haven't you retired?' he asked his thirty-five-year-old hostess.

The most enduring visitor to Old Church Street, however, was E. M. W. Paul – or Paul, as everyone called him – whom Amaryllis had met through the Norwegian pianist Hilda Wanderland. While staying in Malmö for a broadcast with

Hilda, Amaryllis mentioned that she was unhappy with her new cello, an Italian instrument she had owned for little over a year and which she had bought on her own judgement rather than taking professional advice. Hilda's husband, who besides managing a mental asylum in Malmö was a keen amateur violinist, told her of a dealer in England who had found him a magnificent violin. Amaryllis accordingly invited the dealer to her home to inspect the instrument.

When Paul entered the studio he was horror-struck. Her cello was one he had bought from a shop window in Brighton for £20 and had resold for £30 to another dealer with strict instructions that it was not Italian but Flemish. It had duly made the round of four other dealers, each time gaining in price and ancestry until Amaryllis had bought it for £700, certified by Hill's of Bond Street as a Francesco Gofriller. The only trouble, as Paul revealed, was that nobody knew what a Francesco Gofriller looked like. It was Matteo Gofriller who made cellos, while his brother Francesco was only reputed to have done so; thus any Italianate cello of uncertain origin was optimistically tagged as a Francesco. To this day Francesco Gofriller remains the unknown soldier of cello makers. Paul immediately arranged for it to be sold. The dealer with whom he struck a bargain agreed to his sole condition that Amaryllis's name not be connected with the instrument in any way, then sold it very profitably to an Australian on the strength that it was the cello on which Amaryllis Fleming had built her career.

Paul also recommended that she sell her Ruggieri – in the words of Bill Beare, then London's foremost dealer, 'No one has ever made a solo career on a Ruggieri' – and dismissed her Dodd bow with a shake of his head. 'There are Dodds and Dodds. This one won't do.' The Ruggieri went to Rembert Wurlitzer in New York, who found new wood in it, which he removed, thereby improving the tone. The Dodd was replaced by one from the workshop of François Tourte, the king of French bow-makers who had been born in 1747, just ten years after Stradivarius's death.

With the money from her two cellos Amaryllis was able to afford a Guarneri which had belonged to Iwan D'Archambeau, a member of the Rosé Quartet, and which had 'one of the most beautiful scrolls I have ever seen'. Two years later this was discarded in favour of another Paul find: a 1717 Stradivari with a belly and scroll made by the eighteenth-century Spanish maker Contreras, which is the cello she has played ever since. More important than either instrument, however, was the new and vital partner in Amaryllis's life.

An intense, deep-eyed man, whom taxi drivers occasionally mistook for Yehudi Menuhin, Paul had been born in Heidelberg as Paul Rosenbaum. He had trained as a lawyer before fleeing Germany in the Thirties after breaking an SS officer's arm. His entire family, save one brother and an aunt, disappeared into Hitler's camps for ever. Paul escaped lightly, suffering only the indignity of being interned on the Isle of Man as an enemy alien. There he met Norbert Brainin, a fellow internee who went on to lead the Amadeus Quartet and who instilled in Paul an abiding love of music. After the war he worked as a Fleet Street photographer before finding a part-time job with a musical-instrument dealer in Charing Cross Road. It was an unsalaried apprenticeship – Paul was grateful simply to be able to examine the instruments – but a commission was payable if he brought in anything of interest. His first find was a small Ceruti violin and shortly after that he decided to go into business as an independent, home-based dealer.

When Amaryllis first met Paul he was living in Hampshire

with his wife Diana and his daughter Isabella. Diana had never recovered completely from a bout of tuberculosis, and Paul, who himself had a weak heart, spent much of his time caring for her. Trips to London were a welcome escape from domestic duties and his visits to Old Church Street turned from afternoons to days, to weeks and then to months.

Amaryllis took it upon herself to act as Paul's chauffeur and together they toured the country in search of bargains. The Sixties were on the horizon and it was a time when the old was being busily discarded in favour of the new; stately homes were being demolished, attics were being emptied, and the market was flooded with treasures at knock-down prices. For those with the eye, the energy and the luck, there were rich pickings to be had. Amaryllis's Tourte bow, for example, cost only £6 from a Brighton dealer who refused to admit his own mis-diagnosis. On one occasion Paul and Amaryllis drove down from the north of England with fifteen naked cellos stuffed into her Hillman Minx. Another time, in Norfolk, Paul was having his hair cut when the barber tipped him off about an old woman who lived nearby and had a Strad cello for sale. He and Amaryllis found a disintegrating mansion, apparently untouched for over a century, whose deaf occupant, clad in tweeds and heavy walking shoes, greeted them with a stentorian 'You're late!' The cello was English and far too expensive, but she also had a bow that caught Paul's eye. 'It's a Voirin,' he bellowed. She shouted back that it was a Voisin, which she pronounced Voyzin, a maker who had never existed however one said his name. It was a bargain at £100.

Paul's greatest coup, however, was not in the shires but in the very heart of London. While doing the rounds of auction houses he discovered in the showrooms of Puttick and Simpson (now Phillips) a genuine Amati cello which other dealers had dismissed as catalogue deadwood. Amaryllis arrived, disguised in headscarf and dark glasses, and studied the ugliest painting she could find while the cello was smuggled down to the basement for a private viewing. It had been made in about 1600 by the brothers Antonius and Hieronymus Amati, but was unplayable: the bridge had warped; the strings were hairy; the body had been cut down and neglected; and the varnish was lifeless. Yet under the dirt shone the real Amati gold. Paul's feverish request to leave an unlimited commission bid was refused, so he had to chance being recognised and bid for it in person. On the day Amaryllis waited nervously by the phone in Old Church Street. At last it rang; Paul had bought the Amati for £52. After months of painstaking restoration by the Swiss-born repairer Dietrich ('Derek') Kessler, it took its place alongside Amaryllis's Strad.

Despite Paul's near-infallible eye for a bargain he never grew rich on his talent. In part, this was because of his unthinking generosity: when, for instance, he stumbled upon a Rembrandt drawing he gave it away to a friend the next day. It was also due to his practice of selling on to other dealers at only a small profit. Amaryllis decided that it would be far more profitable to cut out the middle-men and sell direct to players. They tried it for a short while, but without success. Musicians either had trouble making the instrument sound or disappeared with it on approval for such prolonged periods as to make the exercise useless. Furthermore, Paul's outspokenness made him an atrocious salesman. 'If you can't play in tune how can you expect it to sound good?' he harangued one famous violinist.

Eventually they reverted to dealers, predominantly two Jewish friends of Paul's: a small, thin man, known only by his surname Rose; and Lou, a large fat fellow who had changed his name from Lewis Solomon to Solomon Lewis to sound

more English on the telephone. Although the best of friends –
Lou acted as a mealtime spokesman for both Rose and his
father, neither of whom would speak directly to the other –
they were fierce professional rivals. Once, when Lou outbid
his companion at a country auction, Rose lay in wait under an
arch and hit him on the nose. They were both arrested and
taken to court, where the magistrate refused to believe that
tiny Rose was capable of striking enormous Lou. They were
always descending on Old Church Street and occasionally
came to hear Amaryllis play. Rose, who also ran a carpet shop
in Brighton, once surprised her by appearing in the audience
wrapped in an antique rug he thought too valuable to let out
of his sight.

Lou had an endearing lack of scruple. On one occasion Paul
instructed him that the cello he was selling him might look
Italian but most certainly was not, and under no circumstance
was he to sell it as such. All innocence, Lou asked how he knew
the difference. Paul replied that the F-holes would be a
different shape. Shortly afterwards, Paul and Amaryllis were
invited to dinner by a very respectable dealer named Alfred
Langonet. 'Now,' said Langonet when they arrived, 'just look
at this wonderful Italian cello I've bought.' They saw the
altered F-holes, recognised one of Lou's many fake labels, and
remembered pressing business elsewhere.

Amaryllis learned a tremendous amount from Paul, and not
only about the chicanery of dealers. He taught her what to look
for in an instrument, how to understand the tools of her trade.
'You must go for quality,' he told her, 'and never mind names.'
He had an unerring instinct for bows, knowing at a glance not
only which was the best on offer but for whom it was best suited.
Once, having heard a radio broadcast by the violinist Patrick
Ireland, he telephoned to say he could give him the very bow he
needed. Ireland plays with that bow to this day.

It was not only stringed instruments that caught Paul's attention. From Florence he brought back a supposedly unimportant Venetian spinet, so beautiful in sound and appearance that neither he nor Amaryllis could bear to let it go. It duly found a place in the sitting room of Old Church Street. His eye for good workmanship was all-encompassing. In a crammed junk shop he could spot, within seconds of entering, the one worthwhile object on display – such as a cracked saucer he made Amaryllis buy for two shillings. 'It's beautiful and it will teach you something.' The simple act of getting out of a car could prompt an observation on the quality of the road surface or the care with which the pavement had been laid. He enjoyed, too, the interplay between different fields of art, particularly that between music and painting. He likened Titian's control of harmony, for example, to that of a musician, and described his *Perseus and Andromeda*, in the Wallace Collection, as holding the solution to contrasts and even offering an explanation for the lack of dynamics in Bach's scores. 'Go at once!' he urged her, adding that she would learn more from that one picture than from any musician, book or recital.

Amaryllis took Paul to Fryern, where Augustus was deeply impressed by his perspicacity. But when, over lunch, Paul began to criticise one of his paintings – an unforgivable and unheard-of sin – Dodo and Amaryllis feared the worst, for even in his eighties Augustus was capable of instigating a bloody fight. To their astonishment, he invited Paul into his bedroom to look at more paintings. For three hours they were closeted together while he elicited Paul's opinion of the heap of canvases he stored under his bed. 'Well, that certainly did Augustus a lot of good,' Dodo said, still unable to believe what had happened.

*

Augustus also extended to Paul the rare privilege of seeing his work in progress. For years he had been trying to capture Amaryllis with her cello, attempting to produce a latter-day masterpiece to rival his earlier triumph with Suggia. Throughout the Fifties his letters had been peppered with pleas for a full-length sitting, 'cello and all'. 'Shall I *never* pin you down?' he wrote in 1955. Five years later, in the summer of 1960, his wish came true. Amaryllis had been portrayed by Augustus before: in the red conté drawings of Tite Street and in another conté portrait of 1952, which included the scroll and finger board of her cello. At her neck was the outline of a Nicholas II rouble given to her by Ian's girlfriend, Lisl Popper. 'It will bring you luck in love,' she had said. 'Coals to Newcastle!' her friend Manoug Parikian later remarked. All three drawings were accomplished, the last especially so. This latest attempt, however, was to be of a different order altogether. As Augustus told Paul, it was going to be his swan song.

For more than a fortnight Amaryllis donned full concert dress and swathed her way through brambles and dew-sodden plants to Augustus's old studio, where she was expected every morning at ten o'clock. On arrival she mounted a rickety model's chair raised on a platform, with a separate easel arranged to hold her cello, and a velvet cushion laid out for Susie, her brown poodle. For three agonising hours at a stretch she was expected to remain absolutely still, balancing precariously over her cello, no longer a human being, let alone a daughter, merely a subject. Meanwhile Augustus huffed and puffed, dancing to and fro in a frenzy of deliberation before lunging forward to deliver a brushstroke of infinite delicacy. Occasionally she saw through the canvas which of her limbs Augustus was painting, and stole the chance to relax the other ones. But before long he raised a brush and with precise, gentle movements guided her back into position. Each session ended at lunchtime with Dodo's congratulations and a large glass of whisky.

The first finished sketch was magnificent, the very essence of music. Paul was overwhelmed by Augustus's magic. For him the portrait's physical accuracy was secondary to the spirit it had captured. He became obsessed by the manner in which Augustus had clarified the distinction between truth and reality, citing the revelation as one more instance of his maxim that 'we go through life like sleepwalkers'.

But from then on the portrait was a disaster. Augustus began to overpaint first the face and then everything else. Sittings became a struggle of revisions, each leading to further indecisions. And then, deciding his triptych would be the perfect background, he painted it in laboriously. It was the death knell. He had been bedevilled by this mural for over a dozen years and when he died in 1961 it was still unfinished, a final, mutative monument to a great artist's waning powers. Swipe after swipe of colour was applied to Amaryllis's portrait until she could bear it no longer. She left, pursued by plaintive demands that she return. The portrait was on the cusp; it was nearly there; it needed only a little more time. But time, to Augustus, was a meaningless concept; Amaryllis could have sat for an eternity. The portrait, huge and unhouseable, rested against a wall of Augustus's studio, and was gradually nibbled away by mice.

Augustus was coming to the end. In that same year Cecil Beaton journeyed over for a sitting. 'I told him that I had recently read a description in my diary of his being at the Eiffel Tower with a lot of young girls dressed as lesbians. "I love lesbians," said John as the door opened to his natural daughter, Amaryllis Fleming, the cellist, a glorious figure of a woman with tumbling curls.'[82] They enjoyed a long conversation about the relationship between Eve and the Marquess, which Beaton relished as being 'infinite in its variations on the theme of love, marriage of convenience and divorce'. The portrait, however, was a failure. As he had done with Amaryllis, Augustus produced a passable first sketch but was incapable of progressing further. When Beaton returned in the late summer of 1961 for a second attempt, Augustus, a 'blinking old man dressed like a French servant in blue', had deteriorated still further. 'Everywhere', wrote Beaton, 'were added signs of weakness. Before he had been able to stand to work – now as he sat he jerked and twitched and his breathing became so heavy that I felt his heart *must* soon give out. Not only was his stertorous breathing agonising to hear but from inside his chest came other sounds of rusty boxes grinding – of wheezing concertinas and rattling combs.'[83]

Beaton was horrified to see the result. 'The canvas was the raving mess of a madman. Nothing was there. Just nothing. A weak daub of entrail-coloured brush strokes that fell far wide of their mark.'[84] It came as an overwhelming relief when 'a letter chewed by a cat arrived in Augustus's shaking hand' announcing that he was so preoccupied by his triptych he would have temporarily to abandon the portrait. But Beaton knew Augustus could never paint again: 'He is a realist and it is terrible to see him living a life of pretence. He must know he can never finish his panels, never embark on another drawing, but if he didn't pretend, and go each day to the studio, what would there be for him to do?'[85]

Beaton was consumed with a premonitory gloom. 'It is the sad time of year when the summer is getting tired, the trees dark and all the nostalgic flowers of childhood's holidays come into being again – and it is the time when I feel I don't want any more to be surrounded by old people – when I need to see people whose laughter overrides all the lurking innate sadness of late summer.'[86] He was Augustus's last sitter. After a brief illness the great artist died at Fryern, of heart failure, in the early hours of 31 October 1961.

At the moment of Augustus's death Amaryllis was driving home from a concert. When the news was broadcast on the radio the following morning she was fast asleep. The first she knew of it was when André and Sylvain Mangeot telephoned to offer their condolences, whereupon she burst into hysterics. Sylvain rushed over, as did Paul, and hot on his heels came Lou, on business, in a pair of brand-new, squeaky, orange shoes that caused further hysterics. Later that day Ian also appeared but for once the legendary charmer had nothing to say. Lost for words, he ripped off his watch – big, expensive and gadgeted about in best Bond style – and thrust it at her. Amaryllis later passed it on to Paul, who wore it until he died. It was the only watch that never stopped on him.

The loss of her father was something Amaryllis had anticipated but for which she had never really prepared herself. The two had got on exceptionally well, thanks, possibly, to the fact that Amaryllis had discovered him so late in life. Augustus, as he told her, had 'no gifts as a paterfamilias'. Stern, overwhelming and unapproachable, he brought his children up in a manner which Dodo described tactfully as 'Victorian'. His granddaughter, Rebecca John, later wrote, 'Augustus had a complete lack of understanding as a father; indeed, scarcely recognised his sons as individuals at all.'[87] Not having grown up under the full force of Augustus's impressive personality, Amaryllis was able to cope better with him as an adult, and perhaps Augustus recognised this. He had written to her before one family weekend, 'I think your company is indispensable to the preservation of my sanity.' But their time together was too short; Amaryllis had had barely thirteen years to make up for almost a quarter of a century of being fatherless.

Augustus's memorial service was held on 12 January 1962 in St Martin-in-the-Fields. Rupert Hart-Davis described the event in a letter to George Lyttleton. 'Apart from an abnormally high ratio of beards to pews, it was all immensely decorous and tasteful, and might have been in honour of any ambassador or social dignitary. A crowd of gypsies on a mountain-top, with plenty of wine and girls, would have been nearer the mark . . . Many of AJ's children and grand-children were there, and I wondered how many illegitimate ones . . . Did you know that Peter Fleming's mother had a child of his? A pretty girl called Amaryllis, with his red hair and Mrs F's features . . . Now she is a cellist of, I suppose, thirty-seven, very good-looking and withdrawn. The most moving – the *only* moving – part of yesterday's service was when she suddenly appeared in the choir, looking very young and slim in black, with flaming red hair, carrying her cello, on which she played some unaccompanied Bach – rather too much I thought.'[88]

Amaryllis was struck by the cold of the church, which seeped from the stone floor into her cello, and by David Cecil squawking nervously like a chicken as he made his address.

SIXTEEN

Treasures in Venice

Although Augustus was dead, his presence rumbled on through the early Sixties. Christie's held two large studio sales and an appeal was launched to raise money for a bronze statue. At the invitation of Vivien Leigh, who had sat for Augustus in 1942 and was a member of the appeal committee, Amaryllis agreed to organise a fund-raising concert. It was a grand affair, held at the Royal Academy in the presence of the Queen Mother, and included the Amadeus Quartet playing music by Haydn and Mozart with Amaryllis joining them for Schubert's Quintet in C Major. But Amaryllis was shocked to find that while she had been invited to the subsequent dinner, the Amadeus Quartet had not. 'What, those little Jews with the Queen Mother?' said the Secretary of the Academy. His words were a sour reminder of the prejudice and snobbery Augustus had so despised.

During the Twenties Augustus had settled on Jelly d'Aranyi as the perfect model for a violin-playing portrait to make a pair with his Suggia masterpiece. Jelly, although famous, was penniless, and her mother had run her up a red dress and matching knickers. 'As Jelly was taking her position,' wrote her biographer, 'she felt an ominous slackening round the waist and the worst had happened. Fortunately John was at that moment called to the telephone, and before he returned she had them in her handbag.'[89] Nothing came of the sittings

198

save a few sketches, but in 1962 there was an echo of the incident during one of Amaryllis's many lunch-hour recitals. 'While I was playing the button burst on my knickers and when I stood up, to my horror, they dropped to my ankles. I stepped out of them and scooped them up on the end of my bow. I was almost incapable with laughter but the *frightfully* English audience looked the other way. When I came back on there was violent applause and I had to play an encore knowing that the whole audience knew I had no knickers on!' Eve was amused to hear of it. 'I think you should wear short pants and keep them on!' she wrote from Monte Carlo. 'Shall I try and send you some? For concerts I mean.'

It was good of Eve to remember her daughter, for her attentions were almost entirely devoted to the preservation of the Marquess of Winchester. She had always said she did Monty a power of good. Under oath she had stated that this irreligious aristocrat had become a keen churchgoer since he met her and that after a period in her care his doctor had pronounced him 'twenty years younger than the last time he saw him'. Possibly there was substance to her statement, for, on 8 June 1961, aged 98 years and 221 days, the Marquess of Winchester tottered into the *Guinness Book of Records* as the oldest peer in history. Alas, he had little time to enjoy the glory. He died in Monte Carlo the following year on 28 June, within spitting distance of his one hundredth birthday. Once again, Eve went into mourning.

There was consternation among the Fleming brothers, none of whom wanted anything more to do with Monty, so Amaryllis was deputed to represent the family at his funeral. When Peter rang she protested that she had not the time nor the money nor any black clothes. 'Make the time,' he insisted. 'I'll pay the fare. Wear scarlet.' So, bundling up her darkest clothes, she went.

On the first day Eve intercepted a glance between her bored chauffeur and her equally bored daughter, which led to Vivaldi's immediate dismissal. Then Amaryllis discovered that her mother wanted her to sleep in Monty's old bed, complete with its hole in the mattress which had been constructed specially for the incontinent Marquess. She refused point-blank, and a camp-bed was swiftly produced. The next day, Eve took exception to Amaryllis's clothes, which, although dark, were not sufficiently so. From her closet she produced an oversized costume in perdition black, which she strung around her daughter. Then they marched solemnly to the funeral. Amaryllis could scarcely contain her giggles as the vicar eulogised Monty's generosity to the poor of Monte Carlo and his magnificent achievement in 'nearly winning the Grand National'. After the service he pressed Amaryllis's hand between his own. 'I know how you must feel!' he commiserated in hushed tones. 'I don't think you possibly could,' Amaryllis murmured back. The next day she flew home, vowing never to return.

Meanwhile Paul had temporarily abandoned his dealing to pursue the research which had long fascinated him: untangling the confusion of names, dates and places which surrounded the history of Venetian makers. He arrived early in 1962 and immediately began delving into the Curia – the church archives – which soon yielded valuable information. It was an unexplored mine which had never been visited during its 160-year existence. The privilege of working alone all day in the Curia possessed him, as every day he uncovered at least one stunning piece of news. His enthusiasm was infectious. Within a few months he had obtained financial backing from Rembert Wurlitzer, the wealthy and erudite son of juke-box tycoon Rudolf Wurlitzer, acknowledged as the world's leading authority on stringed instruments. One day Wurlitzer joined him in the Curia and browsed through a volume of 1640. A name caught his interest and within a minute he had discovered no less than four makers. The finds were overwhelming.

Paul's original plan had been to produce a facts-only catalogue of Venetian makers from 1685 to 1760. But the unexplored depths of the Curia resisted such simplification. One day he discovered Vivaldi's date of birth, which was heralded as a triumph by the Italian press. On another, he found the ancient Venetian unit of measurement carved into a church pillar, confirming that the Venetian inch was different from the Cremonese inch, which in turn led him into a detailed investigation of Venetian proportion. Out of the archives came a welter of fascinating titbits: Tintoretto's bill for painting San Rocco; a lawsuit against Titian for slipshod work; another against Vivaldi's nephew for sleeping with both a mother and her daughter; a number of splendid lies by Gofriller; and a host of court cases all recorded, for the sake of economy, in miniature hand.

Into Paul's magnifying glass sprang the minutiae of Venetian daily life, the more ridiculous aspects of which soon reached Amaryllis: the husband who ascribed his impotence to his wife's wind; the man who married a hermaphrodite by mistake; the priest who got three years for serenading outside his mistress's house; the teacher who held masturbation rallies with his class, then assaulted one of their mothers; the groom who found he was about to marry the public whore; and the sad tale of a noble who married his housemaid but in such secrecy that no one believed him.

Letters flowed in a steady stream between the two. Whether in Waterloo Station or the Curia, a bar in Leicester Square or a brasserie in Brussels, on the train to Hull or the train to Florence, they found time to scribble a note. The extent of

Paul's research was reflected in his postmarks: Cremona, Florence, Trieste, Milan, Rome, Frankfurt, Heidelberg. And Amaryllis's increasingly busy schedule was reflected in hers. By now she was getting concerts all over Britain, Scandinavia and the Continent, interspersed with visits to Fryern and Monte Carlo, summer schools and pilgrimages to Prades.

Since her time with Casals she had often attended his annual festival. 'I *wish* I were coming with you,' Augustus wrote when she set off with Yvonne Hales in 1951. His presence might not have been welcomed by the local taxi driver, who took such a violent fancy to Amaryllis that his girlfriend personally saw her on to the train home. The following year she drove herself, this time with André Mangeot, but due to the traffic they were forced to make an overnight stop. The hotels were as full as the roads, but a helpful night porter came to their rescue. 'Go to the square by the railway, and when you reach the third house on the right knock three times.' After paying the proprietor in advance – '*Et puis je ne regarde pas ce que vous faites*' – they found themselves in a seedy *maison de passe* where 'the walls were stained with squashed mosquitoes, and all night long you could hear footsteps tramping up and down the stairs. In the morning André brought me a cup of coffee made with God-knows-what and said, "Whatever you do you must not go to the loo".' But the festival was as wonderful as ever.

Due to Prades's growing popularity it had been decided to do a recording – on 78 rpm, which allowed no editing and needed a perfect complete take – and Amaryllis was invited to sit in on the Brahms B Major trio with Casals, Isaac Stern and Myra Hess. 'All was fine until the scherzo, in which Casals made a very obvious wrong entry. They finished recording the whole piece and Casals immediately started packing up his cello. Stern went up to him and said, "Maestro, I don't think we can leave that mistake in the scherzo. Would you mind if we played it again?" Looking rather disgruntled, Casals took his cello out and sat down. Off they went and the same thing happened. During the third take Casals came in right but Stern's E string squeaked. Another try and it squeaked again. Finally all went well until the last chord was obliterated by the church clock's chimes. After each attempt Casals seemed quite unmoved by the various imperfections and always started putting his cello away until he was reluctantly persuaded to sit down.'

The advent of recording technology, however antiquated, changed Prades's impromptu charm. The festival was soon absorbed by the very world whose pro-Franco attitude Casals had rebelled against; by 1962, when Amaryllis drove down once again with André, the place was swamped. 'The artists' room is like the crowd at a bull-fight,' she wrote to Paul. 'Every man for himself and choose your own weapons for the attack. The church is packed out and hermetically sealed with no ventilation of any kind. One sits like a sweating sardine and the stench is only to be compared to having one's head under the bedclothes when you've let off a real clanger. I take it that's how the audience expresses its appreciation as there's no clapping.'

André, now seventy-nine, was becoming a bit difficult, and refused to visit anything other than a concert hall or a restaurant. Casals, however, was in excellent form. 'His intonation is still, at eighty-six, so superior to any one hears that it goes straight to the heart, however long the piece.' One night he sat up with Amaryllis discussing his conviction that Mozart had written a cello concerto.

Work was Amaryllis's overriding concern, but whenever engagements permitted she went to Venice to be with Paul. He had unearthed a backwater *pensione* which offered bed, breakfast, dinner and wine for the equivalent of just £1 a day, and whose proprietors welcomed *il professore* and *la signorina* as members of the family. The son Giorgio became their constant companion. A lanky, tweed-clad adolescent, he brought them breakfast in bed, helped Paul in the archives – having quickly learned to read seventeenth-century Italian script, a bit of Latin and the dialect of that period – and when Amaryllis came down with a bad back he rowed her through the canals in a hired *sandalo*, a downmarket version of the gondola. At the time she was having a special cello chair made, and the regular journeys for 'fittings' took on a nightmarish quality. They sat for hours in canal jams. They got hopelessly lost as Amaryllis directed Giorgio from a sketchy tourist map. And at every corner her much-practised cries of 'Oeh!' brought forth only a torrent of abuse from gondoliers who thought Giorgio was stealing their trade.

The end to this convenient arrangement came one autumn morning when Amaryllis was woken by screams and yells from the kitchen. Initially she was unperturbed: every day started with what sounded like a full-scale battle as the family discussed the evening menu. This, however, was something different. Descending in her dressing-gown she found the bailiffs removing the entire contents of the kitchen and dining room, with their next stop the bedrooms. Amaryllis joined the fight. She told the bailiffs she would report them to a high-ranking friend in the government at Rome. They loaded the ovens on to their boat. She threatened to tell the British Consul. They shrugged, and counted the cutlery. Finally she made the proprietors cram as many tables and chairs as they could into her room, then locked the door and refused to let the bailiffs in. Amazingly, it worked. But the damage was done. The family carried on gamely but by the winter, when Paul and Amaryllis had to leave their bedroom doors open to catch the warmth from a stove in the hallway, it was clearly time to move.

Paul's new destination was the Pensione Seguso, whose proprietors soon warmed to *il professore*. Indeed, everybody warmed to the man who had become an all-season fixture in Venetian life. Every time Amaryllis visited he seemed to have met someone new, ranging from tourists such as Lady Epstein to locals such as Giovanni Missana, a wind player in the Banda Municipale, and Dom Cisellini, a monk who worked at the Instituto Cini and was in charge of the Vivaldi archives. Dom Cisellini spoke 'the most beautiful Italian I've ever heard', had a large black beard and slept in a room covered in Giotto murals, which, alas, Amaryllis was forbidden to see. 'Only Signor Paul,' he explained apologetically before consoling her with the news that if she thought it was wonderful sleeping in a roomful of great art she should try it in winter; fires were forbidden lest they damage the paint, and Dom Cisellini accordingly froze to his bunk.

Paul's attraction was as much visceral as intellectual or emotional. He had an inexplicable force, an energy that gave him healing hands, ruined most watches he wore, enabled him to find sources in the Curia by means of a hazel divining twig, and communicated itself clearly to those he met. Amaryllis had much the same sort of energy. She too had healing hands and a vigour that was felt by all, especially Paul, to whom she was his 'darling activator'. They were undeniably meant for each other. But while the subject of marriage was broached, it never got beyond idle chat. To Amaryllis their lives seemed fine as they were. Paul, too, had reservations. Children, however, were a different matter. From a sixteenth-century manual on palmistry Paul read himself a hand foretelling two wives, no money and a host of children. Amaryllis had no objections, nor did her relations.

'Do you like babies?' Augustus once wrote. 'I adore them. If you should ever feel the urge to produce one just give me a nudge and I will do my best even if it took me all my nights to collaborate successfully. Such an experiment might well prove more effective than catching you on the hop with a paint brush.' Ian, too, had urged her on. When she asked who would look after the child when she was away, he dismissed the problem with a wave of the hand. 'Peter and I will give up gin for a week,' he said airily. 'That'll cover a year's worth of nannying.'

SEVENTEEN

High Slow Hymns

While Amaryllis and Paul were discussing their future in Venice, Eve was getting restless in Monte Carlo. Monty's death had brought her last great enterprise to an end and life as a tax exile was losing its appeal. She had nothing to do, nobody to talk to, not even a violin to play, having sold her Strad to concentrate on Monty. She was old, she was tired and she wanted to come home. So, in the spring of 1963, she summoned Ian to escort her back to London.

'She is convinced that she is bankrupt and all her sons millionaires,' wrote Annie Fleming to Evelyn Waugh. 'They live in terror of disinheritance. She hired a room for Ian in the basement of the annexe of the Metropole Hotel, no daylight and much traffic, and such daylight as penetrated was obliterated at 8 a.m. by the parking of his mother's Rolls-Royce outside his basement window, it stood there all day in case she felt like a breath of fresh air. [Ian] did not dare improve his living conditions in case Mama thought he was rich.'[90] Come the morning of departure Ian was horrified to find that Eve expected him to share a sleeper and a packed dinner consisting of 'a dead partridge and half a bottle of *vin de pays*'.[91] He quickly rearranged matters and they left for London in separate compartments, one of which contained Eve and her very heavy jewel case, the other Ian and his mother's gall-bladder X-rays. Far behind, in the luggage van, fourteen cabin trunks bearing the initials E. B. Ste. C. F. thundered northward through the night.

For all Eve's bravura, the Winchester trial had taken a great deal out of her. At one point she had written to Augustus that she was 'in the last depths of despair and can't clamber out', adding, 'No news from A – she hasn't written since wanting more money.' Now, her arteries were hardening, her gall bladder was failing and the first signs of mental deterioration were apparent. It was a weaker, mellower Eve who settled at the Grosvenor House Hotel and tried to collect the strands of her old life. She took up the violin again, using a Ceruti sold to her by Paul – coincidentally the selfsame Ceruti that had launched his dealing career – and visited such acquaintances as she could muster. But most of her old friends were dead or dying and if she had ever wanted a reconciliation with her siblings it was now too late. Both Ivor and Harky had succumbed to cirrhosis and Kathleen was petrifying in Chelsea Cloisters, a slab-faced apartment block in Sloane Avenue of which another inmate, Matthew Smith, had said, 'Once in the Cloisters, you never come out.' Nor did she, on the grounds that she had no suitable clothes, contenting herself with phone calls to the outside world until her death in 1967.

Eve's existence was a pale shadow of her former life. There were no statesmen to entertain, no staff to command, no 'exquisite passion' to set her spirit free; little to do but make doctors' appointments and cross out names in her address book. Her sons had no intention of being sucked back into her influence, her daughters-in-law disliked her, and she had been away too long to cement any relationship with her grand-children. All that remained was Amaryllis. So, tentatively, she tried to patch up matters with her difficult daughter.

Once again she was too late. Amaryllis was blind to the new Eve, and saw her acts of kindness as mere exceptions that proved the rule. She dismissed every peace offering in scathing letters to Paul. Eve ordered flowers for a concert: 'Mum sent a bloody great coffin of flowers from Moyses Stevens which I'm dragging back without opening!!' Eve got on well with Derek Kessler: 'Mum was here and told him all about her ancestors while he had a drink!!' Eve gave her a pen: 'Mum's fucking pen's given out – what's the use . . .' Eve admired her Dodd bow: 'perhaps because it's gold-mounted and a gift'. Eve gave her money to buy some of Augustus's pictures at Christie's second sale of his studio contents: 'I bought the enclosed at the Christie's sale on Friday. It's called the 3 Horsemen of the Apocalypse . . . *Also* 3 little pen and ink drawings (in one lot) of a black and a white girl tit to tit, *ever* so naked and humorous . . . Mum was so horrified at the sight of them that she gave me £100 towards the other one so long as I didn't buy those dreadful things . . . I haven't done too badly – as long as we remember to hide them when she comes here!!' Eve pretended not to notice her daughter's obvious attachment to Paul: 'She was gazing at the washing on the line today, which included 2 pairs of your underpants and a vest. I was frantically thinking up a good story to account for them, such as belonging to Sir Edward . . . but luckily she said nothing.'

There was nothing Eve could say about anything that anyone would listen to; her time had passed. Shortly after her return she went to visit friends in Mexico City – where divorces, Monty had once assured her, were 'good the world over' – and had a stroke, falling head-first against the corner of a glass-topped table. When she awoke it was with concussion and a conviction that her hosts were after her jewels. She fled and, somehow managing to get herself, her baggage and her jewel case on to a plane, arrived at Grosvenor

House, from where she called first a doctor and then Amaryllis.

After a partial recovery, she moved into a flat in Grosvenor Square, a dreary abode looking on to a light well, whose only advantage was its postal code and which was furnished with a few sticks of serviceable furniture Richard and Amaryllis had bought at auction. She began to wander, not mentally but physically, and after an exhausting period during which she spent day and night hammering picture hooks into the wall she was put on tranquillisers and given twenty-four-hour nursing. A succession of pretty young Australian nurses came to Grosvenor Square, only to be sacked when their patient, in a lucid moment, became uncomfortably aware of the contrast she presented. She settled on a solid, plain, English matron, who, because she had a bungalow in Brighton, suggested it would be beneficial for Eve to get some sea air. Eve agreed, and before she left wrote her daughter a short, shaky note: 'My Darling Amaryllis, If I die first I shall always be waiting for you (if I am allowed to) so that you shall not be alone by any chance – I want to do everything for you to make you happy always both here and in the next world. I love and adore you.' Then she was chauffeured down to Brighton, where a room awaited in her last Metropole Hotel.

The night of 25 July 1964 was hot. The temperature outside was in the eighties and in the Albert Hall, where Amaryllis was playing the Saint-Saëns Concerto in A minor at the first night of the Proms, it was even hotter. First-aiders picked their way through the crowds to help those who had fainted and on the conductor's podium Malcolm Sargent was sweating so heavily that his glasses had become opaque. This gave Amaryllis some pleasure for he had just signalled the orchestra to play louder, thus drowning the cello part. It was the last joy she got that evening. After the performance she phoned

Brighton from the artists' room and was told by Eve's nurse to come as quickly as possible.

When she arrived at the Metropole, her mother had already sunk into a coma. She rallied briefly. 'You're marvellous, Ma!' Amaryllis said. 'No,' whispered Eve, 'it's you that's marvellous.' They were her last words before relapsing into unconsciousness. The end was clearly in sight. Would it be possible, wondered the nurse as she held the oxygen mask in place, to have Eve's saucepans?

Eve lingered until the following morning, when, with Peter, Richard and Amaryllis by her bedside, she died. For all of them, particularly Peter, whose face had crumpled into utter misery when he entered the room, it was hard to believe that the woman who had dominated their lives was gone. Eve had had many failings; she had also had virtues. The combination had moulded her children's characters. Whether they liked it or not, they had been taught how to succeed: Peter was the elder statesman of travel writing, Ian had created Bond, the name on everybody's lips, Richard was managing director of his grandfather's merchant bank, and Amaryllis was one of Britain's foremost cellists.

Richard stayed to make the necessary arrangements while Peter drove Amaryllis home. On the way back they stopped to break the news to Ian, who was recuperating after a bout of pleurisy in the Dudley Hotel, Hove. As soon as they entered his room Amaryllis was struck by the aura of death. Ian had always put a cheerful face on illness. After his first heart attack, in 1961, he had sent her a postcard: 'Don't believe everything you read in the papers. I'm having a delicious rest surrounded by beautiful nurses and when in a few weeks I can "go for a drive" it will be to you. Being "ill" is heaven!' On the other side, in a touch of wry humour, was a picture of a skull. This time was no exception. He joked and bantered as usual, but the pretence was painfully transparent. He looked what he was: a man with only weeks to live.

Against his doctor's advice Ian made the journey to see his mother buried at Nettlebed. The funeral was drab and uncomfortable. The organist, despite Amaryllis's entreaty to play the hymns low and fast, played them high and slow. And at the subsequent wake at Merrimoles, Peter's house on the old Joyce Grove estate, Ian remained silent throughout, holding Amaryllis's hand in a fierce grip from beginning to end. He looked dreadful, drained of energy, his face suffused a deep purple. Amaryllis could barely stand his distress. When it was time to go, she asked if he wanted to come home with her. 'I can't,' he replied, then he drove off with Annie. It was the last Amaryllis saw of him. On 12 August he had a fatal heart attack.

His funeral was held at his country home, Sevenhampton, where Annie, distraught and on medication, caused unwitting offence by offering Amaryllis the photograph which Ian had kept by his bed of her playing the cello. Then Peter and Richard went to Scotland, leaving their half-sister to arrange the memorial service. Accompanied by Derek Kessler – afterwards she could not remember quite why she had inveigled him to come – she set out to find a suitable church in London. Perhaps foolishly, she chose a Sunday. The vicars pounced at the sight of new faces in their congregations and when they heard what Amaryllis was looking for their eyes lit up. But nowhere struck the right chord, and as her sherry consumption rose, her heart sank. It was not until she reached St Bartholomews, near Smithfield meat market, that she found what she wanted. The church was old, one of the oldest in London. It had atmosphere. Its vicar barely knew of Ian, let alone that he had died. And he had been to almost all of Amaryllis's concerts. This was the place.

The service, on 15 September, was packed, though the hordes she had anticipated when organising a police cordon never materialised, and Amaryllis, perched with her cello in the organ loft, was terrified. It was a deeply emotional occasion. Peter read the lesson in a trembling voice, with tears rolling down his cheeks, William Plomer delivered the address, the choir sang Thomas Tallis's Lamentations and Amaryllis played Bach's Sarabande in C minor. Then it was time to pay the choir, whose fee was £100, and the agent, whose cut was ten per cent. 'What's ten per cent of £100?' pondered Richard, who would shortly become chairman of Robert Fleming & Co.

Afterwards Peter wrote her a short letter. 'Darling Am – I can't thank you adequately for all you did today for Ian and all of us; but I must thank you. You're a girl in a million.'

EIGHTEEN

The Spirit of Baroque

The first four years of the Sixties had been hard for Amaryllis. In that time she had lost father, mother, brother, and two old friends: Hugo Pitman and Jimmy James had both died in 1963. But the impact was less devastating than it might have been. Throughout her youth she had striven for self-sufficiency. Not even the discovery of her origins and her subsequent freedom from Eve could dent that hard shell of individuality. Moreover, having pinned her identity so firmly to the cello, she had rendered herself almost untouchable. Family and friends would come and go, but music was eternal. She had every defence she needed against bereavement. And as Paul dug ever deeper into the Curia she discovered yet another: Bach's Suites.

Paul's research had all the fascination of a musical whodunnit, centred increasingly on composers as much as makers. Questions were answered which led to yet more questions as to what early composers had been trying to convey. Over hundreds of years that original intent had been lost, with scores being rewritten to suit tastes, to enhance the wallets and reputations of re-writers or simply to replace destroyed originals. Worst affected were the great Baroque composers Bach and Vivaldi, with Handel and Purcell close behind. To Amaryllis all this would have been relatively unimportant were it not that Bach had created the finest cello works known to humankind. As Margaret Campbell wrote in her introduction to *The Great Cellists*, 'During my researches I have read a number of books, waded through a great deal of correspondence and consulted endless press reviews spanning three centuries. I have listened to hundreds of recordings and have attended as many concerts. One overriding conclusion I have reached is that the *raison d'être* of every cellist is the collection of J. S. Bach's Six Solo Suites. It is the cornerstone of the repertoire and many admit they could spend the rest of their lives studying and playing them.'[92]

Given their importance the Suites had enjoyed a strangely subdued existence. Following their creation in the early decades of the eighteenth century, they had been virtually ignored by the musical world on the grounds that they were both too demanding and too dull for most audiences. Occasionally a player might slip a small section of a Suite into a larger, more impressive recital – as a concert encore, say – but on the whole they were seen as mere technical exercises. Not until the beginning of the twentieth century, when Casals brought them to the attention of the general public, did that view begin to change. Yet even in the Thirties they were still treated as studies that were 'good for you', not as something worth performing. It took another twenty years for them to become firmly established as the acme of a performing cellist's art.

But whatever the prevailing opinion of Bach's Solo Suites, whether as studies or music in their own right, they were still considered fair game by re-writers. The first published edition came out in 1825, followed by at least twenty-six other editions, each with its own phrasing, bowing and fingering. Two were even given a piano accompaniment. Amaryllis's experience of the Suites had been moulded by nineteenth-century styles and techniques: 'The leading solo cellists had inherited that firmly in their heads and hands,' she explained in a BBC broadcast, 'and were simply not interested in playing earlier works in any way differently. That was how they succeeded so they saw no reason for change, and we followed.' But in the early Sixties she looked for the truth that lay beneath the Romantic gloss.

She found herself in a musical cul-de-sac. Of Bach's original vision there remained nothing save the Anna Magdalena manuscript, which had been copied by his wife and contained a number of ambiguities 'probably because she was cooking the potatoes for her twenty children at the time'. Amaryllis resolved to unravel the threads of later interpretations and, if possible, to re-weave them into their original whole.

Of all musicians, harpsichordists know most about Baroque music, not by choice but by necessity, little having been written for the instrument since it was superseded by the piano in the eighteenth century. Paul introduced Amaryllis to his friend Basil Lam, who was both a harpsichordist and an eminent musicologist. Musicologists are reckoned a sober-minded breed, but Lam was unlike any Amaryllis had encountered. He drove a motorbike, had a keen sense of humour and 'had nightmares that he was a BBC producer, only to wake up and find that he was'. He liked to arrive unannounced at Old Church Street at all times of the day to show her his latest find. 'Look at this!' he cried one evening, as he stomped excitedly into a dinner party, wearing boots, leathers and helmet. In his hand he clutched a piece of paper on which he had copied out a few bars from a Beethoven Quartet – the MS version which had been printed wrongly in all subsequent editions.

Lam showed her Baroque harpsichord music, and played

through some of Bach's keyboard pieces, and with his help she began to re-decipher the Anna Magdalena manuscript. As Amaryllis soon discovered, reconstituting Baroque music was no simple task. First there was the problem of authenticating the slurs. Then there was the theoretical possibility of alternative tunings, for the music had been written in an age when scordatura, or distuning, was common and rarely marked on the score. To cap it all, the music may have been intended for a five-stringed instrument rather than the more popular four-stringed. In the case of Bach's Suites two of these problems were eliminated, for the composer had not only indicated scordatura for the Fifth Suite but had annotated the Sixth as being specifically '*à cinque cordes*'. Nevertheless, the slurs alone were hard enough, and even when all the detective work had been done there remained one stumbling block: Bach's Suites had been written for a sound which no longer existed.

Since the first true cellos appeared in the sixteenth century, the instrument had undergone dramatic mutations. It had originally been designed as a bass instrument used mainly to boost the harpsichord – a clattering creature, popularly compared to a skeleton dancing on a tin roof, which had trouble competing with the human voice, let alone a violin. Large, with a short fingerboard, no end-pin and four or five gut strings, depending on requirements, these early cellos rested between the knees and were played with an outward-curving bow. In the late seventeenth century, however, when the cello's solo potential was realised, makers went to work to create slimmer, shorter, more manageable models on which players could reach higher positions with ease. Along the way it was found that most notes available on the fifth string could be reached on the fourth, and because fewer strings made for easier bowing it was little time before four-stringed instruments became the norm. The changeover from bass to solo use was a major step forward, and during the late eighteenth and early nineteenth centuries most of the outsize instruments were reduced to conform with the smaller patterns. But the cello received its hardest evolutionary jolt with the arrival of the modern piano in the mid nineteeth century. Against this newcomer's volume, and in the larger auditoria through which it now swelled, the cello was no longer a match. Even the great 'Golden' Stradivarii, legendary for their carrying power, were swamped.

Once again the makers and repairers got busy. The cello's body, already reduced from its original bulk, stayed the same but its 'set-up' was radically altered. The neck was lengthened and angled back to cope with a higher pitch, while the bridge was raised to give a tighter, more brilliant tone. An end-pin was added, allowing stronger strokes to be used. And following the invention by François Tourte of an inward-curving, rather than an outward-curving, bow, cellists had yet more power at their disposal. By the twentieth century, with the development of metal strings, the cello had seemingly reached its apogee. From a soft, fat instrument designed for intimate spaces it had become a lean, powerful aggressor capable of holding its own in the most cavernous hall. And in the process it had lost – like the scores themselves – the true soul of Baroque.

Amaryllis therefore decided to convert her Amati to five strings. Derek Kessler, who had taken such trouble to restore it as a four-stringer, began painstakingly to undo his earlier work. Many musicians scoffed, for despite evidence to the contrary it was widely believed that five-stringed cellos had never existed; some claimed that Bach's Sixth Suite had not been written for the cello at all but for the viola pomposa, an overgrown viola for whose existence there was even less evidence than for a five-stringed cello. But whatever the differences of opinion, all were agreed on one fact: with nothing but guesswork to guide them Amaryllis and Kessler faced an uphill struggle. 'It was terribly complicated. For a start it needed a wider neck and then we found that a normal-shaped bridge acted as a mute. I had about fifteen bridges cut before one worked. Then it was a question of finding the top E string. All the gut strings I tried broke. I tried a Gamba D string tuned up to E and that broke too. I tried harp strings. Nothing worked. Finally I had to settle for a metal string made to order by Thomastik in Vienna but even that wasn't ideal. It sounded that little bit too different from the others.'

After much trial and error they achieved a set-up which, if not perfect, was at least playable. But there still remained the problem of finding a five-string head, an item which, like the instrument it had once served, was almost the stuff of legend. A number of makers offered to carve a new one, but were prevented from doing so by more urgent work. This was fortunate because, after one of her many performances in Brussels, Amaryllis went for a drink at the home of Carlo Jadot, an old friend who had once led the Ysaÿe Chamber Orchestra. There, on his mantelpiece, was an original five-string head. It was Flemish, carved in the shape of a lion's head, and he had picked it up in a flea market for next to nothing. The two dickered back and forth for hours; the more Amaryllis offered, the fonder Jadot became of his fireplace ornament. Eventually Paul came to the rescue with a couple of bows Jadot could not resist. Amaryllis got the head and Derek Kessler grafted it on to the Amati.

When Kessler had finished, Amaryllis was the only cellist in the world – and the first in maybe two centuries – to be playing on a five-stringed Italian original. The challenge began to obsess her. 'Have been going nuts on the 5-string cello – can't tear myself off it,' she wrote to Paul. 'It doesn't sound *right* yet – strings need gauging and I'm sure sound-post isn't in the right place, and maybe bridge is wrong, but all that will have to wait for you. The *quality* is there, but something too gamba-esque about it at the moment. Am getting the hang of it quicker than I expected and this morning learnt nearly all the Bach D Major Gamba Sonata on it, which I think will be a tremendous success with the jangle-box.' Soon everything was coming together: 'Have just collapsed into bed after fetching the 5-string cello from Derek. He's made a new bridge and sound-post, end-pin, nut, and planed the finger-board a bit, but the C still buzzes. However it does sound marvellous, and even Derek had to admit it.'

It was some time before she mastered the art of playing with an extra string, and occasionally she would forget in mid-piece. But as her confidence increased she built up a small repertoire comprising Bach's Sixth Suite, his three Gamba Sonatas with harpsichord and Schubert's Arpeggione Sonata – written, aptly, for another instrument which no longer existed, the six-stringed, guitar-shaped arpeggione which had thrived only briefly after its invention in Vienna in 1823. She recorded the Schubert with pianist Geoffrey Parsons, did recitals – 'Tunes ran off her bow like honey,' wrote Joan Chissell after one performance – and, through Basil Lam, got a number of broadcasts. It was these last that brought her to the attention of music scholar Arnold Goldsbrough.

Then in his seventies, Goldsbrough had been studying Baroque music for the previous forty years. An organist, conductor and harpsichord player, he had long since quit the ratrace of London's musical scene to continue his studies in the more tranquil surroundings of Worcestershire. He was not unknown to Amaryllis; in 1949 he had played a concert with her at Whistler's House in Cheyne Walk, and had arranged a Purcell Violin Sonata for cello which she later played in Paris at Ashley Clarke's apartment. He also conducted the Goldsbrough Ensemble and the Goldsbrough Orchestra (which became the English Chamber Orchestra) and gave occasional talks on the BBC. He was a man of high standards: once, having been invited to speak on recordings of Bach's Suites by several of the world's most famous cellists, he arrived at Broadcasting House and while rereading his notes in the lobby realised that there was nobody whose interpretation he believed in and that he had nothing to say about their performances. He put away his notes and caught the next train home.

It came as all the greater a compliment, therefore, when he wrote to Amaryllis saying that her broadcast was the best performance of a Bach Suite he had ever heard and urging her to come down to Worcestershire to discuss the music with him. A meeting was arranged for the autumn of 1963, when she was playing the Elgar Concerto in Worcester Cathedral. Goldsbrough's enthusiasm burst forth like fireworks. 'Good,' he wrote. 'When you come will you bring any editions you may have of the Suites, including if you have it the Anna Magdalena facsimile – I have one on loan but it should be returned to my cellist friend who owns it. The news about the 5-stringer is excellent! Will you have a flatter bridge too – it can't be like the one on the Bach cellos because of the modern fingerboard but it can be less curved, can't it? Those rasping chords are alien to the spirit of the music, and to hear a highly sentimental slow – and in a sense beautiful – performance of a Sarabande punctuated by great walloping chords is ludicrous. A pianist, if you like, or the clavichord or hpd. player does not lam into the harmonic background like the fiddlers and the cellists, does he?'

It was only with difficulty that she evaded a working breakfast, but the day that followed was overwhelming. Goldsbrough got more and more excited, pulling score after score from his shelves until they were surrounded by a sea of Bach. Every suggestion made by one sparked off ideas in the other. Occasionally Goldsbrough dashed to the piano or harpsichord for an illustration. It was a meeting of minds and when they parted it was with firm promises to go through all the Suites at a later date. Goldsbrough was left in 'a state of excitement, rare even by his standards', according to his friend John Engleheart. 'He talked and talked about their day together. It had been evident to me that the affair of the Cello Suites at Broadcasting House had left him negative and depressed, but now her way with them and the interplay of his ideas and hers at last reinforced the opinions he had developed and cherished.' But due to Amaryllis's busy schedule their later meeting never took place. Dates were pencilled in, inked in, crossed out, put back a week here, a month there. Then, on 15 December 1964, Goldsbrough died.

In the following year there was a series of commemorative concerts at which Amaryllis played a tributary First Suite. But the true memorial to Goldsbrough lay in her dedication to Baroque music, which, after that single day at Worcester, had become a compulsive passion. She wrote to Goldsbrough's wife, 'Arnold has become almost a god for me . . . At last I had found someone who had not only the knowledge but also the feeling and the vitality and the capacity for conveying the essence of Bach, and at last I felt capable of understanding . . . As long as I live I shall never forget that day and everything I learnt. And it will, I hope, bear fruit.'

Her hope was realised. Equipped with her five-stringer, she became the first person this century (and possibly the first person ever) to give a London performance of Bach's Sixth

Suite in its intended form. She was also the first to play the Fifth with its original tuning. Bach became the centre of her life. When she played in a series of chamber-music evenings held at Heal's department store in 1965, Basil Lam described the composer's enduring appeal in a programme note. 'Although Bach did not invent the unaccompanied cello suite ... he raised this seemingly unpromising medium to the highest level, where the enforced economy of a single line of melody with an occasional supporting chord produces great art comparable to such things as, say, Rembrandt's etchings, where the suggestion of a supreme imagination far surpasses the full statements of lesser talents.'

'Her ideas on Bach are absolutely fantastic,' claims Margaret Moncrieff. 'Unlike so many Casals pupils she doesn't try and play Bach like Casals, which has been fatal for so many cellists. Her playing is very vital, very clear. She is one of the few people who knows a great deal about the theory and is nevertheless able to play the works as music. Many of those in the authenticity brigade know so much about the music but play with about as much feeling as a suet pudding. It's one thing to know what strokes to use, another to know how to use them. Amaryllis is very high up on the list. Some of her best qualities come out in playing Bach. But she's not a big player. Although her playing is alive, coloured and passionate, decibel-wise it's not a very big sound. There is more an aristocratic quality to her playing.' And like a good aristocrat Amaryllis decided to pass on some of her wealth.

Teaching is something almost all good musicians do sooner or later, and Amaryllis was no exception. Her rebellious nature prevented her applying for a professorship at the RCM, but from the early Sixties she began taking private pupils. One was Raphael Wallfisch, only fourteen years old when he started with Amaryllis and now an accomplished performer and teacher in his own right. 'She listened incredibly intently all the time,' he recalls. 'She taught me to listen more carefully, made me aware of expressive intonation – things which had impressed her from Casals. I think she considers herself a protégée of his – intonation particularly. I always had to prepare a study every week, which was a rigorous discipline for someone still at school. She hadn't done a great deal of teaching at that time and I was aware that she was very excited about trying things out. She gave me lots of things that I don't think she'd give now to a young person – some exercises which were dreadfully boring and difficult to understand why on earth one had to do them. I don't give them to my pupils because I can see people's eyes glaze over. Ševčik particularly. But I probably learnt something and we tried out all sorts of different things. She was also thinking a lot about her own playing and the lessons were exciting, far from routine . . . She made me very aware of stylistic differences and was very particular over ornamentation. Now everyone is into Baroque, but then she was one of the few who was really interested in more authentic performance. She used gut strings for a long time, which was very unusual.'

The wisdom she handed down was partly aided by Paul's investigations. His letters, sometimes jotted down on paper napkins, revealed changes in slurs, bowings, notes and fingering that had been introduced over the ages into Baroque composers' works. But his research was getting ever slower. The first blow had come in October 1963, when Rembert Wurlitzer's death from a heart attack deprived them of a close friend and vital financial support. 'Suddenly there is a great bottomless pit under our feet,' Amaryllis wrote. A still larger chasm yawned two years later when Paul was admitted to hospital in August 1965. His health had never been good and, at forty-nine, he was assailed by thoughts of human frailty. In one dark moment he recalled the words written by Byron on his departure for Greece: 'Already I am 35! And have accomplished nothing in life.'

Paul had little time left. In the summer of 1966 he and Amaryllis spent their last holiday together in a converted convent south of Naples. Then she drove back for a concert in London and he returned to his work in Venice. That autumn she rang the Seguso to learn that Paul had been hospitalised following a serious heart attack. She flew out the same day with a leading London specialist, but nothing could be done. Paul lingered for a few days, during which Amaryllis left his side only once, to comfort Missana's wife who was dying of cancer. Then, while the specialist was explaining to his Italian colleagues, with the aid of diagrams, the full extent of their inadequacies, his patient died.

She arranged Paul's funeral through the unlikely medium of Thomas Cook, and a black gondola bearing his coffin, Amaryllis, the Seguso's night porter and Missana's daughter, Esmeralda, slipped over the waves to the Isola San Michele, Venice's island of the dead. A 'nasty little monk with dirty toe nails' said a few grudging words of prayer, then Paul was lowered into a grave in the non-Catholic cemetery. Unkempt and overgrown, with wild roses rambling down to where the sea lapped against an unwalled shore, it was the perfect resting place.

For the next week Amaryllis stayed on at the Seguso tidying up Paul's affairs. His wife Diana, and their daughter Isabella, had contacted the British consulate as soon as they heard of Paul's death and ordered his room to be locked and his belongings to be kept out of Amaryllis's grasp. Before that happened Signor Seguso allowed her to remove the ear-rings Paul had bought for her, and a cashmere sweater she had just given him – which she presented to the night porter. Then she flew back to London and slept for the first time in seven days.

The pressure of work filled the terrible gap left by Paul's death. The following day she drove down to Eastbourne for a performance of the Dvořák Concerto with the Royal Philharmonic Orchestra. Then she had to prepare for the Elgar Concerto in November under Sir Adrian Boult. In the intervening period she also had to resolve matters with Diana and Isabella Paul, both of whom were understandably bitter.

'My poor darling Amaryllis,' Dodo wrote that November, 'there is nothing adequate I can say but I send you all my love and sympathy and thank God you have something to keep you going. So glad you did see him and that you had that small holiday together. I shall always remember him. Your loving and devoted Dodo.'

NINETEEN

The Aristocrat's Progress

By the mid Sixties Amaryllis was one of the busiest cello soloists in the country and scores rustled like leaves through 137 Old Church Street. They drifted on any flat surface, piling upon chairs, tables, Paul's Venetian spinet, the kitchen dresser, windowsills. 'Going up those stairs I'd see pieces of music at each landing lying on odd bits of furniture,' Raphael Wallfisch recalls. 'I once saw the Rawsthorne Concerto – obviously just written and sent to her. And whenever she went out of the studio I'd have a surreptitious look to see what else had come in. There was an *awful* lot of music knocking about. If nothing else it taught me a great deal about repertoire.'

One item that would have caught Raphael's eye was the Walton Concerto. Completed in 1956, it had been commissioned from Sir William Walton by Piatigorsky and premièred by him in 1957. A little later Amaryllis met the composer at a party given by Yehudi Menuhin's pianist brother-in-law, Louis Kentner. Walton was keeping a low profile on the party's outskirts and when Amaryllis approached him he refused initially to say who he was, leaving her to fumble until she matched his face to a name. But as they talked she noticed he was steering her firmly round the room. 'It's all right,' he said, 'I'm not playing musical chairs. I'm just trying to avoid Lionel Tertis. I haven't spoken to him for over thirty years and

I don't intend to start now.' He explained why. Having dedicated his Viola Concerto to Tertis, Walton sent him a copy for his approval. It came back by return post with a note saying it was unplayable. The Concerto was premièred in the 1928 Proms by Paul Hindemith and had since gone from strength to strength.

Amaryllis and Walton had immediate rapport, so much so that he invited her to give the second British performance of his work. It was a daunting prospect; the piece had been written very much for (and some would say very much by) Piatigorsky. This giant of a Russian, born in 1903, was one of the most colourful cellists of his time and during the Concerto's eight-month gestation he had left a significant mark on Walton's work. Afterwards the composer wrote to thank him for his patience during 'my darker moments, and some were very dark indeed. And I can assure you that without the confidence and urge with which you inspired me, I very much doubt if I should have finished, at any rate in time . . .'[93] The result was, as Frank Howes wrote in his study of Walton's music, 'the most intellectually challenging' of all English cello concertos this century. The second movement in particular, a scherzo *allegro appassionato*, he compared to 'an eel out of water, a large electric eel, and the only thing to do with it is to cut it up into lengths'.[94] Maybe Piatigorsky cut it into the wrong lengths. For whatever reason, Walton was unhappy with his performance, particularly the cadenzas, and Amaryllis hoped to do better. She took the work home, studied it and, when she thought she had it under control, called the composer in for an opinion. His advice, on one tenuti-packed phrase, was to the point: 'Play more clitorically, darling.'

Walton's Concerto had much the same effect on her career as had Seiber's *Tre Pezzi*, and before long she was playing it all over Europe. Music lovers enthused, not least Amaryllis's gynaecologist, who made his staff stop work to hear a broadcast conducted by Emanuel Hurwitz. Walton, too, was impressed. He invited her to play it at the Festival Hall in honour of his sixtieth birthday, in March 1962, and did his best to secure performances for her elsewhere. Often he failed: 'some nonsense about not being able to have both a foreign soloist and conductor in the same concert', he wrote from Lisbon in October 1963. But even his failures were encouraging. As he wrote the following month:

> I grovel for not having got on to you (in all senses) before I left, but I know you realise how rushed the last 48 hours in London can be.
>
> However, I arrived in Rome in time for the concerto and Sig. Selmi played on the whole well, but not as well as you would have played it, nor did he look a patch on you! Nor would you, I trust, have forgotten as he did (though he had the music in front of him) the 1st cadenza in the last mov. He nearly reached the Pizz G s then dried up and wisely started again (looking at the music). No one noticed or knew except me, who inocently enough thought that he thought the Variation was too short so he added a repeat! Anyhow the notices for a change were pretty ecstatic (enclosed).
>
> I don't think I've a hope of muscling you in for a perf. as it seems he is an old Roman favourite. But somewhere else sometime let's hope.
>
> The garden is full of you (late ones) from pale scarlet to passionate red, *molto esotico ad appassionato* – so let it rest at that.

In 1965 she played his Concerto at the Royal Festival Hall with the New Philharmonic Orchestra led by Hugh Bean. Walton himself was to conduct, which gave her cause for alarm. In her experience composers rarely made good conductors, and a broadcast from Scotland earlier that year, with Fournier as soloist and Walton conducting, had done little to reassure her. Fournier had got lost in the scherzo and Walton was too slow to catch him. On the night of 8 May, as they were about to go on to the platform, Walton suddenly whispered, 'What's the tempo of the first movement?' Amaryllis sang it to him. A few seconds later he was assailed by new doubts. 'You *will* be absolutely metronomic in the scherzo, won't you, otherwise I'll lose you!' To make matters worse, this was the first time she was playing it from memory, and in the artists' room she had found a disturbing message scrawled over her programme: 'Shall be listening – Piatigorsky'. In the event it was a success; Hugh Bean and the orchestra kept with her all the way, despite Walton's some-what erratic conducting; she discovered that the message had been written by her violinist friend Manoug Parikian; and Louis Kentner came up to say how much he preferred her interpretation to Piatigorsky's.

Despite such triumphs, the hurly-burly of a soloist's life was beginning to wear her down. In a letter to Paul, years before, she had given vent to her desperation following a Dvořák performance. 'Playing concertos in these circs is just a farce – 3/4 of an hour rehearsal and no musical co-operation whatsoever. The conductor and the orchestra knew the concerto well but he had no feel for anything and the orchestra was out of tune and paid no attention to detail. I just *can't* play when things are like that. Got through it all right, but considering it's the concerto I know best, it was lamentable – notes out of tune and not enough control. In other words on edge all the time . . . *How* can one make music like that? Think of all the care and thought that goes into a sonata or trio performance, even the "under-rehearsed" ones.' Alan Loveday shared her feelings. Having talked it over they came to the conclusion that 'the only thing worth doing was chamber music and that concertos amounted to a battle for survival against impossible odds'.

There was another good reason for her to consider a shift in career focus. In 1955, while Amaryllis was struggling before a Bolognese mirror, William Pleeth had written a letter of recommendation for the Suggia Award. 'She is the most outstanding cellistic and musical talent I have met so far,' he said of the applicant, 'to which she adds incredible maturity of mind. I am of the opinion that she will have a great career and deserves every help to this end.'[95] The applicant was Jacqueline du Pré, who at the age of ten became the youngest person to win Suggia's bequest. In 1960, she won the Queen's Prize. Her Wigmore début came in 1961 and her Prom in 1962, by which time she had won the Suggia Award for seven consecutive years. Then, in 1965, she played the Elgar at New York's Carnegie Hall. 'From this point,' wrote Margaret Campbell in *The Great Cellists*, 'du Pré could do no wrong.'

Britain embraced du Pré wholeheartedly. The nation, having 'never had it so good' under Harold Macmillan, was now enjoying Harold Wilson's 'white heat of technology', and the future looked rosy. People were buoyant, and wanted music that reflected their mood. Jacqueline du Pré supplied it. Young, glamorous and extrovert, with bow movements which remain unequalled for sheer vigour, she captured audiences' hearts wherever she played. Amaryllis could not compete.

'The prime reason for her ceasing to perform as a soloist', wrote Geoffrey Parsons, 'is that she was superseded by the next generation. Jacky was not better than Amaryllis, but she was perceived to be better. She made a stronger impression in public. Amaryllis presented herself in a very different, very aristocratic style.' But aristocracy was a dirty word in the

Sixties, so Amaryllis stepped quietly out of the limelight.

Her performing career now revolved mainly around chamber music and recitals. In recitals, the musical *crème de la crème*, she had been accompanied for a short while by Gerald Moore. The partnership never gelled, partly because of Moore's high fees, which, besides being higher than her own, tended to price them out of the market, and partly because as the older partner he liked to make people think she was his protégée – a reasonable claim, given his earlier help with her career, but one she resented. Moore also recalled problems with balance: 'The violoncello has to be treated with discretion by the pianist for its lowest tones can easily be swamped by the pianoforte. After an Amaryllis Fleming recital, my friend Hamish Hamilton told me I was sometimes too loud for the cello, "or perhaps", he added, "Amaryllis was too soft for the pianoforte".'[96]

Her next choice was Geoffrey Parsons. An avowed accompanist, with no wish to pursue a solo career, Parsons was mostly interested in singers, 'which is a very special thing', according to Amaryllis. 'You have to prompt them with their words, which means you have to know songs in all languages. Mostly singers aren't very intelligent – with some notable exceptions – so you have to coach them musically, almost give them lessons, while making it seem as if you aren't. I found Geoffrey an extremely unselfish musician, always listening and having ideas about sound and colour.'

But as Parsons' career became more involved with singers, so his place was taken by Peter Wallfisch – father of Raphael and husband of the ECO cellist Anita Lasker – with whom Amaryllis had briefly played in Gervase de Peyer's clarinet trio. Peter was a brilliant but highly-strung musician, given to sudden bursts of *ff* when the music said *pp* and vice versa, and possessed of a pathological need to practise. When he and

Amaryllis went to Sandor Vegh's festival at Cervo, on the Ligurian coast, Peter insisted on a grand piano rather than the upright available. Sandor laughed, then gave a list of the world's most famous pianists who had practised on that same upright. The encounter brought out Sandor's most difficult side, and from that moment he seized every opportunity to ridicule Peter's serious approach to music. If no opportunity existed, he created one. At rehearsals, for example, Sandor altered every agreed idea, then countered Peter's objections with, 'Why do you want rehearsals if you're not going to change anything?' Caught in the bickering, Amaryllis could understand only too well why the Vegh Quartet had folded.

Sandor remained a close friend, however, and became a frequent, but formidable, visitor to Old Church Street. Every chair he sat on broke, and his appetite was exhausting. Food cooked to last three days went at a single sitting and hardly was the last mouthful gone than he would jump to his feet and suggest they play duos. His presence was overwhelming. He gave private lessons in his bedroom – 'he didn't quite have the nerve to steal my studio' – asked Amaryllis to collect his fees and insisted she drive him to broadcasts and concerts. Within two days of his arrival she was invariably wilting. 'Ah,' sympathised his wife over the phone, 'all men are babies, but Sandor, he is a king baby.'

By 1968 Amaryllis had decided to solidify her career in chamber music. The Fleming String Trio was founded that same year with Granville Jones as violinist and Kenneth Essex on the viola, and made its début on 16 June at New College, Oxford. 'The string trio is the most inspiring and most difficult medium,' she told the *Sunday Times* on 26 May. 'And demanding, for it requires three soloists who are also excellent chamber-music players and in sympathy with each other.' But it was a flawed combination. Granville, the son of a Welsh miner, was 'a sweet, quiet man', according to Amaryllis, '*very sensitive and a natural on the violin*'. He even elicited praise from Dodo. 'At last I write to say how much I loved your trio,' she wrote on 27 August. 'Surely the Welsh chap was very good? It's terribly difficult to judge things for the first time. Seemed fine to me.' Granville's sensitivity hid a deep depressive streak. When, in December, Amaryllis and Kenneth had taken their seats for a morning concert in the Hampstead Music Festival, Granville was still closeted in the Gents. 'The minutes passed and he eventually appeared looking white as a sheet. He said he was all right and we began the concert but he was shaking with nerves and couldn't keep the bow on the strings. We'd started with a Schubert String Trio which has very little in the cello part, nothing I could cover up or help him with. At the end I whispered to Ken, "Ask him if he wants to go off the stage." But Granville declined. The next piece was a Beethoven Trio in which I played very loud to try to keep him going but he never recovered his nerve. He'd got the pearlies and his bow was jumping all over the place. The audience didn't know how to react. It was one of the worst experiences of my life.'

She made sure there were friends to look after him on the Tube journey home, and that afternoon he rang her, wanting to come and talk. 'I suggested the next day, hoping that by then I'd be able to talk him out of what I knew was coming – that he couldn't go on and must leave the Trio. That evening he went to a club near his home and on the way back drove into a lamp post. He was killed immediately. People said afterwards that he was drunk. I don't think he was.' Only then did she learn that Granville had been seeking psychiatric help for depression. A series of commemorative concerts was held the following autumn in the Victoria and Albert Museum, the proceeds from which were pledged to the Granville Jones

Foundation, a newly established scholarship for musicians. Scarcely had the concerts finished than the proceeds were embezzled and the Granville Jones Foundation remained stillborn.

In Granville's place came Emanuel Hurwitz, a well-known and highly respected violinist who had led the Goldsbrough Ensemble, the ECO and the Melos Ensemble, among other achievements, and who had an uncanny nose for the ludicrous. 'Manny had his own way of looking at things. He'd spot some ridiculous story in a newspaper and read it out to us. There was nothing you could do but laugh.' Hurwitz had been with the Trio only a few months when he was presented with an unexpected opportunity for humour. In the spring of 1969 he was delighted to hear that Amaryllis, she of the aristocratic tone, the coloured and passionate interpreter of Bach, the sensitive *belle dame* of British cello playing, had been invited by Ibbs and Tillet to act as stand-in for Bette Davis in a film called *Connecting Rooms*.

Amaryllis was no stranger to cameras. Her first brush with the small screen had come in January 1953, shortly after she had won the Queen's Prize. Television was then in its infancy, an exciting, experimental time when most programmes were broadcast live and producers learned as they went along. Music programmes being few and far between, the producer decided to mark Amaryllis's appearance with some special effects. Mist was specified for Fauré's *Après un Rêve*, but without enough dry ice for a rehearsal he took a chance that all would go well during the performance. As she started playing a thick fog rolled across the studio floor. It grew thicker. It rose higher. The crew dropped on their hands and knees to blow it away. Amaryllis played on in increasing obscurity, now and then catching through the smoke a a glimpse of the official BBC accompanist, Josephine Lee, looking pale with terror. The fog cleared just in time for Tchaikovsky's *Valse Sentimentale*, for which the producer had decided to shine a mercury light on her to create a stark effect. He succeeded beyond his wildest dreams – Amaryllis looked not only stark but stark naked.

The programme generated enormous interest. A number of story-hunting journalists called to see if the studio was on fire. 'No; cellist Amaryllis Fleming was not fired by her own enthusiasm,' wrote one disappointed hack. 'The smoke clouds at her feet were a misguided attempt at cloud effects.' The *Sunday Graphic* reporter looked on the brighter side: 'Miss Amaryllis Fleming, young and charming, gave a delightful interlude with her cello on Sunday. Lighting tricks, however, sometimes made it appear as if Miss Fleming was wearing little more than her cello . . .'

David Attenborough, a friend of both Amaryllis and the producer, was delighted, and dined out on the story for months afterwards. The producer, who was sacked the next day, took a quieter line. Following this débâcle, Amaryllis's next appearance, that October, was low-key. The women's programme *Leisure and Pleasure* fitted innocently between a talk on tapestry and *Watch with Mother*. Its star was captioned under a photograph simply as 'a musician'. Even so, she was noticed by at least one attentive viewer. 'There was a pretty cello player with dark, smouldering eyes . . . who looked like a gypsy,' remarked Randolph Churchill in the *Evening Standard*.

Since those days she had appeared many times on television, but had reservations about the medium. While it brought her name and playing to a wider public, it lacked human contact. Moreover, conditions in the studio were trying: 'The heat given off by the lights was intense. You sweated and sweated, no matter how much powder they put on you. And there was always the nightmare possibility of the cello cracking.'

The big screen, however, was virgin territory, so when Ibbs and Tillet suggested she take the part she wanted to know what it would entail. The agency had no idea so the score composer, Johnny Shakespeare, was sent to explain.

Shakespeare collected her in a white Rolls-Royce and sped her noiselessly to Knightsbridge to eat Chinese with the producer and the director. They read her the script, the details of which she immediately forgot, save for one point on which they sought her advice: did she think it better if Bette Davis's screen boyfriend, Michael Redgrave, was sacked from his post as schoolmaster for rape or buggery? 'As the plot was so dreadful I told them I didn't think it would make much difference either way.' She formed an equally low opinion of Johnny Shakespeare's talent when he played her some of his earlier soundtracks, but she needed the money so she took the job. Besides, there was a good precedent: in 1924 Shostakovitch had financed the composition of his first symphony by playing the piano in a backstreet Leningrad cinema, though later he was sacked for stopping to laugh during an American comedy.

Bette Davis was then aged sixty and the days when she had been a box-office queen lay far in the past. As Hollywood gossip put it, her career had been 'recycled more often than the average rubber tyre'. And though a recent cycle of horror movies had put her back in the public eye, they were a far cry from her glory days in the Forties. Vast, blown-up photographs of a younger, more attractive, more successful Davis adorned the walls of her dressing room when Amaryllis arrived to prepare for her scene – busking outside a Charing Cross Road theatre. She put on Davis's clothes, her wig, her shoes – 'all of which were far too big and made me look an awful frump' – then went out with a hired factory cello at two o'clock in the morning to play to a bus queue of extras, her exit cue being Michael Redgrave bearing down with a bouquet. The next day she got a phone call. It was Geoffrey Parsons: 'I hear you're a bit short. Can I lend you half a crown?'

The scene went well but there remained the problem of getting a shot of Bette Davis herself playing the cello. 'She had got into such a state of nerves that she could hardly hold the cello and wouldn't even allow me to adjust the angle. Someone had been hired to teach her how to move but it was no good. "Honey," she said to me, "I've spent forty years learning how to act. I'm still not sure I can do that. And I can *not* learn to play the cello." ' The compromise, reached after much telephoning to Hollywood, was for Amaryllis to kneel behind Davis and play through the arms of her costume. Accordingly the crew moved to Pinewood Studios, where the two women clambered into an enormous sweater still damp from being stretched by the laundry. While Amaryllis bulged around in the steamy sweater, trying her utmost not to laugh, Bette Davis sat with her hands behind her back looking musical.

The experience taught Amaryllis how wearing it is to make a film, and in the interminable intervals between takes she entertained herself playing Bach. Unbeknown to her, Bette Davis had been watching her every move and in the next shot was able to match her head movements precisely to Amaryllis's bowing. Amaryllis was impressed by this, and by her professionalism, but in conversation Davis was a disappointment. Obsessed by acting (*her* acting, in particular) she came to life only when Amaryllis revealed that Celia Johnson was her sister-in-law, whereupon she insisted on an introduction. Celia never forgave Amaryllis for the subsequent lunch.

Amaryllis hated *Connecting Rooms* for its 'dreadful script and cliché-ridden score'. And when it was finally released in London in 1972 she was abroad. When she returned, a few days later, it had vanished. But she retained some stills from the Charing Cross Road scene, half a sweater with 'To AF from BD' embroidered on it, and a fee that covered the cost of a forecourt at Old Church Street designed by Sir Edward Maufe.

The year 1969 ended on a sad note. First, there was the sight of André Mangeot, now in his eighty-fifth year and clearly near the end. 'Eventually, when André became old and ill,' Amaryllis wrote for his centenary concert in 1983, 'I would come round to Cresswell Place as often as possible with my cello. He appeared to be in a state of wandering oblivion, unaware of people or of their conversation. But when I put Anna Magdalena's manuscript of the Bach Suites into his hands, and sitting down in front of him started to play, he would wake up and follow every note with something of his old insight.' His death the following year, only weeks after that of Sir John Barbirolli, was no less sad for its inevitability. Dodo's state of health was of even greater concern. 'For goodness sake do be careful,' Dodo had written in December 1968 after the death of Granville Jones: 'musicians seem too likely to get killed.' On the night of 23 July 1969 she herself died.

Ever since Augustus's death Amaryllis had continued to visit the woman who had become her adoptive mother and greatest friend. She spent Christmases at Fryern and took Dodo on excursions to escape Romilly and his wife Kathy, who looked after her but whose presence, however well-meaning, was resented. Rebecca John recalled that in her old age Dodo 'was still beautiful and mysterious; gliding silently across the dining-room floor in her long dresses, or sitting at the head of the long refectory table at tea-time, smoking a cigarette and laughing softly at some long-past absurd adventure with Augustus that she would sometimes retell. But she found old age trying, so that she was often snappy, especially with her daughters and grandchildren.'

Amaryllis experienced little of this snappiness. Dodo had a hard, independent streak and, recognising the same in Amaryllis, kept the peace. It was a friendship based on equality, unsullied by dependence, and deepened by mutual self-respect. As Paul told Amaryllis, Dodo was 'the only person you love more than me'.

That left Fryern. The house and garden, growing a little more dilapidated with every year, had retained their welcoming charm. But now, without Dodo, they were nothing. None of the children had enough money to repair or maintain the house, so it was sold. And, as always seems to happen with old, much-loved homes, it was modernised and developed. The 'new' studio was made habitable and sold as a separate dwelling, while the 'old' studio and the orchard made another lot. An era had ended.

TWENTY

A Spot of Cancer

Amaryllis claims that she inherited four main characteristics from Augustus: the look in her eyes; a fondness for drink; an inability to remember dates; and a lot of moles. In 1970 one of these moles, on the back of her right upper arm, began to fester. A skin specialist removed it, put it in a test tube and sent it off for analysis. For two weeks the mole lingered unattended in sorting offices while a postal strike ran its course; then, after four expert opinions had been sought, it was diagnosed as malignant melanoma. The shock of finding she had cancer was intensified by the possible repercussions of an operation to her bow arm.

She had one consolation in that Peter too had had cancer and had recovered, with no remission. A tumour had appeared on his neck in late 1962 and the following year, on returning from a foreign tour, Amaryllis found a message to ring him at the Royal Marsden Hospital. She received a typically Peterish diagnosis: 'Oh, it's nothing. Just a spot of cancer.' When she visited him she found she had forgotten her cigarettes, so Peter gave her his pipe, which she solemnly smoked by his bedside. Perhaps remembering his lucky escape, she asked the surgeon if she could fulfil her engagements for the following week before going into the Royal Marsden. 'By all means,' he replied, 'if you want to be dead the week after.'

Amaryllis tried to keep her operation secret lest news of it harm her career. But as the surgeon told her, she needn't have bothered: he had so many people telling him to be careful that he hardly had the nerve to pick up his scalpel. But he did, successfully removing most of the skin and a large part of the underlying flesh from the back of her arm, as well as a number of other possibly cancerous moles. The nurses nicknamed the bandage-swathed result The Wreck of Vietnam or, if she was complaining, as she mostly was, they called her Madame de Pompadour.

When Augustus had been in hospital in 1954, he had sent her vitriolic reports of his stay. 'This is a kind of Hell on Earth,' he wrote from Guy's Hospital, 'and the food is quite the vilest I've ever tried to eat . . . I'm hoping John Davenport will bring me a bottle of wine. I sent him a pound to get some but Caspar thinks he will have used this for his own necessities. His need may be greater than mine. I told the surgeon not to make a new man of me but to ginger up the old one and improve his mileage. This he swore to do.'

Amaryllis took much the same approach. She complained constantly about the filthy baths and toilets, had food brought in by friends, threw fruit at the doctors, insisted the nurses make toast for her caviar, and maintained a large cocktail cabinet. Every night her room was filled with hard-drinking guests who arrived in such numbers that sometimes she had to get out of bed to give them somewhere to sit. The only noticeable absentee was Alan Loveday, who was convinced she was dead.

Richard Fleming was a daily visitor until she told him he was looking a little unwell, which made him so angry he slammed the door and did not come back. As it happened, he was suffering from pleurisy, but admission of illness was never the Fleming way. When Amaryllis telephoned Peter he outlined a typical remedy. 'Pleurisy? Tell him to go for a thirty-mile walk. That'll fix it.' Pleurisy apart, Richard had every reason to feel unwell. In 1969 he had led Robert Fleming & Co. into a deal with Robert Maxwell, unwittingly making the bank party to Maxwell's first major swindle as head of Pergamon Press. Although Flemings were only acting in an advisory role, the repercussions were horrendous. The firm faced a lawsuit for millions of dollars, negligible by modern American standards but then a major part of the bank's capital, and they were forced to pay because the legal costs would have been even higher. Until his death Richard held a grudging admiration for Maxwell: 'You couldn't help but be impressed by him.'

Amaryllis remained blithely unaware of Richard's predicament and continued to enjoy hospital life. She became firm friends with the surgeon, Jean-Claude Gazet, and three years later pressed him into appearing on a radio programme. *Your Record Choice* was a Radio 3 phone-in, where listeners were invited to request pieces of classical music and then explain before it was played why they had made their choice. Commonly known as the Record Sleeve Programme because presenters spent their time studying LP sleeves to improvise when callers dried up, it featured Amaryllis as host in what was pronounced 'Women's Lib Week'. All requests had to be connected with female artistes and her 'guest' – part of the programme's routine – had also to be a woman. The guest was violinist Isolde Menges, leader of the Menges Quartet, whom Amaryllis had admired ever since hearing her at Downe House with Ivor James. She did a preliminary interview, in which Isolde seemed to be perfect radio material. Although terrifyingly old – she died shortly after the programme went out – she started talking when Amaryllis arrived at her home at three o'clock on a summer afternoon and was still in full flood when the sun went down. But her radio performance down the phone was woeful. It proved difficult to reach her – 'Keep talking!' the producer begged as researchers were sent to find an alternative telephone number – and when finally she was contacted her false teeth made her almost inaudible. It later transpired that the friend who shared a house with Isolde was so jealous she had turned off the bell on her telephone extension. The one star was Jean-Claude, whom Amaryllis had earlier primed to phone in with a prearranged request for Ginette Neveu playing the Sibelius Concerto, about which he knew nothing whatsoever. Amaryllis, who delivered her presentation in a high-pitched gabble interspersed with nervous giggles, found the experience of talking to unseen callers 'quite horrific. I think I got through half a bottle of whisky that morning.'

With the loss of both Dodo and Fryern, Amaryllis had spent more time with Peter and Richard, the two remaining Fleming brothers. But in August 1971, barely a year after her release from hospital, came the tragedy of Peter's death from a heart attack while shooting at Blackmount. The news was doubly sad because, although they had been lifelong friends, it was only in the last few years that Amaryllis had really understood him. Reserved almost to the point of rudeness, Peter had always hidden behind a mask of emotionless imperturbability. He never removed that mask but occasionally, on her visits to Merrimoles when brother and sister were alone, Amaryllis had been allowed selective peeks beneath it. He told of the anguish he felt at being head of the family following Val's death, and how he wished he had died instead of Michael. In one moment of despair, he told her that she was the only member of the family who was a true artist, dismissing himself as a mere journalistic hack. But if

Amaryllis tried to probe further, the mask returned. When, for example, she quizzed him about the 'sergeant-major' lecture he had given her on Eve's instructions, he went red and left the room.

Peter's house at Merrimoles had filled part of the gap left by Fryern's sale. Another part was filled by Richard's Gloucester-shire home, Leygore Manor. An architectural hodge-podge which straggled along the side of a Cotswold valley, it contained Richard and Charm, plus varying combinations of children, grandchildren and dogs. It also contained, in a curious harking-back to her youth, Joan Regent, her husband Frank, and Hilda Gee. This trio of old Cheyne Walk-ers had arrived at Leygore in 1960 through an unlikely chain of events centred round Eve's court case with Bapsy Pavry.

Many years later, Richard liked to relate that Bapsy had sent him a note after the trial assuring him that his eighth child would be born with a black mark on its forehead. On 13 October 1959, a few weeks short of a year after Bapsy was denied her final leave to appeal, Charm gave birth to their eighth child, a boy. His forehead was blemish-free, but the birth was a difficult one and to compound matters their staff took the opportunity to leave en masse. In despair, Richard asked Amaryllis if she knew of a couple prepared to tackle Leygore's chaos. She did.

A few years before, while still at The Ovaries, she had lost the services of her artist-manquée-in-residence, Mrs Virgo, who, having announced her intention to take a few days off, had cleared her possessions and vanished into thin air, only to rematerialise a few months later in a Rolls-Royce, bearing apologies, an extravagant bouquet of flowers and the explanation that she 'had found somewhere a little better'. In her place came Hilda Gee, with her moustache and flat feet, who had followed Eve faithfully round the world but who became dispensable when her employer opted to spend the rest of her life with Monty in Monte Carlo, and who had therefore been handed down like a chattel from mother to daughter. Pleasant as she was, Hilda was a slight liability. Her feet seemed to make stair-climbing and cleaning an insurmountable problem and, encouraged no doubt by her new mistress's ingrained thrift, she took to shop-lifting for the groceries – 'I got it free, Miss!' she would exclaim, proudly placing a loaf on the table. When Richard telephoned, Amaryllis saw a way out. She had kept in touch with Frank and Joan Regent, and immediately called them with the offer of a job which, as she euphemistically described it, would never give them a dull moment. She then called Richard to tell him that she could find him a couple but only on condition that he took Hilda Gee too. He agreed. The Regents agreed. And Hilda went to the country, where she sat carpet-slippered in front of the stove, commenting to the Regents on their every move, 'That isn't how Mrs Fleming would have done it.'

Amaryllis got on well with all her Fleming nephews and nieces, with one notable exception: Ian's son Caspar. Although he had become virtually her neighbour, living in an apartment at the top of Old Church Street, Amaryllis had little contact with him, his sole topics of conversation being firearms and Egyptology. Like Amaryllis, he was unable to get on with his mother, Annie, and whenever Amaryllis saw the two together she found their squabbles unbearably embarrassing. The death of his father had affected him deeply and on 12 August 1974, the tenth anniversary of Ian's fatal heart attack, Caspar made an abortive suicide attempt. For another year he hovered, in and out of hospital, before killing himself with a drug overdose in October 1975. Amaryllis heard of his death in Aalborg, the conductor having spotted it in the local newspaper, and immediately wrote a long and forthright letter to Annie telling her not to blame herself for the suicide. Annie took this double-edged consolation with remarkable composure and even wrote to thank and agree.

Amaryllis made little secret of her dislike for Annie, but shortly after Ian's death his widow had casually remarked that Amaryllis was 'the only human Fleming'. The comment would have brought forth approval from all the Fleming brothers. For them Amaryllis was an escape valve, one of the family but free from family constraints, an inside outsider who was able both to accept and to express the emotions they hoarded so jealously. The same held true for their children. She fell into no easily labelled category. At Leygore she was just Amaryllis, a beautiful, red-haired, husky-voiced relation who arrived at Christmas and played her cello during the day, then drank, laughed, smoked, played cards and listened to problems throughout the night. She was different.

In 1973, as if to underline the difference, she bought a house in France – which, to those Flemings who had been weaned on a holiday diet of Scottish rain, swarming midges, long walks and high mountains, was about as different as anyone could get.

TWENTY-ONE

La Musicienne

The farmhouse in Sotteville had no telephone. Nor did it have central heating, electricity, running water or a bath, and the single, purple toilet had yet to be connected. Most of the interior woodwork had rot. A few small windows lit gloomy rooms which looked backwards over a riotous garden of dock and nettles. Springs rose not only in the courtyard but beneath the house itself. The roof leaked. Amaryllis bought it on first sight.

She had stumbled across the village of Sotteville, about twelve kilometres from Cherbourg, purely by chance. In 1973, while staying with André Mangeot's niece Leah and her husband Marcel Grillard, she had been overwhelmed by the beauty of Normandy. The idea struck her that she could buy a house which might serve as both holiday home and picturesque venue for a summer school. So, for fun, she toured the surrounding countryside. Then, again for fun, she inquired at a local estate agent. He, also for fun, before showing her something expensive, whetted her appetite with the dilapidated Sotteville farmhouse. To his dismay she offered the asking price of £4,000.

The idea of running a summer school was a logical extension of her career. Pioneered in 1929 by her old tutor Jimmy James, summer schools, often held at 'real' schools

248

vacated for summer holidays, are a mix of instruction and entertainment which gratifies both pupil and teacher: the teachers enjoy the prestige attached to such an event and the pupils enjoy the prestige attached to the teacher. Participants cram into dormitories or nearby rented lodgings in happy confusion, congregating at a central arena, a hall or marquee, where masterclasses are held, and a concert is given in which the most promising pupils are invited to play. Then all go home fortified by wisdom and alcohol. Or such, at least, is the idea.

For the next few years Amaryllis travelled between London and Sotteville, alternating performances and teaching with the serious business of restoring her new acquisition. To her aid came a Clochemerle collection of local artisans who helped and hindered in equal measure. The mason, Marcel Lepaumier, was a magnificent craftsman but thought it was only enjoyable doing the job if Amaryllis was present. Whenever she telephoned for a progress report, his reply was '*Ah, ça ne sera pas pour demain*', the local equivalent of *mañana*. When he did start work it was usually in Amaryllis's bedroom, into which he would creep at seven in the morning and announce his presence by tickling her toes. One day he hoisted her by the ankles and pretended to throw her into the *lavoir*, the old stone-flagged pond previously used for washing clothes. 'The neighbours can think what they like!' he cried. The carpenter had a similar sense of humour: his favourite trick was to hide in the bathtub until she thought the house was empty, then jump out at her. The plumber was confidently incompetent; his watchword, '*Pas de problème!*', soon became his nickname. Where did he intend to run the soil pipe? *Pas de problème*, through the sitting room. Where was the bathwater going to empty? *Pas de problème*, into the *lavoir*. He later ran unsuccessfully for mayor of the nearby town of Carteret.

Without a telephone – '*Ça ne sera pas pour demain, Madame*' – work moved at a snail's pace. If Amaryllis wanted to contact her builders, she had to bicycle to the end of the spread-out village where a single public pay-box stood in a private courtyard surrounded by dogs and children and with a cluster of hens roosting on its corrugated plastic roof. Any major progress became the talk of the neighbourhood. When a JCB was hired to drain her waterlogged courtyard, the entire village, plus several families from nearby settlements, came to marvel and advise.

Sotteville was defiantly rural. When Amaryllis introduced herself to her neighbours, they stared blankly at her. She was the first foreigner they had ever seen. The couple soon warmed to her, however. She became *La Musicienne*, her barn *La Salle de Musique*. The husband became a regular visitor, setting himself down in her kitchen to regale her with stories of his time as a prisoner-of-war, while his wife despatched regular presents of wood and fresh eggs. The farmer's wife who lived opposite sent donkey-loads of kindling, the occasional basket of jam and Calvados (covered in a cloth lest the other neighbours became jealous) and, once, a whole *boudin noir*, prepared from a freshly slaughtered pig, which was so noxious that Amaryllis had to bury it in her garden.

Another who came to her aid was M Chattel, the local gravedigger, who 'pretended to do my garden'. He took Amaryllis on tours of the countryside – she driving, he waving regally to the neighbours – pointing out features such as his first grave, and the local château whose inhabitants he claimed were great friends of his, an excuse he repeated while urinating against their walls. He took her to her home's original owners to discover its name, *La Minoterie* (The Mill House), then celebrated their discovery by making a pass at his passenger. Amaryllis bundled him on his way and the next morning he brought a bottle of pickles as a peace offering.

His inability to garden stemmed partly from his fondness for Calvados and partly from his consuming lethargy. Once or twice Amaryllis made the mistake of visiting his home to chivvy him along. 'It was like living in treacle. He would slowly go to the cabinet, slowly open the door, slowly take out a bottle and, without asking if I wanted any, slowly pour out a glass. Then he'd slowly pour another for himself. It was impossible to understand a drunken Normandy accent so I sat there going "Mm . . . Ah! . . . Oui", not knowing whether he was talking about his dead wife or the goat. Because he drank so slowly I always finished first and then he'd give me a refill. Once I tried putting my hand over the glass. He slowly poured Calvados over my hand.'

He solved his gardening defects by sending over Michel, his youngest son, aged about fourteen, with an omnivorous goat which grazed its way through everything. Amaryllis became extremely fond of both, especially Michel who had been brought up by his father after his mother had been run over by a car when he was very young. He was lonely, barely articulate, slightly retarded, and fell for Amaryllis, bringing her a glass of warm goat's milk whenever she arrived at the house. In return, she brought him a football from London, to give him a bit of standing among his schoolmates. But such a totem, she found, was not to be wasted on frivolities such as games. Michel hung it from a rafter in his barn and refused even to consider kicking it. She felt sad when the time came for him to get a proper job and they lost contact.

By then, however, Amaryllis had discovered a new play-mate. While attending a summer school at Caen, she and double-bass player Rodney Slatford balked at listening to any more concerts. They trolled the town looking for fun and ended up in a sleazy bar where they became firm friends with

Mona, the resident prostitute. Blonde, bubbly and very entertaining, Mona provided an intriguing glimpse into Caen lowlife. Amaryllis soon learned not to be late for lunch appointments after Mona complained her unpunctuality was costing her clients. She was also amused to note that whenever she entered a restaurant with Mona the men stared fixedly at their plates. She was a stickler for etiquette, refusing to let Amaryllis dance with a man three times in succession because it showed she was interested in him.

Mona sometimes came to lunch at Sotteville, arriving in her sports car with an ever-changing succession of boyfriends. 'Amaryllis, you're a woman of the world . . .' was her usual opener when seeking advice on how to regain absconding admirers. On one occasion, she brought Bernard, a night-mail railway employee who was the son of yet another prostitute and a local philatelist. Amaryllis and Bernard fell for each other at once, thus starting a long and complicated affair which involved Amaryllis getting up at 3.00 a.m. (with the help of four alarm clocks) to meet the mail train at Caen, and which centred around various Caen hotels or, if the town was busy, Mona's 'office', a surprisingly clean and attractive room in one of Caen's prettiest squares. Among its regular occupants, Amaryllis was delighted to learn, were the mayor, *notaire* and *chef de police* of the town.

Throughout the Seventies Amaryllis spent almost as much time in Normandy as she did in England. Not that her music suffered; she continued playing duos with Peter Wallfisch, and struck up new partnerships with harpsichordist Harold Lester and pianists Bernard Roberts – with whom she appeared as featured artist in the York Festival of 1976 – and Michael Gough Matthews, who later became director of the RCM. By the middle of the decade the Fleming String Trio had run its course. Emanuel Hurwitz had become leader of the Aeolian Quartet, a job that was impossible to combine with any other work, and so, reluctantly, the trio disbanded. But in in its place came an even more successful collaboration, the Parikian-Fleming-Roberts Trio.

Amaryllis had known Manoug Parikian for a long time and had the greatest respect for his playing. Five years older than she, he had left his native Cyprus to study at Trinity College, London, before becoming leader of the Philharmonia Orchestra in an era when it boasted conductors such as Furtwängler, Karajan, Boult, Klemperer and Toscanini. His career had remarkable echoes of Amaryllis's own. Like her he had quit a soloist's life to concentrate on teaching, chamber music and recitals, and he had not only studied under Eve's old tutor, Pecskai, but he played the Strad which Eve had sold on moving to Monte Carlo with Monty Winchester. Amaryllis enjoyed a reputation for her aristocratic perform-ances, and Manoug too was renowned for his classical poise and stature, playing with a 'spontaneity and naturalness far removed from flashy pyrotechnics'.[98]

They complemented each other perfectly, a fact which had not escaped Eric Thompson, then deputy music director of the Arts Council. It was he who mooted the group's formation in 1976 by suggesting that they find a third to join them at a celebratory concert to mark the Wigmore Hall's seventy-fifth anniversary. Amaryllis thought immediately of Bernard Roberts, with whom she had played all the Beethoven sonatas at the York Festival that year.

The rehearsals went magnificently, and even before the performance Manoug was suggesting they continue as a group. Afterwards, when they had played Beethoven's *Archduke* to thunderous applause, others made the same suggestion. The trio was born. In December 1983 Natalie

Wheen wrote for *Radio 3 Magazine,* 'In some ways it is extraordinary that they exist at all: a piano trio in the age of the string quartet; a trio ungarlanded with the laurels of the competition circuit, naked of the more dubious excesses of the packaging business ... the Parikian-Fleming-Roberts Trio is rather like some rare and distinguished delicacy from the highest class of delicatessen.' Their reviews were superb: 'The performance was like an intelligent conversation, without a word or gesture wasted, polished and yet taking a full measure of the music's expressive power,' said *The Times*; 'Each of them has a soloist's authority ... but their united musical front betrays neither competition nor compromise' (*Financial Times*). These quotes, immediately plastered over their brochure, described precisely the qualities every chamber musician longs to possess.

The Trio was just getting into its swing when, in August 1977, Richard died. Shortly before his death in August 1964, Ian had warned Annie, 'This is a bad time for Flemings.' It was an uncanny premonition. Robert had died on 1 August 1933, and, in the years that followed, the month of August took on a strange terror for Flemings. By 1977 all but two of Robert's direct descendants who had died of natural causes had done so in August. And on 14 August that year, Richard followed the family tradition. Amaryllis was now the last of Eve's children.

'All the boys were wonderful,' she recalls, 'but Richard was *so* kind. He always went out of his way to help people. He struck me as being the saint of the family and had much more equilibrium than the others. It gave me a shock to think they'd all gone and I was the only one left.' Richard had steered an even course between the extremes of Peter's aloofness and Ian's rakishness, although one magazine article classed him with Ian as being one of the few people in Britain to possess panache. He had even managed to cope with the drive for success which Eve had instilled in all her children. After Amaryllis tried to browbeat one of his daughters into making something of her artistic talent, he took her aside and asked, 'Why? Can't she just be herself?' On such matters they agreed to disagree. But money was something on which Richard took a firm stand. Ever since the war he had acted as the family's financial factotum and in the mid Seventies his responsibilities weighed heavily. Inflation was soaring, oil prices had sky-rocketed, taxes stood at crippling levels, Britain was being subsidised by the International Monetary Fund and Fleming's was still struggling to recoup its Maxwell losses. 'He and Charm were driving me back from somewhere or other,' Amaryllis recalls; 'they were in the front and I was in the back prattling on about musk-rats and *lavoirs* in Normandy, when suddenly Richard said, "I don't care about your musk-rats. I care about your paying back the money for this house. And I don't care if it's a good investment or not. You can't eat houses and you can't eat land. You'd better sell it and you may as well think of selling your Strad because you can't eat that either." I sat in stunned silence for the rest of the journey, visualising life without either Normandy or my Strad. And Charm, who was too embarrassed to speak, seemed equally stunned. When we got to Leygore she rushed upstairs and came down with a matching set of silver-amber Tibetan ear-rings and necklace, which she gave me to make up. I'd never heard Richard so angry, *ever*.'

Had Richard lived a little longer he would have had more cause for complaint because, not satisfied with her French entanglements, Amaryllis was turning her attentions to the London property market. For all its charm Old Church Street had become a nuisance, with its stairs, its upkeep and its procession of au pairs. In 1978, in emulation of her previous coup with Ovington Square, Amaryllis bought the freehold and put the house up for sale. By coincidence this was the year that Sylvain Mangeot died and 21 Cresswell Place became available. Amaryllis had always loved André's small mews house. So, having already taken out one loan to buy the Old Church Street freehold, she now took another to buy Cresswell Place. Her new home needed extensive modernisation – 'It's a slum!' cried one student from the Gorbals – as well as structural alteration to provide a suitable music room. Bills mounted, house prices fell, and Old Church Street remained unsold. Where concerto scores had once drifted like leaves, there now fluttered a confetti of scribbled sums charting Amaryllis's precarious finances. It was two years before she sold Old Church Street, two years during which her loans bit deep and the stress caused her temporarily to lose all feeling in her right-hand fingers. By the time she moved into Cresswell Place she had lost any profit she had made by purchasing her freehold. And there still remained the Sotteville debt.

Seven years after moving into *La Minoterie* Amaryllis managed to get a telephone installed. It was almost the finishing touch. Marcel Lepaumier had uncovered a blocked-in window and an original stone fireplace and had stripped the flaking plaster from the interior walls to reveal their original, beautifully coloured stonework. More windows had been added in the vernacular style to bring light to the gloomy rooms. Hand-made tiles had been laid on the kitchen floor and the carpenter had installed a stable-door leading from the kitchen to the garden. There was now electricity, running water and a septic tank. Musk-rats swam in the *lavoir* and a fleet of timid owls sailed silently in and out of the barn. There were one or two bits and pieces to complete. And the roof still leaked, but Amaryllis had collected enough traditional stone tiles to repair the damage. The end was in sight.

The beginning of the end came one summer when she invited a couple to stay while she was away. One night they were surprised to find Michel at their door asking for an English dictionary. He reappeared the next morning with the same request and was given the same answer: there was no dictionary in the house. That night as they were going to bed a weed-killer bomb exploded in the courtyard. Barely had they extinguished the flames when shots began to pepper the side of the house. Using the newly installed phone, they called the police, who removed Michel to an asylum. But he was soon released. The next year, when Manoug and his wife Diana visited, they found a note from Michel pinned to the door, proclaiming his eternal love for Amaryllis and embellished with pictures of 'various private parts, all labelled and with full descriptions of their use – which made Manoug laugh'.

Unwisely, Amaryllis took no action over the note. The showdown came later that season when she visited Sotteville on her own. She had just driven Leah Grillard to the station and arrived home late at night, when there came a knock at the window. It was Michel, desperate to talk. She told him to come back the following afternoon. But ten minutes later she heard owl cries from the garden, and saw Michel leering through the stable-door with a nylon stocking over his head. 'I have all the time in the world,' he said, before disappearing into the darkness. Amaryllis fled upstairs, pursued by owl cries from the garden, and phoned the police. When they arrived there was little they could do. A search of the garden, which Michel knew like the back of his hand, brought forth only derisory hoots.

Michel was eventually caught and re-committed to an asylum. But the head psychiatrist told Amaryllis when she went to inquire about his condition that they could not keep him there indefinitely. There was only one way in which she could continue to live at Sotteville, and that was if she rang the asylum before every visit, whereupon they would then collect Michel and incarcerate him for the duration. It was an impossible situation. Reluctantly, she decided to abandon her dream.

In fact, Sotteville would never have made a good summer school. It was too remote, too primitive, to accommodate the numbers such events attract. Besides, Amaryllis readily admits that she would have been quite incapable of managing it. She was, by then, a freelance professor at the RCM and her teaching duties combined with her Trio appearances already made travelling difficult. Her closest approach to organisation was a vague agreement with Julian Bream that they play at each other's summer schools in a barter exchange. *La Minoterie* was eventually sold in 1984 to an employee of the French nuclear industry who received free concrete as a job perk. When Amaryllis returned six years later everything, including the *lavoir*, had been concreted over.

Nineteen-eighty-four brought another disappointment, with Bernard Roberts's decision to drop out of the Trio to concentrate on a solo career. Neither Manoug nor Amaryllis wanted to abandon what they had so painstakingly created, so they drew up a list of prospective pianists and crossed them off one by one. At the end, they were left with just one name: Hamish Milne, whom they had heard and admired on the radio but whom neither had met. Hamish was a completely different personality from his predecessor. Where Bernard was outgoing and audience-friendly, Hamish was dry and ironic. The one was thickset, balding and exuberant, the other drawn, bespectacled and intense. But despite the outward differences the music was still of an impeccably high standard. As Amaryllis told Margaret Campbell, 'A succesful trio must consist of three personalities – three soloists. The difficulty is to find a pianist who has the sensitivity of sonority to blend with strings but has a soloist's technique to cope with the very demanding piano parts. The two string players need to share the same mental approach, by which I include style of bowing and anticipation of nuance. I think we have realised the answer to these problems. Our rehearsals are a joy because we aim for the highest standards and we have a sense of humour.'[99]

Although it received rave reviews in both its manifestations, the Trio never made its members rich. One reason, Amaryllis claims, is that the agents did not try their hardest. The agents would no doubt blame the players, all of whom were poor publicists. They would also point out that of all the individuals and groups on their books a piano trio is perhaps the least profitable. Whereas opera singers can get thousands of pounds per night, only the most famous chamber groups even approach that sum. And if they do they are probably a string quartet, a recognisable entity with a repertoire which audiences have become accustomed to. Trios are unpopular, and piano trios are still more so. Their meagre takings are further diminished by the cost of hiring, transporting and tuning a piano. Yet, money aside, the collaboration was deeply rewarding. Amaryllis had started her chamber-music career with one piano trio (the Loveday) and now she had reached a pinnacle with another. Moreover, she was at the very heart of it, if the American cellist Felix Salmond was to be believed when he declared that the cello was '*par excellence* the great poet and singer of the trio . . . unequalled by the piano or violin in its variety and range of tone colour and in its capacity to express music of nobility, tenderness, and declamation'.[100]

Individual prominence, however, was not her aim. Chamber musicians must battle to suppress as well as express their personalities. Playing in a quartet has been likened – only half-jokingly – to being married to three different people. The strain is less for a trio but even so there are compromises to be made, accommodations to be reached, for the modern piano is a product of the industrial age while the violin and cello are offspring of an earlier, frailer era. According to one programme note, it 'is a combination that presents great difficulties to the composer and few succeed always in preserving a satisfactory balance'. That the Trio succeeded in preserving this balance was a tribute to their close rapport, constant rehearsals and their willingness to subordinate self-importance to the demands of a group. In Manoug's words, 'If we had been good at our public image, then perhaps we would never have met as a Trio; we would have been prominent in our own spheres and too busy rushing from here to Hong Kong to San Francisco to Des Moines. You see, it isn't very important in our lives, this question of the image of the individual – in that sense we all feel the same, even though when we're on our own we make a pretty good bash at playing concertos.'[101]

Partly through choice and partly through circumstance, Amaryllis had always lived in an older generation. Now that familiarity with age was reaping its inevitable harvest. The Seventies had seen the loss of a number of friends and relatives. During the Eighties, yet more familiar faces vanished: Ivor Newton and Annie Fleming died in 1981, Celia Johnson in 1982; 1983 claimed William Walton and Adrian Boult; Caspar John and Basil Lam went in 1984, Pierre Fournier the next year and Romilly John in 1986.

Losing Fournier was particularly sad. Since the late Fifties, they had drifted further and further from each other, until their only meetings were those of a professional nature. In the mid Sixties, Amaryllis was called in to take Fournier's place in a performance of Bach's Third and Sixth Suites, after he had caught his forefinger in his trouser zip, but was reprieved at the last moment when he cured the wound by dipping it in a glass of gin. Otherwise, they saw little of each other. Fournier's appearances in London became less frequent as he became older, and his last performance at the Queen Elizabeth Hall was a pitiful spectacle. Amaryllis was in the audience. 'He'd eaten something on the plane which disagreed with him. The doctor said he shouldn't play but he was determined to. He just lacked strength, was changing bow a great many times because he didn't have the control. *I* could see through it to what he had once been. But somebody who'd heard him then for the only time wouldn't have got it.'

The bond that linked them, however, could never be broken. In February 1987 Amaryllis paid tribute to him at a celebratory concert in the RCM. 'In the line of great cellists Fournier was exceptional. His playing was informed with character and individuality and was often so refined and sensitive that sometimes one felt he was walking a musical tightrope . . . As a teacher he was very caring and very, very generous, and his influence was far-reaching. It has certainly become part of me and so it is passed down to my pupils . . . So he lives in us, in our students (even in those who never heard him) and in their pupils. This is not fossilised tradition. It is learning and inspiration transmitted as living strands from past to future.'

As always, Amaryllis let these latest losses wash over her, burying herself ever deeper in her work, but by 1988 that solution had become impossible. On Christmas Eve 1987, Manoug Parikian died of a heart attack, and with him died the Trio. The thought of starting the collaborative process anew for a second time was more than either Hamish or Amaryllis could stand. The repertoire was hard and few newcomers were prepared to learn it, let alone find the time or financial freedom to do so. Then there were the additional difficulties of producing new promotional material, pestering the agents, pushing for work, posing for new photographs. It was all too much. Kenneth Sillitoe, whose playing they both admired, helped them fulfil their prearranged engagements, then they quit.

TWENTY-TWO

Final Chord

The dissolution of the Trio effectively ended Amaryllis's performing career. In the Fifties and early Sixties her name had been on every concert-goer's lips, but since then she had withdrawn first to the intimacy of chamber music and then to the rarefied seclusion of Bach's Suites. Her playing remained of the same high standard throughout but, like the Ševčick exercises which Fournier had given her so long ago, the means had overtaken the end, an audience had become less important than the music itself. By the time of Manoug's death the impetus which had once taken her on whirlwind schedules around the Continent and, in later years, around the more sedate chamber circuit had been replaced by a maturer, more reflective approach. No longer desirous of solo-star adulation, she was content to play the role of musician's musician, known for what she stood for and how she played rather than where she performed, how often she did so and how well publicised those performances were.

This choice was dictated to a degree by arrogance and lethargy. Amaryllis felt that people should contact her rather than her having to approach them. At the same time she was too lazy to hustle her agents to obtain a performance, particularly as hustling required letters. Like her father, who was bedevilled in his old age by the curse of rewriting,

Amaryllis had become a compulsive composer. Her letters, written habitually in the early hours of the morning on the back of other letters, were a mass of crossed-out fulminations which, come breakfast, were usually put to one side. If they reached their target, the message was often obscured by intent. As Christopher Bunting once had to remind her, 'Brevity is the soul of pith.'

There were, of course, other reasons for not pursuing a solo career. According to Geoffrey Parsons, 'A high London profile is terribly important. But how many cello recitals can you do? Perhaps that is why people constantly want new musicians to perform.' Amaryllis was neither new nor young. The concerto circuit takes a heavy toll, especially when engagements are abroad – travelling alone, living alone, eating alone, dealing alone with a foreign orchestra. Gone were the days of her youth when musicians were valued as ambassadors of their country and given a glass of sherry by the airline before being ushered into their seats ahead of the mothers and children. Now it was a question of haggling over the extra ticket which had to be bought for an instrument that could not travel in cargo.

Added to this was the refined quality of Amaryllis's tone, which was better suited to the light strains of chamber music than the din of an orchestra. 'The cello wasn't made to be played with a grand piano or a modern orchestra and despite all the adjustments it still has quite a struggle to be heard. In this respect it hasn't really changed at all. The eternal problem for cellists is that we're all terrified of being drowned.' Despite her tuition by Casals she had not mastered his knack of enhancing the sound of his instrument. 'He had this trick of playing terribly softly at rehearsals, and then complaining that everyone else was too loud. They got quieter and quieter until they were playing pianiss*ississ*imo. Then, at the performance, he would play at normal volume.'

With or without orchestra, there is still the djinn of perfection which hovers over every artist. Augustus was a victim of its influence and so, to a lesser extent, was Amaryllis. 'The more you know the higher your standards become, until they're impossible to live up to. There's so much more to lose than when you're young, and the better your reputation the greater the fear. I've tried to convince myself that you never go below a certain level. Sometimes you go above what you thought you could do and you really play as you've never played before. It doesn't occur to you that you might miss anything. But at other times you have that fear and don't play so well. But even so you've got enough background, enough technique, enough know-how, enough professionalism, not to go below that certain level . . . I think.'

Perfection was something that prevented her from making recordings. As Bernard Roberts told *Radio 3 Magazine* in 1983, 'Why do musicians want to make music? The performance is the essential part of being a musician; a hundred extra ears can make our ears more aware, it stimulates you to do entirely new things on the night – it's live performance which counteracts this blanket of music. No hi-fi can compete.' Amaryllis shared this view, feeling that recordings counteracted the vitality of the music. 'The essence of performance is that you do it once and then the next time it's going to be different – different audience, different acoustic, you feel different, the other players will feel different, which in turn affects you. I don't think music is meant to be played over and over again. In commercial recording you redo all the things that don't go right, and this makes it slightly false. You become ultra-careful at the thought of everyone playing it over and over, picking out all your mistakes. You lose that sense of freedom. In a concert there are always things which aren't absolutely perfect but people don't notice them so much. Paul, for example, could always tell when I'd slipped up because he said I put on a particularly seraphic expression. But he never knew *how* I'd slipped up.'

By the Nineties the musical world had changed enormously from the rarefied one in which Amaryllis had made her mark. 'In the mid Sixties,' according to Raphael Wallfisch, 'there were three or four leading cellists. Today there are about fifteen. There's been a cello revolution since Jacqueline du Pré and there are now between two thousand and three thousand people either learning or playing the cello in this country. Hundreds of people turn up at the world cello seminars and congresses. There's always been a club atmosphere, which has become more like a world brotherhood.'

Amaryllis had never been one for clubs or brotherhoods. Shrinking from the wider musical scene, she devoted her performances almost exclusively to Bach. By this time she had further cornered the market in five-string cellos with the discovery at Sotheby's of yet another Amati. Alerted to the five-stringer's presence by the dealer Charles Beare, she did her usual disguised inspection before bidding in person. The sale was dominated by the presence of a Strad belonging to Lady Anne Blunt – Byron's granddaughter and wife of archaeologist Sir Wilfrid Blunt. But the Amati had not gone unnoticed. Two other dealers had shown interest: one from America, who graciously agreed to stand down; the other from Amsterdam, who also agreed not to bid provided he receive a commission on the sale price. All went well, and the cello was about to be knocked down at £700, when the Amsterdam dealer started bidding. The hammer finally fell at £1,400 to a cry of 'Bravo Amaryllis!' from the auctioneer. Pushing aside her congratulators, Amaryllis ran to the nearest phone booth and begged her bank not to bounce the cheque.

The price was low for such a unique instrument, the only five-stringed Amati in existence which had not been cut down or had its fifth peg-hole bushed. But she was still irritated by what she saw as the dealer's treachery, and was gratified when his son became apprenticed to Charles Beare and was put on to the Amati's restoration.

But even Baroque music was beginning to lose its appeal. 'There's a real bandwagon for Baroque music now. It's become fashionable, which is really rather unhealthy because throughout the centuries it has always been new music that interested people. The old was discarded. Now people are digging out all sorts of third-rate eighteenth-century composers who haven't been played for years – admittedly, this is partly because modern music is so unsatisfying.' Nor did she approve of the direction this trend was taking, concentrating more on the technicalities than the spirit of the music. 'Take the end-pin, for example. Modern Baroque players for some unknown authentic reason choose not to use it, which I can never understand. Besides giving them terrible back pains, it's authenticity for authenticity's sake, which, frankly, is just a load of balls.'

The ready-made solution lay in teaching, which remains the mainstay of her life. 'She's a marvellous teacher,' claims Geoffrey Parsons, 'and that's another problem with a career. When teaching takes such an important part in a life, as it does for her, it's a vocation which is difficult to mix with a career. The Master Class, that's not proper teaching, it's the icing on the cake. But someone has to produce the cake, and that's what Amaryllis does. She's totally dedicated. I think teaching became the strong part of her life not as an alternative to playing but as something she really wanted to do.'

Master classes are the popular apogee of teaching and Amaryllis has given any number of them, some as far afield as

Australia. But she remains dubious about their value. Pupils get welcome public exposure and the chance to learn from a leading artist. They receive fresh ideas and, if they have already been well taught and are receptive, they are able to use them, but the brevity of the encounter can make it more of a gimmick than a useful exercise. There are only so many points a teacher can make in a single lesson and, indeed, only so many faults that can be detected in that short time. The student might leave without having fully understood, in which case the exercise is pointless, or having misunderstood, in which case it is damaging. There is also the danger that some teachers use the class merely as a vehicle for their own egos. Pupils are ridiculed and made to look foolish, or can be placed uncomfortably amid a coterie of the master's long-term pupils on whom the praise is lavished. They leave demoralised and lacking in confidence, which is possibly the worst impediment for a musician. 'I couldn't disapprove of those kind of masters more,' says Amaryllis. 'It's just an ego-trip. Luckily word soon gets around and people avoid those ones.'

Personal, one-to-one teaching is something else altogether. In individual classes Amaryllis tries to rectify the faults in her own tuition. Unlike in the old days when personal contact was shunned and Jimmy James could watch the tears stream down her face for an hour and a half without saying anything, she takes account of pupils' feelings. 'There's quite a lot of psychology involved. You have to draw out their centre, find out what's really in the middle of them and try to make them have confidence in that.' She is a harsh critic, but when praise comes it means something. One twelve-year-old pupil described her system of evaluation: 'When she says "good" it means you're not as bad as she thought you were. When she says "*good*" you've done one thing right. If she ever says "GOOD!" you fall on the floor and don't get up.' Not that lessons are an exercise in disapproval; on the contrary, Amaryllis is smiling, outgoing and informal.

Posture is another important element she has learned not to neglect. 'So many musicians tie themselves up in a bad posture and then get a bad back. You need good powers of observation to see what's being done wrong: elbow too low, failing to use the little finger, neck too tight, frowning, going out to the music. I'm not rigid about making pupils do what I do, so long as what they do works. There's much more concern now for posture and unnecessary tension – but not nearly enough. There are very, very few teachers, for example, looking after young kids' posture.'

She bemoans the lack of opportunity for musicians nowadays. Britain is currently enjoying a boom in cello talent, and more and more students compete for fewer and fewer vacancies. There can be up to seventy cellists trying for one place in an orchestra. Auditions are hard, short – say, ten minutes – and, except for the supremely confident, nerve-racking. Moreover, there is no certainty that the place has not already been filled and is advertised only to satisfy legal requirements. Even if the student wins a place, there is no guarantee they will enjoy it. Amaryllis knows orchestral cellists who have abandoned a performing career because of the twin impossibilities of playing under a conductor they did not respect and finding another post. In stark contrast to her college days, when extra-mural performances were forbidden, she encourages her pupils to form groups and find employment where they can.

She also bemoans the unavailability of good instruments. Back in the early Sixties, as Paul proved, it was possible to find Amatis and Stradivarii at affordable prices. Nowadays, few students have the means to insure, let alone buy, one. Fortunately there are always makers willing to experiment with new designs and new materials. Few are like the Scottish fiddle-maker Amaryllis once met who had spent a cheerful life making violins out of oak (an impossibly unacoustic wood) on the happy premise that birds sing more beautifully in oak trees. Fewer still are like the varnish-maker who blew himself up while demolishing amber in an attempt to recreate the lost Italian varnishes. But enthusiasts often arrive at Cresswell Place asking Amaryllis to test their latest creations. One recent visitor, proffering a cello whose belly was made out of black, iron-hard African timber, clearly believed that there is no logical reason why perfection should stop with the classical masters.

How do musicians stop? *Can* they stop? Some never do. Leopold Stokowski signed a contract for his 100th-birthday concert, only to die ten years before the event. Mieczyslaw Horszowski, on the other hand, celebrated his century by cancelling an engagement in New York's Carnegie Hall.

According to Amaryllis, 'There aren't many musicians who know when to stop. Some have given farewell concerts for years. The last time I saw Casals on television it was terribly sad. He couldn't bear the lights and was putting his hand over his head, and he had lost the strength. It was amazing he could still play at ninety-something but one felt one would rather remember him as he used to be. And the same with Fournier. So I don't want to be like that.'

At what point an artist succumbs to the ageing process is a lottery. Approaching seventy, the great French cellist Louis Duport liked to prove his steadiness by filling a wine glass to the brim and walking round the room with it balanced on the back of his hand. 'All technical skill is acquired and retained by dint of hard work,' he claimed. 'As for the sureness of intonation, I have to thank Nature alone for it.'[102] The first inkling that Amaryllis would never be able to perform the same feat came in the New Year of 1993 when she had a by-pass operation to replace an artery clogged by decades of smoking. The operation was a success, but that March, in the middle of a lesson, she had a stroke. Her pupil continued to play while they waited for an ambulance to arrive. The following morning she awoke in the Cromwell Hospital deprived of the power of speech and able to move only her left hand. Her first coherent word was 'Fuck!' This time the recovery was slower and less complete. By May she knew she might never be able to perform again.

Amazingly, she remained unperturbed. Indeed, it was almost a relief to escape the tyranny of her instrument. A rebel for so long, she had perhaps forgotten the original purpose of her rebellion. She had long since established herself as an individual, forged her own identity and destiny. That the cello had led her to that end was glorious – few are lucky enough to combine their being and their career in such a fashion – but it had been all-consuming.

For many years, she had been tinkering on the fringes of mysticism. The origins of Christianity had long fascinated her, as had the serene depths of Buddhism. Since the late Eighties, after breaking an ankle on holiday in France, she had been enthralled by the wisdom of Jean Gibson, a healer and teacher of self-awareness. She is now Amaryllis's personal guru, having 'taught me more about myself and my playing than anyone in my life'. A trip to Bhutan in 1992 had led her to consider forsaking music in favour of an existence devoted to meditation, but then again the cello had intervened. As Jimmy James said, 'Music is a kind of inarticulate, unfathomable speech which leads us to the infinite, and sometimes allows us to look beyond.'[103] In Bach's Suites Amaryllis had found access to a 'dance of eternity' which became her meditative tarot.

Now the cello may be gone, and with it the Bach Suites. But the hole is surprisingly small. She is now free to explore, to start again, to express herself in different ways that have no connection with the past. As Casals once wrote, 'Music must serve a purpose, it must be something larger than itself, a part of humanity . . . A musician is also a man, and more important than his music is his attitude to life.'[104] Nowhere is this clearer than in the life of Amaryllis Fleming.

Amaryllis still lives at Cresswell Place. Guests find a house which, despite alterations, has much the same atmosphere as it had in André Mangeot's time. Beauty, slight chaos, good art, good wine, good food, informality. A mess of plants is carefully cultivated in cracked pots outside the door. On the window ledge a note for the milkman lurches out of an old wine bottle. It is a place for people as much as music. A constant stream of visitors rattle at her door, ranging from college pupils to Asian royalty. Those who cannot call in person do so on the telephone. 'Don't worry,' she reassures one friend who rings in distress because she has lost her spectacles and is unable to find either her wig or her dentures, 'I'm sure you look very fashionable.'

The house centres on one main downstairs room, the music room. The walls are dotted with her father's art. A grand piano swells from one corner below a case of arthritic bows. Opposite the piano is a walnut cabinet, one of Paul's bargains, which holds a nest of curiosities ranging from strings and music to ping-pong balls and grub screws. Alongside is a stereo system of a certain age, and in the centre of the room are two hard chairs and a pair of rickety music stands. The bare brick walls converge on a disused fireplace topped by a clock which no longer works, a photograph of her old neighbours at Sotteville and a minuscule brass horse looted from a Chinese tomb. Everything commands attention, interest, but the true focus is a small oak table by the fireplace. It is well made, well polished, well used, and stands about eighteen inches high, the level a small child might sit at. It is her nursery table from Turner's House.

NOTES

1. Letter to the author.
2. *The Times*; obituary of Sir Richard Quain, 14 March 1898.
3. *Lady Anne Blunt*; Rosemary Archer & James Fleming (eds.); Alexander Heriot, 1986. p. 171.
4. *The Life of Ian Fleming*; John Pearson; Pan Books, 1967. p. 13.
5. *The Sisters d'Aranyi*; Joseph Macleod; Allen & Unwin, 1969. p. 99.
6. Letter to Val Fleming from Winston Churchill, dated 22.11.14.
7. W. B. Yeats, quoted in *Augustus John. Volume 1: The Years of Innocence*; Michael Holroyd; Heinemann, 1974. p. 263.
8. *The Seventh Child*; Romilly John; Cape, 1975. p. 180.
9. *Augustus John. Volume 2: The Years of Experience*; Michael Holroyd; Heinemann, 1975. p. 90.
10. *Finishing Touches*; Augustus John; Cape, 1964. p. 101.
11. *Chiaroscuro*; Augustus John; Cape, 1952. p. 118.
12. *Ibid.* p. 144.
13. Quoted in *Augustus John. Volume 2*. p. 115.
14. *The Lyttleton Hart-Davis Letters, Volume 6*; Rupert Hart-Davis (ed.); John Murray, 1984. p. 151.
15. *Tears Before Bedtime*; Barbara Skelton; Hamish Hamilton, 1987. p. 140.
16. Letter to the author.
17. *The Times*, 22.7.36.
18. Quoted in *Peter Fleming*; Duff Hart-Davis; Cape, 1974. p. 43.
19. 'Wages on the Nettlebed Estate', written 16.9.68.

20. *Ibid.*
21. *Goodbye to the Bombay Bowler*; Peter Fleming; Hart-Davis, 1961. p. 155.
22. *The Power of Change*; Rupert Hart-Davis; Sinclair-Stevenson, 1991. p. 33.
23. *The Road to Oxiana*; Robert Byron; 1937.
24. Letter to Dodo from Augustus John, 29.8.33. Quoted in *Augustus John. Volume 2*. p. 140.
25. *Sunshine and Shadow*; Cecil Roberts; Hodder & Stoughton, 1972. p. 146.
26. *Ibid.* p. 148.
27. *Ibid.* p. 149.
28. *Ibid.* p. 161.
29. *Celia Johnson*; Kate Fleming; Weidenfeld & Nicolson, 1991. p. 59.
30. *Olive Willis and Downe House*; Anne Ridler; John Murray, 1967. p. 2.
31. *Ibid.* p. 130.
32. *Ibid.* p. 133.
33. Letter to the author.
34. Quoted in *Augustus John. Volume 2*. p. 175.
35. *RCM Magazine.*
36. *Lions and Shadows*; Christopher Isherwood; Methuen, 1982. p. 91.
37. *Ibid.* p. 85–6.
38. *Ibid.* p. 85.
39. Pierre Fournier Celebration Concert, 16.2.87.
40. BBC French Service, 3.12.53.
41. *Overture and Beginners*; Eugene Goossens; Methuen, 1951. p. 99.
42. *Pablo Casals*; H. L. Kirk; Hutchinson, 1974. p. 199.
43. 'Sitting for Augustus John' by Mme Suggia. *Weekly Dispatch*, 8.4.28. Quoted in *Augustus John. Volume 2*. p. 94.
44. *Am I Too Loud?*; Gerald Moore; Hamish Hamilton, 1962. p. 108–9.
45. *On the Contrary*; Mary McCarthy; Weidenfeld & Nicolson, 1980. p. 126.
46. *Finishing Touches*. p. 127.
47. *The Life of Ian Fleming*. p. 131.

48. Quoted in *The Great Cellists*; Margaret Campbell; Victor Gollanz, 1988. p. 214.
49. *My Life and Music*; Artur Schnabel; Colin Smythe, 1970. p. 17.
50. *Ibid.* p. 98.
51. *With Strings Attached*; Joseph Szigeti; Cassell, 1949. p. 6.
52. *Chiaroscuro.* p. 272.
53. *You Only Live Once*; Ivar Bryce; Weidenfeld & Nicolson, 1984. p. 83.
54. *Ibid.* p. 83.
55. *The Life of Ian Fleming.* p. 167.
56. *Chiaroscuro.* p. 273.
57. Quoted in *The Great Cellists.* p. 214.
58. *The Most of S. J. Perelman*; S. J. Perelman; Methuen, 1980. p. 385.
59. *The Secret Life of Salvador Dali*; trans. Haakon Chevalier; Vision, 1973. p. 341.
60. *The Lyttleton Hart-Davis Letters, Vol 6.* p. 151.
61. *Finishing Touches.* p. 12.
62. *Self Portrait with Friends – The Selected Diaries of Cecil Beaton 1926–1974*; Richard Buckle (ed.); Weidenfeld & Nicolson, 1979. p. 328.
63. *The Seventh Child.* p. 184.
64. Quoted in *Peter Fleming.* p. 132.
65. *The Life of Ian Fleming.* p. 192.
66. *You Only Live Once.* p. 114.
67. *Conversations with Casals*; J. Corredor, trans. André Mangeot; Hutchinson, 1956. p. 223.
68. *Ibid.* p. 146.
69. *The Life of Ian Fleming.* p. 368.
70. *You Only Live Once.* p. 114.
71. *A Life In Music*; Daniel Barenboim; Weidenfeld & Nicolson, 1991. p. 66.
72. *Celia Johnson.* p. 134.
73. *Picture Post* Vol. 60, No. 12, 19 September 1953.
74. *Self Portrait with Friends.* p. 256.
75. Quoted by Margaret Campbell in *The Great Cellists.* p. 195.
76. Programme note written by Deryck Cooke, 17.8.59.
77. Letter to E. M. W. Paul.

78. *Octopussy*; Ian Fleming; Cape, 1966. p. 83.
79. *Ibid.* p. 86.
80. These and following extracts from *The Times* law reports.
81. *The Letters of Ann Fleming*; Mark Amory (ed.); Collins Harvill, 1985. p. 209.
82. *Self Portrait with Friends.* p. 327.
83. The unpublished diaries of Cecil Beaton.
84. *Ibid.*
85. *Ibid.*
86. *Ibid.*
87. *Caspar John*; Rebecca John; Collins, 1987. p. 38.
88. *The Lyttleton Hart-Davis Letters, Vol. 6.* p. 151.
89. *The Sisters d'Aranyi.* p. 162.
90. *The Letters of Ann Fleming.* p. 324.
91. *Ibid.* p. 324.
92. *The Great Cellists.* pp. 15–16.
93. *Behind the Façade*; Susannah Walton; Oxford University Press, 1988. p. 162.
94. *The Music of William Walton*; Frank Howes; Oxford University Press, 1965. p. 104.
95. Quoted in *The Great Cellists.* p. 321.
96. *Farewell Recital*; Gerald Moore; Hamish Hamilton, 1978. p. 20.
97. *Caspar John.* p. 217.
98. *The Independent*, obituary by Robin Golding, 30.12.87.
99. *The Great Cellists.* p. 268.
100. Quoted in *The Great Cellists.* p. 153.
101. *Radio 3 Magazine*; Natalie Wheen, December 1983.
102. Quoted in *The Great Cellists.* p. 40.
103. *Ibid.* p. 130.
104. Quoted in *Pablo Casals*; Robert Baldock; Victor Gollancz, 1992.

SELECTED BIBLIOGRAPHY

The Letters of Ann Fleming; Mark Amory (ed.); Collins Harvill, 1985.

Lady Anne Blunt; Rosemary Archer & James Fleming (eds.); Alexander Heriot, 1986. p. 171.

The Barbirollis; Harold Atkins & Peter Cotes; Robson Books, 1983.

Pablo Casals; Robert Baldock; Victor Gollancz, 1992.

A Life In Music; Daniel Barenboim; Weidenfeld & Nicolson, 1991.

My Own Trumpet; Sir Adrian Boult; Hamish Hamilton, 1973.

You Only Live Once; Ivar Bryce; Weidenfeld & Nicolson, 1984.

Self Portrait with Friends – The Selected Diaries of Cecil Beaton 1926–1974; Richard Buckle (ed.); Weidenfeld & Nicolson, 1979.

The Great Cellists; Margaret Campbell; Victor Gollancz, 1988.

The Great Violinists; Margaret Campbell; Granada, 1980.

Joys and Sorrows; Pablo Casals; MacDonald, 1970.

Conversations with Casals; J. Corredor, trans. André Mangeot; Hutchinson, 1956.

Celia Johnson; Kate Fleming; Weidenfeld & Nicolson, 1991.

Overture and Beginners; Eugene Goossens; Methuen, 1951.

Peter Fleming; Duff Hart-Davis; Cape, 1974.

The Power of Change; Rupert Hart-Davis; Sinclair-Stevenson, 1991.

The Lyttleton Hart-Davis Letters, Vol. 6; Rupert Hart-Davis (ed.); John Murray, 1984.

Augustus John. Volume 1: The Years of Innocence; Michael Holroyd; Heinemann, 1974.

Augustus John. Volume 2: The Years of Experience; Michael
  Holroyd; Heinemann, 1975.
The Music of William Walton; Frank Howes; Oxford University
  Press, 1965.
Lions and Shadows; Christopher Isherwood; Hogarth Press, 1938.
Chiaroscuro; Augustus John; Cape, 1952.
Finishing Touches; Augustus John; Cape, 1964.
Caspar John; Rebecca John; Collins, 1987.
The Seventh Child; Romilly John; Cape, 1975.
Adrian Boult; Michael Kennedy; Hamish Hamilton, 1980.
Pablo Casals; H. L. Kirk; Hutchinson, 1974.
The Sisters d'Aranyi; Joseph Macleod; Allen & Unwin, 1969.
Am I Too Loud?; Gerald Moore; Hamish Hamilton, 1962.
Farewell Recital; Gerald Moore; Hamish Hamilton, 1978.
The Life of Ian Fleming; John Pearson; Cape, 1966.
The Wanton Chase; Peter Quennell; Collins, 1980.
Olive Willis and Downe House; Anne Ridler; John Murray, 1967.
Sunshine and Shadow; Cecil Roberts; Hodder & Stoughton, 1972.
My Life and Music; Artur Schnabel; Colin Smythe, 1970.
Tears Before Bedtime; Barbara Skelton; Hamish Hamilton, 1987.
With Strings Attached; Joseph Szigeti; Cassell, 1949.
Behind the Facade; Susannah Walton; Oxford University Press,
  1988.
Dawson of Penn; Francis Watson; Chatto & Windus, 1950.

INDEX